SWEET UNREST

CELIA CROSBY

SWEET UNREST

by

Celia Crosby

This book is a work of fiction. Any references to historical events, real people, or places are used fictitiously. Other names, characters, places, and events are products of the author's imagination, and any resemblance to actual events or places or persons, living or dead, is entirely coincidental.

Cover design © 2023 by Angela Haddon
Text copyright ©2023 by Celia Crosby

For Jason. Again.

The past is never dead. It's not even past.
-William Faulkner, *Requiem for a Nun*

1

The engine of my ancient Subaru had already started making a knocking sound when I crossed into Mississippi. By the time I arrived at the entrance to the long, winding drive of Le Ciel Doux, the knocking had been joined by a whining rattle that I knew wasn't good. I'd been white-knuckling the steering wheel since somewhere outside Baton Rouge, half praying, half begging the rusted-out machine to keep going.

Maybe leaving Chicago in the middle of the night without any real thought other than to get the hell out had been a bad idea. But ending up stuck on the side of the road somewhere in the middle of Louisiana seemed like a worse one.

Which was what I got for letting myself get too comfortable. For hoping that maybe if I went with safe, it would all work out.

I could hardly believe it when the wagon finally coasted into the parking area, shuddering and shaking, before the engine gave out with an undignified clank. Considering that half the dashboard lights were flashing, it was clear the old girl wouldn't be taking me anywhere else anytime soon. But I didn't exactly feel relieved that I'd made it to my destination in one piece, not when the car's certain death meant there was no turning back.

As I leaned my forehead against the cracked leather of the steering wheel, the reality of my situation crashed into me. Even if I wanted to change my mind, now I couldn't. I had exactly one hundred and ninety-six dollars in my bank account, which wouldn't be nearly enough to fix whatever the hell was wrong with the car. The repairs would be expensive, and I'd probably made them worse by not stopping two hundred miles ago.

I tapped my forehead on the steering wheel and let out a string of curses. What had I been thinking?

Clearly, I hadn't been.

I'd been acting on impulse. I'd felt so stupid, so *betrayed* by Matt ending things that I hadn't known what else to do but leave. As quickly as possible.

Things hadn't been quite right for a while—it had been weeks since he'd touched me, months since he'd looked at me with any kind of real heat in his eyes. But that was what I'd wanted, wasn't it? I'd let myself fall into a relationship with Matt—if you could call what we had a relationship—because he felt *safe*. He was stable and boring and nicer than most of the assholes I'd met working odd jobs while I tried to get my art career going. He was *easy*.

After he'd asked me to give up the room I was renting and move in with him, I'd taken a chance. So what if the sex was never that great? That was part of the draw. He was just so damn comfortable that I slept better in his bed than I had in years. Until I didn't.

I should have known it couldn't last. When the nightmares started up again, things changed between us. When I saw the pity and resentment in his eyes, I'd known it was over before the words were even out of his mouth.

Maybe it shouldn't have been a surprise. It was what always happened, wasn't it? But somehow, the end had still caught me off guard. Not that I could blame Matt completely. I'd kept things from him. I couldn't be too angry he felt betrayed by the walls I'd built up over the time we'd been together.

I should have known it couldn't last. I shouldn't have let myself relax, no matter how sweet and safe he'd felt. It always happened the same way—whenever I started to get too comfortable or think I'd outgrown the terrible dreams that had plagued me for most of my life, they'd come back with a vengeance and screw up everything.

Matt had tried to let me down easy, even offered to give me a few weeks to find a new place, but I've been through this particular dance often enough to know that when something's over, it's over. Mostly, I couldn't stand the pity. Frustration, irritation, even disgust, I could have handled. But the soft, sad expression that came over him when he looked at me was too much. At least anger you could fight. Pity just made me feel broken.

So I'd sent the email before I really thought anything through, and I accepted the job offer that had been haunting my inbox for months. Then I'd thrown anything I could fit into my ancient car and started driving. It hadn't mattered that it was the middle of the night or that Matt had begged me to stay long enough to talk things through. I couldn't have stayed in that apartment another minute.

Chicago's skyline had disappeared in my rearview mirror over thirteen hours before, and I hadn't stopped for anything but gas since—not even to sleep. *Especially* not to sleep. But now the Subaru was dead, and I'd reached the end of the road. The exhaustion of too many restless nights and the endless drive hit me hard. If I hadn't already been sitting, I probably would have collapsed.

I let my eyes close. Not to sleep, though. *Definitely* not long enough to dream. Just to block out the world for a minute or two. . .

A sharp knock at my window startled me back to consciousness before sleep could dig its claws into me, and I looked through the grimy glass to find a pair of strangely familiar eyes peering in. They were my dad's hazel eyes, but this particular pair belonged to his older brother, my Uncle Leonard.

"Lucy?" His voice was barely audible through the glass, but I understood his confusion. I'd only accepted the job he'd offered me a few hours before. I hadn't even told him I was on my way.

I waved half-heartedly and, resigned, opened the door to the bright heat of Louisiana in June. The interior of the car had already started to warm, but the outside air was another thing altogether. It was like stepping into a solid wall of humidity. For a moment I wasn't sure I could breathe through it.

"It *is* you," Leonard said with a mixture of disbelief and something almost like pleasure. "I just got your email this morning. We weren't expecting you so soon."

"Sorry," I said, all too aware of how impulsive, how thoughtless it had been to take off without at least warning them to expect me. "I know I should have called or something to let you know, but I sent the email and just thought. . ." *What?* All I'd been thinking was that I had to get out. Out of Matt's apartment. Out of Chicago. Out of the rut my life was in.

I pasted on a smile I hoped wasn't too pained. "I was just too excited to wait."

It was—apparently—the right thing to say. Leonard's eyes crinkled. "Don't you worry about it for a second. I thought I was going to have to warn off some after-hours visitors. This is a much better surprise. Sam's going to flip when he sees you're here."

His partner. I hadn't seen either Leonard or Sam since my dad's funeral. They'd tried to talk me into moving closer to them, but I'd been in college by then, and I hadn't wanted to leave my program or the little apartment my dad and I had shared in the city. I'd thought with the money my dad had left, I could make it on my own.

But here I was, six years later. My dad's apartment was long gone, and so were my delusions about making a living as an artist. Hell, I couldn't even make a living as a wedding photographer, not when the market in Chicago was so competitive and skewed toward the decidedly traditional and boring. And not when my issues with insomnia started interfering more and more with my ability to show up on time.

I could have kept trying—maybe if I'd have been thinking, I *would* have kept trying—but once I'd sent the email, my fate was sealed. I'd accepted the position, made the long trip south, and now I'd live with the consequences.

"Well, let's get you to the house," Leonard said, when I didn't immediately respond. "You look like you could use a cold drink."

He wasn't wrong. The lack of sleep, the drive, and the heat were all conspiring against me. My head was swimming, and it didn't help that I could practically feel my hair starting to frizz. Sweat was already trickling down my back.

"We can drive your car over, if you want?" he said, not so subtly glancing at the baskets of clothes and stacks of half-finished canvases that filled the back of the wagon.

"I'd prefer the walk," I told him, not ready to deal with the reality of my poor, dead car. It had been my dad's—the last thing I really had left from him. But even *I* knew the heap of metal likely couldn't be fixed. "I need to stretch my legs, if the car will be okay here?"

He nodded. "Should be fine. We'll come back for it."

I grabbed my phone and my camera bag from the passenger's seat before locking the doors. Not that there was much to take, but I hadn't exactly made arrangements with Matt about the rest of my things yet. The stuff in the car was all I had.

As we walked across the gravel lot toward the main part of the grounds, I snuck another look at Leonard. He was taller than my dad had been. Thinner, too. And years younger.

If I was being honest, I'd been avoiding him. He and Sam had moved to Louisiana about four years before. They'd invited me down to the plantation museum where they lived plenty of times since then, but I'd always managed to make an excuse. I'd been afraid that seeing him would be too hard, too much a reminder of losing my father. But now I relaxed a little. Leonard wasn't really anything like my dad. The resemblance was there, but that was about it.

Leonard was a historian by trade, a preservation expert, and he'd been hired by the Foundation to help restore the house and grounds of an old sugar plantation. He'd offered me the job as site photographer for the first time last year. The position involved documenting the grounds and helping to catalog any artifacts they found. I'd also be serving as the official photographer for any events held on-site. It wasn't the type of work I wanted to do, but he'd tried to convince me that a steady income and free lodging would give me the time and freedom to keep working on my art.

I'd turned him down four times since he first offered, even though the job made a lot of sense. Money, a home, and enough free time to do my own work should have been an easy choice. But as I followed him around the bend in the path and reached the opening of the long alley of live oaks that lined the wide drive leading to the main house, I remembered all the reasons I'd said no before now.

With its stately columns and overwhelming size, the mansion was your quintessential Southern plantation home. It looked like something straight from *Gone with the Wind*. It was ringed with huge, thick columns that could have been taken from an ancient Roman temple, and its deep porches kept the windows on both levels in shadows. It was a gorgeous old thing. Stately and commanding, it looked like a house that held secrets.

There was something menacing about the whole place,

though. Something more than the violent history that had built it or the play of shadows that darkened its porches. Now that I was there, I knew for certain I hadn't been wrong. This house and its grounds had haunted my dreams—my nightmares—for years before my uncle took the job here. And now that I'd arrived at the one place I'd been avoiding for ages, I knew I'd made a mistake.

LEONARD AND SAM lived on the grounds of the estate in a small picturesque cottage that had once belonged to the plantation's overseer. Their home was a soft yellow stucco, accented with worn dark timbers and slate-blue shutters framing large airy windows. With its welcoming deep veranda, it didn't look like the kind of place where shadows lurked, and for the first time since I'd left Matt's apartment, the tightness in my chest started to unwind.

Before we'd even made it to the porch, the front door opened and a middle-aged man with deep brown skin and bright orange glasses stepped out.

"Holy shit," the man said, his eyes owl-like behind the thick lenses. "That can't be Lucy?"

"Hi, Sam." I gave him a half wave. "Surprise?" I could only imagine what I looked like, considering I hadn't had a shower in nearly two days.

I barely had time to feel embarrassed, though, before he'd launched himself down the steps and enveloped me in a hug. Considering I hadn't seen either of them for years, it should have felt awkward. But somehow, it didn't. Sam smelled of ginger and sage, a scent as bright and happy as the man himself.

They ushered me into the house, peppering me with questions as Sam returned to stirring a pot of something that smelled warm and spicy on the stove. Over drinks and a plate of cookies, I did my best to answer without saying too much about the situation that had driven me to take the job. I especially left out my recent breakup.

"But how have you been *really*?" Sam asked, placing a plate of jambalaya in front of me. "And don't give us that bullshit about being fine. One look at those dark circles under your eyes tells me nothing's been fine for a while." He exchanged a knowing look with Leonard.

"Are you having trouble sleeping again?" Leonard asked, bringing another pitcher of mint-and-raspberry juleps to the table and taking his seat next to Sam.

My dad had explained my insomnia to them, but I didn't know how much they really knew.

A knock at the door saved me from answering. Leonard excused himself, and a minute later he brought the visitor into the kitchen, where we were sitting.

"Mina, I'd like you to meet my niece, Lucy," Leonard said. "She's finally agreed to accept the site photographer position."

"Now that *is* some good news, Leonard," the woman said before she turned to me. "When did this happen?" She accepted a julep garnished with a sprig of mint from Sam.

"Earlier today," Leonard told her. "Lucy, this is Amina Sabourin. Mina's the business operations manager here at Le Ciel, so she'll be one of your supervisors."

Mina was a tall Black woman, maybe in her forties, with dark hair pulled away from her lean, sharp face. With high cheekbones and a generous mouth, she was stunning. Her green linen pants and flowing silk tunic draped over her slim figure, and against her throat and wrists, clunky antique jewelry clinked musically.

Of *course* I'd meet one of my new bosses with thirteen hours of road dust and sweat clinging to me.

Brushing off my embarrassment, I got up from the table and

offered my hand. "It's great to meet you. Thanks again for the opportunity."

"I've seen your work," she said. "I think we're the ones who should be thanking you." She took my outstretched hand with a smile. Her palm was warm and soft, and her grip was surprisingly strong, but when she squeezed my hand gently, I swear something like recognition jolted through me.

I had the sudden unwelcome feeling I'd met her before, which was impossible. I'd avoided Le Ciel Doux for a reason, and my dreams about this place were too vivid to forget someone like Mina.

Luckily, she seemed unaware of the direction my thoughts had taken. Her eyes were a deep, dark brown—the type of eyes that broadcasted emotion clearly. Now they were smiling, like she was clearly pleased to meet me, but then, for the barest whisper of a moment, I thought something move in their depths. Something that made me wonder if she recognized me, too.

"I saw your car out in the satellite lot," she said in a smooth-as-cream voice. "I thought I'd come by and see if Leonard knew who was on the grounds before I locked up."

"I would move it, but I think it's going to need a tow," I admitted. When I felt Leonard's questioning look, I explained the car's earlier death.

"Don't you worry about that," Sam said. "We know a mechanic in town who will give you a good price on repairs."

I nodded my thanks and didn't bother to tell them the car was likely beyond fixing. And even if it could be fixed, it would be a while before I could pay for the repairs.

Leonard waved away my concern. "The car's fine there. We only use that lot for bigger events, and there isn't one of those until later this month. I'll get a couple of the guys to help with your stuff."

"There's no need—"

"Of course there isn't a *need*," Mina said with a wink. "But let the men help anyway. It makes them feel useful." She rustled through her bag for a second and pulled out a blue glass bottle. "I found this today at the flea market in town and thought to give it to Leonard, but now I think it was meant for you."

"Oh, I don't—"

She was already handing me the slim antique blue bottle. "You can hang it in the tree outside your new place. To catch the bad spirits."

"The bad spirits?" She was still holding out the bottle, so I didn't have much choice but to take it.

"It's a local custom," Leonard explained.

Mina nodded. "Sure is. Folk around these parts believe the spirits are an important part of life. Most are good—they help the crops grow and keep the waters back. But a few of them . . ." She paused dramatically and waggled her eyebrows over a sip of her julep. "A few of them are mischievous. Devilish things that like to cause all sorts of troubles."

I glanced between Mina and Leonard, searching for some sign I was being had, but neither of them looked like they were joking.

"Oh, leave the poor thing alone." Sam rolled his eyes as he topped off my glass. "It's just a story, Luce. Kind of a local superstition."

"People around these parts think it's more than a story," Mina said, cutting her eyes in his direction. But her expression softened when she looked back at me. "It'll take a couple of days to get your cabin ready, since we weren't expecting you. But once you settle in, you'll need something pretty to spruce up your new place. And to keep you safe."

The glass was old and delicate, and when I held it up to the lamp, blue light spilled across the floor. I wasn't sure I believed any stories about spirits, but I'd arrived with practically nothing, and the bottle would lend a bit of beauty to wherever I ended up.

"Thank you," I said, meaning it.

"Are you sure you don't want to stay for supper?" Sam asked Mina. "We have plenty."

"Oh, I wish I could, but I have some work to finish up in the office before I head out." Mina turned to me. "You come see me tomorrow, Lucy, and we'll get you all set up."

"I will, thanks." Because as uneasy as I felt about everything, the fact was I *did* need the job. It had been weeks since I'd lost my last one in Chicago. The position at Le Ciel might not be perfect, but it was something until I got back on my feet. Until I could start over.

I can start over.

Maybe I *hadn't* been thinking when I fled the apartment I'd shared with Matt and the city I'd grown up in. But maybe I'd managed to make a good choice just the same. Something in the welcome of my uncle's house made a different future feel almost possible.

2

I'm falling, sinking.

Something heavy is dragging at me, pulling me down into the blackness. The water is cold around me, filled with dirt and the muck of something putrid that makes the dirt seem almost clean. I struggle up, frantic to get to the surface, but every move brings pain. Sharp, ripping pain. So sudden and absolute I almost gasp. *Almost*, because the moment my mouth opens to scream, cold, fetid water rushes in, and I clamp down out of instinct.

I have to survive this. Someone needs me. I can't die here.

But I'm still sinking. I'm heavy. *So heavy*. Something is dragging me down to the bottom, like cruel hands that won't let me go. Pain and darkness and the cold wet of death surround me.

I'm sinking.

I look up, and the dim light of the surface gets farther away.

My lungs are burning, and I only have seconds to think about what brought me here. To remember.

But before I can, my lungs spasm with my body's instinctive need for air, and the water rushes in. Burning and heavy, it fills me.

I see him suddenly, a face rising out of my memories. Essential. Necessary. Golden hair. Eyes as green as emeralds. But I can't think of who he is or why he's important before the darkness takes me in.

3

I woke with a start, lurching upright in the narrow guest room bed like I was still trying to reach the surface. My skin was clammy with sweat, and my face was wet with tears. Then my body convulsed, and I coughed up fetid water.

Against my better judgement, I'd let myself plunge into sleep the night before. There had been too many long sleepless nights leading up to Matt's decision to break things off, and that was before I'd driven south without a break. I dozed off without setting the series of alarms that keep me from sleeping too deeply, that keep me from *dreaming*.

It had been weeks since I'd allowed myself to sleep soundly enough to dream, weeks since I'd been pulled back into the nightmares that plagued me. The last time had been the night things ended with Matt. But those dreams hadn't been as vivid as this.

As I sat shaking and gasping in the damp, sweat-drenched bed, I couldn't pretend it had been a normal dream—not even one of *my* normal dreams. Something had changed.

I'd woken with such utter terror and regret that I couldn't stop myself from shaking. I'd woken with the *river* in my throat, and with the knowledge that drowning was so much less than I deserved.

And I had no idea what any of it meant.

I DIDN'T BOTHER GOING BACK to bed. Once I settled down enough for the shaking to stop, I showered off the sweat and tried to wash away the dream before letting myself out of the sleeping cottage without waking anyone. There were five missed calls from Matt, but I ignored them. I wasn't sure what either of us could possibly say. It wasn't like I could change what had happened to make us fall apart, because I couldn't exactly change myself. I would have already.

On the second day of my new life, I watched the sunrise by the Mississippi. The first hints of dawn came slowly, the light struggling through the dense trees before it painted the sky with orange and crimson. I used to watch the sunrise over Lake Michigan sometimes, when sleep seemed too dangerous back in Chicago. Even on bitterly cold days, I'd take the L downtown so I could watch the sun transform the lake into a pool of diamonds. Watching the sun erase the darkness had always helped me push away the dreams that haunted me.

But that morning, nothing seemed to touch the chill that still clung to my skin.

I tossed back the last of the can of Diet Coke I'd brought out with me. It had grown flat and tepid as I'd waited for the light to peak over the tops of the distant trees, but I choked it down anyway. I needed the caffeine.

From where I was sitting on the grassy levee, miles of fields on the distant bank gradually emerge from the shadows of night. The sun glinted off the water, but didn't transform it. As the sky lit, the river remained a muddy brown, and the tightness I'd been fighting remained solidly lodged in my chest.

Suddenly, I was angry. *Livid*. I'd been dreaming of drowning, dreaming of the mansion behind the alley of trees, dreaming about death since I was just a kid. Doctors couldn't help me. Sleeping pills had only made it worse by trapping me inside the nightmares.

The dreams had wrecked my life. I could never sleep easy, which made sleeping with someone else nearly impossible. Everyone got tired of my nightmares. My mom. Roommates. One boyfriend after another. Everyone got tired of *me* eventually. Even Matt had grown tired of the constant waking, the constant thrashing in bed. And I couldn't even blame him. No one was more tired of it than I was.

And now I was coughing up river water, like the dreams were *materializing*.

I crushed the can in my hand until the sharp edge bit into my skin, and, cursing, I let the can drop. A line of blood welled in my palm as I made my way down the bank to retrieve the can from the water's edge.

It couldn't be a coincidence, my arriving at Le Ciel Doux and the intensification of the dreams. I'd never been to Louisiana, had never even seen the plantation until my uncle started working there long after I'd been dreaming of its columns and shadows. And of some unseen terror or regret hidden among the oaks.

I'd decided to accept the job at Le Ciel in a knee-jerk reaction, but maybe something else had drawn me. I wouldn't call it fate, not exactly. But maybe some deeper need had pushed me to send the email and stop avoiding the place I'd feared for so long.

The thing with Matt had been the last straw. No more running from one bad situation to the next. I was done with letting my dreams destroy my life. I was done letting them control me. I needed to figure out once and for all what the dreams meant and how to stop them.

My camera was sitting next to me, and I picked it up, letting its familiar weight calm me as nothing else could. I took a deep breath and aimed the camera at the sunrise. I knew exactly how I wanted the picture to look. I'd overexpose it, so the sun would be a white-hot hole, obscuring everything else.

4

By midmorning, I'd checked in with Mina at the main offices and filled out the paperwork to become an employee of the trust that ran Le Ciel Doux. Mina had shown me around the offices, which stood on the edge of the plantation's grounds and introduced me to various staff members. Everyone was happy to meet me. Everyone was welcoming and warm. Considering how my morning had started, it all felt so strangely *normal*.

Mina had shown me the line of cabins where some of the staff lived. They weren't far from my uncle's cottage, but far enough away from the main house that tourists wouldn't wander by. One would be ready for me in a day or two. I could stay with Leonard and Sam until then.

It wasn't even noon yet, but the heat of summer in Louisiana was different than anything I'd ever experienced. No matter how clear the night had been, the heat of the day never really dissipated. It radiated from the pavement and the walls, swirled through the ancient trees, and hung heavy in the air. By midmorning, the day was as hot as any August afternoon in Illinois and promised only to get hotter.

I could have taken a couple of days to settle in, but after that first sleepless night, I was anxious to get started. I needed something to distract me.

Leaving the cool hush of the offices, I made my way over to the main house. I wasn't in any hurry to face it—or my fears—but if I was going to accept the job, I'd have to.

No time like the present.

I was glad to find there were fewer shadows in the morning light, and the gloom I'd sensed the evening before when I'd arrived wasn't quite as evident. A small crowd of workers was milling around the lushly green lawn that skirted the house, waiting for the staff meeting to get started.

If I hadn't known the plantation was a living-history museum, if I hadn't expected the costumed interpreters, the effect of seeing fifteen or so people standing around in wide skirts and old-fashioned suits would have been unsettling. Even expecting it, the effect was uncanny, a little like peering into the past.

Lifting my camera, I captured a few shots of the crowd, testing the quality of the Southern light. I thought about making a print for Leonard and Sam, to thank them for all they'd done to welcome me. Landscapes weren't usually my thing, but if I did the print in a sepia tone, maybe burned in and blurred it a little, the final image would probably would look like it had been taken on a day more than one hundred and fifty years ago. Past and present colliding on the same ground.

I found a place on the outskirts of the crowd and forced myself to study the house. The property was named Le Ciel Doux, which roughly meant Sweet Heaven, an apt enough name for what used to be a sugar plantation. Looking up at the gorgeous old structure, I could see why they'd picked the name. It must have felt like heaven to the people who'd lived here—at least those who'd lived in the big house.

Leonard gave a shrill whistle to get everyone's attention, and the employees gathered as he went over the events for the day. I lifted my camera, but as I centered my uncle in the viewfinder, my vision blurred and the picture shifted. Leonard's mop of auburn hair and lanky body transformed into someone else, someone broader and darker, with hooded eyes and a tight, angry mouth.

I blinked, and the scene shifted back. Leonard was there again, same as he'd always been.

Dizzy from the vision, I put the camera down and stared at the crowd again, but everything seemed normal. The sun was hot, and the sky was a clear blue, but dread still crept across my skin. *Recognition*. That was what it was. A feeling that I'd been there, in that place before. That I had seen all of it before.

I shook my head to clear the thought. Lifting my camera again, I studied the crowd, forcing myself to focus on what was real. Art was the only thing that had ever been able to break the hold my nightmares had on me. Taking pictures for the Foundation would have to be enough to distract myself from the strange sensation that had washed over me. If I focused on my work, I wouldn't have any time to worry about the fact I might be losing my mind.

That was when I saw him.

The guy was standing slightly away from the rest of the employees, leaning against one of the tangled ancient oaks that lined the wide alley leading up to the main house. Maybe it was the way he held himself, apart and confident, but something drew my attention immediately.

I felt suddenly even warmer. The man was gorgeous. Even from a distance, his broad shoulders and sculpted cheekbones made my mouth go dry. But his good looks also marked him as exactly the kind of guy I usually avoided. I knew men like that, men who spent hours in the gym, perfecting the cut of their biceps, or in front of mirrors, coaxing their hair into a perfectly disheveled tumble. Men who looked like that usually wanted high-maintenance girls, every bit as polished and perfect as they were. They didn't look twice at frizzy-haired artists with more curves than fashion sense.

None of that seemed to matter, though. My brain might have been saying no way, but my body had other ideas. Sure, Matt and I hadn't really had sex for a couple of weeks. But that didn't seem like a good enough reason for my reaction.

I wanted him. *Instantly.* And with an intensity that left me unnerved.

There you are.

The thought rose inside me, unbidden. *Unwanted.* The voice didn't quite feel like my own, but it had a familiar edge. It held the same desperation I felt every time I woke from one of my nightmares.

If his too-perfect features weren't enough to warn me off the guy, that bone-deep feeling that I knew him probably should have been.

My fingers ached, and I forced myself to release my death-grip on the camera. It was probably the exhaustion or the remnants of the strange dream from the night before. The guy was no one to me, and he was going to stay that way.

But I didn't want to admit the intensity of my feelings had rocked me, so I lifted my camera in defiance. I didn't have to be interested in a relationship or anything else to appreciate the view. I dared myself to look at him again.

Through the viewfinder, the guy came into sharper focus. His easy posture didn't match his expression. He was tense, maybe even angry. The slash of his mouth was set in a hard line over his strong, sharp chin, which was completely at odds with his casual, almost lazy, lounging against the tree.

A study in contrasts, there was something compelling about the scene—something compelling about *him.* Without hesitating, my finger pressed the shutter button, capturing him.

He couldn't have heard the soft snick of the camera—not

from that far away. But the second I took the picture, he looked directly at me as if he had.

Initially embarrassed at being caught, I lowered the camera, but I didn't let myself look away. Instead, I lifted my chin a little, as though daring him to say something. I hadn't done anything wrong. It was my job to document the grounds, and that included the employees. Or, at least that was what I told myself.

The guy's expression flickered, like he was surprised at my defiance. Taking the bait, he tilted his head and began to return the interest, his gaze sweeping slowly down my body—my rumpled outfit, my bare legs, my worn-in boots—leaving a trail of heat every bit as intense as if he'd actually touched me. From the heat of my skin, my cheeks must have been pink, but I wasn't about to turn away, no matter how uncomfortable I felt. He was toying with me. He couldn't really be interested. And I wasn't about to give him the satisfaction of backing down.

When his gaze finally drifted up my body to meet my eyes again, I lifted a single brow, and was rewarded with the hint of a smile. His eyes—a green so vibrant and true that the color was clear even from that distance—lit with amusement. Again, I couldn't shake the feeling we'd met before. That I *knew* him somehow.

That he meant something to me.

Unsettled by the intensity of the thought—my *sureness*—and by the wave of fear that followed it, I turned away so I could breathe again. I willed my heart to slow back down, took a few deep breaths to steady myself, and turned back.

But when I looked up again, he was gone.

His sudden absence felt like I'd just lost something important, but I didn't know why. Suddenly, the day was too bright, the crowd too close. My head started to swirl, and my vision blurred, and then everything went black.

5

I surfaced slowly, like swimming up through mud. Though I could sense the heat of the summer day and the buzz of concerned onlookers, I struggled to break free of the darkness that threatened to drag me under again. Nights of restless sleep, of *lost* sleep, had taken their toll.

"Miss? Can you hear me?"

I didn't recognize the voice. Deep. Rough in timbre with the hint of a Southern drawl. Concerned. But the meaning of the words barely penetrated the fogginess.

"Are you okay?" Sure fingers brushed hair back from my face. "Come on, now. I need you to open your eyes for me."

My ass and elbow ached where I'd hit them on the way down, and the ground was rocky and uneven beneath me. But I was vaguely aware that a solid wall of warmth supported my back. The air smelled of cedar and amber smoke.

No. Not the air. Someone's cologne.

I clawed my way to the surface, but my vision swam as I tried to sit upright to pull away from him.

"Whoa, there," the voice said, its rough timbre stroking something inside me. Strong hands held me steady.

Even with the world tilting, became even more aware of the concerned crowd gathering around me. I had to get up, *immediately*. Before I made a bigger ass of myself.

"Just take it easy a second," the guy said, his molasses and smoke voice like a caress that soothed my rising panic. "There's no rush."

At first, I thought it was *him*, the guy with the green eyes, but I was wrong. The guy supporting me against his broad chest had eyes the color of carmel and dark brown hair that curled around his temples.

He was gorgeous. With his strong jaw and broad soft mouth, the guy was the kind of beautiful that belonged on runways or fashion spreads. And he smelled good too, I thought inanely. *Really good*. It was a struggle not to lean into him, to take another deep breath of that woodsy spice that clung to him.

"Did you just sniff me?" he asked, looking down at me with amusement in his eyes.

"No," I lied. "Why would I sniff you?" I tried to laugh, but it came out as a choking sound. "I'm just trying to catch my breath."

A dimple winked in his cheek, like he knew I wasn't telling the truth. Like he knew exactly how completely I was attracted to him—as in, instant punch to the gut, tightening in my lady parts, and mouth gone dry with lust.

Which was the surest sign I needed to get myself out of his arms *immediately*. If I couldn't make things work with sweet, boring, stable Matt, the last thing I needed was someone who made me feel instantly off kilter.

I tried again to pull myself upright, but he didn't let me. Instead, I was off my feet before I could find them again, scooped up into strong, capable arms.

"Just hold on," he said. "Let's get you into the shade."

A thread of authority in his deep voice had me doing exactly what he demanded—holding on. My arms wrapped around his neck, and I was painfully aware of the muscles bunching and flexing in his shoulders as he carried me. My traitorous body hummed with pleasure at the feel of his broad chest, when I should have been fighting to get back on my own feet.

In a few long strides, we were at the big house, and he settled me on a wrought iron bench beneath the broad shaded veranda. People were still watching, but I barely noticed. The scent of his cologne and of him—something clean and purely male—was too damn distracting to think about anyone else.

The guy was dangerous without even trying to be. A shiver of anticipation ran through me as I considered how much more dangerous he could be if he did try.

"Are you okay?" He was peering at me with a look of concern that had my cheeks warming again, but this time from embarrassment.

"Fine," I said, trying to pretend I wasn't a little light-headed from the proximity. I forced myself to focus instead on taking stock of my injuries—my elbow ached, and my ass was still sore too and likely covered with dirt.

Suddenly, I realized I didn't know where my camera was, and I had a moment of sheer panic when I thought it might be gone. "My camera—"

"Here." A costumed worker stepped forward and handed it over. "It didn't hit the ground or anything. You caught it."

"You went down hard," the guy who'd carried me said. "I was walking up the path there and saw it happen. I thought for sure you'd hit your head." He took my face gently in his hands, not letting me pull away. I felt froze, transfixed, as his fingers gently prodded through my hair, sending little shivers of awareness across my skin as he examined me. "Look at me for a second, would you?"

Dark brown lashes and brows framed warm cognac-colored eyes that a girl could get drunk on. Gold flecks glittered in their depths, drawing me in. He was studying me so intensely that wings took flight inside my chest.

"I don't think you have a concussion," he said, releasing me.

I let out an unsteady breath, feeling stupid. *Of course.* He'd just been looking for injuries. He wasn't really interested, and I wasn't either. I couldn't afford to be.

"Are you sure you're okay? You didn't hit anywhere else?" He reached for my arm, like he was going to continue his exam, but I pulled back. I couldn't handle his hands on me again, without doing something completely stupid, like leaning in and taking another hit of that expensive cologne.

"Really. I'm good."

I definitely wasn't good. I was bruised in places other than my pride, and all I wanted was to get out of here before anything else happened. Mostly, I wanted to get away from my rescuer, whose presence was doing dangerous things to my peace of mind.

"Lucy?" Leonard was pushing his way through the crowd as I got to my feet.

The guy stood as well. He was still close—too close. His arm was slightly outstretched, like he intended to catch me if I tumbled again.

Leonard's expression broadcasted his fear. "Someone said you were hurt, and—"

"I'm fine," I assured him.

"She fainted," the guy said at the same time.

Leonard frowned. "You fainted?"

I shot a sharp look at the guy before turning to Leonard. "It was nothing. I swear. Must have been the heat, or maybe I locked my knees or something." I gave a half shrug. *Or something.*

It took everything I had to not let my gaze drift across the crowd to see if the green-eyed guy was watching the spectacle as well. But he either hadn't stayed long enough to see me go down, or he'd left shortly after.

Neither Leonard nor my rescuer looked like they were convinced, but the dark-haired guy seemed to realize the crowd hadn't dispersed yet. A couple of quick words had most of them scattering.

"You're sure you're okay?" Leonard asked again.

"Positive." I looked my camera over, brushing the dirt from its body.

"Sam said you were up early. Did you get enough sleep?"

"I'm fine, really," I said, ignoring his question. "I'm more embarrassed than anything else."

"Maybe you should head back to the cottage? Sam's still there eating breakfast. Did you eat anything this morning?"

"Seriously. . ." I tried not to sound too irritated. After all, it had been years since I'd had family close by, years since anyone had really taken care of me. "I'm good."

I stole a glance at the dark-haired guy, who'd stepped aside to speak with another of the employees, and my stomach flipped. Up close he was handsome. But the whole package? *Holy shit,* he was hot. Tall and lean with just enough muscle to fill out his clothes to perfection. I was even more embarrassed since he'd been the one to find me passed out in the dirt, but I couldn't really regret that I knew exactly how strong those arms of his were. The way he'd scooped me up? I might as well have been weightless.

Too bad I couldn't afford to be interested. I hadn't uprooted my whole life and left the only place I'd ever really known to start flirting with a guy, even one as good-looking as him. I needed to get a grip on myself. I was here to put my life back together, not to jump into some stranger's bed and end up worse than I started.

But would it be worse to end up in his bed? It wasn't like the sex with Matt had ever been spectacular. Which probably accounted for my insta-lust. It had simply been too long.

"Really, guys. I'm fine," I repeated. "I'm more embarrassed than anything else."

Leonard frowned, as though he didn't quite believe me.

My rescuer had finished up his conversation and wandered over. He looked me over, but it wasn't the toe-curling appraisal the blond guy had given me. It was legitimate, clear concern. But when his eyes met mine, they warmed. My brain might have been telling me not to be interested, but my body wasn't on the same page.

"Your color's looking better," he said. "But you should probably get out of the heat for a while. We have air-conditioning back at our offices. I could take you over there, get you some water? Maybe buy you dinner to make up for your experience here at Le Ciel." He grinned then, flashing that damn dimple of his again. "We take our hospitality very seriously 'round these parts."

I couldn't help but smile in return. The warmth in his eyes made me almost wish I *were* a tourist. It definitely made me wish I were the kind of girl who could fall into bed with someone without worrying about the fallout. But life had taught me otherwise.

"I can make my own way back to the offices," I said. "I work here."

His brows lifted, and his gaze cut to Leonard before returning to me. "You're new?"

"Just started today." I shrugged, feeling suddenly awkward.

"Silas, this is my niece, Lucy," Leonard said. "I told you about her a few months back, remember?"

"The artist." The dark-haired guy—Silas—had a new appreciation in his eyes that made my stomach flutter again. "Leonard, here, showed me your stuff. He didn't tell me you were . . ." He seemed to think better of what he'd been about to say. "You're incredible. Your work, I mean. It's exceptional."

"Thanks." My skin was growing hot under his attention, but I ignored it.

His expression grew more intense. "I'm really glad to hear Leonard finally talked you into taking us up on our offer of employment."

"Silas," I said, finally realizing who I was talking to. "*You're* Silas LaRoux? The owner of this place." Of *course* he'd be my boss.

"Not the owner anymore." If I wasn't mistaken, he looked almost embarrassed. "I put the whole estate into a trust a few years back. I'm just one of the lowly trustees who run the Foundation now."

"Don't be so modest," Leonard laughed. "You're the *head* of the Foundation."

Whatever I might have pictured when I thought of Silas LaRoux, it definitely wasn't the guy in front of me. I'd expected someone older, definitely someone with graying hair or a distinguished set of glasses. Instead, Silas LaRoux couldn't have been older than his early thirties, but he carried himself with the kind of confidence that made him seem more worldly somehow. His hair was dark—nearly black, and his skin was somewhere between a deep tan and a light brown that might be from Mediterranean ancestry, but knowing the area, it could just as likely mean Creole.

Now that I really looked at him, his clothes gave him away. He was wearing the kind of unpretentious but perfectly cut clothes that whispered money rather than screamed it. No wonder he'd smelled good. He smelled *expensive*.

Silas held out his hand, his brown eyes warming. "It's a pleasure to finally meet you, Lucy."

I hesitated only a second, already preparing for the rush of familiarity that everything seemed to trigger since I arrived at

Le Ciel Doux. But when I slipped my hand against his, all I felt was the warm strength of his grip and the same fluttering in my chest as when he smiled at me before. I didn't feel anything else. No twinge of recognition. No spike of adrenaline brought on by unexplained fear.

I practically sighed in relief.

"I'm excited to get started," I said, surprised my words were actually true. Whether I stayed or not, working at Le Ciel would give me a chance to save some money, so I could have a real choice about what I did next. "I really appreciate the chance you're taking by hiring me, Mr. LaRoux."

"Please. My friends call me Sy." He smiled, and I forced myself to ignore just how much I liked him looking at me like that. He was my boss, and with my car a heap of metal, I needed this job. "Besides, I've seen samples of your work. Hiring you wasn't exactly a gamble. I can tell you're exactly what this place needs."

His tone was so confident and his expression so welcoming —so *interested*—that I couldn't stop myself from smiling. "I hope you're right. Sorry again about. . ." I gestured vaguely toward the ground.

"Don't worry about it for a second." He held my gaze for a beat longer than was probably necessary, and the only thing I felt was that spark of anticipation that comes with attraction. But I forced myself to ignore it. Silas LaRoux was my boss, and I needed this job. The last thing I should have been thinking about was what it might feel like to run my hands through those dark curls of his.

He flashed another smile that made me want to rethink my decision to stay away. "I wonder if you might have time for a quick walk around the property. I have a couple of appointments already today, but maybe we could make time tomorrow, before it gets too warm? I'd like to get to know you better."

I should have said no, should have kept a professional distance, but my mouth apparently had other plans.

"Sure," I said, breathier than I'd intended. "I'd love to." Something about the way he looked at me made me light-headed. It made me feel things I had no business feeling.

"I have a few items I want to go over with you," he continued. "Things I'd like documented, so we can update our website."

For the job. He wanted to talk with me for the job. Mentally, I slapped myself.

"Of course." I forced a smile. "I'd be happy to take care of you."

His eyes danced, and I realized my words could be taken a couple of different ways.

"I mean, not *you.* I'll take care of the pictures," I stuttered. "Whatever you—I mean, whatever the *Foundation* needs."

His smile deepened. "I'll hold you to that. And then maybe we can grab that dinner I promised you after?"

I started to tell him dinner wasn't necessary, but Silas had already turned to Leonard and clapped him on the shoulder. "We'll talk later about Thisbe's place?"

"I'm free around two," my uncle said, seemingly unaware of the sparks that had been firing between me and Silas.

"Great." Silas's eyes warmed, and the frank openness of his interest made me feel like some kind of teenager. "I'll see *you* tomorrow. Bring that camera of yours."

"Sure." I gave him a half wave. "See you then."

His gaze held mine for another moment that had my heart squeezing, before he lifted his chin and started back toward the alley of oaks that led toward the parking area. He tucked his hands into his pockets, the picture of ease, and greeted everyone he met as he cut through the remaining costumed interpreters.

"He's a good guy," Leonard said. "He could be making a killing on events, but instead he's losing money every month.

But he's determined to transform this place into something more than some cheap tourist attraction. He's in it for the history."

"Yeah. He seems great," I said, purposely turning my back on the direction Silas had taken and forcing myself to shake off whatever attraction I might have been feeling. I didn't have any business being interested in anyone—not so soon after Matt. But thinking about starting something with my boss? That was the worst idea I'd had in a while.

Leonard gave me a once-over. "You still don't look quite right."

"Gee, thanks," I said dryly.

"Your color's all off," he said, ignoring my not-so-subtle sarcasm. "Why don't you head back to the offices and cool off, like Silas suggested. Better yet, you could head back to the cottage. I'm sure Sam wouldn't mind the company."

Retreating to the cottage felt too much like giving up. I wasn't going to let whatever had happened to me this morning win.

"I think I'll head over to the offices, instead. They're air-conditioned, and I'd like to look through some of the archival materials to get a sense of the place. It'll help me figure out how to set up some of the shots we might want for the website."

"You're sure you don't want to take the day and rest? A nice nap might be just what the doctor ordered."

A nap was the last thing I wanted. "I'm good," I assured him, slinging my camera strap over my shoulder. "Promise."

He seemed reluctant to let me go. "If you need anything—"

"I'm *fine*. Really." I rolled my eyes at him, but I had to admit it was nice having someone who cared. "I'll see you later."

Before he could argue, I took off, toward the offices at the edge of the property. I didn't look back to where Silas had been heading. I wasn't about to ruin a good thing by letting myself go down that road. But I couldn't stop myself from glancing toward the tree where the green-eyed guy had been lounging.

It hit me then, why the guy had seemed so familiar. *Those eyes.* I'd seen them the night before as I was pulled under by the Mississippi. I'd seen his face right before drowning in my dream.

6

I'd been working steadily through the afternoon, carefully making my way through the boxes of pictures and records the Foundation had collected in their main offices. I would be lying if I didn't admit to relief at being indoors, out of the summer heat and away from the big house. The Foundation kept its main offices on the property, but they had the bland, anonymous decor and buzzing fluorescent lights of most industrial parks. I could have been sitting anywhere.

A soft knock on the door drew my attention away from a series of daguerreotypes I'd found in one of the boxes. Etched into silvery sheets of metal placed under glass, the antique images were incredibly delicate, but they were also startlingly detailed. I couldn't help but be impressed with their clarity and depth. This series depicted the plantation in the mid-1800s. Someone had cataloged the mansion's exterior. In the distance, a barge drifted down the river. I could propose a series where I replicated these images, maybe. Past and present together, caught on film.

I lifted the daguerreotype to look at how it was constructed, marveling at how far photography had come and how quickly. The person who'd taken these images couldn't have predicted the darkrooms to come, and they certainly couldn't have imagined how computers would transform photography again. With digital images, nearly anything was possible.

The thought made me remember the images I'd taken earlier. Pulling out my camera, I flipped through the shots I'd captured before I went ass over elbow this morning. *Not bad.* Not amazing, but not a terrible start overall. I could see how the light here was different from up north, and also how I could work with that for better images.

I flipped through again, confused. I'd taken a picture of the green-eyed guy, but—

A knock pulled my attention from the camera, and I'd barely looked up when Mina poked her head into the room. "Can I interrupt for a minute?"

"Of course," I said, setting the camera aside. "What's up?"

The door opened completely, and Mina entered, followed by a younger woman about my age.

"I wanted you to meet my daughter, Chloe," Mina said, nodding to the woman next to her. "She works at the offices in town most of the time, since that's where most of the event staff is located, but she came by today."

Chloe had the same wide mouth and dazzling smile as her mother, and when she turned it on me, I couldn't help but smile back.

"It's great to meet you," I told her.

She was every bit as beautiful as her mother and nearly as tall. Her skin was a bit darker than Mina's, and she wore her hair in long, smooth braids that moved like water when she tilted her head. Some were tipped with silver beads that chimed happily when they clinked together.

"I'm here to rescue you." Her eyes were shining impishly.

"Rescue?" I glanced at Mina. What exactly had she heard about my tumble?

"You haven't seen the Quarter yet, right?" Chloe asked.

I shook my head. "No. I just arrived yesterday."

"So it's *way* too soon for you to be stuck in here working," Chloe said. "You need to get out. See the sights. I'm heading into the city. I thought maybe you'd want to come."

I looked back down at the daguerreotypes I'd been working through. They'd been here for more than a hundred years; they'd likely last another day. The chance to get off the property —to get away from the big house, even for an evening—was too much temptation.

"I don't have a car," I explained. "I wouldn't want to force you to drive back here."

"I don't live in town," Chloe said. "My mom and I have a place down the way, so it's no trouble. I'm coming back anyway. And if we don't feel like driving back, we can always crash at my boyfriend's place. He has a place near the Quarter."

"That sounds great. Can you give me a few minutes to put these things back? And if we could stop by my uncle's, so I could drop my camera?"

"Sure," Chloe said. "I'll meet you out front in twenty?"

DRIVING into New Orleans was a study in contrasts. One minute, we were traveling through a landscape of fields already lush with crops growing in precise rows, and then suddenly we were crossing the wide breadth of the Mississippi with a modern city rising to our right. From a distance, New Orleans looked like any other moderate-sized city. Big buildings loomed over the horizon and told the story of progress. As we drew closer, worn-out houses peppering the view along the highway provided a stark contrast and a glimpse into everyday lives.

Once Chloe exited the interstate, she drove into an area that looked vaguely European. The narrowness of the streets and alleys reminded me this was an old city, not one built for cars and busses. The buildings tumbled over one another, evidence of years and years of growth and development butting up against what had already been there. I loved it instantly.

Chloe knew the French Quarter as well as I knew the Loop. As she navigated through the twists and turns of the narrow streets, she taught me about the different buildings we passed and pointed out some of the important tourist spots. If she was irritated at all about having to play tour guide, she didn't show it. Instead, she seemed genuinely happy to have someone new to talk with, and I could tell in an instant she was one of those people others gravitated to.

You couldn't help it. With her wide smile and easy demeanor, her friendly nature was infectious. In the worn seat of her vintage blue Chevy, I found myself relaxing. Finally, we headed toward the river, where she parked in a large surface lot overlooking the water.

"I just need to stop by the office for a few minutes, and then we can grab dinner," she told me, grabbing her satchel from the backseat and locking the car.

The Foundation's satellite offices were a few blocks away on Decatur Street, across from a triangular park anchored by a statue. The building was flanked by a souvenir shop and a cigar store. It was painted a soft blue, with arched windows and doorways painted a bright white. A wrought iron balcony clung to the second story, dripping with brightly flowering vines.

"It'll be just a minute," Chloe said. "Come on in."

I followed her into the offices, where a woman with deep brown skin and natural coils framing a heart-shaped face sat behind the reception desk. She smiled at Chloe.

"Hey, Shaunda, this is Lucy," Chloe said. "She's working up at Le Ciel. She's Leonard and Sam's kin. She'll be taking pictures for the Foundation. Lucy, meet Shaunda. If you need anything at all, she can work miracles."

Shaunda tipped her chin up to Chloe, as if to say, "You know it," and then extended her hand in greeting. We talked for a few minutes while Chloe ducked back into her office to drop off her things. Shaunda had lived in New Orleans her whole life, and promised to tell me all the best places for oysters and home-cooked food.

We were laughing over a story about her son's first time eating crawfish when something shifted in the room. It wasn't that I heard him or even sensed movement, but I knew before turning who it would be.

"We meet again," Silas said with another dimpled grin that threatened to turn my knees to jelly.

"I'm here with Chloe," I blurted, as though I had to give him an excuse. His brows furrowed a bit, so went on, inanely, trying to explain. "She's going to show me around the Quarter. It's my first time in New Orleans."

"So. . . you're a virgin, then?" He bit his full lower lip and lifted his brows playfully.

"What?" My cheeks went hot before I realized he was talking about New Orleans and not my sex life. "No, I mean, yes. I mean, I've never been to the French Quarter, so I guess that does make me a virgin. In that respect."

He paused just long enough for me to realize my words implied I wasn't one in other respects, and my entire body grew so warm that I thought maybe—if I was lucky—I'd pass out again. But I stayed upright, distracted by Shaunda's cackling laughter.

Luckily, Chloe came out from the back before things could get any worse. "Sy! I wasn't expecting you to come in today. Did we have a meeting or—"

"No," he said, cutting her off before she could get too worked up. "No meeting. I just dropped by to finalize some contracts on the convention planned for the fall. I was going to leave them to be filed."

"I was about to check out for the day, but I can take care of that now, if you need me to," she said, glancing my way with a small shrug of apology.

"Tomorrow's fine," Silas assured her. "They're already signed, and you clearly have plans." He faced me then, his gaze heating. "It was good to see you again, Lucy."

"You too," I said, meaning it.

"We're still on for tomorrow?"

His steady interest was wreaking havoc on my pulse. "Of course."

"Great. There's this great place not far from Le Ciel. Very casual, but the best gumbo you've ever had." He inclined his head toward Shaunda and Chloe. "Ladies." Then he headed back into the belly of the offices.

For a second, no one said anything, and then Shaunda gave me a smirk that was all mischief. "Girl, he's got it *bad* for you."

"It's not like that," I insisted. "I'm going to do some photos for the website. That's all."

"That is *definitely* not all," Chloe said, trading a silent look with Shaunda. "*I* heard he came to your rescue this morning, scooping you up like some kind of princess when you keeled over from the heat."

"He might have helped me up," I admitted. "But he thought I was a tourist when he offered to buy me dinner. I'm sure it doesn't mean anything."

"Silas LaRoux made himself a millionaire ten times over before he turned thirty," Shaunda said. "He doesn't do anything he doesn't mean. And he was looking at you like he most *certainly* meant it."

An answering tug pulled low in my belly as I remembered the intensity in his eyes when he looked at me, the unsettling sureness of his arms caging me in—even if it was only because he'd thought I had a concussion from falling on my ass. "Really. It's not like that. He's my boss."

Chloe laughed. "Like that matters. Look, maybe you're right and there's nothing to it. But let me tell you, if that man has the hots for you, hold on with both hands and do *not* let go."

7

Outside the offices, the Quarter was starting to come alive for the evening. It was a weeknight, but even so, the sidewalks were crowded with a blend of tourists and locals. Women in cocktail dresses walked side by side with families struggling to get strollers over cracked and uneven sidewalks.

As we wandered down the crowded paths, Chloe told me about growing up by the river and close to New Orleans, pointing out her favorite shops as we went.

"We're going to meet Piers at Napoleon House. It's a little touristy, but they have a killer warm muffuletta and a courtyard with some prime people-watching."

"Sounds perfect," I said, more relaxed than I'd been in weeks.

Even before that last night with Matt, I'd known things were tense. I'd had a couple of bad nights a few weeks ago, so I hadn't been sleeping. Maybe if I would have just explained sooner. Maybe if I'd been brave enough to tell him everything, he would have understood. But I'd done what I always did—I'd hidden the darkest parts of who I was. The parts that made me feel broken and more than a little insane.

I understood the truth: if I couldn't trust Matt, a man I'd picked because he was so kind and *easy* to be with, I'd likely never trust anyone enough to let them in. To let them see who I really was.

But the Quarter was so alive, so vibrant, that I could almost forget all that. The thumping music in the air, the murmuring of the crowd, the smell of fried beignets and chicory coffee mixing with cigarette smoke—it was the distraction I needed. It was nothing like Chicago, nothing like the life I'd run from. And it was almost enough for me to forget the dream I'd had the night before.

Napoleon House was a few blocks into the Quarter, not far from the Foundation's offices. The corner restaurant looked like it hadn't been updated since Napoleon's time, with worn stucco and windows large enough to be doors, which opened out onto the sidewalk. As we approached, Chloe waved to a guy sitting at a window table—a guy who could only be her boyfriend, Piers.

He stood when we arrived, unfolding himself from the small chair until he towered over Chloe. Piers had dark brown skin that contrasted beautifully with the lemon-yellow polo he was wearing. His head was cleanly shaven, and his right arm was tattooed down to his wrist in an intricate sleeve of angular designs.

With an almost graceful sweep of his arm, he moved the chair back for Chloe, kissing her softly when she tilted her face up to him.

I took the seat across from them and tried not to interrupt. I was going to turn twenty-six later in the year, and I'd never once had what the two of them seemed to have—the ease of being with someone who simply *knew* you. I certainly hadn't had it with Matt. With him, I'd always been trying—too hard— to be what he needed, what I thought he wanted. And in the end, even that hadn't been enough.

"You're early," she said, kissing him once more before slipping into the seat he'd offered.

He lifted one brow. "You sure you aren't late?"

Checking her watch, she cursed. "Sorry, baby. I had to stop at the office, and Silas was there."

Piers shrugged. "It's fine. I've only been here a minute or two." He offered his hand before he took his own seat. "You must be Lucy."

Thankfully, when his broad palm slid against mine, there was no unsettling feeling of familiarity. I breathed a little easier as Chloe finished the introductions. "I've heard a lot about you."

He glanced at Chloe playfully before returning his attention to me. "All good things, I hope?"

"Nothing but. Chloe couldn't stop singing your praises on the drive out here. You're in grad school at Vanderbilt for anthropology?"

He nodded. "Back for the summer, though. I'll probably continue my internship at Le Ciel through the fall, if Leonard will have me."

"He's already said he will." Chloe said, cutting her eyes in his direction.

From her tone, I sensed there was something else going on between them, but then the tension evaporated, and we launched back into a comfortable conversation.

Chloe was right. The muffulettas were delicious, warm and loaded with briny pickled giardiniera mix that reminded me of the Italian beef that had been a staple of my Chicago childhood. The drinks were maybe even better. Chloe insisted I try a Sazerac, and by the time twilight painted the Quarter in soft tones, my third was softening the edges of everything.

"Where are the two of you off to next?" Piers asked, slinging one of his broad arms over Chloe's shoulder.

"I thought I'd take her to meet Mama Erzulie, and then we'll meet up with Shaunda and hit Bourbon Street before heading back." She tipped her head to his shoulder. "You want to come?"

The softness in his eyes all but disappeared. "You know I've never been a fan of you messing with that old woman."

Chloe pulled away at his words, her mouth going tight. "And you know you're being ridiculous. Especially since you're the one who introduced us in the first place."

Piers frowned. "I didn't know you'd take it as an invitation to start messing around with the spirits. It's dangerous, Chloe. You *know* that."

The irritation in Chloe's expression eased. "Piers, baby, I'm not messing with no spirits."

Piers didn't look convinced. "*Baby*—"

"Oh, crap. We're already late." Chloe checked the time on her phone. "Sorry, but we've got to go. You know Mama doesn't put up with missed appointments."

She kissed Piers intensely enough that he stopped arguing, and then she gathered her things and pulled me out of the restaurant into the bustling night of the Quarter.

"Who's Mama Erzulie?" I asked as Chloe led me through the crush of people already heading out for a night on the town, toward the towering spires of the cathedral.

"She's the best, Lucy. The absolute best. You're going to love her. She's probably the last of the old Voodoo queens left in the city."

"Voodoo?" I laughed. "Seriously?"

Chloe stopped. "Yeah, seriously." She studied me for a second, like she was making a decision on whether she'd made a mistake in taking me out, in offering her friendship.

"Sorry," I said, backtracking. "I just didn't think Voodoo was real."

"There's a lot you Yankees don't understand, you know," she said, still frowning. "All those silly movies and superstitions. Pins in voodoo dolls and all that trash." She wrinkled her nose in disgust. "That's not what Voodoo is all about, and that isn't what Mama Erzulie deals with."

I didn't know what to say to that, so I didn't respond.

"If you're not going into this with an open mind, you shouldn't come," she warned. "I'm not going to insult her like that. You don't have to be a believer, but if you've already made up your mind, then maybe it's better if I go on alone. We can meet up later."

I knew the choice she was offering was more than simply going with her or not. It was one of those capital-M moments when someone made a decision about you. Maybe I should have offered to meet her later, but I'd be lying if I didn't admit I was interested. And besides, I *liked* Chloe. She seemed smart and savvy, and if she said this Mama Erzulie character was the real deal, who was I to say she wasn't?

"Consider my mind open," I told her, lifting my hands in surrender. "Please. I'd like to meet your friend."

Chloe hesitated for only a beat longer before apparently deciding I was serious. "Okay, but we're already late, so we have to move it."

She maneuvered easily past the half-sober groups of tourists browsing through the makeshift galleries that ringed Jackson Square, and I matched her stride. As we walked, Chloe nodded toward the line of ragtag people hunched over tables, each waiting for a tourist to pay to have their cards read.

"There's a lot of fake Voodoo shops around this town, and they make a killing from selling tourists all sorts of stupid things. People come here looking for magic, so they go and buy up phony gris-gris and all kinds of dime-store junk. They hand over a lot of money to have some supposed psychic tell them their future."

She shrugged. "It's good for the city, I guess. The tourists come to find some magic, and their money helps keep this old town on its feet. Doesn't matter they're being taken, as long as they're having fun. As long as money keeps flowing into town, right?"

I wasn't sure what answer she was looking for. "I guess not."

She shook her head. "Mama Erzulie—she's not like that. She's the *real* deal."

"Wouldn't that make her dangerous, then?" I asked, thinking about Piers's warning about the spirits.

"Is a priest dangerous?" She shot me a look that dared me to contradict her. "But you assume Voodoo is because you don't know it."

She was right. I didn't know a thing about Voodoo other than what I might have seen in some old B-movie on late-night TV. I had a vague memory of one featuring a toothless old witch who controlled rotting zombies.

"You're right," I admitted. "I've spent most of my life in one place. There's a whole lot I don't know." But I thought about the dreams I'd had my whole life and how they'd intensified since arriving at Le Ciel. Doctors couldn't help me. Maybe this old Voodoo queen could read my cards and provide some insight. At the very least, she'd be interesting to meet.

8

Mama Erzulie's shop was tucked into the alley not far from the cathedral. There wasn't anything flashy about the place, and the average tourist would have walked right past the brightly colored door with its small hand-written sign that said "Readings and Herbs."

I'd expected a Voodoo queen's lair to be dark and mysterious, but I was immediately disabused of that notion. Stepping through the coral-pink door into Mama Erzulie's shop was like stepping into a sunny day. Brilliant yellow paint covered the tin ceiling, cerulean blues washed the rough plaster of the walls, and the floor was a light oak, worn almost white by time. It was a comfortable space that smelled of sage and the ghosts of pressed flowers. Teak shelves lined the back wall, filled with large clear jars, each holding a different dried herb or flower. Bottles in brilliant jewel tones hung from the ceiling, making me feel like I'd stepped into some magical forest.

"You're late, Chloe!" A call sounded from the hallway that led toward the back of the shop.

"I'm sorry, Mama. We were having dinner with Piers, and I lost track of the time. You know how distracting that man can be." Chloe laughed as she picked up one of the small primitive cloth dolls that rested on a nearby shelf and ran her fingers along it. "When are you gonna give me a love charm to make sure he's always mine?"

A woman appeared from the back hallway, looking irritated except for the beginnings of a smile that tugged at her mouth. "Baby, you know better than to think that's ever going to happen."

Mama Erzulie had to be in her early sixties, with a broad smooth face and dark hair, just beginning to go gray around the temples, pulled back into a tidy knot. Her face was more plump than angular, and she was thick through the waist. She might have been described as a sturdy woman, but no one could have called her fat. Though she wasn't overly large, somehow the room felt almost too full with her presence.

"Aw, Mama," Chloe said, clearly joking. "Just a little one?"

"I like Piers too much for nonsense like a love charm. You bind someone, and you're not talking love. You're talking something else." She tipped up Chloe's chin. A small smile pulled at the corners of her mouth. "*You*, my sweet girl, deserve love. Not that something else."

Chloe smiled and hugged her. "Damn straight, Mama. But can't blame me for trying."

The woman laughed, a heady sound, but she stopped when she finally noticed me. All the joy drained from her expression, and her posture stiffened, like just looking at me had set her on edge.

"And who's *this*?" she murmured, but I couldn't tell if she was talking to Chloe or me, or just to herself.

I tried to paste on a smile, but her staring made me feel like a specimen pinned to a board. "Hi, Ms. Erzulie. I'm Lucy. Lucy Aimes." I extended my hand. "Chloe's told me so much about you."

Mama Erzulie looked at my outstretched hand as though I'd just offered her a live snake.

"Is that right?"

She still didn't take my offered hand, so I let it fall to my side. The pleasant softness from my earlier drinks dissipated, leaving an uncomfortable embarrassment in its wake.

"Mama, Lucy's come to work out at Le Ciel," Chloe said, the false brightness in her voice doing little to dispel the tension in the room. "She's Leonard's people. His niece from Chicago. You remember I was telling you how he wanted to recruit her months ago?"

Mama Erzulie glanced at Chloe. "I remember, but why is she *here*, child?"

"I wanted her to meet you," Chloe said, glancing at me with an *I told you so* kind of expression in her eyes. "We were out for dinner tonight, and since I had our appointment, I thought I'd bring her along. She doesn't know all that much about Voodoo."

Mama Erzulie's dark eyes were sharply focused on me, and examined me the same way someone might if they were trying to determine if a piece of fruit was rotten. "Maybe she doesn't want to know."

"No. I mean, yes. I do," I stuttered. "I'd like to know more, that is."

"Why?"

"Why not?" I shrugged.

Mama Erzulie's lips twitched. "Why not, indeed." She thought about it for a second as she continued to study me, and then, making up her mind, she walked over and sat at the small table in the corner of the shop. "Well, then. You want to know about Voodoo? Fine. You come over here and let me read your cards. Then we'll see how much more you want to know."

～

AT MAMA ERZULIE'S WORDS, Chloe's expression softened, and I had the sense I'd passed a test of some sort. "You're going to love this, Lucy," she whispered as we followed Mama Erzulie over to the small table adorned with crystals. "She's never wrong."

I wasn't convinced, but I didn't want to offend anyone, so when the old woman gestured that I should take a seat across from her, I sat without question or complaint, and I waited for her to work her magic.

Mama Erzulie took out a stack of oversized cards with an intricate design on the back. Printed in ink the color of old blood, delicate lines of angular dark symbols bordered a series of interlocking doors. The markings reminded me a little of Piers's tattoo, and the wear around the edges of the cards, along with their slight discoloration, made them look ancient. "We're gonna shuffle the deck, and then you're gonna draw. Once you have your cards, I'll read them for you."

Mama Erzulie shuffled the deck thoroughly, let me cut it, and then spread it before me, facedown, in a wide arc.

"Pick three and line them up, facedown in front of you." She gestured to the table. "Go on now."

I glanced over at Chloe, who gave me a serious nod of encouragement.

Okay, then. I drew three cards and did as Mama Erzulie asked, placing the cards in a straight line from left to right across the table. In a practiced movement, the old woman swiped up the remaining cards and set them aside.

Her steady gaze swept over my face. "You don't believe this is real, do you, baby?"

I glanced over at Chloe, who looked nervous. If I thought lying would have helped anything, maybe I would have. But I sensed that the old woman would have known. "Not really," I admitted. "But I'm willing to let you show—"

"Bah," she interrupted. "It doesn't matter what you believe. There is. And there isn't. You can choose not to listen, but that

doesn't make what I'm gonna tell you any different. Look here."
She pointed at the discarded pile. "You didn't pick any of these
cards. Why not? Why'd you pick the ones you did?"

I frowned. "I don't know. I just did."

"You didn't think nothing about it, did you?" Mama Erzulie
pressed. "You didn't have no strategy. It's all chance, right?"

"Sure," I said, regretting my decision to come and wanting to
get the whole reading nonsense over with.

"Maybe so." The old woman pursed her lips. "But maybe
something drew you to those cards." She held her hand up
before I could protest. "You got to understand it doesn't
matter what you *think* or even what you believe. It matters
what *is*. You see, girl, there's energy all around us." She
lifted her arms and gestured at the surrounding room like a
magician revealing her trick. "Good energy. Bad energy. It
moves us, steers us. We aren't aware of it, mostly, but it's
there. Everything's energy. You're energy. I'm energy. These
cards, they got their *own* energy deep inside them. That
ain't hoodoo," she said with a sharp tap on the table.
"That's *physics*, girl. Something for you to wrap your head
around.

"Now these cards are just one way of reading that energy
you got inside you. *And* the energy that moves us *all* around."
She paused and pointed to the first card. "See here, this first
card—it's your past."

"But I thought you were going to tell me my future," I
countered.

She looked at me as though I was impossibly dense. "How
can you know where you're going if you ain't know where you
been, girl? You can't have no future without a past.

"Now, as I was telling you, this here card represents that
past." She flipped it over and showed me its face. Unlike the
back of the card, the picture on the face was stunning. The card
was printed in lush colors and iridescent ink that didn't show

any signs of wear from age. When the light hit it, the picture seemed to be in motion.

I blinked, willing my eyes to focus, but the image on the card continued to move. The Sazeracs I'd had earlier were apparently stronger than I'd realized.

Mama Erzulie didn't bother to explain the strange card, but flipped the next card, and the next. "This is your present, and this is your future." She sat and considered the cards, humming to herself. When she glanced up at me, I was surprised to see her original distrust had transformed into something more like interest. Maybe even curiosity. "You're gonna be an interesting one to watch. You drew yourself some very powerful cards."

Leaning forward, I studied the strange cards with their even stranger images. "That's good, right?"

I glanced up at Chloe, who gave me a small promising nod of approval.

But Mama Erzulie didn't answer.

"Look here." She pointed to the upturned cards, tapping two of them with her long finger. "You drew mostly the Major Arcana. That's rare. They're only about a third of the whole deck. But they're the most important cards. The *trump* cards. They mean your life's gonna be of major importance. You're gonna have yourself a higher purpose than most in this world."

Well, that at least sounded promising. And whatever the old woman was seeing in the cards had made her soften toward me. Her expression was still serious, but it no longer held the clear distrust she'd had when we met.

"We'll start here." She pointed to the distant past card. It was a picture of a woman with long raven hair sitting in a chair and holding two long broadswords in a defensive cross in front of her.

"The Two of Swords. This here card shows me that in the past, you blocked your emotions and avoided the truth because you refused to see what was right in front of you." She gave me a look that said she wasn't surprised.

"See here, how the woman is blindfolded? She can't see the truth. She *refuses* to see it. She'd rather hold those weapons than take off the blinders she's wearing, and the swords are crossed over her heart, because she won't allow herself to *feel* the truth either."

"What does that mean?" I asked.

"It means you kept someone or something out, because you didn't trust in your own heart." She reached across the table and tapped lightly on my chest.

She could have guessed. There was no way she could have known the truth—that I kept *everyone* out because it was easier than trying to explain. Keeping myself locked away was so much easier than watching pity replace affection.

Mama Erzulie had already moved on to the next card. "This here card, the Fool, is your present."

I huffed. "Figures."

"Girl, the Fool don't mean you're foolish." She paused for effect, lifting her brows thoughtfully. "Though, maybe you are. Pay attention. Really take a good look at it and tell me what you see."

Chloe was peering over my shoulder at the spread on the table, but I didn't need her confirmation this time.

I studied the card. At first glance, it could almost have been the Joker from a typical deck, but when I examined it more carefully, I saw something more. The fool wasn't wearing the usual court jester hat, as I'd originally thought. The hat was actually his—no, *her* hair, blowing wildly in the wind as she leaped onward. She carried a brilliant crimson bag and was accompanied by a sleek whippet-like dog.

"She seems so free," I murmured, the words coming before I could even think to stop them. Drawn to the image, I touched the card, and as my fingers brushed its worn surface, I swear a breeze rippled through my hair.

The older woman clucked approvingly. "See here, girl, this card means you're starting something—a journey or quest. It's signifying new beginnings and new challenges."

New beginnings...

Her words brought me back to reality. "No offense, ma'am, but it doesn't take a fortune teller to know I'm starting something new. I just moved here." I couldn't shake my doubt.

Mama Erzulie shot me a dark look. "That may be true enough, but I ain't no fortune teller, and your move isn't what I was talking about. It's only part of your journey. See here, how the card is facing away from you?"

I nodded.

"The Fool usually tells you to follow your heart, but the position of *this* card? It's closed. It means you're reluctant to give yourself that freedom. And that reluctance is going to hold you back in more ways than one."

I couldn't help but wonder if she was talking about the instant attraction I'd felt for Silas.

She continued, seemingly unaware of my growing doubt. "This card is your *future*."

I looked at the final card. Where the other cards had been almost alive with color, the last one was a study in darkness. A hooded figure grasped a jagged-edged scythe in its skeletal hands as it stood over the broken and bleeding body of a woman. The only color on the card was the deep scarlet of the blood running from her throat. Behind them, a dark river flowed.

My chest was suddenly too tight. The air in the room was suddenly too warm. There was an entire deck of cards to choose from, but somehow the card I'd managed to pull to predict my future was Death.

9

"So, what? I'm going to die?" I asked, my voice breaking a little as I thought of the dream. Looking at the dark river on the card, I could practically feel the cold, fetid water of the dream I'd had the night before rushing over me, pulling me down.

Mama Erzulie made an impatient-sounding snort that jolted me back into the room. "You're looking at things too literally. You got to look *soul* deep. Death doesn't mean no end. This card shows a *powerful* energy. It means something's gonna change."

"Death is more than a change," I said dryly, trying to cover my fear with sarcasm.

But Mama Erzulie didn't take the bait. "You don't believe that when we die, we just end, do you?"

I thought about that for a moment. "I don't know."

"You don't need to *know*. Can't change what is. That's what this card is showing us. Death isn't nothing more or less than a change. Something was," she said, sweeping out one hand and then the other. "Something new is gonna be. This here card means something big is coming for you, Lucy. A door will close. Another will open." She pinned me with her eyes. "Something is gonna change in your journey. And you'll have to decide whether to sink or swim above it."

"That sounds like I should be worried," I said, no longer caring how stupid fortune-telling and card reading might be. I'd woken this morning with the river in my mouth. I'd pulled the Death card to predict my future. I needed to know what was coming next.

"Well now, that depends, don't it?" Mama Erzulie sat back in her chair and considered me. "You're in for big changes. Scary at times, transformative always, but if you don't turn away from the challenge, you'll be all right in the end. Just remember, you can't start moving into one life until you let go of the other."

I wasn't sure what that was supposed to mean, but before I could ask for clarification, Chloe chimed in.

"Mama Erzulie's always right, Lucy," Chloe said reverently. "She's got the gift."

I looked between the two women, trying to keep my face from broadcasting my doubts.

"I can tell you're having trouble believing this." Mama Erzulie smiled warmly, as though confirming she had read my thoughts clearly. "But you don't need to believe me."

"I don't?"

She leaned forward a bit. "What is, *is*, baby. Not all magic is make-believe. Love is a powerful magic, and it's as real as anything you can touch."

But love had never been any kind of magic for me. Matt wasn't the first guy to think he wanted to be with me, only to turn away the second things got hard—the second he realized I was too much trouble to deal with. He wouldn't be the last.

"You *know* that's the honest truth," Chloe murmured, clearly unaware of the direction my own thoughts had taken. "Read me, Mama, please?"

Mama Erzulie shook her head. "You aren't ready yet, Chloe.

We still got some more work to do before I can read your cards."

I didn't understand why I had been ready when Chloe wasn't, and I could tell Chloe felt the same way. Disappointment, and maybe also a hint of anger, crashed through her expression, but she masked it quickly.

"We still have a little time, though," Chloe said. "Can we still have our lesson?"

Mama Erzulie nodded. "Of course we can. Do you remember where we left off?"

"We'd just started talking about the dreaming," Chloe said.

"The dreaming?" My voice broke, and my unease must have been evident, because both women were looking at me with new questions in their eyes.

Mama Erzulie frowned. "What do you know about Voodoo, Lucy?"

"Not much," I admitted. "Is it a little like . . . I don't know? Witchcraft?"

Chloe took a sharp breath.

"Witchcraft?" Mama Erzulie asked, more curious than horrified. "So you think Voodoo is some kind of dark art? Some kind of hocus-pocus?"

"I honestly don't know."

She shook her head, then tilted it. "Voodoo is *so* much more than that." She glanced up at Chloe. "Tell her, baby."

"Voodoo isn't a bunch of spells," Chloe explained. "It's more of a religion. It's a way of understanding the big powers out there."

"It's a way of *interacting* with the energy all around us," Mama Erzulie clarified. "We got a Supreme Being, no doubt about it, but he mostly stays out of the way. He's got bigger worries than us. But the lesser spirits—we call them the Loa— they *do* get involved in our lives. Voodoo gives those of us who practice a way to speak to the Loa—to ask them to intercede for us. The practice is more akin to praying to saints than any kind of hocus-pocus you might be thinking about."

She turned to Chloe, like a teacher drilling a student. "What is the world made of?"

"It's made of energy, Mama. Energy that moves and changes," Chloe dutifully recited.

The old woman murmured in approval and returning her gaze to me. "You *know* it. Those fancy scientists in those fancy colleges took years to figure out what my people have known for ages. We all just energy. Energy doesn't end. It changes. *Transforms*. A person is many things, but at the base—at the very *root*—we're nothing more and nothing less than energy.

"Those of us who practice believe each human life is made up of a body and a spirit." She lifted one of her hands and then the other, as though balancing the two thoughts in her palms. "One can't exist without the other. Our body, now that's our form in this here world, but it ain't just flesh. It takes a lot of energy to locomote a body, and that energy comes from the life force *all* living things share. That energy is a thing itself, a part of the body but separate from the soul."

She glanced at Chloe. "Tell her, Chloe. What is a soul?"

"It's who we are," Chloe said. "The essential part of ourselves."

"It's who we've *always* been," Mama Erzulie corrected.

"You mean, like reincarnation?" I asked.

"A little like that, yes," the old woman confirmed. "The soul connects our many pasts to our current present. Those pasts, those other lives, they accumulate, and they help determine who we are gonna become in *this* life. When our body dies, our soul goes back to the source of everything until it's ready to start again. It changes, of course, from life to life, but the soul doesn't end."

"But what about heaven?" I wondered. "Why would any soul want to be reborn if it could just stay there?"

"To be the same forever and ever—to never *change*?" Mama Erzulie asked. "That ain't no kind of heaven. A soul ain't nothing but a dream unless it has a body."

"A dream?" I asked, my throat going tight around the word.

Mama Erzulie only nodded. She was focused on Chloe now and their lesson. "That's where we left off, wasn't it?"

"Yes, ma'am," Chloe said. "You were going to tell me about the dreaming."

The old woman took a deep breath and seemed to consider her words. "We already talked about how the soul needs a body, but the life of the body is something of a trial, no doubt about it. That trial is *everything*, though. Because the lessons the soul learns in *this* life will shape who it will become in the next." She paused again before continuing. "But sometimes a soul has unfinished business, something in one of its previous lives that hangs like a weight around its neck. For those souls, they can get drawn back to their earlier pasts when they walk free in the dreaming."

"What's the dreaming?" I asked.

"It's the part of life that lets our souls be what they've always been," Mama Erzulie explained. "When we close our eyes each night, we let go our bodily worries, so our soul can be free."

"So if someone has a recurring dream," I said carefully, picking my words like dangerous fruit, "it might mean something about some past life?"

From the looks the two women gave, I instantly regretted not keeping my mouth shut. But the dreams were back, more intense than ever. I was at the point where I'd listen to pretty much anyone's ideas about what it meant if they could help me stop them.

Mama Erzulie considered my question for a long awkward minute before she finally spoke. "Dreams let our souls walk free from our body, from our here and now. For some, they're a way to re-remember something from an earlier time. For others, they might see glimpses of their future—or of their lives to come. But for most they're simply a way for our souls to roam and play."

There was nothing playful about the horror of drowning in a river.

I thought about the card—Death's skeletal hand reaching for the bleeding girl, the dark water of a river in the background. "Is there any way to tell?" I asked, more urgently than I meant to. "I mean, whether a dream is about the past or the future?"

The past, I could handle. That was over and gone. The future, though? Considering what my dreams were about, that was more than a little worrisome.

Mama Erzulie paused and studied me for another uncomfortable moment, her eyes sharp as knives, before lurching to her feet. "I'm afraid our time's up." She looked at Chloe, her expression softening a little. "We'll pick up again next week. And don't you be late." She wagged a finger at her.

"Yes, ma'am."

"But about the dreams I've been having?" I asked again, interrupting their goodbye.

The old lady stopped my words with the sharpness of her gaze. "Time's up for now." She offered her hands and pulled me up. Her expression was determined and serious. "You have an old soul, Lucy Aimes, and there are hard choices ahead of you. But they're choices only you can make." She squeezed my hands gently before releasing them.

And with that dismissal, Mama Erzulie hugged Chloe before disappearing through the doorway leading to the back of her shop.

Chloe and I stood in silence for a second or two, both of us staring after her. I felt suddenly uneasy and almost painfully sober, and from the ragged exhale Chloe released, I suspected she probably felt the same.

"That was a little intense," I admitted as we let ourselves out of the shop.

I didn't realize how cool the shop was until we stepped back out into the steamy heat of the evening. But even the wall of Southern humidity wasn't enough to distract me from all the old woman had told me.

My phone buzzed in my back pocket, and a message from Matt waited for me. I didn't have any doubt that things were over when I left, but the blunt impatience of the message was the final nail in the coffin.

I sent back an equally terse reply, telling him to just trash the rest of my stuff, and ignored the burning in my eyes as I tucked my phone away.

"That bad, huh?" Chloe asked.

I let out a shaking breath, willing myself not to start crying like some kind of idiot. It was my own fault he was angry—I'd kept things from him, things about who I was, until it was too late. "Worse."

"Come on." Chloe looped her arm through mine and tugged me toward the noise of Bourbon Street. "We need to find Shaunda, and you *definitely* need another drink."

10

We made it back to Le Ciel long after midnight, and I spent the rest of the night trying to avoid my dreams. But every time I slipped back into sleep, I was in the Quarter again, being chased by shadows I didn't understand.

The next morning, I felt every second I hadn't slept. There wasn't enough coffee in the world, but I showered off the grime from the night before and took my camera equipment to report for duty. I still had an appointment with Silas later that afternoon, and I was more than a little nervous. After what happened the day before—first fainting at the morning meeting and then later basically losing my shit with Chloe—I wasn't sure that meeting my too-handsome-for-his-own-good boss to take a walk around the property was the best idea.

Still, even though I shouldn't have, I *wanted* to see him again. I would have been lying if I said I wasn't at least a little interested. Even if getting involved with my new boss was a terrible idea.

Luckily, the morning provided enough distractions that I couldn't think too much about the upcoming meeting. Leonard

took me over to an excavation site on the property and introduced me to the anthropologist the Foundation had hired to dig
up the past. Byron was a middle-aged white man with a gut like
a spare tire and the personality of a log.

I spent the morning running errands and taking pictures of
various artifacts. He kept me too busy to worry or think. By the
time noon came around, any nerves I might have been feeling
about meeting with Silas had been replaced by the need to get
away from Byron. When he finally gave me a lunch break, I
headed off without looking back.

The day had warmed quickly into the kind of heavy, moist
heat that made it hard even to sweat. Tendrils of my hair were
sticking to my neck, and my huntergreen Foundation polo was
clinging to my back, but I wasn't quite ready to head back to
Leonard and Sam's place. Since Sam had the summer off, I
knew he'd be home, and I just wasn't ready to make small talk
about how things were going. Especially considering the last
twenty-four hours.

I decided to take my camera and take a few pictures for
myself, instead. Maybe ease back into everything by trying to
frame the world through my camera lens. Even when things
were at their worst, my pictures had always been able to help
me through.

I grabbed an apple and a granola bar from the offices, and
then took the gravel pathway that wound through the gardens
toward a line of trees before coming to a clearing with a small
pond. It was clearly designed to look like a quaint forest glen,
but I was disappointed to discover that everything about the
space was too perfect and artificial. At the far end of the clearing, one of the oaks that were the trademark of the plantation
dripped its Spanish moss over a bit of land that interrupted the
otherwise-perfect oval of the lake. It was picturesque, sure, but
it wasn't *interesting*.

If anything, something about the tree made me feel even more unsettled and just plain *off* than the big house.

I was about to head back when a warm breeze rushed up from behind me and cut through the stillness of the day, stirring the trees that surrounded the pond and violently rustling their leaves. The current rippled through my hair, grazing me with an unwelcome warmth, and sent a skittering awareness across my skin like a warning. I scanned the tree line across the pond for danger, but didn't see anything that would explain my intense unease. When the feeling didn't subside, I scanned the trees at my back for some sign of danger.

I wasn't alone.

The green-eyed guy from the day before was lying in the shade of the trees not far from where I was standing. His shirt was open, and the sculpted lines of his well-defined chest were bare to the dappled sun. He was sleeping, his face covered by a well-muscled arm, and completely unaware I'd happened upon him.

Mine. The word bubbled up unexpectedly, shaking me with the same urgency I'd felt the morning before. *Finally,* the voice inside me whispered. *Finally.*

I didn't know what that meant or why this guy could evoke such intense feelings. I probably should have left right then. It would have been smarter to turn and pretend I'd never seen him lying there like some kind of Grecian marble. But I couldn't bring myself to look away. My feet wouldn't move.

When the breeze finally stilled, the clearing went silent once again, something had shifted in the atmosphere. It felt almost like this clearing was separate somehow from the rest of the world, a pocket of stillness untouched by the bustling work of the estate. It seemed almost natural for the guy to be there, a part of the scene—like he was meant to fit just so, there resting beneath the tree. Or perhaps it was the other way around—the diamond-clear water of the pond and the spread of wildflowers around its edge could as easily have been designed to serve as a setting for his too-perfect beauty.

I *definitely* didn't belong there. I had the inexplicable urge to get as far away from there, as far away from Le Ciel, as I possibly could.

Panic clawed at me as I fled from the clearing, but before I could make a complete escape, a twig snapped under my foot, shattering the silence. The green-eyed guy woke, pulling himself upright in a quick, graceful movement. His eyes locked on me almost instantly, and sudden recognition pulsed through me again. This time it, though, it was even stronger.

"You came." His voice was warm and rough, and the low rumble of his words rubbed at some long-forgotten memory.

I should have been terrified. Part of me was. But there was almost an inevitability to the moment, like I couldn't have run from it—from *him*—even if I had wanted to.

Again, I remembered the dream from my first night. The terror of drowning. The mystery of his emerald eyes looking at me through the murky depths. Somehow it was all connected— my nightmares, this place, and *him*. But how?

Neither of us said anything else at first, but there wasn't any awkwardness to the silence between us. Could he feel the same strange pull? The same familiarity? Did he feel the same startling *want*.

Somehow, I doubted it. He was examining me again. When his brow creased into a frown, I fought against the impulse to smooth down my curls and tug at my sweat-dampened shirt. But from the tightness around his eyes, I wasn't sure any amount of preening was going to improve his impression.

All at once, he seemed to make up his mind. He broke eye contact first and pulled his shirt around his bare torso. With quick, efficient movements, he buttoned it. His eyes were sharp, and I got the distinct feeling he was calculating something. But I didn't have a clue what it could be.

Finally, he spoke again. "I was beginning to think you would not come." He spoke formally, and his voice held the hint of an accent—maybe French?

I frowned. "I didn't know I was supposed to." Maybe I'd missed something. But if I was supposed to meet him out here to help with something for the Foundation, maybe I'd misread everything.

"No?" He smiled softly then, but his eyes remained too serious.

"No. No one said anything about meeting you here." I gave him an apologetic shrug. "Is there something Silas wanted shots of? That tree, maybe, or—"

He started to move closer, and my mouth went dry. I completely forgot what I'd been saying. He was close enough that I could see his eyes weren't simply green. His irises glinted with different shades of emerald, and the combination gave the effect of surprising depth and emotion.

Another gust of warm air coursed around us, setting the trees in motion and lifting his honey-blond hair from his brow.

"Or?" he asked, echoing me. But I still couldn't remember what I'd intended to say.

A strange energy was building in the heavy, humid air—one that almost crackled between us. As sun glinted off the stone-smooth surface of the water, a breeze rustled up the dappled underbellies of the leaves again. The moment felt strangely familiar. Even if it didn't quite feel safe.

"Or the pond," I finished weakly, my voice betraying my nerves. I willed myself not to take a step back. "Have you been waiting here long?"

He nodded, but didn't offer any other explanation.

"I'm really sorry. I didn't mean to keep you. If I'd have known you were expecting me . . ." His expression didn't soften, so I shrugged again. "They must have forgotten to mention it back at the offices."

He simply stared.

"Look," I said, holding out my hand. "Let's start again. I'm Lucy."

He tilted his head, but he didn't accept my offered hand. An amused smile tugged at his mouth. "Ah, so you are the Light."

"What?" I dropped my hand.

"Your name, it means light." He gestured to the sky. "Like the sun."

"Right," I drawled. He wasn't wrong. "Actually, I was named after this woman—a suffragette named Lucy Stone. Some historian or someone said she had a soul 'as free as the air,' and my mom decided that's what she wanted for her daughter."

I was officially babbling. Oddly enough, though, he looked intrigued.

"And do you?" he asked.

I blinked, confused. "Do I what?"

"Have a soul as free as the air?"

"Oh." I thought about it for a second. About the nightmares that haunted me, about feeling that being there at Le Ciel had always been inevitable. About everything Mama Erzulie had explained about souls and the lives they led before.

"You know, I think my mom got it wrong. I think my soul has been pretty stuck for a while now."

It was more honesty than I'd intended, but the way he was looking at me made the words feel right—almost necessary.

If he was surprised by my frankness, I couldn't tell. His expression never so much as flickered. "I quite know the feeling."

There was a stark sadness in his tone that suggested he understood.

"I am Alexandre."

The rolling cadence of his soft accent gave the name a sophisticated edge that pulled at another memory in the dark corners of my mind. Another flicker of recognition, of familiarity that I couldn't completely dismiss.

"You're not from around here?"

He shook his head and stepped closer. "But I have been in this place quite a long while."

I wasn't sure if it was the intensity in his expression or his nearness—if it was excitement or fear—that made my heart unsteady in my chest. The space between us was charged with a peculiar energy, and I thought he might close the distance between us and touch me.

His crooked grin told me he had recognized the direction my thoughts had taken, and I don't know if it was the angle of the light hitting his face or the tilt of his mouth, but again, recognition glimmered.

"It is very nice meeting you, Lucy." He turned to go, clearly dismissing me and our entire conversation.

I sighed. "Likewise, Alex," I muttered.

He stopped. Hesitated for a moment before turning back to me, his expression unreadable. "What did you call me?"

I shrugged, trying for a nonchalance I didn't at all feel. "Sorry. You just look more like an Alex."

I hadn't really noticed the tension in his body until his shoulders relaxed and his eyes softened. His mouth pulled up— just a little—at the corners. Not enough to be a real smile, but enough to show he was amused. "As you wish, *ma chère*." He gave me a small ridiculous bow and then headed off through the trees on the far side of the pond.

Still unsettled, I lifted my camera and captured his tall form as it receded into the woods, a stark figure against the darkness of the trees beyond. He looked back as the shutter snapped, but when I looked up from the viewfinder, he was gone.

11

"I have good news."

I glanced up from the box of antique photographs I'd been sorting through. Mina was standing in the doorway.

"Oh? What kind of good news?"

"Your cabin—" She paused, frowning. "You're not really going to wear that for your meeting with Silas, are you?"

"What do you mean?" I looked down at the green polo the staff wore while on duty. "What's wrong with it?"

"Nothing," she said, her brows lifting. "If you're trying to send the clear message that you're not even a little bit interested in a young, handsome, and eminently eligible bachelor like Silas LaRoux, that's exactly what you should wear."

I pressed my lips together to keep from laughing. "And what if I'm not interested?"

"I'd say you're a terrible liar." She smirked. "Or an idiot. But I don't think you're an idiot."

"Thanks for the vote of confidence. Did you have some news about my cabin?"

"Oh, right." She pulled a set of brass keys from her pocket and placed them on the table in front of me. "Your place is ready."

"Seriously?" I picked up the keys, measuring the weight in my hands. After leaving Chicago with practically nothing? They felt like freedom.

"The cabin's not much—none of them are. But it's clean and has its own plumbing. We can get some of the guys to help you bring your stuff from Leonard's."

"I can take care of it," I told her. "There's not that much."

She nodded. "If you need anything, just holler. But in the meantime, think about finding something a little less . . . *corporate* for this afternoon's meeting?"

IT WAS PROBABLY A HUGE MISTAKE, but I took Mina's advice and changed into a breezy silken tank top and a pair of loose linen shorts before meeting with Silas. After the embarrassment of our first meeting, I figured it couldn't hurt to make a better impression. The outfit was dressy without looking like I'd tried too hard, and the shorts let me move and crouch, in case I'd misread the invitation and actually needed to take pictures during our walk.

I grabbed my bag to head out, but when I caught sight of myself in the hall mirror, I decided to take an extra minute and swiped on some makeup. There were dark circles under my eyes from too many sleepless nights, and the warm, bronze skin I'd inherited from my Dominican mother looked almost sallow from exhaustion. A little concealer and blush perked up my complexion, and mascara helped make the blue of my eyes pop against my tawny skin. Sometimes I wished I had the same warm hazel that ran in the Aimes family, but I couldn't regret the soft grayish-blue that came from my mom. Though, more days than not, I regretted getting her unruly curls. Since arriving, I'd come to realize fighting the Louisiana humidity was a losing battle, so I tied my shoulder-length hair back into a low, loose knot to keep it off my neck and out of my face.

I took another look at myself in the mirror. I'd have to do. It was a business meeting, not a date, I reminded myself. And I wasn't interested in Silas LaRoux. I couldn't be.

Silas was already there, finishing up some paperwork in his own private office, when I returned to the Foundation's on-site building.

"He said to go on back," Mina told me with a small nod of approval.

I knocked softly at his open door and tried to tell myself it didn't matter that my heart raced at the sight of him sitting there, concentrating on the papers in front of him, or that his expression lit when he looked up and found me standing in the doorway. Still, I felt that same instant and overwhelming attraction, and my whole body felt like a live wire when his gaze traveled from the scoop neckline of my tank to where my shorts hit the top of my thighs, the soft brown of his eyes darkening with appreciation.

He swallowed, visibly, and looked almost as bowled over as I felt.

Good. At least I wasn't alone in feeling whatever this was between us. Even if I couldn't let it go anywhere.

"Give me a second to finish this, and then we'll go."

"Sure," I said, suddenly more nervous than I had been before. I was feeling that heady mix of anticipation and excitement and uncertainty that came with attraction. "I'll just wait out front."

I was a coward, but I needed a minute or two to pull myself together and to prepare to spend the afternoon by his side. Especially if I was going to follow through on my plan to keep things professional.

The heat of the day was just starting to ebb when we left the offices and headed toward the big house. The last of the day's visitors were framing their final pictures with the ancient live oaks and the mansion lurking off in the background.

"I'm not sure how much Leonard's explained about this place, or why I bought it," Silas said as we walked along. He smiled at a couple reading the inscription on one of the many plaques around the estate.

"He's explained a little," I told him, underselling the details my uncle had filled in for me. I wanted to hear them from Silas himself.

"What did he tell you about me?" There was a larger question in his tone.

"I knew you bought the place a few years back and that you're trying to save it, but until you came to my rescue yesterday, I didn't know who you were."

"Clearly," he said, biting back a smile.

My face warmed as I thought of our first meeting and how I'd acted like a complete idiot. He'd definitely caught me sniffing his cologne like some kind of addict. Even now, I had to force myself to resist leaning in and taking another hit of what seemed to be his signature scent, warm and woodsy and so damn mouthwateringly good.

"I'm sorry—"

"Don't be." His eyes filled with humor. "It was refreshing."

"Sure . . ."

"It *was*," he said, and this time his expression grew serious as he stepped toward me. His scent wrapped more tightly around me, and I wanted to step into him, to accept whatever he was offering. "New Orleans is a big enough city, but out here?" His voice was soft, but its deep timbre sent skittering awareness across my skin. "Everyone knows everyone's business. They all especially know *my* business. The fact you didn't. . . ?"

He took another step closer, until I could feel the warmth

radiating off his body. "The fact you were attracted to me even though you *didn't* know about my bank account?"

"Who said I was attracted to you?" I asked, sounding every bit as breathless as I felt.

His mouth kicked into a smile. "Are you saying you aren't?"

I forced myself to take a step back and tried to ignore the hammering of my heart. "I'm saying it doesn't matter, since you're my boss."

"That's what I thought." His smile grew even brighter. "Come on. Let me show you the mansion."

Up ahead, the late afternoon light drew slanting shadows across the house, like the bars of a prison. The mansion was beautiful—there was no denying that. Everything about the architecture and design was intended to be visually stunning. But a heaviness, a foreboding hung over the entire estate, something larger than my own personal nightmares.

As he gave me a tour of the mansion, pointing out specific features he wanted cataloged and documented, Silas told me about the history of the estate. With how aware of him I was, it took all my concentration to listen to his story instead of imagining what it would be like if he simply pressed me against one of the heavy wooden doors and kissed me senseless. Somehow the tale of Jean-Pierre Dutilette, the French sugar farmer who established the plantation couldn't hold a candle to my clearly sex-starved imagination.

By the time Silas was telling me about how Jean-Pierre's son, Roman, took over in the 1840s and built the house, I'd almost managed to get ahold of myself. *Almost.* Thanks to Silas's smooth-as-molasses drawl, I'd never been so turned on by a history lesson in my entire life. Luckily, Silas didn't seem to notice. Or at least he pretended not to.

"It was a miserable existence for everyone but the Dutilettes," Silas continued as we walked the property. We stopped to look out over land that would have once been sugarcane but was now planted with soybeans. To the right, the Mississippi rolled silently by. "Sugar might grow readily in the Caribbean, but this far north it's harder to cultivate. It took a lot of manpower and a tremendous amount of brutality. There's blood on this land that can't be erased."

Something in his voice had me turning toward him. "Then why buy Le Ciel?"

His eyes met mine, and I saw the thread of steel that must have been the cause of his success. "Someone had to."

"But why you?"

His brows drew together. "The family that owned this place before me was making good money, but they were tired of managing it. In the forty or so years since they bought the land, they'd turned the estate into a tourist trap like most of the other plantations left on the River Road. They'd tried to erase the worst parts of the past—tore down all the cabins where enslaved people lived, bulldozed any sign of their graves or existence, and wiped any mention of them from the tours." His beautiful mouth tightened. "Apparently, tragedy isn't good for business.

"I don't blame them, exactly. I get that the house is beautiful. The land is too. Look there, how the river curves." He pointed out over the fields to where the Mississippi flowed steadily south. "This time of day, when the sun hits it? There's not much that can top this place. It must be why the Roman chose this spot. But it's not right, forgetting what happened here. Erasing it."

"You want to preserve that past," I said, understanding. My heart clenched. "To make sure no one can ever forget."

"Exactly." He seemed almost relieved that I got it, that I understood.

"It's commendable, what you're trying to do here." Why couldn't he just be gorgeous? Why did he have to be truly good as well?

"It's damn expensive," he said wryly. "I had to bid against an events company who wanted to corner the special occasions market, so I paid more than I should have. But it needed to be done. I want to make sure people can't forget. That's where I'm hoping you can help."

I'd been fighting my attraction to Silas's easy good looks, but listening to him talk with such dedication, with such intensity, had only made things worse.

"I'm not sure I can do more than you already are." I was more aware than ever of exactly how different we were. I'd coasted into town with nothing but a carful of possessions to my name, running from myself and everyone else. I didn't know what I wanted from life, much less how to go about getting it. And he had . . . all *this*. Not just the money or the estate, but a reason for doing what he did.

"You forget—Leonard's shown me your work. Something about it struck me—the truth and emotion in it. I knew you'd be a good fit here. I'm the one who asked him to reach out to you about the job."

All along, I'd thought the job offer had been Leonard's doing. It was one of the reasons I'd resisted so long—the last thing I wanted was family charity. "The job was your idea?"

"Sometimes people need more than words to understand." His expression was serious now. "You're very talented, Lucy. What capture in your pictures and in your other work . . . I think you can help more than you realize."

We started back toward the estate again, my brain awash with this new information as Silas explained in more detail what he was thinking. Photos of the present day superimposed on the past. He wanted to create a virtual museum as well as the one he was building here. He wanted Le Ciel to have a reach beyond the grounds.

"It has to be more than simple stock photography," he explained. "People aren't going to come if they aren't moved.

But then, not everyone *can* come. I want to make sure this place —its history and past—is accessible for everyone. I want the whole world to understand what happened here, what was sacrificed to create the beauty everyone admires now."

We rounded back onto the manicured lawns, cutting through a carefully designed garden bursting with summer color. "We've already done a lot to restore what the previous owners destroyed. But it'll take more work yet. I want it all documented. You've seen the images we've collected so far?"

I nodded. "You have some really amazing pieces. Some of the daguerreotypes look like they were taken a week ago."

"So . . . now you've seen a little of what I want to preserve." He stopped at the mouth of the alley of oaks. His gaze swept over the scene before us, the elegant trees and stately mansion. But the expression he wore wasn't exactly pleasure. "This place still gets me every time I step foot on it. You know these trees were planted nearly a hundred years before the Dutilettes even dreamed of their house?"

"No." I studied the perfectly aligned row of enormous oaks with a sort of wonder. "I hadn't realized."

"There's something almost timeless about this place. Something bigger than any single family's story." He paused, silent and thoughtful, before turning to me. "Anyway, that's what I'm thinking. The Foundation's done a lot of work to push back the commercialization. I've stopped the weddings and parties. The café is focused on producing food that pays tribute to the history of the local cuisine. But the Foundation can't keep bleeding money. We need grants and other funding to finish what I've started here, and to get them, we need to prove what we're doing is worthwhile. Your pictures are going to help with that."

"I'll do whatever I can," I promised. The job wasn't quite what Leonard had described when he said I'd be a staff photographer—it was better. Silas didn't want stock photographs. He wanted images that would move people emotionally. Maybe the job wasn't the work I'd once imagined for myself, but there was room for creativity in what Silas was describing. Working on his vision wouldn't be a burden.

And the Foundation's mission was genuinely good. There was, as Silas said, a lot of pain in that land, but he seemed determined to create something important and lasting from that pain.

"So . . ." He gave me a roguish look. "Now that we've got the professional obligations out of the way, dinner?"

"Mr. LaRoux—"

"Silas," he corrected, stepping closer again.

"What?" I asked, a little unsteady as he moved toward me.

I'd barely gotten my body's reaction to him under control, but now that he was back in my personal space, my heart stuttered again. I had no choice but to tip my face up slightly to look him in the eye, and I couldn't help but wonder what it would be like if he leaned down just a little.

He leaned down, just a little. "Call me Silas, Lucy."

I could feel his breath on my lips, and it was just enough to set off warning bells. "You're my boss," I reminded him, sounding far too damn breathless for anyone's good.

"That doesn't mean we can't be friends." The dimple in his left cheek threatened to appear as the corners of his mouth twitched.

He had a beautiful mouth, with full lips set into his otherwise angular face. It would have been easy enough to rise on my toes a bit and see if it was as warm and firm as it looked.

"Doesn't it?" I forced myself to step back.

His smile dimmed. "It's just dinner, Lucy. It doesn't have to mean anything."

But I wasn't so sure that was true. *Not with him.*

"Fine," I told him, because I couldn't quite bring myself to say no. "We can do dinner, but nothing too fancy, and I'm paying my own way."

"Absolutely not," he said, victory flashing through those gold-flecked eyes of his. Then he tipped his head to indicate I should follow.

12

I f I needed a reminder of why I shouldn't act on the attraction I might feel toward Silas, his car definitely helped. The Audi was a sleek beast of a machine with supple leather seats and burnished wood accents that reminded me *exactly* how different we were. My car was still sitting in the satellite visitor's lot, a two-ton paperweight that would cost more to fix than it was worth.

We were from different worlds, going different places, and I'd do well to remember that. Especially after things with Matt had fallen apart so spectacularly. I'd gotten too comfortable with him, started to rely on him. And when it was over? I'd been left with nothing.

So when Silas pulled into the gravel lot of a low-slung building clad in weathered clapboard ten minutes later, I was surprised. Silas had kept his promise—the place was little more than a low-country juke joint surrounded by soybean fields. Its neon sign was missing a couple of letters, but enough were lit for me to read "Creole House."

"Not what you expected?" he asked, his low voice betraying his amusement. "Disappointed?"

"No," I said honestly. "Much, much better."

The manager knew Silas on sight, and after a couple of minutes of friendly banter, she showed us back to a corner booth, far enough away from the noise of the bar that we could talk. I detected the slightest hint of curiosity, maybe even jealousy, as she dropped off some ice water and a basket of fresh rolls before she took our drink orders.

"You come here a lot?" I asked, wondering at the familiarity between them.

"Some." He reached for one of the soft, pillowy rolls and slathered it with the honey butter provided. "Eugenie and I went to high school together."

I didn't bother to mask my surprise. "You're from around here?"

He nodded, taking a bite of the bread. "I grew up a little west of here, in Plattenville. Just me and my mom." His otherwise cheerful expression dimmed a little. "But she's been gone for almost ten years."

"I'm sorry," I told him. "My dad died when I was nineteen."

"Twenty-three, for me." He paused, as though remembering. "Your mom still alive?"

I nodded. "As far as I know. She and my dad met when she was an exchange student at the University of Chicago. She was a little younger than him, though, and I don't think she ever really intended to settle down or be a mother. She didn't stick around. I don't really remember her. Last I heard she was off somewhere in Senegal."

"I'm sorry," he said.

"I'm not. Not anymore, at least." I selected a roll from the basket as a distraction. "My dad was more than enough. I got lucky."

"He died young, though?"

I nodded, focusing on tearing the bread in two perfect halves so I wouldn't have to meet his eyes. It had been six years, but the loss still felt too fresh. Grief had a way of creeping up on me. "Cancer." I took some of the butter to keep my hands busy and watched it melt into my bread. "It was his pancreas. He went fast."

"I know what that's like."

His tone had me looking up at him, and from the pain in his expression, maybe he did. "Your mom?"

"Ovarian," he said. "She died before we sold the app, though, so she never knew what I made of myself."

"You're a software designer?" I don't know why it surprised me, but nothing about Silas screamed tech bro. Still, I'd wondered how someone so young could have made enough money to buy an entire plantation or start a foundation.

"I was." He nodded. "A friend and I created an app that matched customers with local freelancers, and it took off not long after I graduated from Tulane."

My mouth fell open. "You're not talking about Get-Got?"

"It's a dumb name," he laughed. "We were drunk when we came up with it, but it's done pretty well."

"There were a lot of months I made rent because of that app."

The task-share app had exploded a couple of years back, and I vaguely remembered hearing about the young up-and-coming design team that had created it. If I remembered right, once the app went viral, they'd sold it to a major software company for millions. I'd known Silas had to have money to afford what he was doing at Le Ciel, but this was more than "having money." He was likely wealthier than most people could even imagine. And I barely had two hundred dollars to my name. It was yet another reminder we were living in completely different worlds.

Maybe I should have felt overwhelmed by this new informa-tion, but the Creole House was so worn and comfortable, and

Silas seemed so at home here that it was hard to picture him as someone who could probably buy a small town.

"I'm glad our little app could be of service," he said, an almost shy smile tugging at his well-formed mouth. "That's what we wanted—an app that could do good out there." His expression faltered. "Sometimes I wonder if we should have held on to the rights."

"You're doing good with the money you made from it, though, right?" I asked, as I shoved some of the bread into my mouth. The warm yeastiness mixed with the sweetness of the butter registered on my tongue, and I moaned softly before I could stop myself.

His expression grew heated. "Good, yeah?"

"Yeah." My cheeks warm, I licked the remaining sweetness of the honey butter off my lower lip. I didn't miss how his gaze darted down to my mouth. "If the free bread is this good, I can't wait to try the food."

He glanced back up, meeting my eyes. "If you have that reaction to the rest of what we order, neither can I."

Damn, if I didn't like his clear interest. There was something about the guilelessness—the directness—of it and him that I couldn't help liking. But the timing was all wrong. I wasn't even a week into this new job. The last thing I should be doing is hopping into a new relationship, even if the guy was Silas LaRoux.

"Silas—" I started, but before I could explain to him all the reasons we shouldn't, Eugenie was there with our drinks, the longneck bottles already damp with condensation. She eyed me not-so-subtly as she took our orders, but I pretended I didn't notice.

The conversation between us was easy—maybe too easy—as we waited for the gumbo special Eugenie had suggested. Silas had a calm sureness about him that made it easy to confide in him. But I had a lot of practice at keeping up my walls, and even

Silas LaRoux's charm wasn't enough to dismantle them so quickly. When the gumbo finally arrived, I had to admit he was right about the food. It was the best thing I'd eaten in a long time.

"People must have been pretty happy to see a local boy make good when you bought Le Ciel," I said, sopping up the last of the peppery gumbo with one of the rolls. But instead of the pride I'd expected, a shadow crossed his face.

"Maybe if I'd have kept things as they were." He set his spoon down, like he suddenly had no interest in eating. "But not everyone wants to stir up the past, especially around here. There are families who have been in this area since before the Civil War, and a lot of them don't want to be reminded of how things were. They'd rather move on and remember the good parts—hoop skirts and all. But the darkness? The terrible things that happened on this land? They don't want to go there, and they certainly don't want to think about the ways their current lives are built on it." He tapped the side of his beer, frowning thoughtfully.

Silas had beautiful hands, as well formed and strong as the rest of him, with almost elegant long fingers tipped in well-manicured nails. I didn't want to be interested, but as he traced the curve of the bottle, I couldn't stop myself from wondering what it would be like if he touched me like that. If those capable hands traced my curves, his fingers soft and sure against my skin.

He drained the rest of the beer in a long swallow, and I looked down at my empty bowl, willing the heat that had risen to my cheeks to subside.

"Spicy?" he asked.

I practically choked. "What?"

"The gumbo." He grinned as he nodded toward the bowl. "Sometimes the pepper hits harder than people expect, if they're not used to Cajun food. Your cheeks are all flushed."

I pressed my hand to my warm cheek and laughed softly. "I blame my dad's side of the family for my ability to light up like a tomato."

"He was Leonard's brother?" he asked. "I never would have guessed you were Leonard's niece when I first saw you."

I picked the damp label on my own beer. "My dad and I got that a lot when I was younger. I look a lot like my mom."

"But your dad raised you." Understanding lit his expression. A man as pale and russet-haired as Leonard raising a little girl with light brown skin and a head full of dark curls. There were plenty of times I knew people were looking at us, trying to put it all together. "Chicago, right?"

"Yeah. I grew up there. My dad and I had a small place in West Lawn. It was close enough to the airport that the planes would rattle the windows when they came into Midway." I smiled at the memory of our apartment. It had been in a four-unit building—two upstairs, two down. It hadn't been much, but it had been home.

The smile slid from my face. "When I started college, I had to take out a second mortgage on the place," I admitted. "And when my career as a world-renowned artist never took off . . ." I didn't want to remember, didn't want to admit that the one thing I'd had left of my dad was gone.

His hands covered mine, warm and sure as I'd known they'd be, and he gently took my fingers away from the mangled label.

"It was my own fault." I started to pull away, but his fingers threaded through mine, holding me in place. Pinning me to him. It was too damn comforting, but I didn't want his pity, didn't want his comfort—I definitely didn't deserve it.

But I couldn't help myself. I didn't fight him.

"Maybe it was," he agreed, surprising me with his words. "But you were just a kid. That must have been a lot. And besides . . . all that brought you here."

I glanced up, and my throat went tight when I saw how he

was looking at me. With understanding and warmth, yes. But there was no pity in his eyes. No judgement. There was only unmistakable desire that echoed my own.

He released my hands and leaned back in his seat, and I tried to ignore how much it felt like I'd just lost something.

"There's another thing I wanted to talk to you about," Silas said.

"Oh?" I willed my heart to settle back into its usual rhythm. "What's that?"

"Like I said, I've seen some of your work, Lucy. It's good. *Really* good. You know, there's a pretty strong market for art in the city. The Quarter's full of galleries. I know some people in town who might be interested in what you do. I think we could get you set up with a show."

I couldn't have possibly been more surprised by his words. I should have been excited about the offer. But I learned a long time ago there's nothing more dangerous than hope. And I already owed him too much. "Oh, I don't think—"

"It would be connected to Le Ciel, of course," he continued, ignoring my protest. "Your work, especially some pieces focused on the property, and the Foundation's artifacts displayed together. It could be mutually beneficial. You'd get introduced to the art community here in New Orleans, and the Foundation would get its mission in front of possible donors. Win-win."

It would have been one thing to reject his charity, but when he put it like that? It was harder to say no when I'd be helping him and the Foundation. "You really think it could benefit the work you're doing?"

"I do." His lips pressed into a firm line, determined. "I believe in what I'm doing here—what the Foundation is doing—but I'll be honest with you, Lucy. I can't keep bankrolling the project if we keep bleeding money. I would if I could, but I'm not old-money wealthy, you know? I made bank cashing out on our app, but those funds are finite. We need new donors, fresh blood in the mix. I think a show featuring your art—maybe some other local artists—could be good for us both."

"I'll think about it," I promised. "Thanks."

"No reason to thank me. You're the artist." He nodded toward the camera I'd placed next to me on the banquette. "Speaking of . . . Have you managed to get anything good yet?"

"Maybe," I said, lifting the heavy body of the DSLR and switching on the display. I pressed the button to look at some of the shots I'd taken in the last day or so, showing him a couple as I went. A few were pretty decent, but I could do better. When I reached the end of the images of Le Ciel, Matt's face filled the display.

"What's wrong?"

I quickly deleted it and then flipped back to an image of the mansion. "Nothing," I lied, focusing on the camera. But something was off. Another inspection of the shots I had confirmed it: I was missing pictures.

"You don't look like nothing's wrong."

"It's just . . ." One look told me he'd know if I tried to hide it. "I thought I got a shot, but it isn't here."

I'd taken a picture of the green-eyed guy—Alexandre. I *knew* I did. That first morning, it had been the click of the shutter that had drawn his attention to me. Even a novice couldn't miss a shot that well set up. But he wasn't anywhere to be found in the images on my camera. It wasn't the only image missing, though. Another quick look confirmed that the picture I'd taken of him by the pond was missing as well. There were pictures of the trees and mansion, but no picture of Alex himself.

"I must have deleted them somehow," I told him, trying to convince myself. "Maybe when I fell yesterday, I hit a button or something." But that didn't explain the picture I'd taken later.

Silas was watching me. "Can you recover deleted images?"

Shaking my head, I flipped back and forth through the

pictures again, as if going through them once more would change the truth. There was the shot of my uncle talking to the crowd, the group of costumed interpreters looking like the past come to life. There was the tree Alex had been leaning against. And there were images of the pond itself. But none of the green-eyed guy. "No. Once an image is deleted, it's gone."

He frowned. "It wasn't anything important?"

Immediately, I realized how bad this looked. I'd lost the pictures I'd taken as part of my new job, and I'd gotten so comfortable around Silas that I just admitted as much to the man I worked for. "No," I said. "None of them were important. They were just some practice shots." But the words felt like a lie.

WHEN SILAS DROPPED ME OFF, he walked me to Leonard and Sam's door.

"Thanks again for tonight." I stopped in front of the steps leading up to their porch. "Next time, though, dinner's on me."

Amusement lifted his mouth as his eyes grew heated. "You're saying there *will* be a next time?"

I felt that familiar tug of desire from the look he was giving me, and as nice as it was, it set off warning bells in my mind. "Silas . . ."

"Lucy . . ."

I smiled softly. "I like you, Silas. But this is a bad idea." Too bad my voice was a hell of a lot huskier than I'd intended.

"Doesn't seem like a bad idea from where I'm standing." He closed the distance between us. "Looks even better from here."

"You're my *boss*."

"I'm not really. I'm just one of the many trustees who run the place you happen to work."

"I need this job."

He frowned. "I would never do anything to put that into jeopardy, Lucy."

"I know, but . . ." I sighed. "You're a great guy. An *amazing* guy. A girl would be an idiot to turn you down."

Amusement flickered in his eyes. "You aren't making a very compelling argument."

"I'm a mess, Silas. I coasted into town on fumes. I basically have a carful of crap to my name, and I just got out of a relationship. And you're—" I gestured toward him: his perfectly cut clothes and broad shoulders and warm eyes and good-down-to-his-toes soul.

He lifted his brows, waiting. "Devastatingly attractive?"

I couldn't stop the smile. "*Humble.* I was going to say you're very, very humble." But then I grew more serious. "We're in such different places right now, and I just don't think this is a good idea."

"I know," he said, but he didn't seem all that upset by it.

"You do?"

He nodded. "Which is why I'm not going to kiss you right now, even though I want to."

I blinked at his bluntness, and my confusion must have shown. "Oh," I said, more than a little disappointed. "Good. That's *good.* We should keep this professional."

He tucked his hands into his pockets, almost like he was trying to keep himself from reaching for me. His words were playful, but his tone was anything but. "Lucy, nothing about whatever this is between us is professional. But when I kiss you for the first time—and I *am* going to kiss you—you're going to want it. No hesitation. No misgivings. Just you and me."

Before I could even sputter a response, he was already walking away. He tossed a smile over his shoulder. "You have a good night, Lucy Aimes. Dream of me."

I stood there for a solid five minutes, watching until he'd cut through the line of trees that separated the employee area from the rest of the estate. But even after he was long gone, I couldn't make myself move for a long while. Music on the T.V. drifted softly through the closed door.

Finally, turning to go in, I shook my head. It would be good to move into my own cabin. But my hand had only just touched the knob when I paused. Something pulled at me, drew my gaze to the line of trees Silas had just entered. It wasn't Silas standing there, though. Alexandre's eyes glinted green in the twilight, but his sharp features were otherwise unreadable in the shadows.

Without even thinking, I stepped toward him, but as my foot hit the stair below me, I realized what I was doing. Every cell in my body urged me on, to go to him, which was about the surest sign I shouldn't. It took everything I had to stay where I was, in the safety of Leonard and Sam's porch. I closed my eyes against the urgency that rose inside me, wild and almost unhinged. And when I opened them again, Alex was gone.

13

T hat night, I slept more deeply than I had in weeks. I didn't have one of my usual nightmares. I didn't dream about drowning or bone-deep guilt. But despite his request, it wasn't Silas I dreamed of.

The dream started out so dark that, at first, I thought I was drowning again. I expected to feel the cold pull of the water around me, but it never came. Instead, stifling air surrounded me, tainted by the sharp bite of a chemical I couldn't identify. With a click of the door, light flooded the darkness. I was in a darkroom of sorts. It didn't look like the equipment I'd used back in art school, when I took a traditional photography course one semester, but I recognized it anyway. The fumes were far more intense than anything from college, though, and I needed fresh air.

I walked out of the darkroom into the oppressive heat of a large studio—an attic room with high, unfinished ceilings and antique furniture. One end had French doors, which opened onto a narrow balcony made of delicate ironwork and overlooked a street somewhere in the Quarter. A breeze filtered through the doors, but it offered very little relief from the heat.

This dream was every bit as vivid and real as the nightmare that had haunted me for most of my life, but the colors were strangely muted, like one of those old Kodachrome pictures that had faded over time. Everything was washed out, overdeveloped.

I moved through the dream without consciously meaning to, setting the large camera-like contraption I'd been holding on a long table with other equipment. The photographer in me wanted to reach out and examine the different pieces one by one until I understood how they worked. Instead, a mirror hanging over the table caught my attention. Its pitted surface reflected a stranger with hair the color of ebony that was pulled back from her heart-shaped face in a long, thick braid. Here and there, a curl threatened to break free. With its bow-shaped pout, her mouth was more delicate than my own, and her nose was a bit rounder and slightly turned up at the end. Her skin was a light brown, like she'd spent her days in the sun.

We looked completely different, yet there were unmistakable similarities. My dad never kept pictures of my mom around when I was young, but I'd found one once. A photo from when they'd first met and she was barely twenty. This girl could have been her sister. Mostly it was in the eyes, I think. They were precisely the same grayish-blue I looked at in the mirror every day.

This dream wasn't about me, though. I mean, I was *in* the dream, but I wasn't myself. I was a passenger and observer, but not a participant. I could feel everything she felt, knew everything she knew, and that duality—being both completely myself and completely someone else, all in the same moment—was almost more jarring than the deep waters that often pulled me down during the night.

As I was still contemplating her features, a loud rap sounded at the door, making her—us—jump. She looked at the clock in confusion. There were no appointments that morning, and she wasn't expecting any deliveries. Uneasy with the disruption, she calmed herself by tucking back the last stray curl and removing her heavy apron, which covered a dress flecked with tiny blue flowers. Then, steadier, she headed to the door.

An impeccably dressed gentleman waited on the other side. *Alex.*

Or a version of him conjured by my subconscious. He looked larger and more imposing, somehow, and his features were a bit less angular. He wore a dark morning coat expertly tailored to fit his wide shoulders,

The girl's breath caught and her cheeks warmed as he flashed a rakish grin. Her body responded instantly, and it felt so much like my own response to him—immediate and familiar and every bit as dangerous as drowning.

"What are you doing here?" she whispered, the words tumbling out in a panicked rush. "If anyone sees you—"

"I am looking for Monsieur Lyon," he said, his voice loud enough to carry to anyone who might be listening. "I'm interested in engaging his portrait services."

The girl remained squarely in the doorway, torn between desire and fear. She should send him away before they were found out, but instead, she played along. When she finally spoke, her voice was softer, huskier than she'd intended. "This is Jules Lyon's studio, but he's not available today."

"Is that so?" Alex asked, his eyes serious and heated.

"Unfortunately, Monsieur Lyon has traveled out of the city for at least a week."

"That *is* a pity." The playfulness of his tone was at odds with his words.

The girl paused for a moment, considered her choices. "I am more than capable of assisting you if you are inquiring about the services he provides." She spoke with a practiced calm, making sure that she was loud enough for any passerby to overhear. "Perhaps there is something I might help you with?"

His green eyes glinted with victory. "Perhaps there is."

The girl hesitated a second longer before stepping back to allow him entrance to the studio. She shut the door, leaning into the worn wood as the bolt latched, and took the moment to compose herself—to be sure.

When she finally faced him, Alex was already prowling through the small room, moving from one portrait to the next before examining the camera obscura sitting on a table nearby.

She was in far over her head, but she couldn't bring herself to care that she'd made a mistake in not sending him away.

"Why are you here, Alex?" Before now, they'd only met in public. They were in unfamiliar territory. By inviting him in, she'd crossed some invisible but absolute line. By locking the door behind her, she'd stepped out of her prescribed role, tossed the script aside completely.

He turned back to her then, fixing her with flashing green eyes, and then stalked toward her slowly, as confident as a jungle cat on the hunt. "As I said, I came for a portrait."

They'd never been this close before. She tilted her head up to look at him. The well-tailored cut of his suits had concealed exactly how much larger than her he actually was.

A shiver of awareness coursed through her. She should take a step back. But her body refused. She could no more have stepped back from Alex, from the moment before them, than she could have stopped breathing. Wild horses stampeded through her chest, yet she did not move.

He was not a man for her—could not *be* the man for her— but it didn't stop her from leaning the tiniest bit closer to breathe in the warm spice of his cologne. Sandalwood and berg- amot. And something else, something expensive and unusual that made her forget the closeness of the room, the stink of the Quarter's hot and cluttered streets.

He leaned in as well, and for the space of a heartbeat they were caught in the moment, there in the empty studio. He lifted his hand and brushed the back of his fingers along her cheek.

She could not have stopped her eyes from fluttering closed or the soft sigh of utter desire that escaped her lips if she had wanted to. But she did not want to.

"Where shall we do this?" he murmured.

"What?" Heat flared in her cheeks as her eyes flew open.

"The portrait," he explained, his eyes glinting with amusement

"Oh." The girl forced herself to step back. His proximity had apparently addled her brains. She had thought he'd meant . . .

She wouldn't allow herself to think about what she'd thought. Men like him didn't take women like her to wife, and she had sworn years ago she would not find herself in the same position as so many of the other girls who went off to their first Quadroon Ball with stars in their eyes and ended up with a white man's babe in their belly.

Alex's smile faltered, and his expression grew serious. "Unless you've changed your mind."

She wasn't sure if he was asking about the portrait or about the heavy desire between them. "No," she told him, answering both questions. "I haven't changed my mind."

He stepped back from her then, and she felt suddenly bereft. But she could almost breathe without him so close.

"Show me." When she didn't immediately respond, he grinned. "The *portrait*, Armantine. Show me how it works." Amusement danced in his eyes at the effect he'd had on her.

"You *truly* want a portrait?"

"Among other things," he admitted, his voice low and wicked. "But we can start with the portrait."

She blinked, trying to pull herself together. A portrait she could do. A portrait she could handle.

"It's not difficult. You simply sit before the camera obscura." She gestured toward one of the pieces of equipment he'd been examining. "The small lever there opens the aperture and exposes the plate to light, and the image is transferred."

"There's nothing more?"

"What more could there be? It's a fairly short process, though it can be somewhat tedious for the subject, who must hold perfectly still."

"There are some who believe taking an image of a person using a machine like this is akin to a sort of alchemy or magic," Alex said, running his finger along the camera's body as he examined it.

She could not stop herself from imagining how it might feel if he touched her with that same curiosity, that same care.

He glanced up at her. "Some believe that you can trap a piece of a person's very soul in a photograph."

The girl bit back a smile. "There are some who believe a great many things. But that's a machine. There's not witchcraft or alchemy involved. There's no risk at all."

"I believe I'll need proof."

"The materials are very costly, Alex. Jules will notice if they're missing."

"I'll gladly compensate Mr. Lyon." He moved toward her again. "You did offer your services, did you not?"

She studied him carefully, refusing to cower or back up even with his large body crowding hers. "Very well. Why don't you have a seat over there, and we'll begin." She went to retrieve the camera, but his large hand latched on to her wrist. Its warmth sent a shock of awareness up her arm, and when she faced him, he seemed just as thrown off as she felt. He took a breath and released her, but did not step back.

"You misunderstand. I wish for a portrait of *you*." He leaned over until his scent enveloped her again, the sweet warmth of his breath against her neck.

An absurd burst of pleasure filled her. "Do you?"

He pressed his lips softly against the side of her neck. "You know I wish for a great deal more."

The girl couldn't help herself from leaning back into him. "And if a portrait is all I can give?"

He kissed her neck again, nuzzling his mouth close to the sensitive curve of her ear. "Then I'll have to settle for the portrait and hope against hope that it captures a bit of your soul."

The girl forced herself to step away from him to keep from doing something truly stupid, but she couldn't hide the wanting —the willingness—in her eyes.

She swallowed hard, remaining out of his reach as she focused on showing him how to work the camera. "When you're ready, you simply depress this lever. After three minutes, you'll lift it back up."

With a deft swish of her skirts, she moved to a chair set in front of a wide sweep of velvet drapery and arranged herself. "Whenever you're ready . . ."

Alex's eyes never left hers as he engaged the small lever to open the camera's aperture. "While this is open, you must remain there?" he asked. "Silent and still?"

She met his gaze silently in confirmation.

"You cannot move?" He wandered closer, remaining just out of the camera's range. "Or speak. Not without ruining the quality of the image."

Again, she was silent, but she never looked away from him.

"I wonder," he murmured, "if you have any idea what you do to me."

Her heart skipped at his words, but she remained perfectly still and immobile. Caught in the camera's unerring eye and in the fragile moment spinning out between them, she could barely breathe, waiting for his next words.

"I've thought of nothing and no one else since our first meeting.

All day long, I yearn for you. I imagine having you as my own—to have the right to touch you, to claim you." His eyes grew heated, the green deepening into the shade of verdant jungles. "I think of your scent, lavender and cloves. All day long, thoughts of you haunt me. I listen to my sister's inane chatter and pretend to care about my brother-in-law's business, but my thoughts are of you.

"I think of the curve of your neck where it meets your jaw. I wonder what you must taste like there, how sweet your skin would be. I wonder what it would be like to take the pins from your hair and thread my fingers through your wild curls. I imagine what they would feel like against my skin. All day long, thoughts of you *haunt* me, but it's worse at night."

Her heart was unsteady in her chest, her breathing so ragged now that even he must have noticed.

"At night you visit me." His jaw clenched. "In dreams you come to me without worries or inhibitions. Last night you came. Do you remember?" His gaze held hers, and because of the camera, she could not turn away. "Do you dream of me as well?"

The girl couldn't answer, but the heat in her cheeks must have given away the truth, because he did smile then.

"Ah, but are your dreams as wicked as mine?" he asked. "In mine, you're a temptress." His expression grew serious. "I find that I almost wish this contraption *could* take a piece of your soul. I would do nearly anything to claim even a small part of you."

The short minutes of exposure time ticked on endlessly, and the girl had become breathless listening to his words. She was fully clothed, but she might as well have been completely exposed under his steady, all-consuming gaze.

After an eternity, he finally closed the aperture.

"Now what happens?" he asked.

Her legs were unsteady when the girl stood, but she

managed to keep her hands from shaking as she removed the camera from its stand and secured the plate.

"Armantine?" He was behind her, close enough that the heat of his body warmed her back. Softly, he brushed a curl from her neck. "What happens now, Mademoiselle Lyon?"

She looked up at him, It was already too late to stop herself. "Now we see what develops." Then, before she could think better of it, she lifted onto her toes and pressed her mouth against his.

14

I woke tangled in my sheets, with the dream still thick around me. My body was damp with sweat and pulsing with need. With the antique canopy of Leonard and Sam's spindly guest-room bed overtop of me, I thought I was still there, still *her*. I reached between my legs. My hands were his hands, and his mouth was on me—on her. It didn't matter. We were one and the same, and it wasn't until my own release crashed through me that the dream faded. None of it had been real.

Well, the orgasm I'd given myself had been real, but everything else had been nothing more than a fantasy. But it had *felt* so real. As I lay there, my chest heaving and my body tingling and boneless, I swear the faint hint of bergamot hung in the air.

The sun was pouring into the room, though. I'd slept longer and later than I had in ages. The the dream had been every bit as real and vivid as any of my nightmares, but it hadn't felt dangerous. But I couldn't shake the memory of being in her skin. I needed a shower hot enough to burn away the last bits of her—of *Armantine*—but I didn't have time. I was late.

I threw on some clothes and tried to finger-comb my mess

of hair, but a single glance in the mirror showed me how point-less it was.

Maybe Silas won't be around today.

The thought made me pause. In the wake of the dream, I'd almost forgotten about Silas. I'd gone to bed with him on my mind, but I'd dreamed of someone else. I'd gotten myself off to a fantasy of someone else. If I needed yet another sign that starting something with Silas was a bad idea, that seemed like a pretty obvious one.

I was suddenly grateful he hadn't kissed me the night before. The Foundation he headed was paying my salary, and Silas himself had offered me an opportunity to get my art into the important galleries in the city. I'd be stupid to mess that up.

Sam was still finishing up his breakfast in the kitchen when I emerged from the guest room. He offered me a muffin, and I snagged a Diet Coke from their fridge along with it.

"Mina said my cabin is ready." I drank some of the Coke and waited for the caffeine to hit. "So I should be out of your hair later today."

"You were never in our hair." Sam frowned. "We've really enjoyed having you around these last couple of days."

"I've liked being around," I admitted. "I'm sorry I stayed away so long. It was just hard, you know? With Leonard and my dad. . ."

His expression softened. "I know. We both understood. But now that you're here, you're welcome in our home at any time—day or night."

"Considering how amazing these muffins are? You might want to put a few restrictions on that offer." I snagged another muffin before heading off to the Foundation's offices.

I might have been running late, but it was early enough that the grounds were still quiet. The first big tour groups of the day wouldn't roll in until closer to ten.

I'd taken a look at the Foundation's website before I went to bed, and had found plenty of places where I could help improve it. I'd already made a list of a bunch of pictures I could replace, but first, I wanted to look through more of the antique photos for inspiration.

After talking with Silas the day before, I had a better sense of what the Foundation needed from me. I liked his vision of what Le Ciel could be and I liked that my work could help him achieve it. I had this idea for having the web designers create an interactive feature, so when visitors slid their cursor over the images, the pictures would transform from the present to the past. But for the idea to work, the two would have to match perfectly.

As I approached the offices, I couldn't stop myself from checking the parking lot for Silas's car—it wasn't—or seeing if Alex was around—he wasn't. And I was glad. I needed space and time to think. Between the sparks I'd felt with Silas and the desire that had thrummed through the girl in the dream, I was more than a little on edge.

At least it wasn't another nightmare. But the vividness of the dream had been almost equally as unsettling. I had the strangest, surest feeling that something was beginning. And I wasn't sure I could stop it.

But I also wasn't sure I'd want to, even if I could.

I'd started having the nightmares when I was just a kid, not long after my mom walked out on us. All the doctors ascribed it to that—at first. When my teenage years hit, they thought it was just puberty. Or unresolved trauma. Eventually I reached a point where I just hid the dreams from everyone, my dad included. It wasn't like we had the money to keep throwing at shrinks who couldn't help me, and I didn't want to worry him any more than I already had.

The dreams—the nightmares—became my own secret burden. I could manage them for the most part, but they always broke through when I least wanted them to. Anytime my life finally felt like it was under control, the dreams would pop back up, worse than ever. This latest situation with Matt had only been the last of a long string of others—of broken relationships and lost jobs.

So even if I wanted to be interested in Silas, even if I undeniable sparks that had flown between us over dinner, taking a chance on him wasn't worth the risk. It couldn't be. He seemed like a great guy, almost too good to be true. But there wasn't any point in starting something, because I already knew where it would end—the same place all my relationships ended. But if things went badly with Silas, it would make it damn uncomfortable to stay at Le Ciel. And I needed this job.

There was no sense even thinking about Silas LaRoux as long as the dreams were still plaguing me. My dreaming destroyed everything.

My dreaming.

What Mama Erzulie had told me about souls walking free when they dream suddenly rose in my mind. She'd said that sometimes we can still be connected to our past lives in our dreams. I made a mental note to go back to the Quarter and find the old Voodoo queen again. I had questions for her. Maybe I was delusional, but what if she had real answers?

I'd never really been much into religion or even spirituality. I had a hard time believing in anything that wasn't right there in front of me. But Le Ciel *was* there, and there was no denying I'd dreamed of this place long before I knew of its existence. It probably would be saner to think maybe I'd seen it in a movie or a travel brochure or something when I was young.

The newest dream wasn't really disturbing. I'd likely just been running on empty for too long, and my too-exhausted subconscious had placed the seriously gorgeous and completely unattainable Alex in my dreams.

Too bad I didn't actually believe those explanations. Not when I'd dreamed of Alex before I saw him as well.

The offices were quiet when I arrived. Most of the staff was out on the property, so I let myself into the back archive room, where a bouquet of flowers waited with my name on them. A note from Silas was attached, a brief and breezy "Looking forward to next time." My stomach did a happy little flip at the promise in his words, but then overwhelming guilt hit. I hadn't chosen to dream of the green-eyed Alex on purpose, but the vividness of the dream was still so close that I couldn't stop feeling I'd done something wrong.

Setting my guilt aside, I worked for a while with the flowers for company and tried not to think about what they meant. But my thoughts kept drifting—to Silas, to Alex. By the time a soft rapping sounded at the door, I'd managed to tie myself in knots. But seeing Silas there in the doorway made all of my guilt, all of my doubts vanish. Right along with my determination to stay away from him.

"I see you found the flowers?"

"I did," I confirmed, touching one of the silky petals. "They're beautiful, but you absolutely didn't need to."

"Flowers are never about needing to." That dimple flashed in his cheek, and I was right back where I started—wanting him despite my better judgement. "I'm heading to the airport, but I wanted to stop by and make sure you got them."

"You're leaving?" And damn if that didn't take the air right out of whatever happiness I might have been feeling.

"Just for a few days," he said, looking almost embarrassed about it. "My partners and I have some business to deal with out west. Walk me out?"

He didn't need me to walk him out—he owned the whole place. But with the happy daisies and roses keeping me company all morning, I couldn't exactly say no. I didn't really want to, either.

As we walked the short distance to his car, I explained my idea for the sliders on the website. He said he loved it and promised to get the IT guys on it as soon as I gave them the images.

"It shouldn't take me too long," I promised. "I've already pulled a couple of the historical shots. I just need to set up the retake and then finalize the files. Maybe a week, tops, for the first—" Something drew my gaze to the trees, and I stopped short. A flash of gold. A shiver of movement.

"For the first?" Silas came up next to me. "Lucy?"

I blinked away the overwhelming unease. "Sorry. I thought I saw . . ." I shook my head. "Nothing. It'll take a week for the first four images. I can work on more if we get increased traffic."

He was still studying me. "You're sure you're okay? You're not going to faint on me again?" His voice was light, but the crease between his brows betrayed his worry.

I *hated* that he was worried. "Seriously. I'm fine."

By the time we made it to his car, he seemed to finally believe I was okay. "I'll be back sometime late next week. Maybe we can grab dinner in the Quarter?"

"Maybe." I bit back a smile. "But pick something cheap. You don't pay your employees enough for me to afford Galatoire's."

"Sounds like they should get a raise."

"I don't know about that," I said dryly. "From what I hear, you're bleeding money. Actually, I'm not sure you can afford Galatoire's either."

He barked out a surprised laugh, and I looked up at him, unaccountably happy that I could make him smile like that. The moment hung between us, fragile and hopeful. For a heartbeat, I thought he might kiss me.

I thought I might even let him.

His eyes were smiling at me, but there was heat in his expression, too. It would have been easy enough for him to close the distance, to put to rest the question once and for all. Instead, he stepped back.

My disappointment must have shown, because he laughed again. "Not yet, but I think you're almost ready."

"What's that supposed to mean?" I demanded, though I knew exactly what he was talking about.

"It means I don't think it'll be much longer before I get to see what that mouth of yours tastes like."

Before I could formulate a response, he slipped into his car and shot me another devilish grin before turning over the ignition.

"You're too confident for your own good." I tried—and failed —to look unamused.

"Maybe." He grinned. "But I'm not usually wrong about most things. And *this*, whatever this is between us. I'm not wrong about that either."

I watched as he pulled away, my arms wrapped around myself, like that could keep me from flying apart.

It had been too long since I'd felt an attraction like this—one every bit as comfortable as it was exciting. But I was still dragging the last bits of the dream along with me through the day, and nothing felt quite right.

15

I tried going back to work, but my brush with Silas had apparently scrambled my brains. Instead, I took the rest of the day off to start moving my things into my new home.

The employee cabins weren't much to look at, but when I brought the first load of my things in, I couldn't keep from welling up. It had been a while since I'd had a place that was mine—not a friend's or a boyfriend's. Inside, the cabin was decorated in warm, neutral shades, with enough room for a bed, a small kitchenette, and a seating area with a worn but comfortable armchair. It was perfect.

By dinner, I'd managed to get all my things—which, admittedly wasn't much—into the cabin. I was hanging the blue bottle Mina had gifted me on the myrtle tree outside my front door when, as though summoned by my thoughts, she and Chloe came into view, heading my direction.

"It looks good there," Mina said, touching the bottle and sending it swaying gently.

"Are you all settled in?" Chloe held a potted orchid and glanced over my shoulder to peer through the open doorway.

"Mostly," I told them. "Not that there was all that much to settle."

"Do you need anything?" Mina asked.

I shook my head. "No, thanks. This is great, really. I'm glad the Foundation had an extra cabin for me to stay in. It's been a huge help."

"We brought you a little housewarming gift," Chloe said, offering the orchid.

I thanked her as I took the small pot, but my dismay at keeping something alive must have shown on my face.

"Oh, don't worry so much," she told me. "These are super easy to take care of."

"If you say so. But I can't make any promises about keeping this poor thing alive."

"Just put one ice cube on the soil once a week," she explained. "Couldn't be simpler."

I gave the plant another doubtful look. "Come on in, if you want. I'll just find a place to put this."

They followed me into the tiny cabin, and I was suddenly conscious of how little I'd actually brought—how little an impact I'd made on the otherwise sparce room—as they looked around.

"The window would be perfect," Chloe instructed. "You'll get enough light there to keep it happy."

By the time I finished settling the plant, Mina was studying the canvases I'd propped next to the wall, the ones I'd grabbed before fleeing Matt's apartment in the middle of the night.

"These are yours?" Mina asked.

I nodded, moving closer. I loved photography, but these were mixed media pieces—a new technique I'd been playing with in recent months. I'd layered prints into a collage with found objects and heavy, thick slashes of acrylic paint. I wondered if Mina noticed the painting's resemblance to the columns of Le Ciel.

Mina glanced at me, a question in her eyes, but she never voiced it.

"Well, I should be getting back to the office." Mina's dark eyes remained trained on the canvases a few seconds longer before finally returning to me. "If you need anything at all, let me know, and I'll take care of it."

"I will, thanks," I said, but as she was leaving, another thought hit me. "Hey, Mina?"

"Yeah?"

"Was I supposed to be getting pictures of the pond or something the other day?" I explained how I'd wandered out there and how Alex had made it seem like he'd been waiting for me, but then he never really said what they needed pictures of.

"Alex?" Mina's brows bunched.

"Yeah. French guy with blond hair?" I frowned when she didn't immediately respond. "I just wanted to make sure I didn't miss something."

Mina considered me a moment longer. "I wasn't aware of anything that needed documenting out by the pond."

"Oh, okay." A stillness about her made me think maybe I'd said something I shouldn't. "Well, if you need anything documented?"

"I'll let you know." She glanced at Chloe. "You coming home for dinner tonight?"

Chloe nodded. "Should be back by six."

"That sounds fine." With another glance toward my canvases, Mina was gone.

"Who's Alex?" Chloe asked. She wandered over to my sitting area and ran a finger along the spines of the handful of books I'd stacked on the table.

"I don't know?" I said honestly. "Some guy who works here."

Glancing over her shoulder, she lifted her brows in my direction. "Some guy who had your cheeks going pink when you said his name."

"It's not like that," I said, pretending that my face wasn't hot.

"I hope not," she said with a laugh. "Only a complete idiot would throw Silas LaRoux over for some marginally employed actor. But I have to applaud you for playing the field a little. It wouldn't hurt to keep Silas on his toes."

"Silas is my boss," I reminded her. Again.

"For now," she said, with a too-knowing smirk. "But you can't tell me you aren't tempted."

No. I couldn't tell her that, so I didn't tell her anything.

She laughed. "Fine. Keep your secrets."

I forced a brazen smile. "I will, thank you."

"Whatever." She laughed again. "You'll tell me all about it soon enough. They always do."

I didn't doubt it, but I'd never been good at opening myself up to people. There was a part of me, though, that wanted to change that.

"So what are your plans later?"

"Not much," I admitted. "I'd like to finish getting settled, maybe stock up on some groceries."

"I could give you a lift to the store, if you want?"

"That'd be great."

"I have a few things to work on at the on-site office, but we could go when I'm done?"

"Sure. That's perfect." I hesitated for a second while she headed toward the door, but I stopped her before she left. "Hey, Chloe?"

"Yeah?"

"Any chance you're heading into the Quarter to see Mama Erzulie again sometime soon?"

Her brows lifted a little. "I didn't think you believed in Voodoo?"

"I'm not sure I do, but she said some things that got me thinking. About dreams and dreaming."

Chloe was silent, thoughtful, as though waiting for me to say more.

"I've had the same dream for as long as I can remember," I admitted, venturing into uncharted waters.

I usually didn't tell people about my dreams right away, but I wanted things to be different. I'd already reconnected with the family I'd been avoiding, but I wanted friends as well. I wanted to have people I could trust in my life. Besides, if Chloe went into full-blown pity-and-run mode, better now than before we got any closer.

Gesturing toward the canvases on the floor, I went on. "I dreamed about this place—Le Ciel—before I even knew it existed. A long time before Leonard got the job here." I met her eyes. "They aren't exactly good dreams."

She studied the canvases, their dark slashes and violent splatters of paint. "I see," she murmured, and I thought maybe she did. When her eyes met mine, I was relieved to see nothing had changed. She wasn't looking at me like some poor, broken creature. "And you think Mama Erzulie can help?"

"I don't know," I admitted. "Probably not. Nothing else has helped. But all her talk about the dreaming? Maybe she knows something all the doctors I've been to don't."

"That's for sure," Chloe said. "I have a pretty tight schedule this week, but I'm going to the Saint John's Eve festival next week. Mama Erzulie is usually there, if you want to go?"

Something eased inside me at her words, the part of me that had wondered if Chloe would turn away like everyone else if I risked telling her. "That'd be great. Thanks."

"It's a plan," she said. "I'll swing by later, and then we can take care of that pathetically empty fridge of yours."

16

F or the next few days, my life took on a steady if not
uncomfortable pattern. I didn't think I'd ever really
adjust to the crushing heat of the Louisiana summer,
but I'd learned to manage it. I spent my mornings out on the
property, trying to reenact the various shots from the archival
collection the Foundation had amassed. When the day started to
warm, I'd return to the on-site office, where I'd spend the afternoon working on the images I'd taken in the morning or
consulting with the web guys about how to best use them. My
evenings were free. Occasionally, I stopped by to chat with
Leonard and Sam, and once I had dinner with Chloe, but
mostly, I stayed to myself.

I wasn't lonely, though. For the first time in a long time, with
my own cabin and a steady paycheck, I had time to work on the
art I'd been neglecting for too long. Each evening, it was almost
effortless to slip into a steady pace of work, and I'd surface
hours later, covered in paint and damp with sweat but happy
with the canvas in front of me. Until one evening I surfaced to
find my latest piece didn't feature the bar-like columns of Le

Ciel, but the bright green eyes of the guy who'd been haunting my dreams.

I hadn't seen Alex again since that day by the pond, not in person at least. I'd avoided asking around about him anymore, because I didn't want word getting back to Silas that I was possibly interested in someone else. But every night, fantasies of Alex overtook my dreams. I no longer woke with nightmares clawing at my throat. Instead, I woke hungry and needy, wanting a man I'd barely spoken to and didn't know. Or at least, wanting the Alex who appeared in my dreams. The Alex Armantine knew.

For the first time in my life, I looked forward to going to bed. Every night, I went to sleep, hoping to see Alex. Hoping my dreams would reveal the missing pieces of the puzzle I'd found myself in. And each night, the story of Alex's relationship with Armantine slowly knitted itself together.

I learned her name was Armantine Aurelia Lyon, an orphan adopted by Jules Lyon. He was French-born, a freeman of color and entrepreneur uninterested in limiting himself to the community of freemen in the Quarter. He'd needed an assistant, someone who could help him slip past the defenses of the white Creole society. One look at little Armantine's delicate features and effortless grace, and he had his answer. She was little more than a girl when he took her in, but by the time he opened his studio in the Quarter four years later, she had grown into her beauty and her role in his life.

Her life with him was a happy one, but in a society where blood was destiny, she occupied a precarious position. Still, for the most part, her life was ordinary and far more peaceful than most women of color enjoyed, even in New Orleans. Or at least it was until the day Alexandre Jourdain flipped her world on its head. Armantine couldn't have stopped herself from wanting him, and she didn't try. She came to understand that men like him were why women fell. Men like him, with his golden

SWEET UNREST | 113

complexion and piercing eyes, with his soft words and lofty promises, were why women left the safety of everything they knew for the risk of what could be.

Each night, I slipped into bed feeling better than I had in ages. I had my own place, a path toward a new future, and even a friend who hadn't immediately treated me like I was broken when I told her about my nightmares. But I let myself relax too much and got greedy for the dreams that woke me needy and wanting. Alex might have been a threat to Armantine, but a dream man—a figment of my imagination—wasn't really a threat to me.

I stopped setting my alarms. I started believing maybe my nightmares were over. And then one night it wasn't Alex I dreamed of, but the Mississippi on fire.

Yellow-gold flames jumped high into the dark sky and transformed the murky waters into a path of light. Wood smoke and sulfur filled the air, and when the wind shifted, a haze blew across my vision and stung my eyes. Captivated by the sight, I was drawn to the banks. Slowly, carefully, I picked my way through the brush and walked toward the river. Only as I came closer did I understand it wasn't the water that burned, but small bonfires lining the shore.

A woman waved to me, and I felt suddenly calm, elated that she recognized me from such a distance.

"Armantine!" she called, waving again with pleasure.

With her greeting, I knew I was back in the other girl's body. Armantine's. But this was nothing like the dreams with Alex. I wanted to look around to see if Alex was there as well, but Armantine's eyes remained focused on the small woman with light brown skin. She was clad in a worn but fairly tidy dress, and her curling dark brown hair was plaited close to her head.

"You came! I didn't think that uncle of yours would ever let you out again." She was sitting with others, a few yards from the fire to escape its heat. In the flickering shadows stood tables laden with food.

Armantine's pleasure at the girl's greeting was immediate, so too was her guilt that it had been so long since she'd last visited. "He needs my help most days," Armantine told the other girl. "He's been working on documenting some of the important families in town."

"That so?"

Armantine nodded. "Word must be spreading. He can barely keep up with the demand."

"I'll never understand why anyone lets him take their likeness like that," the girl remarked in a voice thick with caution.

"You know that soul-snatching stuff's not true, Lila," Armantine said gently. Lila was younger, but she looked older than her seventeen years.

Lila made a low, throaty hum of disapproval. "You can't be taking people's likeness without taking some of their spirit in turn."

Armantine knew she couldn't convince Lila that the only thing harmed by the daguerreotypes her uncle produced was the person's bank account. The price the rich Creoles paid to have one of the new portraits was truly astounding. But Lila still believed in the old ways. In the spirits and rituals carried across oceans and passed down through family lines.

Armantine didn't have much faith in the old ways, but she respected them enough to let the promise of good food and strong drinks bring her out to the banks of the Mississippi on the summer solstice. And she knew it was pointless to try convincing Lila otherwise.

"*Oooh*, look," Lila said in reverent tones. "Here comes Thisbe."

Armantine looked up as a row of dark shadows came out of the trees. A woman stood at the center, and around her arm coiled a large snake. The woman was old, with ashy brown skin hanging from her slim bones. Thick lines were carved into her face from years of laboring in the sun. Armantine couldn't help but smile at Thisbe's sense of drama as she walked silently with slow, measured steps toward the people waiting by the fires.

Everyone knew Thisbe was the daughter of a local plantation owner, even if he'd never claimed her as such. For most of her life, she'd been enslaved by him, but when he died, her father had freed her in his will. He'd also given her a small cottage to live in at the edge of his land and an even smaller bequest to keep her fed and clothed. Rumor was he'd done all that because he'd feared her. Rumor was he was right to.

Thisbe's freedom gave her a great deal of power and influence among the enslaved people who lived at the plantations on the River Road. Since she was free, she didn't answer to the planting seasons and could help tend to the sick or ailing while their loved ones toiled all day. Since she was independent, she could help those whose masters didn't provide for them well enough. Since the people believed she had the gift of sight, they listened to her. And they feared her for all sorts of reasons.

The fire threw shadows across the angles of her wizened face, and when Thisbe drew near enough that I could make out her features clearly in the firelit night, she raised her hands and chanted an eloquent invocation. When the invocation ended, a drum sounded from the darkness, and Thisbe began moving on surprisingly nimble feet to the driving beat. Little by little, others joined her in the dance.

Lila grabbed Armantine's hand. They danced through the night, and time tilted, as it often does in dreams, until the sun started to rise.

Armantine woke on one of the long rough benches the dancers had rested on throughout the night. The fires were still smoldering, and bodies draped comfortably across the ground and each other, huddled for warmth in the almost-cool morning air.

She stood and stretched her sore limbs, swayed for a minute as the world spun, and tried unsuccessfully to rub the ache from her head. She'd stayed far too long and had missed her ride back into town. Jules wouldn't be happy if she missed their afternoon appointments as well.

Testing out her balance, she headed toward the road. At a brisk pace, it would take the better part of the morning to walk back to the city, unless someone came along and offered her a ride. She looked back over her shoulder. Visible now in the morning light, the huge mansion rose from an alley of trees. Armantine shivered. She never did like that place, and would have done anything to get Lila free of it, if she could have. Lila had certainly gone back already. There would have been breakfasts to deliver and chamber pots to clean out for the people she served.

As Armantine walked, the stiffness of the night worked itself out of her muscles. She needed a bath herself. Maybe some breakfast. She hoped Cook would have some fresh beignets or some fruit she could eat before the work of the day began.

Deep in thought about the day ahead of her, she didn't notice the men at first as she rounded the bend. Had she been paying attention, she would have moved to the other side of the road to avoid where they crouched, examining something in the reedy wildflowers.

But she didn't notice until it was too late to look away. Too late to move to the other side. Too late to miss Alex glancing up at her, holding a knife darkened with something unspeakable. Too late to avoid seeing Lila's body crumpled in an unnatural pose, her eyes blankly staring at the heavens, and her blood blooming dark as death from a line across her once-elegant throat, across her bared and bloodied chest.

17

I arrived at the office early the next morning before most of the staff. But after the terrible image of Lila's bloody body, I hadn't wanted to go back to sleep. I couldn't have stayed a moment longer in my too-small cabin. Not when the dream was so close—so real.

"You're up early," Mina said as I entered the staff break room. She was the only other person around so far.

"Couldn't sleep." I shuffled over to the coffeepot. I needed something stronger than my usual Diet Coke. My nerves were still strung tightly with the residue of the dream.

It had seemed so *real*. I could almost feel the heat of the morning and hear the buzz of the flies that had already found her. And I couldn't stop seeing Lila's body—her dress torn open, the angry map of strange symbols carved into her chest and arms.

Suppressing a shudder, I tried to dismiss the image, but when I closed my eyes and took a deep breath, it rose in the darkness, even more vivid than before. Her body had been left like a broken doll, each dark mark glinting with blood that had congealed in the morning sun.

"Do you have trouble sleeping very often?" Mina asked, concern shadowing her expression.

I focused on pouring myself a cup of the bitter coffee and then lightening it up with a heap of cream and sugar. "Not really," I told her.

I don't know why I lied. Maybe because she was my supervisor, and I didn't want her to doubt my ability to do the job.

"I'm still getting used to my new place." I took a sip of the steaming cup to give myself a moment before finally meeting her eyes.

She stared at me for a few seconds longer before the tightness in her expression eased. "You know, I have some tea that might help. Chamomile and lavender. It usually puts me right to sleep."

"Thanks. That's really kind of you," I said, not bothering to correct her mistaken impression. Getting to sleep wasn't my problem. What happened behind my closed eyelids was my issue, and I doubted chamomile was going to help that.

I started to head out, but stopped at the door.

"Hey, Mina?" I said. "I had a question for you—about the family who lived here before. Did the wife have a brother by any chance?"

She frowned. "I suppose it's possible. We don't know much about Roman's wife Josephine, much less about the rest of her family. Most of the records we've uncovered have been focused on Roman's family—the Dutilettes. I don't think there's any record of a brother, though I guess it's possible." Her expression shifted. "Why do you ask?"

"I thought I might have found some mention of him in the archives," I told her, not wanting to confess I was asking her about a dream. "But maybe I misread. It's been a while since my high school French classes."

She considered me carefully. "Maybe. I can help look into it for you later this afternoon, if you want?"

"Maybe," I said, echoing her own words. "It's not really important, though. There's no rush. Thanks again for making the coffee."

I retreated to the cramped room that held the archive. After the night I'd had, I wasn't in the mood to take any new pictures. And besides, I was still curious about the Dutilettes. *Did* Roman's wife have a brother? Or had I simply created a narrative about a random hot guy in my dreams?

I hadn't found much when Leonard came by and hour or so later. "Lucy—just the person I was looking for."

I glanced up from the pile I'd been sorting. "Did you need me for something?"

"As a matter of fact, yes. The Foundation just finalized the purchase of a parcel of land with a structure that's original to the property. Silas didn't want us to wait until he's back later today to get started on it. He needs to have the property and building documented before we start any restoration, so you'll need your camera."

At the mention of Silas's name—and the reminder he'd be back from his business trip later today—my heart skipped. I'd been spending my nights having explicit dreams about Armantine and Alex. They'd been a nice change from my usual nightmares, and a pleasant enough distraction from my own frustrating lack of a love life. But now that Silas was returning, I wasn't sure what it meant that I'd slipped so easily into dreaming about some other guy. Or what I wanted to do about the one I actually had a chance with.

"I thought the Foundation was losing money," I said as I finished gathering up the photographs I'd been sorting. "Why did they spring for another piece of land?"

"This purchase has been in the works for a while now, but it's taken a long time to finalize everything. There was some disagreement about whether the parcel was part of another plantation, and the paperwork was pretty much a nightmare to track down. But Silas wanted it, so he made it happen."

"What's so important about the land?" I asked, following Leonard out through the offices.

"In part, it has a freestanding structure that likely dates to the early eighteen hundreds. That alone would make it interesting for Silas's larger project, but the owner of that building is even more interesting. Apparently, a freewoman lived there who was important to Le Ciel."

"Thisbe?" The name came out before I even had a chance to think about it, but the instant I said it, I knew I was right. I just didn't understand how I could be right.

"Yeah." He seemed as surprised as I was at the mention of the name. "I'm surprised you know about her."

The air in the offices suddenly felt very close as disjointed images from last night's dream flashed in my mind. A tall woman wearing a snake and calling forth who-knows-what powers. The angry slash of blood across an innocent throat.

I grasped my now empty cup of coffee with both hands to keep them from shaking. "I must have read about her in the archive." I'd gone through so many old papers in the last couple of days, it *was* possible her name had been in the records.

It was the only thing that made sense. I must have read her name somewhere, and then my subconscious must have put that name together with Alex, but I shuddered when I thought about *how* it had put the two together. Was just my imagination, or did the faint scent of sulfur and sweat really hang in the air?

Leonard didn't seem to notice. "Anyway, Thisbe owned this good-sized patch of land between Le Ciel and the next plantation over. Locals around here still talk about her. Some think she was a witch."

"Was she?" I asked, remembering the figure I'd seen the night before in my dream.

"I'm not sure I could say for certain. There's not much official documentation about Thisbe, but there's plenty of stories," Leonard said. "People in these parts haven't forgotten what a powerful conjure woman she was. Marie Laveau might be New Orleans' most famous Voodoo queen, but people out in these parts? They talk about Thisbe."

"What happened to her?" I asked, focusing on the cup in front of me.

"No one's really sure." He shrugged. "There's no real record. As far as anyone can tell, one day she just disappeared."

18

To my surprise, Chloe's boyfriend, Piers, was waiting for us outside the offices.

"Lucy, you've met Piers?" Leonard asked.

I smiled at Piers in greeting. "Chloe introduced us the other day."

"Good. We're lucky to have someone with his experience on this project."

"Oh?" I glanced at Piers.

"Absolutely," Leonard said as he clapped Piers on the shoulder. "He studied with Doctor Lamott in Haiti, so he's more familiar with occult rituals from that area than I am."

Piers looked embarrassed by the praise. "He's overselling my expertise. I'm just a lowly grad student glad included on this project."

Leonard led the way, since the parcel of land was close enough to walk. We passed beneath the cool canopy of the trees just beyond the gardens, and as we circled the pond, I couldn't help but scan the trees. The last time I'd been here, I'd stumbled upon Alex.

We finally stopped about half a mile from the big house, at the edge of a small grove of spindly trees. Through intertwined branches, faded bottles hung from rust-red cords. Some had fallen, and multicolor shards of glass glittered in the overgrown yard that surrounded the building within the grove.

"Watch your step," Leonard warned, leading us through the tangle of weeds and debris.

It was already in the high eighties and humid, but the whole place gave me the chills. Heavy foreboding hung over the parcel of land, and as we approached the cabin, I took some shots of the grime-covered bottles to keep myself from looking too closely at the house itself.

It was a small, squat structure with a single-gabled roof covered in rusted-out tin. It didn't look like much now, but to a woman once enslaved by her own father, it must have seemed like a mansion. The front was anchored with the same deep porch characteristic of houses in that part of Louisiana. It featured two sets of French doors, and had one of its double chimneys not fallen down, the cabin would have been a study in symmetry. But the whole place seemed to be grinning darkly at me.

"Hey, Piers. Come take a look at this." Leonard pointed to the doorway.

"Red brick dust. Believers think scrubbing your steps with it or putting a line in front of doors and windows will keep out both spirits and people who mean you harm," Piers explained. "Look here, by the window. There's more."

I crouched to take a closer look and documented the strange line of fine rust-red powder in the doorway with a couple of clicks of my camera. "It's funny how it's still so neat. I mean, if this Thisbe person disappeared more than a hundred and fifty years ago, you'd think it would have blown away by now."

"This was done recently," Piers said. "This kind of charm

needs to be reapplied fairly regularly to retain its power. That's why the steps are that funny russet color while the rest of the porch is just worn wood. Someone must still be scrubbing these steps with dust on a regular basis."

"Who would go to so much trouble to protect an old shack?" I wondered.

"Could be any number of people around here," Leonard admitted. "More than a few in the community didn't want Silas taking possession of this land. Like I said, people around here were brought up on stories about Thisbe. They feel a certain kinship and protectiveness toward her."

"That's also probably why the cottage hasn't tumbled down to nothing by now," Piers added. "A hundred and fifty years of Louisiana summers, and this old place shouldn't be anything more than a ruin." He bounced a bit on the porch to demonstrate his point. It lurched, but held.

I looked up at the pitched roof, the faded shutters. It wasn't in great shape, but Piers was right. The cabin could have been far worse. "So, someone's been taking care of this place?"

"Looks like," Leonard said. "We'll have to alert security about that." With a swipe of his foot, he scattered the red line before he opened one of the French doors and went in. "Come on in," he called from somewhere deep inside the house.

Piers and I followed, stepping carefully over the threshold as we entered the dark coolness of the cabin. Leonard directed me in taking some shots of the entry, while Piers drifted farther back into the cabin.

"This is incredible," Piers said when he returned to the front door. "It looks like someone abandoned this place last week, not last century."

Other than a thick coat of dust and wisps of gauzy cobwebs draping from every surface, the house looked untouched. Everything was surprisingly well preserved, considering how long it had been standing empty.

"Someone must have been living here," Leonard said. "Squatters."

"Maybe," Piers agreed. "But if that were the case, you'd think there'd be trash or some evidence of them lying around."

"Maybe someone's been treating it like a shrine," I ventured as I took some more pictures of the entryway.

"I wouldn't doubt it," Leonard agreed.

We took our time picking through the musty darkness of the empty cabin, until we came to a long room lined with shelves. At one end were the remains of one of the two brick fireplaces; on the other, a low, cot-like bed and a roughly made table.

"What do you make of this?" Leonard was examining a wooden box he'd pulled from an ancient cabinet. Mold had blackened its exterior.

Piers took the box from him and pried it open gently. Inside, he found a small gnarled starfish. I lifted my camera to document the artifact and saw it was actually a small primitive doll. Rust-red string had been wrapped around its torso, under and around its arms and legs, so it formed an inverted star against the figure's body.

"Looks to be hand carved." Piers studied it thoughtfully as he turned it over in his hand. "I've seen a lot of old dolls and poppets, but I've never seen one quite like this."

"What's different about it?" Leonard asked.

"These markings, for one." Piers pointed to the series of tiny indentions in the doll's arms and legs. "If I didn't know any better, I'd say it's some kind of additional charm. I'd have to do a little work to find out what it means. Doctor Lamott might know more."

"I'd appreciate anything you could dig up," Leonard said.

I took my time documenting the various furnishing in the room from multiple angles. It wasn't the kind of photography I usually did, but it also wasn't difficult. Actually, there was something soothing about the monotony of it. I didn't have to think about my dreams or Thisbe or anything else while I was cataloging the room.

"Well, what do we have here?" Leonard said from the other side of the room.

He pulled out a small trunk from under the narrow bed and worked it open. Inside was a pile of decaying fabric. Even with his careful, gentle touch, he couldn't keep the mass from crumbling as he unfolded it.

"It's a coat," Piers said as the shape of the garment became more apparent.

"There's something in this pocket." Leonard eased his fingers into a flap in the material and extracted a small booklet. "*Amazing.*"

I knew what it was before he opened it. I recognized the embossed design bordering the cover almost instantly, and a wave of panic ran through me. Behind the fragile cover would be a single image, and I knew exactly who it would depict. My mouth went dry as I stared in disbelief, wishing futilely that no one would open it.

Leonard opened the booklet and gasped. "Amazing. It looks like it was made just yesterday."

I didn't move at first while the other two huddled over it. I *couldn't.*

"Do you think this could be a picture of Thisbe?" Piers asked, oblivious to my distress.

"I doubt it," Leonard said. "According to the records I've seen, Thisbe should have been much, much older than this girl when this technology was being used."

I forced myself to inch closer on unsteady feet. I had to know for sure. But the room felt like it was spinning, and both Leonard and Piers sounded very far away.

As the two men debated the age of the image, I peered over Leonard's shoulder and met the gaze of a girl with dark hair and flawless skin. A girl whose eyes burned with desire. If the portrait had been in color, she would have had eyes the exact color of my own.

Armantine.

It was the last thing I thought before my vision went black.

19

P ain and darkness and the cold wet of death surround me.
And I'm falling, sinking until my lungs burn with the fetid
water that has pulled me into its embrace.

"Luce? Lucy . . . Come on, now. Wake up for us." Leonard's
worried voice sounded through the depths, pulling me *up*.

Up toward the starry night above. Up toward the world.

"She'll be fine, Doctor Aimes. It's probably the heat that got
to her," Piers's said, his voice rumbling through the liquid and
buoying me as well.

So close.

"I think she's coming to." *Leonard's voice.* "Lucy? *Lucy*, can
you hear me?"

My eyes fluttered open and then shut tight against the
brightness of the day. "I'm fine," I mumbled.

Strong hands pushed me up to a sitting position as I tried to
figure out how I'd gotten outside and why I was lying on the
porch. "What happened?"

"You fainted." Leonard's expression was tight with worry,
even as his voice was gentle. "Is this something that happens a
lot? First the other morning, and now—"

"What?" I blinked. "No. Really. I don't faint." *At least I never used to.*

Piers gave me a wry look. "I could definitely testify otherwise."

"The heat must have gotten to you again," Leonard said. "Did you have anything to eat this morning?"

"Coffee," I muttered.

"That isn't breakfast." Leonard was frowning at me. "You need to eat something."

"Really," I muttered, pushing away. "I'm fine."

"Still. I think that's enough for you today. I'm officially giving you the day off. Get into the air-conditioning and get some rest."

I tried to ignore his concern, but he was adamant. After a few minutes, I didn't have any choice but to gather my camera and equipment. Before I could sling the bag over my shoulder, Piers plucked it out of my hands and added it to his load.

"You don't have to—" I began, but the look he gave me stopped my protest. "Thanks," I said instead.

"Should we gather the artifacts before we go?" Piers asked.

Leonard shook his head. "We'll need to leave them for Byron to catalog. You two go on back, and I'll lock up here."

Piers and I started off through the field again, and I looked back only once. As we headed into the thick line of trees, I was glad to finally have the cabin behind me.

"What's an Armantine?" Piers asked, coming up to walk next to me.

"Who?"

He glanced at me. "So it's a who?"

"I . . . uh . . ." I blinked at him.

"Armantine," he repeated. "You said it right before you went down. I'm assuming it's a name."

"I'm not sure," I hedged. "Maybe it was a name I saw somewhere."

It wasn't a lie. Not *really*. I didn't know for sure the girl in the image was the same one from my dreams. Old pictures have a tendency to look the same, and there was no way of telling if a girl named Armantine had ever even existed.

Or that's what I told myself. But I knew deep down—in that place where we know things instinctively—the uncanny familiarity of the image threatened all the careful, rational explanations I'd been constructing about my dreams.

We were nearly back to the main part of the property when movement drew my eyes to the edge of the forest. Alex was leaning against a tree, watching us. The midmorning sun cast dark shadows over the angles of his face, and the light filtering through the trees picked up the gold that ran through his hair, highlighting the tones of his skin. Again, I was swamped with a rush of familiarity, a burst of *wanting* so intense I nearly gasped. My fingers itched to capture those contrasts in a photograph—the angles and softness, the shadows and light.

Since I awoke from the dream of him over Lila's body, dread had been winding itself around my chest. At last, it loosened. As he stood there bathed in dappled light, he didn't look any more capable of murdering someone than I was. I raised my hand to wave to him, but he shook his head, silently urging me not to draw attention to his presence.

"What is it?" Piers asked. Apparently, he was still watching me with those sharp eyes of his.

"What is what?" I turned to look at him.

"It looked like you saw something over there." He pointed to the edge of the forest where Alex had been just moments before.

There was no sign of him now, though.

Had I imagined him?

"It was nothing," I lied.

"You're sure you didn't hit your head?" Piers asked.

"I'm fine," I assured him, but he didn't look convinced. "I thought I saw someone, but I must have been wrong."

Piers frowned as he studied the line of trees. "There shouldn't be anyone this far from the main part of the property." I couldn't tell if he was talking to me or to himself. "But considering the state of that cabin, we should probably let Leonard know."

"It was probably just the light hitting the leaves." The last thing I wanted was to get anyone into trouble.

His expression was serious. "Still. It wouldn't hurt to have security come through occasionally."

We resumed walking, with Piers slowing his pace to match mine again. I felt decidedly unsteady—from what had happened in the cabin, from the dream about Lila's murder, from thinking I'd seen Alex near the trees. Leonard and Piers were probably right. I needed to get out of the heat, maybe get something to eat.

I did look back again, one more time, but Alex was gone. If he'd ever been there to begin with.

20

I tried to take the day off, like Leonard had instructed, but after about an hour trapped in the tiny cabin I now called home, I was feeling more than a little stir-crazy. While I was happy to have a space of my own, there was no denying it was cramped. I grabbed my tablet, a bottle of water, and a sun hat, and I headed outside. I planned to find a quiet place to work on some of the images I'd taken at Thisbe's cabin and get them ready for Silas when he returned.

I'm not sure what drew me toward the pond. I wanted to avoid the tourists wandering the property, for one thing, but the pond also simply felt like where I needed to be. It was where I'd first seen Alex, and it had been a nearly a week since I managed to miss those first pictures of him. I stepped through the line of trees that separated the pond from the main house hoping to run into him, but the was clearing empty.

I brushed off my disappointment quickly enough, though. The shade beneath beautiful old oak at the far end of the pond was calling my name. There, the ground was covered with soft, thick grass, and the breeze rustling the branches was almost cool. I made myself comfortable and powered on the tablet to get to work. I'd downloaded the pictures I'd taken earlier, and I would use the afternoon to figure out which I could use for the Foundation's website.

Flipping through the shots, I started to relax into the steady rhythm of work. There was a particularly good shot of Leonard talking to the employees that Sam might like, and I adjusted the color until it looked almost antique. But when I came to the pictures of Thisbe's cabin, the same unsettling unease hit me that I'd experienced standing at the threshold of the real thing.

Though I tried to push through, the pictures of her cabin were uncomfortable even to look at. I decided to take a quick break. It was probably exhaustion, and Leonard was probably right—I really did need to rest. If I closed my eyes for a couple of minutes, I hoped the feeling would pass.

But I must have been even more tired than I'd thought, because when I opened my eyes again, the slant of light told me it was twilight.

To my surprise, Alex was sitting next to me, as golden and beautiful as he had been earlier. His jaw no longer held the tightness of earlier, and his eyes were clear and bright. Their green depths reminded me of the lushness of forests in the north—a living, fertile color I hadn't encountered anywhere else in the overheated Southern summer. He was looking at me with such intensity that it fairly took my breath away.

Mine. The word came again, right along with the unaccountable wanting. Which was insane. But I couldn't dismiss the feeling, the sure knowledge that being there with him was exactly what I was supposed to be doing.

Love. Hope. Safety. The feelings coursed through me with reckless abandon. I *loved* him.

It was a completely ridiculous thought. I didn't even *know* him. But the feeling was there, deep inside me, and so sure I couldn't dismiss it.

That was when I knew I was her again—Armantine. Alex

wasn't really there, and neither was I. It was all just another dream, and in that instant, I hated Armantine

But my brief burst of anger couldn't survive the desire—the love—welling up from her in the dream. I was swept away more absolutely than by any nightmare. What she felt for him was like drowning—I couldn't fight against it. And I couldn't help but feel it, too.

They were sitting under the oak, inches apart. His hand was close to hers, his finger tracing small circles against her skin. I could feel her delight—the little frissons of excitement and anticipation that burst along her skin. Armantine pretended to be unmoved by his gentle coaxing, but desire pulled low in her belly. She wanted him—his lips against her mouth. His hands trailing fire along the rest of her skin. But she didn't want him to know how badly she wanted him. How she *needed* him.

She was so afraid. The strength of her fear warred with her desire. She'd already given him so much—*too much*—and she was terrified of what could happen to her if Alex ever truly understood how completely he held her heart.

Alex looked at me—her—and smiled. It wasn't the half-cocked mocking grin I'd gotten from him the other day by the pond, but the slow, confident smile of a man who knew what he wanted. "You can trust me, you know," he told her, his voice softly urging.

But Armantine *didn't* know. Doubt kept equal measure with her hope.

"Truly. I could never hurt you, *chère*." His words were serious, but the promise and the endearment rolled off his tongue too easily. He didn't understand how powerless she was—how powerless he was in turn. There was nothing he could do to stop the world from hurting her.

"You may not mean to, but . . ." Her voice came out deeper, huskier, with a breathless quality it hadn't had before, in the studio. "I should go back."

His eyes flashed devilishly as he took her hand and brought it to his lips. "Stay, love. Stay with me a little while longer."

Armantine's breath caught. "Alex," she whispered, but even she didn't know if she was asking him to stop or to go on.

He placed a heated kiss at the pulse point of her wrist.

"I shouldn't," she said, more breath than words. Pulling her hand away, she reminded herself who she was. With him, it was so easy to forget.

She looked over her shoulder, back toward the big house. If someone had seen the two of them. . .

"I never should have come here," she whispered as she gathered the charcoal pencils that had fallen into the grass near her skirts. She tucked them, along with sketches she'd made of the pond and of him, into her bag. They were the only thing she would ever really have of him. The only things she *could* ever have.

He was watching her with confusion and thinly veiled frustration. "Armantine—"

"I should not be here with you." She avoided his gaze as she finished gathering her things. It had been a mistake. She had wanted too much, had *risked* too much. "I can't. *We* can't."

"And why not?" he asked, his voice sharp enough now to make her pause.

She heard the confusion—the *hurt*—he did not bother to hide.

"Was this all simply a game to you?"

"No." Moving toward him, she shook her head, willing him to understand. She took his hand in hers and considered her worlds carefully. "Can't you see I have nothing to offer you?" She paused to meet his eyes. "What future could there be for us?"

His brows drew together as he puzzled out the meaning of her words, and then surprise—Or was it uncertainty that crashed through his expression. "I thought you understood?"

"What is there to understand?" Her voice was gentle, but it carried all the pain of her regret. He eased his grasp on her arm.

"Do you think this is a game for me? I am not toying with you, *mon coeur*," he murmured. He lifted his hand and traced the line of her jaw with a single fingertip.

"I want you." His fingertip followed the line of her throat, down across her collarbone until he reached the edge of the neckline of her dress, and his mouth curved when her breath hitched. "Just as I know you want me."

"It does not matter what I want," she whispered.

"No?" His finger traced the neckline of her dress, dipping to the soft swell of her breasts and then back up, her skin like fire everywhere he touched. "Then you feel nothing when I touch you?"

She swallowed past the desire that tightened her throat, but she didn't speak.

Tugging gently at the neckline of her gown, he bared more of her skin. A little farther, and the nut-brown circle of her areola would be bared to him.

"Can you tell me you don't want this—*me*?" he murmured, leaning steadily toward her, looming over her as she shifted back.

She licked her lips, a nervous dart of her tongue. His gaze flicked down, growing heated. But she couldn't deny that she wanted him.

He tugged her frock farther still, until her breasts were bare to the sunlight. Her nipples grew tight from the coolness of the air, from how badly she wanted him. Still, she didn't speak.

Slowly, torturously, he brushed his fingertips lightly across her skin as he looked at her. "I will not lie to you, Armantine." His touch was soft as a butterfly's wing but singed her even so, as he traced the swell of her breasts. "Not a moment goes by that I do not think of you. Of your beauty and your fire and the light you have brought into my life. Not a moment passes that I do not think of what it would be like to have you as my own," he whispered.

"Alexandre." She murmured his name, her voice hitching with desire.

It was all the encouragement he needed to lower his head and take one of her nipples into his mouth. Heat flooded through her at the feel of his tongue and teeth, greedy and demanding, and she could not stop herself from pulling his head closer. Threading her fingers through the silken locks of his hair, she pinned him to her and let him take what he would.

Breathless, he finally drew back, victory shining in the emerald depths of his eyes. "You belong with me."

"I wish I could imagine the future you see." Reaching up, she brushed a stray lock of hair back from his smooth forehead.

But he caught her wrist, pinned her gently to the ground as he loomed over her. "Can you not learn to imagine it?"

She ruthlessly crushed the hope his words inspired, until it was no more than a pinpoint of light in her otherwise dark future.

"How can you not see this is impossible?" she whispered, her voice trembling with regret and her eyes stinging with unshed tears.

They stayed like that for what felt like an eternity—her breasts bared to the evening air, the heat of the day swirling around them, and Armantine waiting for him to turn away from her.

Because she knew one day, he *would* turn from her. Eventually, he would leave.

Suddenly, he released her. She barely had time to sit up and arrange her dress to cover herself before he'd reached down to his boot and withdrawn a knife. It flashed in the sunlight, the blade as bright as his eyes had become. Fear bolted through her as she remembered him crouched over Lila's broken body, a bloodied knife glinting in his hand.

She knew he hadn't killed Lila, but there was a new fierceness in his expression she'd not seen before. Afraid to move, she watched and waited for what he would do.

But he didn't strike her. Instead, he walked to the oak and stabbed the blade into it again and again. Wary of the violence with which he assaulted the tree, she inched forward, trying to figure out what he was doing. When she reached him, he'd already finished carving two lopsided and primitive-looking interlocking letters into the weathered trunk. The tightly coiled spring in Armantine's chest eased at the sight.

"I promise you this," he told her, his voice thick with emotion. "I have searched for you too long to let you go now. I will find a way to make you believe in my promises, and someday long from now, we will bring our grandchildren to this very spot and show them this tree, this place where I pledged myself to you."

"Alex—" Her voice shook, and I knew what she was going to say. She would refuse him again, even as she wanted to accept him completely.

"No, *chère*. There has been enough talk. Enough fear." He pressed her back against the tree as he framed her face with his broad, strong hands. "Tell me you don't want me, and I'll release you."

But she couldn't.

"Tell me you don't love me, and I'll walk away right now."

She closed her eyes. With her next words she would damn herself.

Maybe she could have held the words back if she hadn't opened her eyes and seen the fear—the vulnerability—in Alex's expression. But the moment she saw everything he felt for her, she was lost.

"You know I'm yours. In every way I can be."

His lips were on hers then, fierce and hungry, and this time he did not hold back.

Neither did she. Her mouth opened for him, their tongues tangling as neither relented. His hands were everywhere. One hand was already pulling down the top of her gown again to grasp and knead her aching breasts while the other found her skirts. He brought his mouth to her breast again as his hand climbed higher, laving his tongue across her nipple as he hiked her skirts up. As he teased her aching nipple with his teeth, his fingers slipped through the split in her drawers and stroked them against her most sensitive skin.

She was at the edge of something she could not take back, and if she tumbled over, it would likely destroy her, but in that greedy moment, she didn't care. Instead of pulling away, instead of putting the distance between them that would have allowed her to think, she moaned her encouragement. Pulled him tighter to her breast. This moment might be all she ever had, and she wanted more. She wanted *everything*.

He didn't deny her. He slipped one finger inside of her, stroking deeply until a need she could not have explained was building and she was writhing against him, pressing herself into his hand as his fingers slid against her slick, oversensitive sex.

Throwing her head back, she was only barely aware of the rough bark of the tree biting against her skin or the heat of the day shimmering in the air around them. Her arms held him tight to her until he brought her to some point she could not return from. He seemed to know exactly what she wanted, what she *needed*, because when she was almost there, almost ready to crest that summit, he pulled back slightly and forced her to look at him. "You're mine, Armantine. *Mine*."

She was too far gone, too wound up with desire to refute his claim. A need built inside her, so sharp and desperate that she wanted to scream. "Please," she whispered.

"Tell me," he demanded, withdrawing a little. "Promise me. Body and soul, you belong to me."

She could only nod her agreement as the world shattered around her.

21

I woke up gasping, my body strung so tight with need that I was already moving, almost by instinct, to touch myself. To release the terrible wanting the dream had stirred up in me.

I probably would have done just that. I probably would have gotten myself off right there in the middle of the clearing before I even fully came to my senses, if the sound of someone clearing their throat hadn't punctured the haze of the dream.

"Please . . . don't feel you need to stop on account of me." The familiar voice spoke nearby, and I froze. Whatever spell the dream had cast around me was shattered, and cold reality set in.

When I finally summoned the courage to open my eyes and look, I half expected Alex to be wearing the black suit from my dream. But this version of him was no dream. He was there, flesh and bone, wearing the same clothes all the costumed interpreters wore—a freshly laundered linen shirt and crisply pressed gray trousers.

"You really shouldn't sneak up on people when they're napping, you know." I lifted one eyebrow in his direction, affecting a wryness I didn't really feel.

He lifted his hands, a smile curving his mouth. "I didn't realize you were sleeping, *chère*."

He looked different than I had dreamed him. The dream's faded tones had dampened the intensity of his green eyes and washed out the gold spun through his hair. In the dream it had been brushed back, away from his face, but now it fell lazily over his forehead

"I thought maybe you'd fainted again," he said.

He *had* been there that first morning. I hadn't imagined him.

I sat up and stretched my stiff muscles, trying to ignore my reaction to him. "I don't faint."

I didn't want to want to admit the effect he was having on me. He was a complete stranger, but he felt familiar. Too familiar. Like I'd been waiting for my entire life for this moment. And after the intensity of the dream? There was a part of me that wanted to pick up where we'd left off. I could almost see it, how easy it would be to crawl over to him, to press him to the ground, and to finish what the dream had started. I could peel off his shirt, expose the chiseled muscles of his chest and explore every inch of him with my hands, my mouth.

I could satisfy the need burning inside me.

Which was, of course, ridiculous. He was gorgeous, sure. But I didn't *know* him. My emotions were still too close to the surface because of the dream—too close to what *she* had felt.

But he was here. I hadn't imagined him, which made me wonder about the daguerreotype we'd found earlier this morning in Thisbe's cabin. Had there ever been an Armantine, or had I only invented a similarity between the likeness in the image and the girl I had been dreaming about?

"Truly . . . I'm sorry to have intruded," he said, frowning slightly. "But I wasn't sure if you were well."

It was hard to look straight at him, not with the dream still clinging to me. "I'm fine," I said, not quite making eye contact. "I must have dozed off while I was working and . . ."

I wasn't going to think about "and."

"Anyway," I said. "I'm fine."

"This," he said, pointing to the open tablet. The screen displayed an image of the house, its columns like bars caging it in. "This is your work?"

I nodded. "Yeah. I'm the Foundation's new photographer."

"Of course you are." He seemed amused. "Will you show me?"

I usually didn't have a problem showing people my unfinished work, but this was different somehow. I'd been trying to find him for about a week—I'd been dreaming about a version of him for just as long. It felt like something bigger was at stake.

"I don't know," I said, considering his request. "What are you offering in return?"

His brows lifted. "What is it you want?"

A good hard fuck against that tree.

Humor sparked in his eyes, like he'd read my mind too clearly. But I swallowed that response and ignored the heat in my cheeks.

"I'd settle for some answers," I told him instead.

"To what questions?"

"Well, you could start by telling me why you keep following me."

"Perhaps I'm not following you intentionally," he said slowly, carefully. "Perhaps you simply happen to be where I am."

"Are you telling me it's a coincidence we keep running into each other?" I asked, doubtful.

His eyes were serious. "Would you believe that?"

"I don't think I would."

He smiled fully then, unable to hide his amusement. "Please." The word came out easier this time for him. "I would very much like to see your work." He gestured toward the tablet.

I thought about refusing, but he looked so earnest in his request, I eventually relented.

He settled next to me, and I detected the familiar scent of bergamot as I started flipping through the images I'd taken since arriving at the plantation.

He studied them carefully. "You have captured the secretive quality of the mansion, yes?"

"I've tried."

"They're quite striking, these pieces. Beautiful, yes, but they give the feeling of being trapped by the grandeur of the place."

"That's exactly what I was going for," I told him. "I wanted the shadows to look like the bars of a prison. The house seemed so intensely malevolent that day. Here, look at this one." I flipped to another image, hoping his reaction wouldn't disappoint.

It was the image of the large fountain in the south garden. Light pooled around the statue of a young girl holding her hands to the sky. I watched him out of the corner of my eye as he studied it, afraid if I looked at him directly, he would see how much I wanted him to get it. To understand this one, too.

He didn't respond right away. His brows were creased above those startling green eyes of his, and his jaw was tight. And then, all at once, his face seemed to unfold, and he glanced up at me, his eyes no longer shadowed or evasive. And in that moment, I had the feeling he saw more than just what I was doing with the photograph. I had the uncanny feeling he saw me, too. *Really* saw me.

There was too much in his gaze—too much intensity, too many questions, just . . . too much. I couldn't help but look away.

After a long, expectant moment, he cleared his throat and spoke again. "She looks like some sort of ethereal being in this one. But you make it a question. Is the water lifting her or pulling her back?"

I bit my lip to keep from smiling like an idiot as I kept my eyes trained on the image.

"You're quite talented," he murmured.

I released a breath, and something inside me released along with it.

When I moved to the next image, he stiffened beside me. It was a portrait of Thisbe's cabin, and even looking at it now, something about the plot of land and the cottage that stood on it made me want to shiver.

"You should stay away from that place," he said, his voice sharp. Stony. "The old witch's cabin isn't safe."

The Alex in my dreams was a gentler, more idealized version of the Alex sitting next to me, his jaw like flint. Maybe my subconscious had evened out his rough edges and softened his intensity.

"Yeah," I said, trying to brush off the unexpected ice in his tone. "It wasn't exactly my favorite place."

"You can't go back there." Real anger heated his expression now.

My hackles rose at his presumptuousness. "I might have to. It's my job to take pictures."

He opened his mouth, like he wanted to argue, but then the anger seemed to drain from him and he closed it without another word. A strained silence stretched between us.

Suddenly, I didn't want to be there, alone in the clearing with him. I closed my tablet and began repacking my bag.

"I've upset you." His voice was still strained and tight, but it was also tinged with something like regret.

"No," I lied. "I just need to get back. I need to check in with the office."

As I stood to leave, I resisted looking at him. I *liked* the Alex in my dreams, but I wasn't going to make the mistake of confusing dreams with reality.

"Please," he said. "I will go. Stay and enjoy the afternoon."

"It's fine—" I grabbed my bag from the ground, but he was faster. Before I could leave, he was already backing away. He gave me a final, tentative wave before he headed toward the woods on the far side of the pond. When he stepped into the shadows of the trees, I lost sight of him. And I was alone again.

All at once, the heat of the day pressed in on me. The clearing was unsettlingly empty without him. Even in the dream, the clearing had felt more complete with him in it.

The dream.

The whole time I'd been talking with Alex, I couldn't quite shake the intensity of Armantine's feelings. The girl's emotions about her Alex had been so stark, so *strong*, they'd colored my every reaction. But there had been something else. Now that he wasn't there distracting me, the details were coming back.

The ancient oak, dripping with Spanish moss was still there, just as it had been in the dream. Carefully, I searched the trunk, running my fingers over its rough bark, but I didn't find what I was looking for.

"Just a dream, then." I breathed easier at the thought. Because the alternative . . . I didn't want to think about it.

Slinging my bag on my shoulder, I started back toward my own little cabin. The lack of two interlocking letters on the tree's gnarled trunk was confirmation I *wasn't* crazy. I wasn't having dreams about some long-dead girl and a guy who looked uncannily like the guy I'd been talking to. Armantine was only a figment of my overactive and sleep-deprived imagination. She hadn't actually sat under this tree with another Alex more than a hundred years ago and—

Almost two hundred years ago, the tree would have been smaller.

For a second, I thought about not going back. It would have been easier to just keep walking, to forget about the tree and my theories. But I couldn't let it go.

It took me a few minutes to figure out how to get enough of a foothold on the trunk to hoist myself up. At first, I almost missed it. At first, I mistook the marking for part of the rough bark, but as I ran my fingers over the shallow, jagged lines, I knew nature couldn't have designed those deeply gouged angles. Dark with age, the two intertwining letters—*A* for Armantine, *A* for Alex—had somehow withstood the march of time.

"Lucy?"

My name echoed through the air, shattering the stillness of the clearing, and I peered through the branches. Silas was standing on the other side of the pond. His hand shaded his eyes from the sun, and he was looking up to where I was perched.

"Lucy!" He started toward me, and I waved before lowering myself back to the ground, sorting through my jumbled thoughts.

I scooped up my bag from beside the tree, and headed to meet him. I don't know why I wanted to keep him away from the oak. I hadn't done anything wrong—it had only been a dream—but I didn't want him there, so close to where I—where *Armantine*—had been with Alex.

"What were you doing up there?" he asked, glancing up at the branches.

"Just checking out a shot."

He looked past me, frowning as his eyes studied the tree's enormous canopy. "We could get you a ladder or some scaffolding, you know. We may be bleeding money, but there's no need to take risks."

I pretended to laugh off his concern. "It's fine. I already got what I needed."

His gaze kept shifted to the clearing beyond me and the enormous live oak again.

"How was your trip?" I asked, trying to pull his attention back toward me. The tree and what I'd discovered sleeping in its branches were mine for the moment. I wasn't ready to share the discovery yet. Maybe not ever.

Silas hesitated a moment longer, still staring at the tree before he blinked away whatever questions he'd been asking himself and smiled down at me. "Too long," he said, his expression softening. "I'm glad to be back."

"I'm glad to have you back."

"Yeah?"

I nodded. I didn't know what the letters in the tree meant about my sanity, but I knew for sure the man in front of me was real and good and a hell of a lot safer than whatever dreams had walked into my waking.

He slung a cool arm over my shoulder, and the scent of mint and his woodsy cologne wrapped around me, brushing away the rest of the dream that had taken hold of me during my unintended nap. "I like the sound of that."

Together, we headed back toward the main part of the property, leaving the clearing and whatever questions I had for another day.

"Leonard said you got some good shots of the new property? Thisbe's place?"

At the mention of Thisbe's cabin, my steps faltered, but I recovered before Silas had to catch me.

"I got a few pictures," I hedged. "Whether they're any good, I'll have to leave it up to my boss to decide."

I didn't let myself glance back over my shoulder as we left the clearing. I tried to focus on Silas, but my thoughts were a jumbled mess. I'd convinced myself that knowing Thisbe's name might have been a coincidence. I could explain away the girl in the picture as an overactive imagination . . .

But the carvings in the tree? I knew for certain no one had told me about it. And if those carvings were real, if those things really might have happened long ago, it meant my dreams might be more than just dreams. It meant Alex shouldn't—*couldn't*—still be alive. It meant I really needed to talk to Mama Erzulie, and I needed to talk to her soon.

22

After that day in the clearing, something changed. Maybe because Silas was back, or maybe because we settled into an easy flirtation that felt normal and safe, I managed to set aside the question of the letters in the tree. Or maybe it was because, for the handful of nights after, I didn't dream at all. My sleep wasn't interrupted by nightmares, and I didn't wake each morning aching for someone who might not even be real.

After a couple of days, I started to wonder if I'd imagined the letters in the trees. Maybe I'd seen what I wanted to see, just like I'd seen a girl from my dreams in the daguerreotype in Thisbe's cabin. Well rested for the first time in, well, *ever*, I felt almost like a different person. But as Saint John's Eve approached, I remembered that there would be an opportunity to talk with Mama Erzulie. But did I even still want to?

When Silas learned about the Saint John's Eve outing, he talked Chloe into an invitation. That's how the four of us—me, Silas, Chloe, and Piers—all found ourselves dressed in white and riding together in Silas's Audi toward New Orleans.

"What time did you say the party starts?" I asked, looking

back to where she and Piers were snuggled together in the backseat.

"Please don't let anyone tonight hear you calling it a party," Chloe said, glancing over at me. "It's not a party. It's a *ritual*. And it starts around sunset."

The word ritual brought with it images of snakes and fires. Of limbs moving rhythmically to tribal drumbeats and blood blooming across lifeless, broken bodies. "Fine. What, exactly, does this *ritual* entail?"

"It's a celebration of the summer solstice. Mama Erzulie will ask the spirits to intercede for a good harvest. She'll do a ceremony on the bridge that crosses Bayou Saint John, and then we'll all eat and dance." She frowned. "Okay, maybe it is a little like a party."

I laughed at her expression. "I won't tell anyone, promise."

She cut me a look, then burst out laughing too.

THE CEREMONY WAS HELD on one of the many inland tributaries that sprouted off Lake Pontchartrain. When we finally arrived, people dressed in white were already gathering at a large steel bridge that crossed the bayou at its narrowest point. They looked like initiates preparing for an old-time religious revival.

As we walked along the bayou toward the growing crowd, Silas slipped his hand into mine. The warm strength of his fingers eased something inside me. I glanced up to find him watching me and smiled, feeling somehow surer. There was a steady sureness to him that appealed. A strength and forthrightness that I couldn't resist.

It was a bad idea to fall for someone like Silas. None of my problems had disappeared just because I wasn't having nightmares lately. I was still the same old Lucy, a hot mess most of the time. But that night? I couldn't think about anyone or anything else but him.

"All these people practice Voodoo?" I asked Chloe.

"Some," she said, waving at someone in the crowd. "But a lot of people come out because it's a good time."

"You don't have to be a believer to enjoy the food," Piers said. "Speaking of—" He brought their interlocked hands to his lips. "I'm going to look at the spread. You want anything, baby?"

"I'll get some later, after I say hi to Shaunda. You go on ahead."

"You want to get in on this?" he asked Silas. Silas looked torn between keeping a hold of my hand and going with Piers to explore the long tables piled with plates of food.

"Go," I laughed.

"Come on," Chloe said, looping her arm through mine once the guys had taken off. "I thought I saw Shaunda down front. Maybe she's saved us a spot."

Chloe pushed her way through the crush of bodies until we finally made it to the mouth of the bridge, where Shaunda was waiting. "Took y'all long enough." She gave Chloe a hug and then wrapped me in one as well. "You ready, Yankee girl?"

"I have no idea," I told her honestly.

"Oh, stop it," Chloe said to Shaunda before turning to me. "There's nothing to it, I promise. First, the priestess will come from over there and cross the bridge. When she gets to the center, she'll do the invocation to the spirits, and then she'll invite the rest of us across."

"The spirits?"

"You know, what Mama Erzulie told you. There are all kinds of spirits out there," Chloe reminded me. "This time, we're calling to the light, to the helpful Loa who will bring strong harvest and keep us safe from storms the whole season through."

On the bridge, someone had already set up a small makeshift

altar that was draped with a vibrant aquamarine cloth. Burning candles covered almost every inch. Most of the candles were white, but a few others had already splattered bloodred wax on the field of blue.

Chloe must have seen me studying them. "The white is for purity and protection, but the red is for power."

Drums started in the distance, and their driving cadence sent a shiver of recognition through me. As the rhythm of the drums became more distinct, I realized the group of people approaching the bridge from the far end of the bayou weren't walking, but dancing toward us. Movement at the far edge of the water caught my attention. Before I could figure out what I was seeing, a flame erupted.

"They light the bonfires to guide the way for the priestess," Chloe whispered.

Sure enough, as the drumming grew louder and the group drew closer, more fires sprang to life on the bank of the bayou. One at a time, they ignited, each closer than the last, until the drumming was loud enough to vibrate in my chest and the group of dancers stopped on the far side of the bridge. They parted then, and a woman stepped forward dressed in an elaborate white turban and long, flowing white skirts—Mama Erzulie.

She raised her arms and sang out to the skies above in a rich, warm song. I couldn't tell what she was saying, but her voice rolled over the crowd. A man stepped forward to drape a large snake over Mama Erzulie's shoulders, and everyone around us stilled. But I gasped as my vision blurred. For a moment the Voodoo queen's dancing became Thisbe's. Her graceful rhythm was replaced by Thisbe's more erratic and disjointed movements. But then almost as quickly as the vision had come, it dissipated quietly into the night, leaving me shaken.

"Don't worry so much," Chloe told me, mistaking my reaction to the vision. "There's nothing evil going on here. In

Voodoo, snakes represent one of the most powerful of the spirits—Damballa."

I didn't correct her mistaken impression, but instead watched Mama Erzulie, who had left her entourage behind her and begun to dance toward us. With writhing, rhythmic motions, she twisted her body in a sensual imitation of a snake as she approached the middle of the bridge. It was reminiscent of Thisbe's dance, but Mama Erzulie's face held none of the angst or desperation that had been clear in Thisbe's.

"When she reaches the middle of the bridge, she'll do an invocation to Saint John the Baptist and any other spirits around." Chloe pointed to the altar. "The snake will go there, as an offering."

"She's going to kill it?" I wondered, unable to keep the tremor from my voice.

Chloe shot me a dirty look. "Of course not. It's just going to stay there so it doesn't get trampled on," she huffed. "Seriously, Lucy, you have watched way too many horror flicks."

"You said offering."

"Yeah, *offering*. Not sacrifice." She shook her head, more amused than truly irritated. "Honestly. We're celebrating the birth of the man who baptized Christ, not Beelzebub. Just watch."

Mama Erzulie danced her way across the bridge until she stood in front of the altar. Slowly, she lifted the snake from her shoulders and raised it high over her head as she knelt before the candles. She called out again, her voice soaring over the stillness of the bayou, and then she set the snake into a depression I hadn't noticed in the altar. After she covered it over again, she stood and faced us.

Her voice rose then, articulating strange syllables in a language I didn't understand. With each call, the crowd responded in kind, Chloe's and Shaunda's voices loud among them. They repeated the call and response, with more of the observers on our side joining the chant each time Mama Erzulie raised her arms, and I found myself swept up and chanting right along with them.

The chant changed suddenly, and the drumming resumed. She raised her hands, and the crowd gave her back her chant. Then she began a new dance.

It wasn't the sensual writhing of a snake now, but a joyful celebration. The people continued to followed, moving across the bridge to where Mama Erzulie waited. She raised her arms again to those on our side of the bridge, but most of the people were already dancing in time to the pulsing drums.

"This is the best part," Chloe shouted. She smiled at me and raised her own arms in the dance.

I laughed and began to move in time to the music. By the time we made it to the center of the bridge, my arms were in the air and my body was moving freely to the rhythm of the drummers. We'd lost Shaunda somewhere in the crowd, but I caught Chloe's bright smile before we got separated, mixing with the other bodies on the bridge. Dark arms tangled with light ones, and the drummers became part of the dancers as the rhythmic sway of the crowd swirled around the small area.

We danced faster then, spinning alone and together, and the air filled with laughter to complement the driving beats of the ever-present drumming. It became its own music in the waning light, punctuated by ecstatic shouts that echoed in the sticky night air, reverberating like a remembrance of something already past.

At some point, strong arms wrapped around my waist. I turned and smiled up at Silas, as his muscular body pressed against mine, moving in time to the music. Drunk on the moment, I leaned into him, let myself relax into the steady rhythm of our bodies. As the urgency of the beats increased, we pressed even closer, our bodies fitting perfectly together, and I felt suddenly and inexplicably free. Like a weight had been taken from me.

I wrapped my arms around his neck and pulled him down to me, until I could smell the mint on his breath. He leaned in, but didn't kiss me. Instead, his lips grazed mine, brushed along my cheek until his mouth was close to my ear. "You're sure?" he whispered, his voice no more than a breath against the shell of my ear. But I heard both the question outright asked and the one implied.

If I said yes, there wouldn't be any going back. I couldn't get swept up in the moment now and regret it later.

The light had grown more golden as the sun inched toward the horizon, and the frenzy of the drumming had increased, but the two of us had gone completely still. He pulled back a little, his eyes serious as he waited.

Was I sure?

The drums were singing so rapidly now that the individual beats were indecipherable, the sound a thrumming roll.

I opened my mouth, and had only just started to answer him when a sharp, high-pitched drum broke the mood with rapid, gunfire-like beats and the crowd fell silent.

Silas and I stood together, caught in the stillness, when Mama Erzulie's voice broke through, shattering the silence.

"Nou tout se zanj O!" Her voice echoed through the bayou, like ripples on the surface of the river. She shouted again, and again, repeating her call over and over, until the words became a rich chorale, a blessing for the crowd. She was standing at the edge of the bridge, her hands extended over the water.

"What's happening?" I asked Silas.

"It's the final invocation," he explained, his eyes still serious, waiting. "She's telling the Loa we're all spirits."

"Spirits?" I asked, my mind immediately bringing up an image of Alex.

"In Voodoo, spirit is just another name for life." He pointed to the horizon. "Look there, the sun's almost gone."

Mama Erzulie continued her invocation until the remaining sliver of fire sank below the horizon, and then she went silent. She walked to the middle of the bridge, the crowd parting silently as she came. "We celebrate tonight the great spirits who will bring us a long growing season and an ample harvest."

The drums punctuated her words with a single beat.

"We celebrate another year, another chance to perfect our souls." Another beat sounded.

"We ask the Loa to intercede on our behalf. To guide us on our earthly journey until we can return to the Great Beginning." The drums rolled then, a low rumble like thunder in the distance.

"Something's coming, my children," she called. "Something that has been waiting for a long while to walk among us again. We ask the great spirits to guide us. To protect us in the days ahead." A final beat sounded, and she dropped her arms. The silence over the bayou hung heavy as the night sky, and we waited for what would come next.

"And now," she said in quieter tones, a broad smile crossing her face. "*Now*, we eat."

Silas was still holding my hands, waiting for my answer, but Mama Erzulie's words had reminded me of everything I'd been through since leaving Chicago, since even before that.

Something *was* coming. Maybe it had already arrived.

I gave Silas a weak excuse for a smile and took a step back.

The drums started again, but their song was less frenzied and more like a conversation. People mingled on the bridge, some placing their own small offerings on the altar, others dancing again with old friends and new. We crossed the bridge to where the banquet was set up between two of the small bonfires. Chloe and Piers were already there.

She lifted her plate in greeting. "The food's almost better than the ritual itself. Y'all need to get some before it's gone."

She didn't have to tell us twice. I couldn't quite sense what Silas was thinking, but he didn't mention the moment that had almost happened between us as we piled our plates high. Having grown up in the area, he took it upon himself to point out the different dishes. It was a mix of old world and new, African and Creole, the Caribbean and the Bayou, all mouthwatering and fragrant. The headiness of garlic mixed with smoky cumin and the spice of cinnamon and cloves. And the intensity of the scents—the savory mixed with sweet, the sharp bite of chili cut with the earthiness of rice and plantains—was so thick in the air, I could practically taste it on my tongue.

We ate together, the four of us laughing in the firelight over plates laden with food, as we watched the crowd grow. Occasionally, the rhythm of the drums would change or someone would start another bluesy call-and-response round.

"Thanks for inviting me tonight," I told Chloe.

"You liked it?" Her eyes glinted with clear joy as she leaned into Piers.

"I *loved* it."

After a while, the guys took our empty plates and went off to find some fresh drinks. Once they were out of earshot, Chloe leaned in. "You're looking good tonight, Lucy. Those dark circles you used to have under your eyes are almost gone. Have you been sleeping better?"

I blinked at her bluntness.

I hesitated. How much should I say? "For the last couple of nights? Yeah. Much better." I took another sip of my drink, hoping she'd drop her questioning.

"So that dream you told me about?" she asked when it was clear I wasn't going to say anything more. "It's not plaguing you anymore?"

My face was growing warm. "Lately it's been . . . different. Not so bad."

Chloe nodded. "Did you still want to talk with Mama Erzulie about it?"

Did I?

There in the bayou with the festival still swirling around me, I didn't want to think about my dreams. I wanted to be there, in the moment, without my past or anyone else's chasing after me.

But before I could answer, a shadow passed over us, and we looked up to find Mama Erzulie standing there. I didn't know how much she'd heard or seen, but her face was solemn, almost stony in the firelight.

"Chloe, you give the spirits your offering yet, baby?" she asked. She didn't stop looking at me even as she talked to Chloe.

"Not yet," Chloe said easily, taking another long pull on her drink. "But I'm going to soon."

"What you waiting for? An invitation? Go on," Mama Erzulie told Chloe, finally glancing at her. "Lucy and me, we gonna talk for a bit."

As Chloe stood and started toward the makeshift altar on the bridge, Mama Erzulie gave a jerk of her head, indicating I should follow, before walking off toward the darkened part of the park.

23

Bayou St. John was in a mostly residential area lined with apartments and houses, but the side we were on was a long stretch of the park not lit by streetlamps or bonfires.

"This bayou is an important place for believers." Mama Erzulie spoke to me through the darkness. "Marie Laveau started coming here with her followers around about the time Louisiana became a state. Back then, it was just a bunch of wildness with some people trying to tame it." When we were a good distance from the other revelers, she stopped. "Course, Marie had a gift. Some people said it was the sight. Other people, they think she just knew what to look for. You know what I mean."

I didn't, but also didn't want to interrupt.

"Now some say Marie wasn't nothing more than a good showman. Legend says a *real* conjure woman lived upriver a ways. Lots of legends about those places that line the River Road, though. You put that much pain and suffering in the land, and a place can't hardly get clean of it.

"Chloe, she tells me you been having some dreams." Her voice was steady, and not a muscle on her face gave away what she was thinking, or what her intent was in asking the question. "Dreams are tricky things," she continued before I could respond. "But I suspect you know that well enough?"

"Yeah." I looked out at the dark bayou beyond. She hadn't asked me what they were about, and now that we were alone, I couldn't find the words to tell her. "If I just knew why I keep having them. Or . . ."

I thought about Alex, about the afternoon by the tree, about the girl in the picture. About the idea that maybe my dreams had really happened, once long ago. But now that the moment had come, I didn't know how to explain any of it without sounding completely insane.

"If I just knew what they meant," I said instead.

"Well, see, child, that's the thing. It's near impossible to know when it comes to dreaming. Sometimes we dream the past. Sometimes we dream our futures. Sometimes we dream our deepest desires." She grasped my upper arms and leaned down a bit so her face was close to mine. "But sometimes dreams are dangerous."

I knew that already. I thought of Alex and the temptation in his smile, and of the suffocating pull of cold, dark water. I wasn't sure which I should worry about more.

"The problem with dreams, child, is they let us free from our earthly bindings. That can be tremendously powerful, but power is always a slippery thing—the second you try to hold on to it, you might find it holding on to you. You get too caught up in dreams, you might never find your way back."

"But how am I supposed to know what's real and what's just a dream?" I asked.

"If you get to the point you start asking that question, you're already going down a dangerous path." She paused, squeezing my arm gently. "I know you're staying out there at the old Dutilette estate, and I hear you've been digging around at Thisbe's place, too. You need to be careful with yourself and remember not all the spirits around these parts are good ones. You stir up the wrong ones, and you'll end up in a world of hurt." She released me and, without another word, started back toward the lights of the gathering.

"But what do I do?" I hurried to catch up with her long strides. "I just want the dreams to stop."

She paused. "You can't make the dreaming stop any more than you can make living stop. You end one part of life, and another begins. Two sides of the same coin. The bigger question is what you're gonna do with them. You enjoy the rest of the evening, now, Lucy. We'll talk some more later, when you come to see me again."

I was thrown off by the abrupt change in topics. "But, I—"

"Tonight is for celebration, child. Tomorrow there'll be time enough for the rest. You come see me again one of these days, and we'll talk some more." She left me there, alone on the dark bank of the bayou.

As she walked back to the people still gathered by the bridge, I realized that I hadn't asked her half of what I wanted to. But I hesitated to follow her again. I wasn't ready to leave the almost-comfortable silence of the park or to put on a happy face and pretend everything was okay. I waited until Mama Erzulie's silhouette disappeared into the brightness of the crowd, and then I waited a bit longer before heading back myself.

Near the bridge, Silas waited in a halo of light beneath one of the lamps that lined the bayou. He didn't make any move to meet me halfway, just watched me with those steady, sure eyes of his, his expression a mixture of thoughtfulness and concern.

"I brought you another drink," he said, offering the unopened bottle when I was finally standing in the circle of light with him.

"Thanks," I said, accepting the beer. It was wet with condensation and already half warmed.

"Chloe told me you needed to talk to someone." There was a

question in his tone, and the concern—the worry—was still there in his expression.

This time, it didn't spark my usual urge to pull away.

I thought about the words Mama Erzulie had just said: that I couldn't stop the dreaming any more than the living. If I was being honest with myself, it had been a long time since I could really consider whatever I was doing *living*. I'd been pushing down the broken parts of myself, hiding them and covering them up, for so long that I'd mostly been existing. Even the thing with Matt—I hadn't ever really let myself lean into what we had together, because I'd already been waiting for him to walk away.

"Sorry I disappeared on you," I said, twisting the cap off the bottle. "The opportunity popped up so fast . . ." I sipped, grimacing at the bitterness of the tepid beer.

Silas's mouth curved. "You don't have to drink that."

"It's fine," I lied, and tipped back the bottle for another long drink. I needed something to take the edge off anyway.

Silently he took the bottle from me and tossed it into the nearby bin. Then he stepped closer, his hand lifting to brush back a curl that had come loose from my usual low knot, tucking it behind my ear. "You're sure everything's okay?"

"Yeah." This time, I stayed still and waited, not allowing myself to pull away. "I think it is."

You get too caught up in dreams, and you might never be finding your way back.

Mama Erzulie was right. Somewhere along the line, I'd wrapped my whole life around my nightmares—protecting myself from them, hiding them from anyone who tried to get close. For too long now I'd been plodding through my days, anticipating—dreading—what would happen when I closed my eyes. I'd been so worried about dreaming that I'd forgotten there was more to living.

Maybe she was right. Maybe there weren't any answers to why I had the nightmares or what the dreams meant.

But maybe I'd been asking the wrong questions all along.

Here was a man who wasn't some figment of my imagination. Silas was solid and warm and real and *terrifying*. If I took a chance on him, if this went wrong, I wasn't sure I could stay at Le Ciel. And I didn't have a backup plan.

I took a step toward Silas anyway. I was tired of sleep-walking through life.

"You said you wouldn't kiss me until I wanted you to." I tilted my face up to him.

"I might remember saying something to that effect," he said, his eyes growing heated. "You saying you want me to?"

I lifted on my toes just a little and brushed my mouth against his. Softly. A question and an answer all at once. His lips were warm against mine, smooth and supple, but he didn't respond at first. "Maybe I do," I whispered against his mouth.

He cradled my face in his hands, threading his fingers into my hair. "You don't think this is a bad idea?"

"I'm sure it's a terrible idea," I whispered. "But I don't think I care anymore."

His eyes glinted in victory, but he still didn't make a move. I thought that maybe he wouldn't.

"Please, Silas," I whispered.

And then his mouth was against mine. This time, his lips were sure and confident, and I couldn't stop myself from winding my arms around his neck, from digging my fingers into his hair and anchoring him to me. His tongue brushed against my lips, and I opened for him, drinking in the taste of him as our mouths collided, our tongues sliding in a rhythm that had me drawing him closer, *closer*. Until our bodies were pressed together, and it *still* wasn't enough.

Kissing Silas was like sinking into a dream—all consuming. His scent wrapped around me, warm and woodsy with a bite of spice, as his hands slid down my body, cupped the curve of my ass, and held me tightly to him. I could feel how much he wanted me, his arousal already pressing against my body, hard and heavy and deliciously large.

I was only barely aware we were moving as he backed us out of the halo of light into the darkness of the park, until my back hit something immovable. A tree. I leaned against it, accepted its support as Silas surrounded me. But it wasn't enough. Instinctively, I hitched one of my legs up over his hip, so he was cradled between my legs. He shifted until the hardness of his arousal was fit perfectly against the notch between my legs and began moving, steadily thrusting the hard length in a tantalizing rhythm until I was dizzy with need. I hitched my leg higher and pulled him closer to the spot that ached. Desperate for more, for *him*.

"You taste like honey." His voice thick with the same need I felt spiraling through me, as his mouth trailed kisses down my neck. "I knew you would. I saw you that first day, and I knew your skin would taste like sunshine and sweetness."

He brushed his lips over the sensitive skin of my neck, licking and biting gently as he worked his way down my throat. I moaned softly in response, barely recognizing myself the throaty hum of my pleasure as it shattered the silence of the park. It had never been like this before. No one had ever made me feel so needy, so desperate for more. Not this quickly. Not this desperately. I needed him against me, flesh against flesh. I needed more. *More.*

Maybe it was because I'd never let myself go like this before. I'd always been careful, cautious. But with Silas, that didn't seem to be an option. I ran my fingers through his curls, anchoring him in place. Urging him on as his mouth made my skin come alive.

My body felt like a live wire, and I was only barely aware of the buzz of the crowded party in the distance. But I couldn't bother with worrying if anyone could see us, if anyone might wander by and discover us tangled in the darkness, not when his lips were on me. He sucked gently where my neck met my shoulder, and desire shot straight through me.

"Oh god," I whispered. "That feels so good."

"God, Lucy, I didn't plan this," he said, his breath hot against my neck. "I really didn't. There was going to be a bed. Flowers. Music. But I can't make myself stop."

"*Don't.*" It didn't matter that we were fully clothed and thirty feet away from a crowd of strangers. "Don't you dare stop."

He smiled against my neck. "Yes, ma'am."

Silas's mouth against my skin, his hands roaming my body, made me feel more grounded, more real than I had in a long time. He wasn't some figment of my imagination, no man shaped from dreams. He was real and solid, and he was *there.*

Silas's hands ran up my back, under my fluttery top and when he discovered I wasn't wearing a bra, he stilled. "You're going to completely kill me, Lucy."

I kissed the strong angle of his jaw, nipping slightly to urge him on. "I hope not. I need you alive."

The truth was that I needed this, *him.* It had been so long since I'd felt anything real, and with Silas's body against mine, his mouth against my skin, I ached in a way I never had before. Then his hand traced upward, along my torso, over my ribs, until finally he cupped the curve of my breast. When his thumb brushed over my already tight nipple, when those elegant manicured fingers plucked and twisted gently at the aching tip, the ground fell out from under me.

My vision went white, and suddenly I was back at the pond, the bright sun overhead and the breeze barely stirring the leaves above me. The tree behind me was that other tree, Silas's hands were other hands, and I was there again, Alex thrusting into me —into *her*—until she shattered—*I* shattered—and the vision broke along with me.

I was only barely aware that Silas had stopped kissing me. Night fell over me again, and little by little I came back to myself. The coolness of the evening air on my sweat-slicked skin. The stars winking overhead. But when I came back to myself, Silas's hand was no longer touching my breast. He hadn't stepped back yet, but he was holding himself completely still, with a stiffness and distance that hadn't been there a moment before.

I didn't understand what had caused the sudden distance between us.

He eased away from me, his expression unreadable. "Is Alex the guy you left back in Chicago?"

"What?" My stomach dropped, and the buzzing pleasure of the moment before drained away.

"You said his name," Silas told me. "*Alex.* My hands were on you, but you said some other guy's name."

"I didn't—" My brain was still scrambled. I didn't remember saying anything, but from the frustration—the *hurt*—on Silas's face, I knew he wasn't lying.

"He's no one." My voice shook, exposing the lie. "I didn't mean—"

But Silas's blank expression had the words dying in my throat.

"We should get back," he said, stepping away from me slowly. Deliberately.

"Silas." I moved toward him.

"It's fine, Lucy. You warned me you weren't ready," he said, backing farther away. "I should have listened."

"Silas . . ." I stepped toward him, but his posture was stiff and closed off. "Please, I—"

A scream shattered the darkness, cutting off my words.

His gaze lifted beyond me, to the crowded gathering, and his brows drew together. "We need to go."

24

By the time we got back to the bridge, I wasn't even close to having pulled myself together. I'd let Silas kiss me. I'd let him do a hell of a lot more than kiss me, and then the vision had pulled me under and I'd apparently said Alex's name.

My skin was still hot and my legs weren't even close to steady as I followed him back toward the gathering. I'd tried to push the dreams aside, but they'd pushed right back.

Silas glanced in my direction as we shoved our way through the crowd, looking for Chloe and Piers. But a new cautiousness lurked in his eyes, and I regretted the space between us that hadn't been there before.

"Lucy!" Chloe called, dodging through the frantic crowd to get to us. Piers wasn't far behind. "Thank god. I didn't know where you'd gone off to, and—"

Sirens wailed in the distance.

"What's going on?" Silas asked, craning his neck to peer over the crowd.

Chloe grabbed me. "Have you seen Shaunda?"

I shook my head. "No. I was with Mama Erzulie, and then Silas and I—" That didn't matter now. "What's happened?"

"There's a body in the bayou," Piers told us.

"A body?" I could practically feel my lungs seize, like I'd been plunged back into the cold black water of the dream.

"Do they know who it is?" Silas asked.

Piers shook his head. "They're keeping everyone back, but I heard it's a woman."

"We have to find Shaunda," Chloe said, her voice betraying her panic. "I haven't seen her for a while now."

I nodded to Chloe, but Piers caught her arm. "You're not going anywhere without me."

"Baby," Chloe said. "I need to find my friend."

"We will," he said, but his jaw was tight. "But I'm going with you."

"It wasn't an accident?" Silas asked.

Piers shook his head. "I heard someone say her throat was cut."

Gone were the cold fingers of the water pulling me down, and in their place, Lila's body flashed through my mind, as vivid and real as the light thrown by the fires surrounding us.

"We'll help," Silas said. "Y'all go check over there, and we'll search the crowd on this side."

I barely heard what they were saying. Instead, I was feeling the heat of the bonfires and remembering the warmth of the day and the buzzing of the flies and the sticky blackish blood at Lila's throat.

"Lucy?" Silas was looking at me expectantly. He must have said something I'd missed. His expression hadn't regained any of its former warmth. "I asked if you're ready?"

Nodding, I followed him through the crowd, searching for Shaunda.

Rumors spread like fire all around us—it was a ritual killing. It was a crime of passion. The girl had her eyes cut out. Or her tongue. She was young. She was old. By the time the police interviewed everyone, and then made us leave the area, we'd heard so many rumors that we didn't know what to believe. But every time one of the rumors came close to my dreams, my skin prickled with awareness and Lila's face flashed through my mind.

We never did find Shaunda. When the police finally made everyone leave the area, we left without answers.

WE DROPPED Piers and Chloe off at Piers's place in the Quarter. They wanted to stay closer to town, in case Shaunda finally decided to answer our texts and needed a lift. Chloe hugged me before getting out, and I made her to promise to call if she heard anything at all.

Once the two of them were gone, the empty silence of the Audi was almost unbearable during the long drive back out to Le Ciel. Silas didn't say anything, and I couldn't figure out what I was supposed to say to fix what had happened between us— what I'd done to ruin it. For a long time, all I could do was stare out the window, watching the lights of town give way to the darkness of the River Road.

When we finally arrived at the wrought iron gates of Le Ciel, I gathered my courage and glanced at Silas. His jaw was set tight, and his eyes were steady on the road ahead. He had one hand on the wheel, and the other was gripping the shifter, and pure lust flushed through me as I remembered what it had felt like to have those hands against my skin.

But I'd ruined everything, just like I always did.

"Silas?" I said his name softly as he drove onto the estate's grounds. "I'm sorry about earlier."

"It's fine." The clipped tone of his words said otherwise, though.

"It's not," I pressed. "What happened between us—"

"Let's just drop it, okay?" He kept his eyes focused on the road. "You told me you'd just gotten out of a relationship. I shouldn't have pushed. I should have listened when you said this wasn't a good idea."

He was right, but I hated it. It *wasn't* a good idea, but that didn't make me want it any less.

The tires crunched along the gravel of the drive as the headlights illuminated the alley of oaks, the sweep of gardens. He pulled the Audi to a stop at the mouth of the path that led to my cabin.

"None of this is your fault." I reached out to lay my hand over his. He glanced up at me, and I withdrew my hand back. "And the guy I broke up with in Chicago was Matt. I wasn't thinking of him. When your hands were on me like that, I wasn't thinking about anyone but you."

A muscle in his jaw ticked. "Then who's Alex?"

"It's a long story," I said, sinking back into the seat.

"But you won't tell me."

How could I? I'd tried to explain my dreams to Matt, to others before him, and every single one of them decided it was too much—decided that *I* was too much. And that was back when I was only dealing with nightmares. The dreams I'd been having since arriving at Le Ciel were more complicated, maybe even more difficult to explain. "It doesn't matter."

"When you're in my arms calling someone else's name, it matters." He glanced over at me. "To me, that shit matters."

"It was a mistake."

"Maybe it was." Silas's hands tightened on the steering wheel. "You were right there with me, and then you weren't. At the end, it wasn't me you were thinking about." He shook his head. "I'm not interested in playing games, Lucy."

He got out of the car and came around to open my door for

me, ever the gentleman despite how the evening had gone. When I stepped away from the car, he followed.

"My cabin's just over there," I reminded him. "You don't have to—"

"A woman's dead, Lucy." Silas's tone was sharp enough that I flinched, but then he closed his eyes, like he was gathering himself. "Let me walk you to your door. Please."

I nodded, and we ambled together down the short path in silence. When we came to my cabin, I turned to him. "I really am sorry about . . . everything," I said finally. "If I could take it back—"

"You would?" he asked, his hands tucked into his pockets.

"Well, only that last part," I said, pressing my lips together. "The rest of it? I wouldn't change a thing."

His shoulders sank a bit, like the fight had gone out of him. "I like you, Lucy. I like you a lot, but if there's going to be anything between us, I need honesty. I've been around too many people who are only interested in what I can do for them."

Anger spiked through me. "I don't know how you can say that. *You're* the one who pursued me."

"So this is *my* fault?"

"No. That's not what I'm saying." I let out a breath and started again. "Look, I'm sorry about how things ended. I don't know why I said that name. If I could take it back, I would."

"You weren't thinking about anyone else?" he asked.

I could have lied. Maybe I should have. All I had to do was say "no." *No*, I wasn't thinking of anyone else. *No*, I didn't *want* to think about anyone else. The vision of what had happened between Alex and Armantine in the clearing had crashed into me without warning. I hadn't asked for it. I hadn't wanted it. But standing there with the moonlight throwing shadows across his face, I couldn't make myself say the words.

"Look, there's a lot you don't know about me. There are

things I'm still dealing with, things that go way back." I wrapped my arms around myself. "I'm still working through it all."

"But you're not ready to trust me with it," he said, hurt flashing in his expression. "I get it."

"You *don't* get it." I tipped my head back and looking up at the darkened sky. Clouds had moved in, and there wasn't a single star to be seen.

I felt him move closer. "Then help me get it, Lucy."

I wanted to. God help me, I did. But how could I? The last guy I'd started to trust had ended the same as the rest. I'd take Silas's anger over his pity any day.

He must have seen the answer in my eyes.

"Right," he murmured, taking a step back from me. "Okay, then."

"Silas—"

"I think there could be something really good between us, Lucy. But I won't push you. I won't force this."

I nodded, unable to speak.

"I'll let you know if I hear anything about Shaunda," he told me. "You have a good night."

I wrapped my arms around myself as he walk back toward his car. But he never looked back.

25

I didn't sleep that night. I sat up, waiting to hear something, but a call never came. And then Piers showed up at my cabin early the next morning, and I knew before he said anything. The girl they'd found floating in the bayou was Shaunda. And her death hadn't been an accident. There were rumors the cops didn't think it was a simple murder. There were whispers she'd been sacrificed as part of some dark Voodoo ritual. They'd taken Mama Erzulie in for questioning, but they'd released her the same day.

Together, Piers and I went over to the house Chloe shared with her mom to check in on her. They lived on a wooded piece of land about a mile from Le Ciel, outside the city proper. Set back from the road, the small white house was surrounded by a grove of trees with bottles hanging from brightly colored string. Two worn rockers sat on the deep porch, and the front beds burst with herbs and wildflowers, which gave the whole place a cozy, lived-in feel.

Mina met us at the door and nodded toward the back of the house. "She's in her room and won't come out."

"How's she doing?" I asked.

Mina looked tired, her heavy jewelry clinking in rhythm with her movements. "She'll be better now that you're both here."

We found Chloe curled in her bed, covered almost completely by a thick faded quilt.

"Chloe? Baby?" Piers's voice was gentle as he sat next to her and pulled back her covers to expose her face.

At the sight of him, she burst into another round of tears, and in response, he wrapped her in his arms. He rocked her for a few minutes, until her sobbing died down to a breathless whimper.

"Is there anything you need, Chloe?" I asked from the edge of the bed.

"Lucy?" She looked up from Piers's now-damp chest. "I'm so sorry, Lucy." She barely got out the words before the tears started again.

"Chloe, you don't have anything to be sorry about."

"Oh, god, Luce. It's my fault she was there. It's my fault *we* were there," she moaned miserably. "It was my idea. I invited you, and I invited Shaunda. She wouldn't have been there otherwise."

"Maybe you'll remember that next time you think of going off again to that woman." Mina's voice came from the doorway.

The ice in her tone had me glancing back at the entrance to the room. Mina stood with her arms crossed and an expression like ice.

Chloe moaned again. "I know, Momma." The tears started again, this time more forcefully. "I'm sorry I didn't listen to you."

"You should be sorry. I warned you about messing around with that old witch!" Mina's voice had grown firmer, her tone sharper. "I've told you time and again that charlatans like her aren't to be trusted. She thinks she has any control over the spirts? She has no idea what she's doing. Maybe now you'll understand that and stay away."

"Ms. Sabourin." Piers was calm as he continued to comfort Chloe. "Maybe now's not the best time for this? Chloe's still upset."

"She *should* be," Mina snapped. "I thought she knew better than to go out without protection on a night like Saint John's Eve, when spirits walk free."

"Please." His tone was firmer now. "Not now."

Mina lifted her hands, as though surrendering. "Fine. If you think you're man enough to tell me what to do in my own house, then you deal with this. But I'll tell you one thing—all that book learning of yours isn't going to save you from what's out there. Something's starting, and pretending otherwise isn't going to stop it." Mina glanced in my direction, and then she left.

"She's right, you know," Chloe said, her tone dull and flat. "If I would have listened to her and stayed away from Mama Erzulie, I wouldn't have been there last night. *Shaunda* wouldn't have been there, either. She'd still be alive."

"Chloe, you can't think that way," Piers said, rubbing her back in slow circles.

"This isn't your fault," Chloe, I said gently.

"You heard about how they killed her, didn't you?" Her eyes were bloodshot when they met mine. "They carved her up. Somebody sliced symbols and runes all over her body."

"Whoever killed Shaunda isn't sane, baby," Piers said. "Come on, lie down here and close your eyes. Nothing bad is going to happen now."

But I wasn't so sure he was right. I'd been thinking all night, and I didn't like where my thoughts had gone. First I'd dreamed of Alex, then the portrait of Armantine, and then the letters on the tree. One by one, they'd all shown up again in my own present. I'd dreamed, too, of a girl with her throat cut on the night of Saint John's Eve long ago. I had the uneasy feeling Shaunda's murder was connected—that it was *all* tied together. But I didn't understand how—or why—it was tied to me.

26

The mood around Le Ciel following Shaunda's murder was markedly different from when I'd first arrived. Even though she'd worked in the French Quarter offices, people out at the estate had known her well. Everyone seemed to be walking around in a haze of grief and fear. It didn't help that the authorities didn't have any leads about her death, and they weren't releasing any additional information about it. Not that it stopped the rumors. Everyone from the French Quarter to Baton Rouge was on edge.

Silas didn't come back out to Le Ciel in the days following Shaunda's murder. I saw him briefly, at the memorial service in town, but other than trading a long meaningful look, we didn't speak. Not that I would have known what to say, anyway.

Chloe all but disappeared as well. She wouldn't return my texts or calls, and Mina told me she was struggling with grief. That I should give her some space. She'd taken a short leave from the Foundation, and she even started to avoid Piers.

I ran into Piers on the grounds a couple of times in the weeks that followed, but for the most part I was on my own except for the evenings I spent with Leonard and Sam. But witnessing the quiet steadiness of their relationship night after night left me strangely unsettled. I'd been avoiding any real commitment for years, but now, seeing how happy they were—how they supported each other—I wondered if maybe I'd been wrong to build up so many walls around myself. Maybe the guys weren't all to blame, and maybe I had been missing out on more than a satisfying sex life by keeping them out.

And now, I was repeating the same mistakes with Silas.

My days were full, though. With the summer season in full swing, the grounds of the plantation were busy with tour groups and other tourists. I was working steadily on the photos Silas had wanted for the new website and was making good progress, but his brief professional emails somehow made me feel worse than if we hadn't been in communication at all. I did the job I had been hired to do, but I never touched my art. I couldn't, not when it I felt like I was sleepwalking through most days, going through the motions without really being present.

But the nights—those were something else. After the murder, my dreams returned, more real and powerful than before. And once again, those dreams focused on Armantine and Alex.

I hadn't actually seen Alex since the day he'd warned me away from Thisbe's cabin. I couldn't help but wonder if that was because he'd only ever been a figment of my imagination or because Silas had fired him. But I didn't want to ask around—I was afraid that might get back to Silas and make things even worse. I did manage to look at the employee schedule in the offices one day, but there was no sign of his name.

My days had grown so empty, so monotonous that I started living for the nights, when I could slip into my bed and into Armantine's life. At least there, I felt something other than sadness and loss. There, I watched the drama of their lives play out as the world slept around me.

Their story came to me in fits and starts. A shy glance across a crowded ballroom. A chance meeting at the market. A fervent kiss tucked into a bare palm. But little by little, I started to piece together the story of their love.

They'd met by accident, but Alex had pursued her with a dogged relentlessness that Armantine couldn't fight. Still, it was a relationship that had to be kept a secret. She knew it was a mistake to fall for him, an impossibility, considering she was a free woman of color and he was a white Frenchman destined to return to his native land. But as I watched him through her eyes night after night, I began to understand why she couldn't stop herself from wanting him—why she had allowed herself to hope. It was the same reason I'd hoped Silas would return to Le Ciel in the days after Shaunda's death. Because sometimes it was impossible not to.

Again and again, Armantine tried lock her heart away, but fate or chance continued to push them together. When Alex appeared at Jules Lyon's shop one afternoon long before the day at the pond, Armantine somehow found the strength to refuse his invitation for an outing to his sister's estate. Until Jules burst into the room unannounced and accepted for her.

"Are you an imbecile?" Jules shouted as soon as they were alone.

Armantine didn't answer as Jules kicked over her easel, sending the small canvas she had been painting to the floor.

"Do you know how long I have been trying to catch a patron as rich as Roman Dutilette?" He let out a ragged breath and stepped back. "That boy is the answer." His hands clenched into fists, and she forced herself not to flinch. "You *will* go to lunch with the young man. You will smile, and you will charm him. You will make sure you do all you can to entice him to come back. You will do your *job*." He retreated toward his office, but before he entered it, he paused. "Don't forget what you owe me, Armantine. I picked you up from the gutter and made you what you are. I can unmake you just as easily."

"Yes, Uncle," she said, her head bowed, her eyes fixed on the canvas he'd knocked to the floor. Lila's eyes stared up at her, daring her to be ungrateful.

But Armantine wasn't convinced that Alex could do anything to convince Roman Dutilette to become Jules Lyon's patron. She'd heard stories from Lila about life in the big house, stories that painted Roman as vicious and cruel as he was rich, and his wife as haughty and spiteful as the day was long. Their only interest in beauty or art was in possessing it so others could not. But Armantine owed everything to Jules, so she did what he commanded and tried, without luck, to keep her heart locked firmly in her chest. And as she fell for Alex, I couldn't deny I did too.

"And you have always lived with your uncle?" Alex asked, tucking her arm through his as they strolled through the park.

Armantine shook her head.

"Your parents, they're—"

"I don't remember my parents."

It was almost the truth. Sometimes she could imagine a woman singing sweetly to her, but other times she thought it was only a dream. She didn't remember anything from before the orphanage with its crowded beds and filthy floors and the sisters with veils that reminded her of shrouds. "Jules is my family now."

"I see. My family lives in the south of France—by the sea." He smiled softly and looked away. "They sent me here to check on Josephine, but I think it was their way of directing me toward the life they intend for me."

Armantine didn't want to ask. She didn't want to be so curious. "And what have they intended that is so terrible?"

"My father is a farmer. He works the same land his father worked, and his father before him, so . . ." He shrugged. "They are quite impressed with what my sister's husband has built here, with the success his family has had in West Indies. I think they hoped it might inspire me." But something about his tone was off.

"And has it? Inspired you?"

His brows drew together, and he stared down at the grass, his expression unreadable. "No," he said simply. "I think it has done quite the opposite. I find that I cannot stomach the lives they lead, nor the excuses they make for their cruelty."

Silence settled between them. Armantine didn't know what to say, because any response felt too dangerous.

He visited her in the Quarter the next day and the day after that for one reason or another, and it became more and more difficult to come up with reasonable excuses to avoid him. Jules would not have allowed her to anyway.

They would walk along the river or find the shade of a tree near the *Place d'Armes* to sit and eat tart cherries that tasted as dangerous as each moment with him felt. She found herself telling him things she had never told another soul. Despite knowing better, she wanted to trust him.

One day she brought her folio and charcoal pencil with her, and he dozed in the shade while she sketched scenes to paint later.

"You should bring your paints out to Le Ciel." He lifted the hat he had tilted across his eyes and watched her as she worked.

"I couldn't."

When he took her hand, the familiar thrill raced through her blood at the warmth of his touch. Although she had become accustomed to being with him, she was always surprised at the jolt on those rare moments when he touched her.

He brought her hand to his lips. "Please, *mon coeur*." He rubbed his lips gently across the top of her hand with no more pressure than the brush of a butterfly's wing.

She jerked her hand away and returned to sketching in a feeble attempt to put some distance between them. "You shouldn't do such things."

"Why is that, love?" He took her hand again. "Do you doubt your beauty? My desire for you?"

She doubted neither. Without her beauty, Jules might never have chosen her. But her beauty was also a constant danger. Plain women were usually overlooked, ignored. Her looks had never been ignored, however much she wanted them to be.

"It's not proper," she whispered.

"I never said it was." He grinned wickedly, and her heart lurched a little at the sight.

But the truth was he would not have taken such liberties with a different woman, one protected by her family and station.

"Come out to my sister's house for the day," he said again.

She huffed an exasperated sigh. "You know very well it is one thing for you to come to the city and for us to see each other here. It is a very different thing for me to visit your family's home. It's not done, Alex."

"I don't care about what is or isn't done. I want to see you there. There's a pond, just beyond the trees. It's perhaps the most peaceful spot I've ever found in all my travels." He glanced at her, his expression soft and sincere. "I've imagined what you would look like there with me."

"*Alexandre.*"

She started to turn away, but he caught her chin. "Don't. Don't shut me out because you are scared. Think about it. Please."

She met his eyes, but didn't respond.

"Come to Le Ciel. *Tomorrow.*" He smiled crookedly. "If it will make it easier, I shall speak with your uncle and hire your services. I find I would very much like a painting of the pond to take with me when I return to France. A memento of my time here." He kissed her hand. "You have a passable skill with paints."

She shot him a tart look. "Passable, is it?"

He chuckled. "Much more than passable, and you know it." He kissed her hand again and then covered it with his own. "Will you come? Will you do that for me?"

She wanted to say no, but she couldn't find her voice. She *should* say no, but this was exactly what Jules had hoped for. And if Alex spoke to Jules about it, she would have no choice.

He took her silence as assent.

During the next few weeks Alex would come for her early in the morning and drive her the plantation. He would sit near her quietly and watch as she sketched. By lunch, he would have grown impatient enough to begin tempting her. A brush of his thumb across her ankle. His hand tracing the curve of her calf. His lips nipping at the tender skin beneath her ear as she swatted him away.

Despite her fears, no one bothered them. No one ventured toward the pond when they were there together.

The clearing by the pond became their haven, far enough from the rest of the world that Armantine could almost forget who he was. Who *she* was. There, she was only who she became when he looked at her, when he pressed her back into the soft grass and covered her mouth—her body—with his own.

Each afternoon, he would return her to the Quarter in time for her to help her uncle with the afternoon appointments. It became an almost comfortable routine for her, despite the impossibility of the situation. Jules, of course, was beside himself with anticipation.

One morning late in the summer, the carriage appeared with Solomon, one of the enslaved men who worked in the big house, but no Alex. Solomon explained the master had something to attend to that morning, but wanted her to continue working on his painting. The thought of being alone on the grounds of Le Ciel made her hesitate, but Jules would not hear of her wasting an opportunity.

They rode in uneasy silence, and when they arrived, Solomon helped her out with a blank expression. She walked toward the pond, aware Solomon walked behind her, watching her silently, and she found her usual place under the oak and set to work with her pastels. Solomon stayed as well. She could feel his cold gaze, watching her from the trees, as the morning drew on.

She didn't know how long she had been working when she realized another person had joined them. At the edge of the clearing stood Alexandre's sister, Josephine. When their eyes met, Josephine started toward her.

Armantine got to her feet, wiping the dust from her fingers as Josephine approached. There was a cold gleam in her eye. She was dressed in the finest silk, her fair hair perfectly tamed into an elaborate chignon, and Armantine smoothed her own plain cotton skirts, suddenly painfully aware of the differences between them.

"Madame." Armantine inclined her head, keeping her eyes trained on the ground.

"Please sit," Josephine commanded with a dismissive wave. "I did not mean to interrupt your work."

Armantine returned to her place on the ground, but instantly wished she had remained standing. Josephine was a small woman, but standing over Armantine, she seemed more imposing.

"I had heard you were here and thought to pay my respects." The woman's voice was clear, with the same musical cadence coloring her English as Alexandre's, but there was no mistaking the ice running through it. "My husband and I were so pleased with the image Monsieur Lyon prepared for us."

"Yes, Madame." She glanced up, but couldn't quite bring herself to look Josephine in the eye. Hers were the same startling green as her brother's, but where Alex's were the verdant green of a summer forest, Josephine's reminded Armantine of the cold sharpness of a jewel.

"And now, I hear you are creating a painting of our lovely pond for him. How delightful," she said, sounding not at all sound delighted.

"Yes, Madame. Monsieur Jourdain was very eager to take a piece of your beautiful home with him when he returns." It was not as easy as it should have been for her to slide back into the practiced persona—not after Alex had helped to free her from it. Meek. Polite. Subservient. She concentrated on these qualities and hoped she could bring them to the surface once more.

"I'm sure he is quite eager," Josephine continued, her voice a few degrees cooler. "But my dear brother is not quite so aware of things as we women are. I worry you might misunderstand his interest in your work as something more. He's leaving very soon, you see."

She could not stop herself from glancing up at Josephine, whose expression had grown even sharper.

"Did he not tell you?" She smiled, cold as a knife. "He's a charming man, my brother, but I would not want you to misconstrue his charm for real affection."

"Of course not, Madame." Armantine's cheeks burned with shame, with embarrassment. He was leaving. He had not told her.

"He has a life back in France. My parents have already arranged a match for him, and he'll be married on his return." She gave Armantine a pitying look. "My brother may spin fairy tales for himself, but he knows what is expected of him. He knows his place in the world. And I'm sure you know yours?"

"Of course. Yes, Madame." Armantine wanted to escape. To return to the Quarter and never even think of Le Ciel again.

"Just as I thought." Her voice was sweeter now, and her cold green eyes dipped to the sketches scattered around

Armantine. "Such a delightful talent. Perhaps you will come back and paint the house after my brother has returned to France, yes?"

It was everything Jules had wanted. And it was all wrong. "I'd be delighted to." Her heart was lead in her chest.

"Wonderful." Josephine made the word sound like a threat. "I'm glad we have had our little talk, *ma biche*. Enjoy the rest of your day here. I am sure you will have more than enough sketches by the time you return."

Her meaning was clear: Armantine was to leave. She was not to return.

"Yes, Madame."

She kept her head down, her eyes steady on the glass-like surface of the pond until she could no longer hear the swish of Josephine's silken skirts. Armantine had predicted this would happen, and cursed herself for allowing it to. Her entire life she had avoided situations that could make her feel small and inferior. It was her own fault that it was happening. She had broken all her own rules going to Le Ciel for Alex, and she had never felt more humiliated in her entire life.

She had to leave immediately, before Alex arrived and made her forget all the reasons she could not stay. But she couldn't quite bring herself to move. She sat in silence, taking in everything she could about the scene, the moment. When she left this place, she would be leaving Alex as well.

The sun was high in the cloudless sky when he finally appeared. Silently he walked to her, his beautiful mouth twisted into an angry line. Without speaking, he sat next to her and stared out over the water.

"I am sorry I wasn't here," he said after a long, silent moment. "She should not have spoken to you, *chère*. She had no right—"

She turned to him then, realizing with a heartbreaking finality how fundamentally different they were. "Of *course* she had every right. This is her land, her world. Her words were no more than I deserved for overstepping my bounds."

He took her chin, gently, forced her to meet his eyes. "With me you have no bounds, Armantine."

She pulled away. He was a fool. They both were fools. He was already promised to another. "I have tried to explain to you . . ." She shook her head, unable to finish her thought. What good were words?

She had already gathered her things, and now she collected her bag and stood, no longer able to face him. She had wanted him, more than she'd had any right to. She had allowed herself to fall, even though she had always known it would come to this —that she would eventually pay the price.

"Please, Armantine." His expression looked as fragile as she felt. "You can trust me, you know."

But she didn't.

Her voice was surprisingly steady as she backed away. "This can't happen any longer." She put up her hands when he moved toward her. If he touched her, she'd lose all resolve. "No. Stay there."

He stepped toward her again. "*Chère—*"

"No!" More forcefully now.

"At least allow me to escort you home—" His voice was soothing, but it was tinged with disappointment. Hurt, or something very close to it, flashed in his eyes.

"No." Took another step back, toward the long road back to the city. Toward a life without him. "No, I need to walk. I need to *think*."

He took a step closer, his hands fisted at his sides, but the shake of her head held him fast. "Let me at least find someone to take you back. You should not be on the road alone." His voice was gentle now. "It's not safe."

The image of Lila's body flashed in her mind, and she nodded, reluctantly.

"Go up to the gate. Someone will be there soon."

She placed one shaking step in front of the other, when he called her again.

"Armantine." His voice was steady, but she continued on without looking back. "We are not done."

She didn't answer, and left the clearing on unsteady legs.

It did not take long for Solomon to arrive with a wagon. When he yanked her roughly to sit up alongside him, she couldn't meet the old man's eyes. They didn't speak as the wagon rolled along the uneven dirt road.

Twenty minutes later, they came upon Thisbe. Solomon stopped the wagon and helped the old woman climb aboard with noticeably more respect than he'd shown Armantine.

She sat silently while the two talked about people they both knew on the plantation. Thisbe asked after his wife and promised to make him up a gris-gris to help protect her from an overseer beginning to show her too much attention. Armantine focused on the horizon and tried to forget she had left part of herself behind.

"I've seen you around here with that girl who got herself killed," Thisbe said, addressing Armantine with cloudy eyes. "But you ain't from the house. Or from the fields, either."

"No, ma'am." And she wouldn't be returning to that house ever again.

"You don't worry yourself none about your friend, though. Her spirit is where it needs to be." The old woman patted Armantine's knee with an ashy hand. "She has a purpose now."

"Yes, ma'am," she said, not really listening to the old woman's words. She could not think about anything but Alex now that she'd finally walked away from him.

Thisbe chuckled, a dry, rasping sound that put Armantine on edge. "You ain't much for conversation, I see, but people around here have been talking about *you*. They say you're trying to snare yourself the master's brother. They say you're gonna move right up into that big house like you belong there, don't they?" She nudged the driver.

Solomon snorted in derision.

"I know my place," Armantine said quietly.

"Obviously not, or you wouldn't be walking away from it so easy."

Armantine didn't respond, and after a few moments of silence, Thisbe clucked and patted Armantine's leg again. "You think I can't see it? It's as plain as day to someone who knows what they're looking for." The old woman's hand was still locked onto Armantine's leg. "You listen to ol' Thisbe. When you're ready, you come to me, and I'll help you with what you need."

Armantine didn't answer. She watched the low-slung buildings of the city grow larger on the horizon and concentrated on the painful process of stitching her heart back together.

And when I woke, the ache that had been so sharp in her chest had settled in mine.

27

I would have happily stayed away from the parcel of land that held Thisbe's cabin for the rest of forever, but the Foundation would start work on the building soon, and they wanted more documentation first.

Leonard and I walked out to the cabin together, and I was more than a little surprised to see Silas waiting with Piers and a couple of other people at the edge of the property. One was Byron, who I'd helped before, but the other was a woman. As we drew closer, I recognized the long colorful skirt and statuesque posture easily as Mama Erzulie's. But any thought of what she was doing there fell away when Silas's eyes met mine.

I hadn't seen him for more than a week, not since Shaunda's memorial service, and the sight of him in his perfectly cut clothes was enough make my throat tighten. His shoulders were squared against the bright blue of the sky behind him, and I realized in that instant exactly how much I'd missed him. It didn't matter that I barely even knew him. I'd been living in my dreams too long. And I'd screwed up something that could have been real and good with Silas because of it.

His warm brown eyes met mine across the distance. Was

there any way to go back? To start over? But by the time Leonard and I joined the rest of the group, Silas had already turned his attention back to business.

"Leonard, this is Ms. Erzulie," Silas said by way of introduction. "She's a local expert in Voodoo, and I invited her here today to consult. I believe you've already met Lucy," he said to the older woman.

"Chloe introduced us a few weeks back." She smiled warmly at me. "I haven't seen you around like I thought I would." She spoke formally, but her voice held the barest hint of reproach.

"I haven't had a chance to get back into town. Not since the memorial." I felt Silas watching me, but I didn't look in his direction. I didn't think I could without broadcasting everything I was feeling.

"You'll come see me soon, though?" It wasn't so much a question as an order.

"I'll try," I hedged. "But it might be a while until I can afford to get my car fixed."

"You can always use one of ours," Leonard said cheerfully.

I nodded ambivalently, not really agreeing. They'd helped me enough, and I wasn't exactly sure they needed to know anything more about spirits or my dreaming.

"I want to thank you all for taking the time to meet this morning," Silas said, his tone formal. "The Foundation would like to start working on this piece of land, but after the initial survey and some interactions with the local community, we decided to call in Ms. Erzulie."

"I know a little about Haitian Vodou, but I'm not really knowledgeable about the kind of artifacts we found last week," Piers explained.

"We want to make sure we're preserving as much as we can without whitewashing or misunderstanding anything we might find here," Silas said. "The Foundation's goal is to represent the history of this place as accurately as we can, and we can't do that without understanding the local customs and beliefs."

Mama Erzulie was studying the building. "You're gonna need a good cleansing ritual before you mess with anything else in there. You never know what you might have stirred up the first time."

"I should have thought of that," Piers said.

Neither Silas nor Leonard seemed thrown off by the suggestion.

"I'll leave that to you, then," Silas said. He addressed me directly. "I'd like to get images documenting the whole process. Nothing too staged or posed. Photojournalist style, if you can manage it?"

My throat had gone tight at the dispassionate way he was looking at me. "You're the boss," I told him, my voice flat.

He stared at me a beat longer, and I thought some emotion flickered in his eyes, but his jaw clenched as he turned to speak with Leonard. "Let me know if you need anything else, will you? I'm heading out for a few days, but my assistant knows to take your calls." He held his hand out to Piers, who gave him some dap. "See you later, man."

He thanked Mama Erzulie again before he left. Before I could think better of it, my legs were moving and I was jogging to catch up with him. "Silas!"

His steps slowed, and he faced me, his curling dark hair stark and shining in the sun. Something like hope shone in his eyes.

I'd caught up to him, but I didn't know what I wanted to say.

"Did you need something?"

You. The word rose in my throat, but I swallowed it. "You don't really believe there are evil spirits lurking around, do you?" I said instead.

His expression went carefully blank. "Why do you ask?"

I had no idea. I just didn't want him to leave. Not yet. Not like this.

"All this talk about spirits and Voodoo . . ." It reminded me too much of my dreams, and I think there was a part of me that wanted him to tell me it wasn't insane. That *I* wasn't insane. "You're paying her to cleanse the place," I started again. "You must believe some of it."

Disappointment clouded his eyes, but he didn't walk away. Instead, Silas seemed to consider his words carefully. "I grew up in these parts, Lucy. The ideas aren't all that strange to me, but it doesn't really matter what I believe."

"No?"

He stepped toward me, and my breath caught as he settled his hands on my arm. But he didn't pull me toward him. Instead, he directed me, gently turning me to look out over the far side of the field, beyond Thisbe's grove. A group of locals had gathered just beyond the edge of the property across the road to watch.

His voice was soft when he spoke again, his mouth close enough to my ear that I could detect the woodsy cologne he always wore. "No. But it does matter what *they* believe."

He pulled back, leaving me achingly bereft. "This land's important to the people around here, and many of them *do* believe in spirits. If letting Ms. Erzulie perform a ritual here helps to ease their minds about what the Foundation is doing? I don't see how that can hurt."

His explanation made sense, but the whole thing still made me uneasy. But maybe if he wasn't opposed to ideas about spirits and the supernatural—

"Is there anything else you needed?" he asked, all business again.

"I really am sorry," I whispered. "About everything."

"Me too, Lucy." He tucked his hands back into his pockets and took a step back. "Me too."

He waited a moment longer, the silence between us heavy and expectant. But when I couldn't bring myself to say anything more—to explain—he gave a small nod. "Well, then. Let me know if there's anything else. I have to get back."

I let him go, watching as he made his way back toward the main part of the property, his broad shoulders hunched against the blue sky. I wasn't even thinking when I lifted my camera and centered him in the viewfinder. A single solitary figure against the expanse of the empty sky. As I pressed the shutter, he looked back over his shoulder, and his gaze held mine as I lowered the camera again.

But I stood there like an idiot and let him turn and walk away.

"Lucy!" Leonard called me back.

When I rejoined them, Piers sent me a questioning look, but I focused on my camera instead of answering.

"We'll start with a simple invocation for protection," Mama Erzulie was telling Leonard. "And then I'll scrub the whole place here with sage. Never hurts to be too careful."

I focused all of my attention to documenting the moment as Mama Erzulie began chanting. Her eyes closed, she lifted her hands to the sky. Then she lit a stick of sage, which released an earthy smoke as it burned. I took the pictures Silas wanted as she worked the braided stick of herbs over the threshold of the grove, up the path to the cottage, and over the porch.

When she was finished, she extinguished the sage using some red dirt she'd brought with her in a jar. "That should do it," she said.

"Silas wanted you to take a look at what we found last week." Leonard directed her toward the building. "If you have some time?"

Mama Erzulie nodded, and together we headed back into the stale darkness of the cabin so they could examine the blackened box and primitive doll.

"I've searched all my sources," Piers explained. "But I couldn't find any markings in them that matched these. Any idea what they are?"

I raised my camera and zoomed in on the doll, trying to capture the carvings on its surface. This time, as the carvings came into focus, my vision swam.

Lila's body. The bloody symbols carved into her chest.

I lowered the camera, shaken. But no one seemed to notice—they were all too busy watching Mama Erzulie examine the tiny figure.

She flipped it over in her hand, her smooth face creasing as she studied it, and then made a low noise in her throat that sounded like disgust. "These marks don't have anything to do with Voodoo."

"But it *is* a voodoo doll, isn't it?" Leonard sounded surprised.

"That's nothing more than tourist nonsense." She waved her hand dismissively. "True believers don't use this kind of magic. If this is what I think it might be, you're dealing with something dangerous here. Something dark."

"What do you think it might be?" Piers asked.

I raised my camera again, focusing on the moment in front of me instead of on the images of Lila that kept threatening to surface in my mind.

"I don't exactly know, but it reminds me of stories I've heard. Stories about witches who used black magic to control the makings of life itself. In those stories, they used to bind their spells with thread, like this here, usually made from the silk of charmed insects or soaked in the blood of the innocent. For those who practice dark magics, blood is a powerful tool because of its connection to the life force. A thread like this? Soaked in the blood of a sacrificed innocent and charmed with the right words, it could bind a person's very soul." Her voice had taken on a hypnotic quality. "This piece reminds me of those old stories. It feels like it once was touched by that kind of darkness."

Clearly captivated by the idea, Leonard turned to Piers. "Maybe we could get some documentation on those old tales and put them together in a display in the visitor's center."

"I don't know." Piers's unease was palpable.

Mama Erzulie was looking at Leonard liked he'd lost his mind. "You want my opinion? You'll get rid of that thing right now. Burn it or bury it, but don't let it out in the light of day."

"Oh, we couldn't do that." His opinion of Mama Erzulie had clearly just dropped a few notches. "But we'll take your recommendations under advisement. Thank you again for your help today, Ms. Erzulie. You'll have to come back when we get everything reconstructed."

Mama Erzulie seemed to get the message. "If that's all you needed, I best be on my way. Lucy, would you mind walking me out?"

Maybe I should have stayed to take more pictures, but I was more than happy to get out of the creeping gloom of the cabin and away from the creeping unease the plot of land inspired.

Together, we started out across the field, heading back toward the main house. When passed through the trees and stepped into the sunlight of the clearing by the pond, Mama Erzulie finally spoke. "I'm serious about you coming to see me again."

"I don't know—"

"That's obvious," she said dourly. "But you need to *start* knowing. You're already on your road, but you can't see what's waiting for you on the other end. You need to figure it out, and soon." Her gaze shifted from me to something over my shoulder. When her expression hardened, the nape of my neck pricked.

I didn't know what was behind me, but I was somehow unsurprised to see Alex standing at the edge of the woods when

I finally looked. His usually tousled hair glinted darkly in the sunlight, and my heart lurched as surely as Armantine's would have at how familiar the strong lines of his face had become to me.

His eyes weren't on me, though. They were focused on Mama Erzulie.

"Stay away from her," he told the old woman, his voice a low, guttural growl.

Mama Erzulie ignored the threat in his tone. Interest shone in her eyes. "Well, well now."

"I said stay away, old woman." He glanced at me. "Lucy, please, come away from her. You're not safe with her kind."

"And you think she's gonna be safe with you?" There was a thread of laughter in Mama Erzulie's voice. "What do you think *you* can do to protect her?"

His expression hardened, the beautifully sharp planes of his face solidifying into a dangerous mask. But he didn't answer.

"That's what I thought." She gave me a soft, conspiratorial smile. "When you're ready, come see me. We got ourselves a lot to discuss, child."

I shifted back, uneasy with how sure of herself she seemed. How similar her words to me were to Thisbe's words to Armantine. When I glanced over at Alex, his hands were clenched at his side.

"Lucy, you must stay away from her."

I'd spent so long in Armantine's mind, experiencing Armantine's emotions, that when I saw him standing there, I'd felt only relief. But the steel in his voice brought me back to myself.

I wasn't Armantine. I didn't have to feel for him what she felt. And I didn't have to stand for him growling orders at me, like some kind of alpha-hole male.

"What is your problem?" I asked. "I don't even know you. I'm certainly not going to take orders from you."

Alex blinked, clearly surprised by my reaction.

I gave my back to Alex and faced Mama Erzulie. "Come on, I'll walk you the rest of the way to your car."

Mama Erzulie laughed. "You're gonna be an interesting one to watch. With the company you're keeping? Who knows what's gonna happen."

I wasn't sure I was any more pleased with Mama Erzulie, but I didn't shy away when she slung her arm across my shoulder as we walked. I didn't look back to see whether Alex would follow. I'd had enough for the day.

When we reached the parking lot, the old woman withdrew her arm and rested her hands on my shoulders. "How's Chloe?"

"Not good. She doesn't want to see anyone. Not even Piers.

Mama Erzulie's eyes clouded. "Try to get her to come see me, too. She needs some healing to get through dark days like this. Here." She handed me a small pouch. "You give this to her and tell her I said it'll keep her safe."

The bit of burlap was surprisingly heavy in my hand. "You said back there I wasn't safe with him," I said carefully. "What did you mean by that? Do you know him?"

"Just what I said, child." She touched my cheek softly. "You come see me, you hear? You've been letting your dreams walk all over you. I can help you with that. And be careful with that boy there. I don't see how nothing good can come from it. Nothing at all."

28

A fter Mama Erzulie's purple van rolled out of the gate, I headed back toward the pond. I was tired of going in circles. I was sick of my dreams taking over my days.

"Alex!" I shouted when I reached the clearing. My voice was eaten up by the stillness. "Alexandre Jourdain," I called again, taking a leap. "I know you're here somewhere. I want to talk to you."

I waited in the stillness of the midmorning heat. The trees rustled faintly in some undetectable breeze, and then, just when I thought he wouldn't appear, he emerged from the tree line beyond, his hands in his pockets, his shoulders rounded.

I took a few steps toward him, attempting to hide my fear by putting every ounce of my frustration into the fire in my eyes. But the fire couldn't hold.

There you are, I thought, wanting to reach for him. To hold on to him this time. But I pushed my feelings—*Armantine's* feelings—away. I needed to focus on what was here, what was *real.*

Alex, at least, had the grace to look doubtful. He also looked tired. He was thinner than he'd ever appeared in my dreams. Dark smudges lay beneath his eyes, and I wondered if maybe he'd been sick these past few weeks. Was that why he'd been missing?

"What *was* that earlier?" I asked without any preface. "You don't even know me."

"Don't I?" he asked, his emerald eyes shadowed.

I wanted to say no. He *didn't* know me. We'd only talked a couple of times. But something stopped the words. Something made them feel like a lie.

"That woman is not your friend." His voice was suddenly cold. "You should stay far from her kind."

"What's *that* supposed to mean?" I demanded.

His jaw tightened. "She's a witch, Lucy."

"She's not a witch." But his use of the word—the same one Mina had used to describe Mama Erzulie—sent a shiver of unease down my spine.

He shook his head, as though he couldn't believe what I was telling him. "You, of all people, should know better. That woman can't offer you anything but pain. Stay away from her."

The authority threaded through his tone made my hackles rise. "Let's get one thing straight, *Alex*. I will do what I want, when I want to do it. And if I want to go run around and chant Voodoo spells at the top of my lungs, naked under a full moon, you won't have a thing to say about it. Got it?"

A ghost of a grin tugged at the corner of his mouth. "Naked?"

I huffed as my cheeks went hot. "You know what I mean."

"I understand. But you don't seem to understand how dangerous a woman like that can be."

"Just like I don't know exactly how dangerous *you* might be?"

"You would think that of me?" He looked genuinely surprised.

"I don't know *what* to think of you! That's the whole point." I jabbed a finger toward his chest. "You're here and then you're not. You tell me half-truths and keep secrets. Sometimes I think you're a figment of my imagination," I finished softly, finally giving voice to my greatest fear about him. "I don't understand why I'm drawn to you. I don't understand what this is between us, Alex."

He studied me for a long moment before running a hand through his golden hair. He looked every bit as exasperated as I felt.

"How can you possibly be so blind?" His voice was tired and brittle, but a glint of anger burned in his eyes. "You look through your little camera and draw out the life in everything around you, and yet you cannot see what is right in front of you. What you already *know*."

His words infuriated me. "Then maybe I should look at *you* through my *lee-tle* camera," I threw back at him, mimicking his cadence.

"Maybe you should." His voice was flat. Cold. "Look at me now and see me. Stop ignoring what you know to be true."

I hesitated, but eventually raised the camera and focused. He was wearing an expression somewhere between anger and lust, contempt and admiration, or maybe it was all those things together. It made the hairs on the back of my neck stand on end.

The shutter release snapped, a satisfying *click* that obscured Alex's face for a moment as the viewfinder went black. When I lowered the camera, he was gone. But the sadness in his voice when he said I was blind—that still echoed clearly in my mind.

29

I still felt shaken when I made it back to the offices, were I'd been working on the images for the Foundation's website on a more powerful Mac in the back office. Unlike the tablet, it had a large, high-definition screen and a lot more computing power.

Mina was sitting at the front desk when I came in, but I could barely manage a greeting as I brushed by. I hated being rude, but I was too stirred up. I was on the edge of something important, something that could change everything.

I closed the door behind me and left the lights low as I sat at the desk and booted up the computer. In a matter of seconds, I had signed in. With my hands shaking, I removed the storage card from my camera and slid it into the computer. I clicked on the files and waited a few seconds longer as the large image files loaded. Then I pulled them up one at a time.

There was the cabin, stark against the white smoke of Mama Erzulie's sage. The darkened hallways within the small cabin. The thread-wrapped doll.

Impatient now, I skipped ahead, mentally calculating how many files there should be. My hands trembled as I brought up three other pictures before finding the one I wanted, the image of Alex by the pond. I opened two other files to be sure before I returned to it. Certain.

I thought of the first pictures I'd taken of him, the one strangely missing after I fainted that first morning and the one I'd taken by the pond. Somehow, I wasn't surprised, but my skin went cold just the same when I expanded the image on the screen. Where Alex should have been, stark and clear as day, there was nothing but a wide arc of almost pure light, as though the sun itself had come out of the clouds the instant I had taken the shot and overexposed it.

But that wasn't what had happened. The sun *hadn't* come out, and I hadn't missed that shot. I hadn't missed *any* of those shots.

But Mama Erzulie saw *him.*

A manic huff of laughter escaped me. Mama Erzulie was a woman who believed in the spirits. She made a living interacting with them every day.

I zoomed in on the image. There was no mistaking what I was seeing. It wasn't the sun or a smudge on my lens. I was too good to make a mistake that big.

I had not wanted to believe that Alex was anything but a real, flesh-and-blood man. Even with the dreams, even with the photo in Thisbe's cabin and the letters carved into the trees, I had not wanted to see what was right in front of me all along, but I couldn't deny the truth any longer. I hit print and listened to the whine of the inkjet as I stared at the picture that should have shown me the face of a man but instead showed me nothing but light. The picture of a ghost.

30

I don't know how long I sat like that, before I finally forced myself to close the file. I didn't understand any of it, not the dreams or how I was connected to this place, but I had to do something—I was strung too tight to just sit here—and when I don't know what to do, I usually turn back to my art. So I picked a few shots I'd taken that morning and I worked on finishing those for the Foundation as my brain tried to make sense of what my gut knew was true.

The first image was the picture I'd taken of the doll, but those carvings reminded me too much of the dream of Lila's murder—and too much of the descriptions of how Shaunda had died.

So I moved on to some other shots I'd taken around the grounds in the week before of happy tourists examining the plaques or listening to their guides. Before I knew it, I'd pulled up the shot I'd taken of Silas earlier that day.

The camera had caught him perfectly. His sharp profile was gorgeous against the blazing sky, but my heart ached from the sadness in his expression as he met my gaze through the camera's lens. It was a good picture of him, one that captured his sureness and strength, and before I could think too much about it, I got to work. I burned in the edges a little, centering the composition around him. With the color faded a bit, he looked like a modern man caught in the past. When it was perfect, I hit print.

I wasn't sure what I would do with the picture. Maybe the Foundation could use it on their site, a portrait of their founder. Or maybe I could give it to him personally, a gift. An apology.

But when the printer finally spit the finished image out onto its tray, I knew I'd never give it to him. How could I?

What was I supposed to tell him? How was I supposed to explain?

Funny story. It wasn't another guy's name I said when you were kissing me that day. I'm just being haunted. By a really hot French ghost. Who invades my dreams. Every night. And I feel like maybe he's here. On the plantation. Invading my waking too.

This was so much worse than nightmares.

I leaned my head back and stared up at the ceiling. I was officially losing my mind. The nightmares had been bad, but this was worse. And I couldn't shake the feeling everything was connected.

"Lucy?" Mina knocked, and before I could answer, she was opening the door to the small office.

I minimized the image I had up, leaving one of the strange carved dolls on the screen instead, and tried to be subtle about sliding the picture of Silas I'd just printed under the one of the empty clearing.

"Yeah?" I said, turning in the chair. "Did you need something?"

"Sorry to bother you." Her gaze drifted to the screen behind me before returning. "Chloe stopped by, and I thought you might want to say hi."

I jolted a bit at Chloe's name. I hadn't seen or really talked to her since that morning at her house. "Yeah. Of course. I'll be right there."

She took another look at the computer screen, her expression unreadable.

But before she could ask any questions I didn't have answers to, I stood, blocking the screen. "Actually, I can come now."

Chloe was sitting in the front office, talking softly with Silas. She looked up, causing him to turn as well. When our eyes met, I couldn't move. I couldn't even breathe.

"Hey, Luce," Chloe said, drawing my attention back. She smiled in greeting, but it didn't reach her eyes. There was still something empty in her expression, something broken that time hadn't fixed yet. I wondered if it ever would.

"Hey," I said, fully aware Silas was looking at me. "How've you been?"

She shrugged. "You know." Her voice was flat, lifeless. "I'm starting back at work next week."

"That's good," I said. "I know everyone's missed you in the office. I've missed you, too."

"Why don't you take the rest of the afternoon off," Mina suggested. "We were going to grab lunch, but I have so much to take care of here. Maybe the two of you could go get something to eat together?"

"Sure," I said, glancing at Chloe.

"You don't have to," she hedged. "I'll be fine on my own."

"You've been on your own enough," Mina chided. "Go out with your friend. Stop wallowing."

Chloe's jaw clenched at her mother's tone. "I can drive," she said flatly.

"I just need to close up the files I was working on," I said.

But Mina waved me off. "I'll lock up the room. Your things will be fine until you get back."

I didn't especially want to leave my camera behind, but with everyone looking at me, it felt weird to argue the point further.

"Great," I said. "I guess I'm ready, then." I pasted on a smile, but inside, I was still thinking about that picture. And shaking like a leaf.

~

I COULDN'T GET over how much Chloe had changed. As we drove along the back roads, she was uncharacteristically quiet. Her whole expression was closed off, like she was on a mission and determined to be successful at it. I had once thought we had the beginnings of a friendship going, so if I could help her deal with Shaunda's death by being here for her, even in an uncomfortable silence, I would do my best.

But things only got worse when she pulled into the small café not far from Le Ciel. After we ordered, the silence between us resumed. Everything about her seemed different. Her eyes seemed dimmer, her skin sallow, and she had yet to flash the smile I'd come to identify as pure Chloe. I tried again, hoping to brighten her mood.

"Mama Erzulie came out to Le Ciel this morning," I said. "Silas had asked her to help with Thisbe's place. She did some sort of cleansing ritual, or something. She asked about you."

Chloe's eyes were no longer flat, but instead of brightening, as I had hoped they would, they flashed with anger. "That so?"

"Yeah," I continued, not knowing what I'd said to offend her. "She wanted me to give you something," I told her, remembering the small heavy pouch Mama Erzulie had entrusted me with. "It's back at the offices, with the rest of my stuff. I can grab it when we get back."

"I don't want it," she said. "And it's not a good idea for you to be messing with her, either."

"You introduced us," I said, confused.

"It was a mistake," she said flatly. "That old witch is nothing but trouble. You'd do well to stay away."

Her change in heart surprised me. "You don't really think Mama Erzulie had something to with Shaunda's death, do you?"

She frowned, her face creasing as though she was struggling through some idea. "All I know is that if I'd have stayed away from the bayou that night, Shaunda might still be alive right now."

"Chloe." I reached out to lay my hand over hers, but she pulled away. "You know it's not your fault, right? You're not responsible for her death. You can't always stop bad things from happening, no matter how safe you try to be."

Chloe looked at me with barely veiled contempt. "And how would you know that, Lucy?"

I blinked. "I'm sorry. I was just trying to help."

"I don't need your trying," she said through gritted teeth. "And I certainly don't need your help."

"Fine." I raised my hands in surrender. "I just thought maybe you needed a friend. I'm sorry if I overstepped."

"I don't think I'm very hungry anymore." She tossed her crumpled napkin onto the table. "Maybe I should take you back."

"Maybe you should," I said slowly, not understanding the abruptness of her moods.

We left without eating, and she drove me back to Le Ciel in complete silence. If she had been anything like the old Chloe, I might have tried to tell her about Alex, about the strange pictures and even stranger dreams. But this Chloe had a wall of thorns built up around her, so I kept my secrets to myself. When we got back to the offices, she didn't bother turning off the car. I didn't offer to get the gris-gris I had for her.

"It was good seeing you again." I meant every word. Whatever was wrong, I'd missed her.

"Same goes." But she didn't look at me when she said it, and nothing in her tone told me she meant it.

I went to shut the door, but she called out to me.

"Yeah?"

"I just wanted to say you should be careful," she said, her voice low and conspiratorial. "Shaunda's killer hasn't been caught yet. She didn't die easy, you know. Throat cut. Arms and chest all sliced up."

I'd heard rumors, like everyone else, but Chloe sounded so sure. "Did her family tell you that?"

She didn't bother to answer. "Anyway, you best be careful. I'd hate to see you end up like her."

Her words sent a chill through me, even though she'd softened her voice. She reached over and pulled the door shut.

I'd barely backed away before the tires spun, and her car shot down the long drive. It passed through the heavy gates and disappeared onto the main road.

Unsettled, I returned to the offices. Mina wasn't here and neither was Silas. I was still thinking about what Chloe had said —how strangely she'd been acting—when I got back to the room where I'd left my camera. It was still sitting there, waiting, just as Mina had promised it would be. I saved the files I'd been working on and shut everything down. I was halfway back to my cabin before I remembered the prints I'd made, but when I went back, they were nowhere to be found.

31

Everywhere I look, I see blood. It's splattered across the tall grass like some demented Jackson Pollock. It runs into the dark earth like a tiny macabre river. And the smell. I don't think I'll ever forget the smell of it, like rust and death. A putrid stench mixed with something sickeningly sweet coats my tongue, makes me gag. It's the sweetness that seems even more obscene.

The girl's body is arranged at an unnatural angle. Arranged is the only word for it, because no one could possibly fall that way. Her neck is twisted to the side, as though she's trying to look over her shoulder. As though she was trying to escape from death itself and made the mistake of looking back. Across the delicate line of her throat is a deep gash. Across her chest, angular symbols have been carved into her skin. She's been gone for hours now, and the blood has stopped welling, has gone thick and sticky. When I realize the flies have already found her, I think I'm going to be sick.

Someone's screaming. A high, plaintive, wailing. Then I realize it's me. My throat is sore from it, but I can't stop.

Strong arms band around me as I scream, and a soft voice whispers into my hair. "Shhh. Shhh. It's okay."

I know that voice, but he was holding the knife. He was standing over Lila's poor, broken body with the knife that had killed her. The image is burned into my mind. I'll never be free of it.

"Shhh. Shhh. You have to stop screaming."

I don't think I'll ever be able to stop screaming. But I do. And then I'm only numb. I can't feel anything. I may never feel anything again.

32

It was still dark when I woke with the smell of death in my nose. It hung in the air of my bedroom, thick and almost sweet with the scent of rot. I couldn't stay in my tiny cabin. I couldn't *breathe*. I needed air so desperately that I didn't think about the danger, just pulled on some rumpled shorts and went outside.

The night was warm, and gray clouds hung heavy above me. Heat lightning flickered across the sky, lighting up the tops of the trees and throwing them into sharp relief, like claws reaching up into the momentarily bright sky. The stars were hidden behind the heavy clouds, and the only light was the glow of the path lights behind me.

I took deep breaths, trying to steady myself. I needed to relax. No, I needed to *move*. I needed to walk off the uncomfortable energy jangling through me, but I didn't want to go anywhere near the woods or the pond, so I headed instead toward the big house. There were more lights around the grounds there, especially in the manicured gardens.

By the time I reached the center of the gardens, I was feeling a little better. The clammy fear that had coated my skin in sweat had started to lift, and now that I was out in the humid night air, the dream was fading. But I wasn't quite ready to return to the small cabin or my own bed. I found a wrought iron bench tucked into a softly lit corner of the garden, and I lay back against the cool metal.

Out of nowhere, Alex's voice broke through my thoughts. "You shouldn't be here, *chère*."

I jumped, but somehow, it almost felt inevitable he'd found me there. After all, I'd known all along this moment would come. Ever since I saw the blur of light on the picture, I'd known I would have to face him again and confront what he was—but I hadn't planned doing it in the dead of night.

"I'm sorry. I didn't mean to startle you." The furrow between his brows and the tension in his jaw betrayed his worry. "The night's not safe, Lucy. Especially not for a woman alone."

"Is that a warning or a threat?" I struggled to keep my voice even, even as I swallowed panic. I thought of Lila, of Shaunda.

I didn't know what I expected from him, but it wasn't the pained smile he gave me. "I couldn't hurt you."

His words—and the truth of them—hung in the night air between us, and a little of my fear eased. "No. You couldn't, could you?" I said slowly.

He shook his head, for once refusing to meet my eyes. "What are you doing out here, *chère*?"

I could have refused to answer. I could have turned back and ignored what he was, what the dreams meant. Or I could keep going, cross into unknown territory, and finally understand. I needed to understand.

"I had a bad dream," I offered. "I came out here to get some air."

"It must have been terrible to drive you from the safety of your bed, out into the night." He didn't come any closer, but it felt like this moment was some kind of a test.

"It was."

"But it was only a dream, yes?"

That was the question, wasn't it? "I don't know," I whispered.

I took a deep breath and looked at him. What was I doing? What could I *possibly* be thinking? Sitting alone in the dead of night, talking to a man who was likely a ghost.

But I couldn't deny everything was connected somehow— the nightmares I'd had my entire life, the dreams of Alex with Armantine, and this place.

"The dreams I've been having . . ." It was impossible to even say the rest.

"Please," he urged. "Go on."

I should have been terrified, yet I wasn't. Not really. It felt like maybe it was always supposed to happen this way.

Finally, I gathered up enough courage to speak. "I think the dreams I've been having are more than just dreams. I think I've been seeing things that happened a long time ago." I swallowed hard and then forced myself to say the words I'd been afraid to say out loud. "Things that happened to *you* a long time ago."

He didn't immediately respond, and his face remained that blank mask he reverted to when he wanted to hide his emotions.

"I've had nightmares for my entire life," I continued. "Terrible dreams about drowning, about dying. And about this house." I watched his expression for some sign of understanding, but he didn't betray even a flicker of emotion. "When I got here, though, the dreams changed. I started dreaming about *you.*"

"Me?" Interest sparked in his emerald eyes.

"Yes, *you.* I fall asleep every night, and I dream about people I shouldn't know. I dream about you with people I shouldn't know." I paused, silently willing him to say something.

He stepped closer. "I'd very much like to hear about your dreams of me, Lucy."

His proximity sent a shiver of awareness through me, but it

wasn't fear. With him so close, it was too easy to remember Armantine's desire—to *feel* that same desire. With the heat of the night licking against my skin, it took everything I had to pull myself back from him. But I refused to let myself fall into her feelings for him again.

"They aren't so easy to talk about," I whispered.

Because the truth was, even if my dreams were really about the past, I didn't know the man standing before me. And yet, he *felt* like the Alex from my dreams. The one who had looked at Armantine and treated her as an equal when no one else had. And no matter how many questions I still had, being with him there in the dark, the coldness that had settled in my chest from the dream was easing.

"I dream about you. And about a girl named Armantine."

When I said her name, pain flashed across his face before he could hide it. His reaction told me everything.

"She's real, then." It was no longer a question.

He nodded, his jaw clenching.

"And you knew her."

But he only stared out to the darkness beyond.

The unease grew in the hollow pit of my stomach. "Years ago. You knew her, and she meant something to you."

At first, I thought he wouldn't admit anything, but then his voice floated across the thick air of the night, barely a whisper. "She meant *everything*."

"What happened to her?"

He looked up at me, his eyes dark with grief. "It doesn't matter anymore. She's gone."

"But you're not," I said, moving closer. "I'm dreaming of things that really happened, aren't I? You should have died over a century ago. But you're still here. *Why* are you still here? Do you have some kind of unfinished business or—"

"I'm not a ghost, Lucy."

I frowned at him. "Then what are you?"

"I don't exactly know anymore," he said, sounding utterly lost. "The witch did something to me, something I've never quite understood. Somehow she's trapped me here. But the answer is out there." He gestured toward the darkness beyond us. "In the witch's house. There's something about that place that keeps me here."

"What do you mean, it keeps you here?" I asked.

He was looking at me, but I knew he wasn't really seeing me. I wasn't sure if he was trying to invent an answer or figure it out himself. I saw in him, then, a fragility I hadn't noticed before. One that had probably always been there, just below the surface.

"Here. In this place. On this land." He gestured around me. "I can only go a short distance from the witch's house before I'm pulled back. The pond is about the farthest I can go comfortably. Being here, near the house, is . . . difficult. And going beyond the gate—impossible."

"And you think something in that cabin is causing it?" I thought for a moment about the voodoo doll Leonard had found, but dismissed it as a possibility. It wasn't in the house anymore—they'd secured it in the main offices right after Mama Erzulie had talked about burning it.

He nodded. "I know there is. But I'm not sure what. There's nothing I can do on my own to discover what's happened to me." He looked utterly lost. "I can't even cross the threshold to search."

"I could help you," I offered. "I've been in there. What if I help you find whatever it is you're looking for?"

"It isn't safe," he told me, shaking his head.

"There's nothing in that house that can hurt me, Alex. But if there's a way to figure out how to free you from whatever this is," I said, waving vaguely toward him, "I'll do it." And maybe, in the process I could free myself.

"I couldn't allow you to put yourself in danger, Lucy." His jaw was tight again, and real fear shone in his eyes.

"You couldn't really stop me, though, could you?" I asked.

"Lucy—"

But I didn't want to argue. I wanted answers. "Will you tell me about her?" I asked, before he could say anything more. "About Armantine?"

His expression shuttered, as securely as a house preparing for a storm. "Hers is not my story to tell."

"I think it is." I took another step toward him, but he didn't retreat. "I want the truth, Alex. I've been dreaming about you and Armantine for weeks now. I need to know why."

"Are you sure, *ma chère*? Now, your world is safe and whole. If you discover the truth, how many of your illusions might shatter? Once they do, there is no going back."

But my illusions were already shattered, my world already tilted wickedly on an unfamiliar axis. I had no delusions it was ever going back. But I was ready to go forward. "There's already no going back."

He considered me for a moment, indecision clear on his face. "I only have my truth to offer, but what I have is yours." Tentatively, he reached out, gesturing for me to take his hand.

I hesitated for a moment and then took another step forward. And grasped air.

33

The moment I touched the warm air where his hand should have been, I was tossed back, suddenly, into Armantine's world. But I wasn't seeing it through her eyes any longer. This was Alex's world, his memories. The room had large windows overlooking the river—her studio, I realized by the art supplies and half-finished paintings propped up around the edge of the floor.

It was sometime after that day by the pond with Josephine—I recognized the sketches spread on her worktable as the same ones she'd done that day. She hadn't started the painting yet, though.

There, sitting in front of a small blank canvas without moving, was the girl—Armantine. He knew she could sense him, yet she refused to turn.

He thought he had remembered what it felt like to be near her, how his blood thrummed in his veins and his heart reeled when she was close. But those memories were nothing compared to the reality of being there in her presence. The whole room smelled like her—the sweet, floral scent cut through with the faint burn of the turpentine she used to clean her brushes.

I could feel the weariness in his bones, the sheer exhaustion born of days of worrying about her. She seemed to sense it too. Finally, she turned to him.

"You've not been sleeping?" she asked, her stormy eyes narrowing in concern.

He walked over and traced the shadows that lay beneath her own eyes. Her skin was so smooth, it reminded him of a petal. "I could ask the same of you."

When she began to turn away from him, he grasped her chin gently in his hand and refused to let her hide. He searched her face for some clue. "What cause have I given you to doubt me?"

"You've done nothing." She stepped back just the same.

"Then help me understand." His voice was soft, an urgent plea. He stepped closer and lifted her hand to his lips and kissed the underside of her wrist. "Explain it to me, Armantine."

But she pulled away instead. She walked to the window and studied the street below, closing him out. "Your sister told me about your betrothed."

He straightened. "Josephine spoke out of turn. She had no right—"

Armantine faced him. "Did she lie?"

"I have no interest in submitting myself to my family's plans," he said through clenched teeth. "My father thinks he can direct my life, but there is only one person I wish to take to wife, and she isn't the simpering fool daughter of my father's neighbor. You are the one I love, Armantine. I'll not marry another."

She laughed then. A dry, hollow sound that held no joy. "I'm not a Creole, Alex. I'm not even one of the poor Americans who trail into our city like fleas on a dog. I'm a free woman, true, and my skin may look no different than yours, but my blood binds me nonetheless." She took a breath. "We can't marry. Blood means something in these parts."

"It makes no difference to me. It doesn't change what is between us." He stepped closer. "You must know that. You must feel even a little of what I feel?"

She wouldn't answer him.

"Armantine," he whispered. He was losing her. "I cannot simply forget about you. I cannot let you go."

"And I will not be kept," she whispered, defeated. "I know other girls are. I know we could come to some agreement that would assure my future. Then, when you tire of me, I would be assured a settlement. A home, perhaps. Money for any children that might result."

The mention of children shocked him. "And you think so little of me that you believe I would agree to this? That I would willingly give you up? Give our children up as well?"

"It is what is *done*. Men do not grow old with their mistresses. *This* is what women in my position are faced with. What *I* am faced with. These *agreements*," she hissed, her eyes flashing with fire. "They are the one thing I've refused to contemplate for myself. No matter that they've been offered. Many times. By men far richer and more important than you. But for you . . ." Her voice softened. "For you, I would consider it. Please, don't ask it of me."

He stared at her, shocked, and then, unable to hold back any longer, he wrapped her in his arms and pulled her close, pressing his lips into her hair. "In a week a ship sails to France. I plan to be on it." He stroked her cheek gently. "I had hoped we could be married before the sailing."

"It's impossible, Alex. The laws—"

"We can be married once we are at sea," he countered. "If you would rather, we could wait until we arrive in France." He did not want to wait until France.

She pulled back, frowning up at him. "You would truly

marry me?" she asked, shock clear in her expression. "I thought—"

"Yes, well," he said dryly as he took her hands in his. "I'm beginning to get an idea of your thoughts." He squeezed her hands gently, feeling how small, how delicate they were in his. "Come with me, Armantine. In France we could be together. Think of it, a life with me. We could go to Paris—a city filled with the art you love, a life we could build together. And no one need know anything about you—about us—but that I adore my wife." He could see it—truly. The vision was there, so brilliant and perfectly within reach.

But she pulled away once more. "But your family—what will they think? You could not keep my past a secret from them, not when Josephine knows."

He tilted her chin up, forcing her to look at him, and placed the lightest of kisses upon her lips. "My mother and father will adjust themselves to my choice. I'm no farmer, love. I never was. And they will welcome you. How could they not love you as I do?" And if they did not, it would not matter. "I wish I could give you more time, *mon coeur*. But I cannot stay here any longer. Come with me."

She didn't respond, and panic shot through him. She would refuse him. He could not allow her to send him away, not yet. He could not lose her.

"I brought you a gift," he said, pretending he didn't see the regret in her eyes. Ignoring his own clawing panic. Before she could refuse, he took a blue velvet pouch out of his pocket. "This was my grandmother's. She said I was to give this to my intended when I found her." He paused, searching for the right words. "I've found her."

Armantine's expression softened, just a little, and victory coursed through him.

He pulled a delicate chain with an ornate silver locket from the pouch. How many times had his grandmother shown it to him when he was a boy? How many times had he imagined this day? "This is my gift to you, whatever you decide. It's an old custom, but I've put a lock of my hair in it for you. A piece of me for you to keep. We are two halves of a whole, Armantine. Nothing can change that."

"I can't—" she started to say.

"You *will*." He was already fastening the delicate chain around her neck. "Whatever you choose, this belongs to you. If nothing else, it will serve as a remembrance of someone who will love you always."

Armantine's hand closed over the locket, and she lifted it to examine it. "It's beautiful," she whispered.

"Honor me by wearing it by my side?"

"I need—"

"Time," he finished for her. "There is still much I need to arrange, so you shall have your time. In six days, I will come for your answer."

She nodded, unable—or unwilling—to find the words.

"But know this—if you do not have an answer for me in six days, it will not matter. I would gladly wait six lifetimes for you." He cupped her face gently and kissed her. "You are mine, Armantine. Nothing will ever change that for me. *Nothing.*"

He leaned in again and kissed her, softly at first, and then when she didn't pull away, he kissed her again. This time, she melted into him, her lips parting, allowing him access to the heat of her mouth. She tasted of the cherries she loved so much and of something unmistakably like herself. When her tongue met his, he pulled her to him.

All at once, they were tangled together, her arms grasping him closer and her greedy mouth urging him on.

"Tell me that you're mine," he begged her as she nipped at the column of his throat. He ran one of his hands up her torso, over the swell of her breast. The stiff peak of her nipples hardened for him beneath the layers of clothes. He would die if he couldn't touch her. "Tell me. *Promise* me."

"Alex—" Her voice was little more than a breath. "Please, Alex—"

He moved one thumb over the peak of her breast again, teasing her—teasing them both with the promise of more. It wasn't fair of him, but he couldn't bring himself to care.

"Say the words," he whispered into her neck, kneading her breast gently as he sucked gently on the delicate skin above her collarbone. "Tell me that you're mine, and I'll give you everything you want, love."

"Yes," she whispered, her hands tangled in his hair, holding him to her, urging him lower.

"Yes, what?" he asked, his hands tugging on the front of her gown as he followed the urging of her hands, trailing kisses down the slope of her breast.

"I'm yours," she said finally, her words breaking as he bared her breasts.

Their eyes met for a moment, and he saw his future in the stormy blue of hers. "*Mine*," he agreed, and then captured one of her pebbled nipples with his mouth as he lifted her onto the table. He couldn't stop himself from smiling at her sharp gasp of pleasure, at the pinch of her nails gripping his hair, pinning him in place.

She whimpered a little when he pulled back, and her eyes darkened with unmistakable need. He looked down at her, propped as she was on the edge of the wide table. Her skirts were hiked up, exposing the soft skin of her spread legs, and her bared breasts rose and fell with the unsteadiness of her breath.

"Tell me that you love me," he said, running the tip of a single finger over the slope of one breast, over the nipple swollen and tender from his mouth. He palmed her, grasping the sensitive tip and rolling it between his fingers until her breath hitched. "Tell me, Armantine."

She licked her lips. "I love you," she whispered, her eyes never leaving his.

Relief flooded him as he kissed her, pressing his nearly painful erection against the place where her thighs met. He kissed her again, their tongues sliding and tasting, as his other hand slipped up under her skirts, over the smooth skin of her thighs, until he brushed against the curls covering her sex. He dragged the pad of his thumb through the slick heat there, until Armantine moaned against his mouth.

"Please," she whispered, rubbing herself against his hand as she pressed against him.

"Tell me again that you love me," he said, greedy for the words and for her. His thumb brushed over the swollen nub, and she gasped again. "Tell me I can make you mine."

She was nodding, but he needed the words, needed to hear them from her own lips.

"Say it, Armantine." He kissed her again as his fingers stroked against her heat. "Give me your promise."

"I promise," she said, her voice unsteady. "I love you." She drew back to look at him, expression desperate as he felt. "Only you."

He dropped to his knees and pushed the skirts up her legs.

"Alex—"

Need tinged her voice, a wanting that echoed his own. He pulled open the slit in her drawers and exposed her. "One day soon, I'm going to make you mine, Armantine," he said, running a finger through the slick folds of her sex and watching her body quiver in response. "Soon, there will be nothing and no one between us, love."

He wanted to take her there and then, in the bright light of day with the Quarter humming just beyond the windows. Wanted to free himself from his too constricting trousers and plunge into her heat, so she could no longer deny what was between them. Soon, he promised. Soon, he would bind her to him, a brand upon his heart. But until then . . .

He moved closer until he could smell the sweetness of her musk. Then he pressed his mouth against her, and the vision shattered around me.

34

I came to on the bench in the garden, my skin hot and my body desperate. Every muscle, every nerve was strung tight and ever cell wanted. The dream still clung to me, so close and thick I could hardly breathe.

Had it been a dream?

It felt different somehow, more immediate. More like a vision or a memory than anything else. Alex's need—his desire and desperation—was still thrumming through my own veins, too close to the surface. And when I moved, my own nearly painful arousal made gasp as my vision swam.

"Lucy?"

At first, I thought it was Alex's silhouette standing above me in the soft morning light, and my body reacted almost instinctively. My breasts felt heavy, my nipples painfully hard. I almost reached out, almost let my mouth form the word *yes*.

But as my eyes adjusted, I realized it was Silas standing there, and somehow that made the desperate need deep in my core worse. He was dressed in a crisp white polo that made the tawny brown of his skin look even more warm and inviting. It was cut perfectly, like all his clothes, the sleeves snug against the curve of his bicep, and the desire that had overwhelmed me during the dream rose again as I looked at him.

I couldn't seem to make myself understand Silas LaRoux wasn't for me.

"What are you doing out here?" he asked.

"I couldn't sleep," I said, trying to will away my arousal. It seemed wrong somehow, feeling so needy and desperate for Silas when it had been inspired by someone—some*thing*—else.

I didn't understand completely what had just happened. I had asked Alex for the truth, yes. And he had certainly given me something. I'd been in his skin, seen what he felt—or at least what he'd wanted me to.

I started to stand, but my legs were unsteady beneath me. Silas caught me against his side. Heat flashed across my skin where our bodies touched, and it took everything I had not to lean in and take a deeper breath of the cologne teasing my nose.

"Whoa, there," he said, strong hands gripping me, setting me upright. "Are you okay?"

"Honestly?" I shook my head. "I don't know."

My nerves were jangling with everything I'd just seen, everything I was still feeling. I felt completely out of control. My body was a live wire, but at least my brain knew the wanting wasn't mine—or it wasn't *all* mine.

Without warning, my eyes pricked with tears. I'd thought I could start over here, had hoped to solve the mystery of my nightmares, but I'd managed to tumble into something far bigger and more confusing. Likely something more dangerous than I'd ever imagined.

It was all too close, too *immediate*. Alex and Armantine. Alex and *me*. And I had no idea how to make any of it stop—or how to get back to myself.

His eyes softened. "It's okay, Lucy. Whatever it is, it's going to be okay."

I just shook my head. He couldn't know that. And in this moment, it felt like nothing would ever be okay again.

But Silas didn't back away. He brushed my hair back from where it had fallen, wild and tangled, into my face, before he wrapped me in his arms. Nothing about the embrace suggested it was for anything but comfort. But that didn't matter. My body was on fire. I couldn't stop myself from sinking into him, from reveling in the solid *realness* of him.

I didn't want to be drawn to him, but I was. I had been since the first day. But I was such a mess. He didn't deserve the issues I dragged along with me.

That didn't seem to stop me from leaning into the comfort he offered, though. His body reacted almost immediately. It didn't seem to matter that he also knew I was a mess. As we stood there, I felt the unmistakable bulge of his erection hardening against me.

I forced myself to step back before I did something truly stupid, like press myself into him, rub myself against him. I resisted the urge to glance down.

He was studying me, clearly searching for some indication of what was going on, but I didn't even know where to start. After a long moment of silence, he let out a deep breath that didn't mask his disappointment.

But I couldn't read what had disappointed him more—that I hadn't explained what I was dealing with, or that I'd stepped back.

"Let's get you back to your place," he said softly.

As Silas guided me back to my small cabin, there was no sign of Alex. I was grateful for the Frenchman's absence, but a part of me felt like I'd lost something important. I wasn't sure what I would do if Alex appeared now, with Silas walking next to me in the dark, my body strung tight with need, and the memory of Alex's mouth on Armantine still clear in my mind.

When we arrived at the cabin, Silas took my key from me before I could open the door and escorted me inside.

"You don't have to—" I started to say, but he leveled a silent, steady look in my direction. I sat on my bed without any further protest.

Silently, he poured some water in the electric kettle before locating a chipped mug in the small cabinet, along with the lavender tea Mina had given me a few days before. He scooped some into the mug as he waited for the water. I didn't miss when his attention caught on the canvas propped against the wall—the one that featured Alex's brilliant emerald eyes.

"It looks like you have some pieces coming along," he said, his voice strangely rough. There was a question there, but he never voiced it.

"A few." It felt wrong somehow to have Silas standing there in my home with Alex's eyes watching us. "Nothing I'm really ready to show yet."

"I've been putting out some feelers." He put his back to the canvases. "One of the galleries on Royal Street has already shown some interest. I think they'll offer a show before the month's over."

"Really?" The news seemed too impossibly good to be true. It was what I had always wanted, what I'd worked so hard for back in Chicago. But somehow, none of it felt right. Not with everything happening.

"Nothing's for certain yet, but . . ." He glanced back at the canvases. "I think it'll work out."

When the kettle was ready, he poured the water into the prepared cup and brought it over to me. I wasn't sure what to even say to him as I accepted it, other than thank you. But thank you didn't seem like nearly enough.

We sat in silence for a while, him watching me carefully as I sipped the tea.

"The grounds open in an hour," he said finally. "You're lucky someone else didn't find you."

I couldn't read the emotion in his voice. Curiosity maybe? Or frustration?

"I'm sorry you had to be the one." I kept my eyes on the contents of the mug instead of him. But I could feel him studying me, could practically feel his unspoken questions.

"That's not what I meant, Lucy." He let out a tired-sounding breath. "Did you sleep at all last night?"

I was too aware he was still maintaining his distance.

"A little." I brought the steaming mug up to my face again, breathed in the chamomile and lavender of the tea and wished it were enough to make my body relax. To dispel this needy feeling like a fire about to erupt. "Not really," I confessed.

"How long have you not been sleeping?"

I looked up at him, took in the expectation glimmering in his eyes, and considered my options. I could lie. It's what I would usually do, but my whole body was still on edge from my vision in the gardens. I was so tired of holding people at arm's length, so tired of being alone. I needed *something*, so I did something I'd never done before. Not for Matt and not for the handful of guys before him. I gave Silas the truth.

"For a while now."

I knew what was coming next—the look of frustration or pity or confusion. I'd been through this all before.

But Silas surprised me. "Take today off," he said instead. There was no pity, no frustration or anger in his expression. "You look like you could use it." He gave me another long unreadable look, and then he headed for the door.

He was almost out the door before I called out to stop him. I don't know what made me do it. I don't know why the sight of him walking away from me yet again was enough to make me take another risk I hadn't before.

"It started with nightmares," I told him. "All my life I've had them. I've seen a hundred doctors, tried meditation and medication, and every sleep therapy you can imagine. Nothing works."

His shoulders settled a little, and his expression had softened when he faced me again. But there was no pity in his eyes. Only curiosity. It was enough to keep me talking, and suddenly the words gushed out, like a river rushing over its banks.

"It's always the same—or it was. I dream of drowning and wake up feeling guilty. Sometimes I dream of this place." I paused, gathered my courage. "I dreamed of this place before my uncle ever worked here. It's why I didn't want the job at first."

His hands were tucked into his pockets, but he didn't turn away from me. Nothing in his expression spoke of doubt. "Why'd you finally decide to accept it, then?"

I shrugged. "I was out of options. I'd lost my last two jobs because the nightmares were getting bad. I'd either oversleep and miss my shift or fall asleep during it. And my boyfriend— my ex— he was done, too." I laughed, dry and humorless. "There's only so many times you can get woken up from a dead sleep by someone screaming before you've had enough."

"He kicked you out?" Silas's brow creased.

"No." I shook my head. "But it was his place, and I knew we were over." I kept my voice light, to make it seem like it didn't bother me. "It happens," I admitted. "Sometimes the nightmares go away for a while, and I got complacent. I'll begin a new relationship or let people in, and just as I her comfortable, the dreams come roaring back. Like they can't leave me alone.

"It happened about a month ago with Matt," I explained. "I'd given up the room I'd been renting to move in with him. I'd promised myself that this time things would be okay. That the dreams were over. But they weren't. We'd barely been living together for a month before I started having the nightmares again. I'd wake up screaming night after night." I glanced up at him. "Eventually, he couldn't handle it. That's when I knew I was never going to outrun them. I accepted Leonard's offer and headed here, the one place I'd avoided since I learned it existed. Because I didn't have anywhere else to go." I looked up at him.

"Matt's a dick," he said flatly, his jaw tight.

I blinked at the anger in his voice. "He was a nice guy. A sweet guy."

"He was an idiot to let you go." Silas's eyes darkened. "Are you over him?"

I blinked surprised by his intensity. "I never really thought we would go anywhere," I admitted. "We were together because he felt safe. Easy. I thought maybe that could work."

"I can't say I'm sorry it didn't." His tone softened then. "Since you arrived here, are you still having the nightmares? Is that what happened last night?"

"Kind of." I swallowed the memory of the dream that had chased me out into the gardens. The scent of death and rot hung in the air. "Ever since I arrived here at Le Ciel, the dreams have been different, though."

"Different? How?" He was studying me, but I couldn't read anything but interest in his expression. There was no pity, no judgement in his eyes.

"More intense, for one."

He waited, patient and unblinking. "And?"

I took another long sip, and the scalding liquid warmed my throat and chest. "How much do you believe in what Mama Erzulie was talking about—evil spirits and witchcraft and all that?"

"I grew up around here, Lucy. 'All that,' as you put it, is just part of the fabric of life." He frowned thoughtfully. "I wouldn't exactly say I'm a believer, but I don't know that I'd discount it either."

I pressed my lips together, gathering my courage before I spoke again. "I think I'm starting to believe. More and more."

His expression didn't so much as shift. He simply waited for me to continue, and his lack of judgement, his patience, loosened my words even more.

"I think the nightmares—the other dreams, too—I think I'm dreaming about the past. About what happened here, on this land." I hunched over the mug, suddenly impossibly cold despite the balmy summer morning. "I'm being haunted by dreams about a past I shouldn't know about—about *people* I shouldn't know about."

"The girl in the picture Leonard found in Thisbe's cabin?"

I nodded.

"Leonard told me about that. You're sure it's her specifically you're dreaming about?"

"I wasn't at first, but now . . . yeah. I'm sure." I licked my bottom lip. "And lately, the dreams are starting to break through even in my waking. At first, I thought maybe coming here I could figure out why I've always had these nightmares, but lately? I feel like I'm losing my mind," I admitted as the first tear broke loose.

The bed dipped under his weight, and Silas wrapped his arms around me, pulling me into the hard planes of his body.

"*Shhh,*" he whispered into my hair as I rested my cheek against his broad chest.

I should have pulled away. I should have put distance between us before I got him any more tangled up in my mess. Instead, I looked up, intending to thank him. But a need simmered in his eyes that echoed my own. Before I could think about what a bad idea it was, I kissed him.

35

Silas froze when my lips touched his. His whole body went perfectly still, and at first, I thought he'd pull away. But then, with a soft groan, he pressed his mouth against mine, hungry and urgent, as he answered my question of a kiss with his own.

I already felt like a live wire from the vision Alex had shown me. He and Armantine together in her studio, her breasts bare to him, his mouth on her center, and his need so thick and potent it had sparked my own. But when Silas deepened the kiss, I was lost.

His hands framed my face, his fingers combing through my thick, wild curls as he pulled me in. His mouth opened, his tongue hot and demanding, and he devoured me.

Before I knew what I was doing, I'd turned and straddled him, my legs bracketed his hips, and his arousal was cradled against my own sensitive flesh. I moved, pressing myself against that hard ridge, needing something more than dreams, and was rewarded with another soft moan against my mouth as his hips bucked beneath me.

His hand moved to my breast, and the pressure there as he

cupped me, kneaded, had me aching against him as my own hands roamed over the strong curve of his shoulders, the well-defined planes of his chest. But I needed to be closer. I needed *more*. Our mouths tangled, a battle of will and want, as I slipped my hands under his shirt and felt his skin, hot and smooth and softly dusted with hair.

His breath hitched as my fingers ran over his nipple, and then his lips were on my neck, sucking gently as his hands moved lower to grab my ass. He pulled me so his arousal pressed into the cleft between my thighs even more, and need rocketed through me so sharp that I gasped. He nipped my neck in response, but his hands were moving again, up . . . up beneath my shirt. They gathered the thin cotton until it suddenly he pulled it up and over my head, and my breasts were bare to him. Only then did he pause.

For an endless moment, he pulled back and simply looked at me. His caramel eyes seemed to burn and his expression was hungry as his gaze locked on my naked breasts. Then his eyes lifted, and my breath hitched as his gaze locked with mine. Without ever looking away, he touched me. Softly. Tenderly. His fingers traced, feather light, over the curves of my breasts, as though he were memorizing the shape of them.

The memory of Alex doing this same thing to Armantine made everything about this moment somehow—sharper, more intense. My whole body ached, *wanted*. And it was almost too much to look into those honey-brown eyes as he watched me quiver under his hands.

I leaned my head on his shoulder, kissed his neck tenderly as he palmed my breasts and kneaded gently. When he twisted my aching nipple, it sent a bolt of heat and need straight to that place between my thighs, where I needed him most.

"Yes," I whispered, urging him on and grinding against his hard length until my sex ached. Until I could feel my own wetness dampening my shorts, and until I thought I might burst into flames from wanting—needing—more. Needing his skin against mine. Needing *everything.*

His grip tightened, and when he pinched my aching nipples again, harder now, the sharp burst of pleasure had me seeing stars. Suddenly, I was her again—Armantine—writhing under Alex's hands beneath a blue sky. I was myself, my body spinning tighter around the need Silas's hands were creating. I was there, with Silas, his hands and mouth stoking my need, setting fire to my skin. And I was with Alex, in the clearing. On the table of an overheated studio. Past and present crashing together, until I didn't know who I was, or where I ended or began.

Silas's hand moved up the leg of my cotton shorts, and his long fingers slipped against my wet flesh. Pleasure bolted through me, and I shifted to give him more access. In that instant, I thought of Alex, his fingers breaching the slit in Armantine's undergarments, but then it was Silas sliding his fingers against me, *into* me. Drawing me back to the present —to *him.*

His fingers were still inside of me, filling me and stretching me, when I began unfastening his belt. But suddenly, Silas withdrew his hand and laid me back. He paused only long enough to peel off his own shirt."

"I need to feel you against me," he said, his voice rough.

"Pants," I urged as his hand ran down my torso.

But he didn't obey. Instead, his fingers parted my slick folds before he cupped my sex again. I ground myself into him, and the heat of his broad palm made me feel like my need would burn me alive if I didn't have more of him against me. *All of him.* "Pants, Silas. Take off your damn pants."

That damn dimple of his flashed as he finally obeyed, lifting himself off the bed so he could finish unfastening his pants. I watched, my mouth dry and my body wound tight, wanting and impatient, as his trousers fell to the floor. His cock strained against his silky black boxer briefs. And then he rolled them down.

For a moment, he stood naked in my tiny home, taking up too much space, and simply let me look as he studied me in return. I wasn't sure what he could be seeing that darkened his eyes like that. But the way he was looking at me? I felt beautiful. I felt powerful, too.

I ran my gaze down over the sculpted planes of his chest, the tight muscles of his stomach, to where his heavy cock jutted free, long and hard. My breath caught when he grasped himself and stroked his strong fingers over the length of his erection. Once. Twice. His head lolled back as he tightened his hand tightened around his arousal, pumping slowly until the broad head glistened.

It took everything I had not to reach beneath the waistband of my thin cotton shorts and touch myself to relieve some of the almost painful need building there. But I let my need build as I waited. I wanted his hands on me. His skin against mine.

My eyes lifted back to his, and I didn't miss the satisfaction in his expression—or the wanting and need that echoed my own. His muscles bunched and moved beneath his smooth skin as he bent, retrieving his wallet—a condom—from the pocket.

But when he bent over, my gaze caught on one of the half-finished canvases behind him, the one I'd painted late at night, haunted by emerald green eyes and dreams of the past. It was as if Alex was watching me—watching *us*—and I don't know why that made me suddenly unsure. Suddenly unsteady.

There's somewhere else I need to be. Someone I need to help—

The thought came like a dousing of ice water, abrupt and far too immediate to ignore. I didn't even realize Silas had put the condom on until the bed dipped with his weight and he was shifting over me.

But his body brushing against mine brought me back to the present. Whatever guilt or fear I'd felt looking at the sight of

Alex's painted eyes faded with the heat of Silas's body rising over me. The heavy weight of his erection dragged against me, as he tugged my shorts down, leaving me bare to him. But then he paused, taking a long moment to simply look again. His gaze like fire as it settled on my breasts, my open thighs . . .

"Silas. . ." My voice was husky, a plea and a command all at once.

Then he was nudging my legs farther apart, cradling arousal against the slickness of my sex. His eyes had gone dark with need, but he held himself back, a question in his expression as he waited for some sign it was okay—that we were okay.

In response, I tightened my arms, pulling his face down to me, so I could capture his mouth with my own as I wrapped a leg up over his hips, anchoring him against me, until there was nothing between us but the need and wanting driving use both to the edge. I lifted my hips, urging him on, and this time, he didn't hesitate. With a slow, sure thrust, he filled me.

My fingers dug into his back, and I gasped, holding him tight as my inner walls quivered at the intrusion. At the over-whelming feeling of him sheathed to the hilt. His hips moved as he adjusted, and I gasped from the sheer pleasure of it.

"Are you okay?" he asked. He withdrew a little, checking on me.

"Perfect." I nipped at his neck. "Don't you dare stop."

This time his expression wasn't so guarded. "Yes, ma'am," he said, giving another slow, torturous thrust until he was completely seated inside me again.

I'd already been wound tight, dizzy with need because of the vision Alex had shown me, but the heat of Silas, the feeling of him inside of me, filling me, was almost too much. If I'd wandered out into the night feeling empty and lost, now I felt anchored. Full and complete in a way I'd never experienced before. And that thought probably should have scared me— should have absolutely *terrified* me. But he thrusted again, and every thought was replaced with a spiraling pleasure and a need so sharp it could slice me in two.

His hips moved, slow and steady, making my body hum. I was so close to tumbling over some invisible ledge, so close to shattering.

"Please," I begged, only halfway aware my words echoed Armantine's. I no longer cared if her desire had sparked my own. I only cared that it was Silas with me, real and true and so good at what he was doing that I would probably die from it.

"God, Lucy. You feel so good," he said, thrusting faster now. "So damn tight and wet. But if you keep clawing at my back, I'm not going to last long."

"Good." I bit the curve of his shoulder and angled my hips to take him deeper. "I don't want slow. Not this time."

I needed hard and fast and reckless. I needed him to anchor me to this world and push away every fear, every nightmare and memory that threatened to pull me into a past that wasn't my own.

"So you're saying there'll be a next time," he asked, a smile in his voice as his fingers tweaked my aching nipple.

I gasped and then smiled against his neck. "Depends on how this time ends."

"Then I better make it good." He kissed me, his hips driving into me, pushing my need higher and higher until he shifted his body so that every time he thrust, he rubbed against my clit. My head fell back and my body tensed, as I came closer and closer to the edge, until suddenly I started to break apart.

My world shattered, and my body went right along with it, breaking into a million pieces as my release careened through me. I was only barely aware of Silas still thrusting as my muscles clench around him, but his low moan in my ear told me he was there as well, tumbling over the same cliff. I held on as he pushed into me, my arms wrapped around his broad, strong back, feeling the play of his muscles beneath my hand. His breathing was heavy as his movement slowed, and with a final thrust, he collapsed onto me.

For a minute, we lay like that. Still. Sated. Completely at peace. Even with his weight pinning me and our bodies pressed together, I didn't have my usual moment of panic. There was no room left in my brain to think about dreams or ghosts or some other couple's stolen moments. In that moment, there was only room for him.

When he finally shifted to roll off me, I felt like whimpering. I watched him cross the room and dispose of the condom, but my gaze caught again on the canvases with the bright green eyes. I shivered a little, though I wasn't sure if it was from the loss of Silas's body heat or the sense that those painted eyes had watched everything, *seen* everything.

When Silas returned to bed, he pulled me into his side, spooning me against him. "Where are you right now?" he asked.

I looked up at him. "What do you mean?"

"You were right here with me, but just now . . . you weren't." He nuzzled his mouth against my neck. "What are you thinking about? Where did you go?"

"I wasn't planning on any of this." My gaze trailed back to the eyes watching from the incomplete canvas. "I wasn't planning on you."

"Do you regret it?" he asked, his voice careful.

Maybe I should have. I'd fallen into bed with a man I barely knew, one who lived his life in the stratosphere, when I was stuck firmly on the ground. He was stable, successful, and so damn *good* I wanted to cry. He was trying to make a difference in this world, and I was just trying to make it through the next day. I should have heard the usual warning bells going off, the ones that warned me to back away before the nightmares returned. I should have felt absolute panic.

But I didn't. Lying there in his arms, my body still tingling from the release that had just torn through me, all I felt was calm.

I turned away from the watchful emerald eyes to face him and shook my head. "No, Silas. I don't regret anything."

"*Will* you regret it?"

I rolled over and smiled softly. "That depends on what comes next, I guess."

Relief flickered through his expression. He studied me, his eyes serious. "What does come next, Lucy?" He brushed a stray curl back from my face. "I'm not going to pretend I don't like you. Or that I didn't feel an immediate pull toward you the first time I saw you. Hell, I couldn't stop thinking about you, even after you said someone else's name. There's something real here, between us. I feel it, clear to my bones. I don't know how you feel, but this is something different for me. I want to see where it goes. But I know you're starting over. I know you might not be ready, so it's your call."

But it was too late for me to back out now or put on the brakes. My dreams might still be haunting me, but now that I'd had Silas, I couldn't simply give him up.

"I'm a mess, Silas." I sighed. "You don't deserve a mess."

"What if I want one?" He touched my cheek tenderly and then leaned in to brush his lips softly against mine. "For the record, I don't think you're a mess. But let me in, Lucy. Let me help you."

"I'm not sure you can." The truth of those words made my skin go cold. "I'm not sure anyone can," I whispered.

I started to untangle myself from him, but he caught my arm gently, pulled me back into his.

"I'm not going anywhere, and neither are you. *Tell me.*"

I could have said no. I could have kicked him out and built my walls back up, but my body was still humming with the pleasure we'd just shared and his arms were still around me, pinning me to bed, to him—to what was real. So, god help me, I told him everything. Slowly, painstakingly, I explained my dreams, painting a picture of Alex and Armantine and the past they shared—a past I shouldn't know about.

But I stopped short of telling him I'd seen Alex, that I'd spoken with him outside my dreams. I wasn't quite ready to admit I'd seen a ghost.

"Alex," he said, frowning. "He's from your dreams? Not one of your exes?"

I shook my head. "Not an ex. Just a figment of my overactive subconscious."

"I don't know whether to be relieved he's not real competition or worried I'll never match up to your dream man."

"It's not like that," I protested.

But I wasn't so sure that was the truth. Alex wasn't real. Or, if he was real, he wasn't alive. At best he was a figment of my imagination. At worst, he was some kind of haunting. There was no future between us. He couldn't complete with Silas. And yet, living in Armantine's skin night after night? I couldn't help but feel something for him, this pull to him that I still couldn't explain and couldn't quite be rid of. This guilt that I' d just been with another man while Alex Jourdain was on my mind.

"I don't know why any of this is happening. I don't understand why I knew Le Ciel before I ever knew *of* Le Ciel," I confessed. "I don't know what my connection is to this place or why everything has gotten so much worse since I arrived. I'm sorry I didn't tell you this before. But I didn't know how to explain. We'd only just met, and I *liked* you. I didn't want to like you, but I couldn't seem to help myself. And then after Saint John's Eve . . ."

"I was an ass," he said softly. "I pushed you too fast and then blamed you for not being ready. My ego got in the way of my head."

"You scare me, Silas."

"Me?" He looked surprised.

"You make me feel more steady and real than I've ever felt. And that scares the shit out of me."

"Why does that scare you?"

"Because I think you're right," I admitted. "There is something between us. But I'm terrified I'm going to screw it up if I don't figure myself out first. Whatever's happening, whatever is causing these dreams, I need to find a way to bring it to an end. Or it's just going to keep haunting me."

He leaned in, until his forehead was pressed against mine. "You don't have to do this alone, you know?"

Before I could respond, his discarded pants began buzzing on the floor. He ignored it at first, but when they buzzed again after the second missed call, he groaned and rolled out of bed. I tugged the sheet up around myself as he retrieved his phone and punched up the voice mail. He still wasn't wearing anything, and I couldn't help but admire the lean strength of his body, the smooth expanse of his light brown skin. His very presence made my small home feel even smaller, somehow, even as he made me feel more expansive.

"Shit," he said, listening. He reached for his boxers as he held the phone to his ear. When he was done listening, he set it aside and started putting on his clothes. "I'm sorry, Luce, but I have to go."

"Is something wrong?" I wrapped the sheet around myself.

"I'm not exactly sure yet," he said. "Something about the property we just acquired—Thisbe's place. Leonard and Byron are out there now. I have to go deal with it." He stopped short of fastening his pants, his hungry gaze taking me in. "I'm sorry. I want to stay, but—"

"It's fine," I lied, staving off the stab of disappointment. A part of me wanted to beg him to stay. I felt steadier than I had in ages, but I'd never been the type to beg. And the last thing I needed was for Leonard to find out Silas hadn't been available because he'd been in my bed.

My cheeks warmed at the thought, at the memory of Silas's hands on my skin—his body against mine.

I watched as he finished dressing.

He slipped his phone into his back pocket and came over to the bed, bracketing me with his arms. "Look, I have to go now, but we're not finished talking about any of this yet, okay?"

"Silas—"

"We're *not*," he repeated, and no judgement, no pity clouded his eyes. "You don't have to do this alone, Lucy. I believe you, and I want to help you." He kissed me, his mouth opening against mine until I couldn't help but kiss him back.

He nipped at my lower lip before pulling away. "We're going to figure this out. *Together.* You're going to take today off and try to get some rest, and when I get back tonight, we're going to figure out a plan."

"You don't have to—" I started to say, but he silenced my protests again with his lips.

I should have pushed him away, but I leaned into his kiss instead. Suddenly, nothing else mattered but the warmth of his mouth, the taste of him on my tongue. If anything waited for me outside the small, snug confines of this cabin, it no longer mattered.

When he finally pulled back, he gave me a determined look. "I just found you, Lucy. I'm not giving you up to some ghost."

36

T didn't exactly follow his instructions and take the day off. I stayed in bed for a little while longer, until the bliss of the orgasm died away. But then, I started getting antsy. I had to do something.

I'm not giving you up to some ghost.

Silas's words repeated in my mind as I went through the actions of showering and getting myself breakfast. He was willing to fight for us—for *me*—and I needed to do the same.

I'd spent my life avoiding getting too serious, because every time I did, the nightmares would rush back and destroy whatever relationship I'd built. Maybe Silas was right. Maybe Matt had been a dick for turning away instead of understanding, but I wasn't completely innocent. I'd spent so long pushing everything I was dealing with down until it eventually erupted and destroyed everything.

There was something different about Silas, though. Maybe it was just the intensity of a new relationship, but instinctively I knew that if I let my past—my dreams—ruin a chance to find out what was between us, I'd regret it. I was tired of letting my

246 | CELIA CROSBY

dreams destroy my waking. I couldn't claim any kind of future as long as I was still living in some distant past.

I didn't wait for Silas to get back. He'd texted me when he was done out at Thisbe's place, but he had to put out some fires with the Foundation.

Maybe I should have waited, but Silas's belief in us made me bold. I'd told him everything—well, nearly everything—and it hadn't changed how he saw me, or how much he seemed to *want* me. It was enough to make me hope that maybe I wouldn't always be alone with my nightmares. But as much as I might want to lean into Silas, this wasn't his fight.

I didn't want it to be his fight.

Of course, it was just my luck that the sultry heat of the overcast early morning had turned to rain by the time I headed out. The pelting rain splattered against my skin and destroyed my curls, but I ignored it as I hurried across the narrow field to the grove of trees surrounding Thisbe's cottage. In the gray haze of the rainy morning, the worn façade of the decrepit building seemed even more faded. The coppery plink of raindrops hitting the metal roof beat out an uneasy rhythm.

All around the cabin, shards of glass now gleamed in the overcast light. Someone had cut down every last bottle that had hung from the trees and smashed them on the ground.

Somehow I wasn't surprised to see Alex waiting for me on the porch, his golden hair a spot of brightness against the dreary scene.

"You shouldn't be here, Lucy." His expression was like flint. "I already explained—"

"We're going to finish this, Alex." I hugged my damp raincoat closer as I mounted the steps. "Whatever's keeping you here, we're going to find it." I hesitated at the doorway. "Have you ever been in there?"

"Once. Long ago." His jaw was set in a hard line, and his

brows were bunched together. "Until recently, I couldn't even mount the steps."

Probably the red dust Piers had wiped away. "Well, let's get this over with."

"You don't have to," he said, his eyes betraying his fear.

"But I do," I argued. "You and me, we're tied together somehow, and I think it has to do with whatever is keeping you from moving on. *I* need to move on, Alex. I've been haunted by this place for too long. It's time."

Pain flickered in his expression, but after a moment he nodded.

As though he could have stopped me anyway.

A chill skittered down my spine as I stepped into the musty darkness of the cabin, but this time the sense of foreboding was stronger. If I hadn't been so determined, I probably would have turned around and left. I got the sense Alex felt the same way; it took him even longer before he finally followed me across the threshold.

With the shutters closed and locked, the interior was too dim to see clearly, so I used my phone's flashlight. The walls were now covered with graffiti. All around the entry, strange runelike symbols had been inscribed in circles and rows, and I couldn't ignore that the feeling of foreboding was stronger.

"We shouldn't be here," Alex said through gritted teeth. "Can't you feel it?"

I could, but the memory of Silas's mouth against my skin, his determination to stand by me, made me bold.

"I'm not leaving. Do you feel anything else, anything that could help us figure out what we're looking for?" I waited for his direction. "The sooner we find it, the sooner we can get out of here, Alex."

He must have realized there was no arguing with me. "This way," he said finally, motioning toward the back room, where we'd found the crumbling coat and the box with the primitive doll.

I followed him carefully through the dark corridors. The markings continued through the building, but the dank mustiness of the entry gave way to a sharper, more cloying scent that reminded me of old pennies. *Blood.* The markings weren't paint. They'd been drawn in blood.

When we came to the back room, Alex pulled up short. "I can't go any farther." He pointed down. "I think that's some kind of spell."

I peered around him. The carcass of a snake had been flayed open and stretched across the threshold of the room. Someone had nailed it in place. *No wonder Silas ran off in a hurry.*

But I needed to hurry too. It was likely the Foundation would have someone patrolling the place in case whoever did this returned for more.

My stomach churned as I stepped over the bloody remains, and the feeling of dread only increased when I entered the small back room where we'd found the portrait of Armantine a few weeks before. Alex remained, still as a statue, on the other side of the threshold.

"Where should we start looking?"

"I remember this." He stared into the darkened room. Then he shook his head, like he was clearing his thoughts. "There, I think." He gestured toward the fireplace.

I bent to look, but the hearth was empty. "I don't see anything."

"There's something there," he insisted. "I can feel it. Look again? Please."

Carefully, I ran my fingers along the stones that made up the fireplace. "I don't think—" And then I felt something.

One stone was larger than the others, smooth as onyx and round. And if I pressed, it wobbled a bit. It took some work to pry it up, but eventually it came free.

When I lifted the stone away, it revealed a small depression that held a small loosely tied sack, darkened with age and grime. I didn't have time to open it before Alex called to me.

"Someone's coming, Lucy."

Floorboards creaked in the hallway a second later. "Alex, we should—" But he was already gone.

Chloe appeared in the doorway. "Lucy?"

I jumped up. "Chloe?" My heart was pounding, and I brought one hand up to my chest, like I was trying to keep it contained. "Wow. God, you scared me."

"You're not supposed to be here." She frowned, her brows bunching over her dark eyes. If she was disgusted or creeped out by the dead snake or bloody runes around her, she didn't show it.

"I was, uh . . . looking for something I lost the other day—a lens cap for my camera." I tucked the small package into the back of my waistband, under my jacket, as I spoke. It was surprisingly warm against my cool, rain-dampened skin. "What are you doing here? Are you on-site today?"

She ignored the question. "Did you find it?"

"Find what?"

"What you were looking for." Her voice was emotionless.

"Oh—Not yet." I tried my best to look disappointed.

Chloe narrowed her eyes. "You need to go. You're not supposed to be here."

"Chloe, are you okay?" I asked, inwardly cursing Alex for abandoning me.

She just stared at me.

"Look, I'm sorry that I overstepped the other day. I shouldn't have assumed I could help when we don't really know each other that well. I didn't mean to upset you—"

"I'm fine," she said, her voice flat and emotionless.

"Okay. That's good." We stood in a tense silence for far longer than I would have liked.

"You need to go, Lucy."

"Right. I know. I was about to leave."

She backed away from the doorway, so I could step over the dead snake again, and then she followed me down the hall and back out onto the porch.

I wasn't sure what I wanted to say, what I even could say. No one at the Foundation would be happy with me poking around in an active crime scene.

"Maybe we could not mention this to Silas?" I asked, glancing in her direction.

She stared at me. "You need to stay away from this place, Lucy. Nothing here concerns you." Then she pulled the hood of her burgundy raincoat over her hair. "You'd best make sure you remember what I told you."

I'd hate to see you end up like her. She'd been talking about Shaunda, and at the time I thought she was probably just worried about me, with a killer on the loose. But now I wondered if she wasn't telling me something more.

The downpour had somehow gotten even stronger while we were inside the cottage. The usual Louisiana heat was turning it into a swampy mist, which gave the entire grove a heavy, unearthly quality. Chloe walked away, a dark red smear against the even darker forest. Then she stepped through the tree line and disappeared.

I sank onto the porch, my legs no longer able to hold me, and leaned back against the door. I pulled out the package, which had grown almost hot against my back, and examined it. "Alexandre Jourdain, this better have been worth it," I said to no one but the rain.

37

The rhythmic swish of the wipers helped calm me as I navigated Leonard and Sam's Volvo through the sparse New Orleans traffic. After getting back to my place and changing into some dry clothes, I'd finally worked up the courage to open the package I'd found at Thisbe's cabin. Inside was a tiny carved figure with faded rust-red string circling its neck. It had the same strange carvings as the other figure—the same symbols that had been carved into Lila's body. But where that other effigy had looked like a starfish, this figure was clearly carved to resemble a man.

It was an ugly, grotesque little thing, all gnarled and blackened. The string tied around its neck gave it the appearance of being strangled. When I took it out of the sack for the first time, I dropped it because of the way it had pulsed warmly in my hands.

When I picked it up again, I knew it wasn't my imagination —the thing really was pulsating with heat. Turning it over in my hand, I looked for an explanation, but it defied logic. Eventually, it grew so warm that I had to set it down. Alex had asked me to find this, but he'd never reappeared after Chloe left me at Thisbe's cabin. Though I'd called for him at the pond, he stayed away. Which meant I was left to deal with the strange figure on my own.

Alex believed something was keeping him on the land, tying him to Thisbe's cabin. Was this it? I probably needed help to figure it out, but Piers didn't answer my text and I didn't want to sit around just waiting all day for Silas to get done with whatever meetings he had to ask him. In the end, I decided to talk to the only other person who might know something— Mama Erzulie.

It took me a few wrong turns before I found the street in the Quarter where her shop was located. By then, the summer rain had slowed and the air was thick with humidity. I hesitated outside her door, briefly considered heading over to the Foundation's offices and finding Silas instead. But after Chloe's reaction to finding me at Thisbe's place, I decided against that plan. I needed to understand as much as I could about what I was dealing with before the Foundation swept the strange effigy beyond my reach, so I set my shoulders and walked into her shop.

The same scent of flowers and sage perfumed the air. Chimes tinkled as the door closed behind me, and Mama Erzulie's voice rang out from the back.

"Just a minute! I'm coming, I'm com—" Her face lit. "Lucy! You finally came to see me." But her gaze flicked down to the bag I was carrying, and her brows drew together. "What'd you do, child? What did you bring me?"

I swallowed hard as I grasped the bag more tightly. "I need your advice about something."

She pursed her lips. "I see you do. Come on back and show me what you've gotten yourself into."

I followed her to the back of the building. The shop was narrow, but it was deep, and the hall eventually opened into another room, this one even larger than the shop's showroom.

The back room was as bright as the entryway, but it was more comfortable. Against one wall, a low sofa was piled high with Caribbean-bright pillows. Two deep chairs in a muted plum flanked the couch.

"Sit." She gestured to the couch.

I eased myself into the plush cushions, while she rattled around on the other side of the room and produced two mismatched, steaming mugs filled with a liquid that smelled like a spring bouquet. She handed me one and then perched on the edge of the chair, like a queen holding court.

"Let's see the trouble you brought with you," she commanded.

I took the small package out of my bag, carefully unwrapped it, and showed her the tiny figure. As before, it pulsed in my hands as I set it on the low coffee table between us.

Mama Erzulie didn't bother to hide her shock. Slowly picked up the charm up, holding it delicately between two fingers. "Where'd you get this, child?"

I hesitated for a moment, not sure how much of the truth I should tell her. Alex didn't trust this woman, Chloe had stopped trusting her, and Mina had never trusted her. "I found it," I said, settling for vague.

"*Where?*"

"I'd rather not say."

She studied me for a moment. "And I'd rather you not tell me no lies, so I suppose we'll leave it be. For now."

"What is it?" I asked.

She put the figure back down softly, like she was afraid to jostle it too much. "It ain't nothing good, I'll tell you that much." Her unease filled the air, matching my own.

"I know that. Something about it doesn't feel right." I didn't only mean because of its strange warmth.

"There ain't *nothing* right about that little bit of juju." Her voice grew serious. "You're in deeper than I suspected, if you're messing with magic like this."

"I don't want to mess with anything. I just want to make it go away. Can you tell me what it is?"

"It's a binding charm," she said, her expression still broadcasting her discomfort.

I looked at the strange figure. "What does it bind?"

"Well, binding charms can do lots of things. Some help people focus by binding their thoughts from drifting around. Other kinds keep things where they supposed to be. This one is made for a darker purpose, though. It's intended for people."

"You can bind a person?" I thought of Alex stuck on the plantation.

"Of course. How do you think those love charms people are always asking for work?" Her brows drew together. "This wasn't meant to bind a body, though. This one here—it's meant for a soul."

I wanted to reject her explanation, but I already knew the truth. I'd seen Alex, hadn't I? "Why would someone do that?"

"Any number of reasons, though people who deal in black magics don't necessarily need rational ones." Mama Erzulie paused thoughtfully and took a sip from her mug. "A person might want revenge. Or maybe they just want someone to suffer."

"You mean, by making someone a ghost?"

"A little bit, but ghosts have a choice. They hang around because they're trying to finish something they left undone. The soul that's bound with a charm like this, it doesn't have any choice. Never did."

"You mean, it's just trapped, forever?"

She let out a great sigh. "Well, now, forever's a mighty long time. Magic like this, powerful as it might be, usually doesn't last much longer than the person who cast it."

"But then once the person who cast the spell died, the

trapped soul would be free?" I asked, thinking of Alex and wondering how this charm fit into his story.

Mama Erzulie nodded.

It didn't make sense. If my dreams were right, whoever had trapped him should have been dead and gone long ago. Alex should have moved on already.

"But this one? The magic's still working," Mama Erzulie explained, frowning. "The heat you feel there? That's a warning."

"You mean, whoever made this—they're still around?"

She eyed me. "Looks like, don't it?"

If whoever had made this was still alive, it had to have been made recently. And if that was the case, I was even more confused about how it was tied to Alex. "Is there any way somebody could keep another person's spell going?"

Mama Erzulie pursed her lips a bit, thoughtful. "Anything in this world's a possibility, child." She shook her head. "But that isn't likely. Each person's magic is their own."

"It doesn't make sense," I said, more to myself than to her. It wasn't possible for someone to have bound Alex almost two hundred years ago and still be around for the charm to work today.

"Magic as dark as that doesn't need sense," Mama Erzulie said. "You best watch yourself, child. Someone wicked enough to perpetrate some soul-stealing like that isn't anybody you want to be messing with, and souls trapped in the in-between can sometimes be as dangerous as the person who trapped them. A soul is wanting for a body. You best be careful he doesn't try yours on for size."

I didn't miss the "he"—she knew. She'd seen Alex. She must have immediately recognized him for what he was.

"How dangerous is this thing right now?" I asked, ignoring her comment.

"To you? Probably not very. Bad energy like that isn't

anything I'd want to mess with, but the more important question is who created it? Now, *that* person would be mighty dangerous. I'd want to steer clear of them for sure. If I were you? I'd steer clear of the whole thing."

"I don't know if I can." Not if the charm was connected to my dreams. Not if I had a chance to finally stop them. "Can the binding be broken?"

"You can destroy the charm, sure enough. Destroy the charm, destroy the spell. But if you do that, the person who made the charm might know." She shook her head. "I don't think you're anywhere close to ready for that."

"How would I destroy it?" I asked.

"You aren't listening, Lucy. You're not even *close* to being ready to deal with this kind of darkness. You best leave it here with me. I'll take care of it." Her voice was calm, but she seemed too eager to take the charm from me.

"No. I can't. It doesn't belong to me." Technically, it belonged to Le Ciel and the Foundation, so that much was true at least.

For a moment I didn't think she would let it be, but then she sighed. "You're sure enough on your way." She shook her head and motioned me to follow her.

I scooped up the figure and hurried back down the hall after her. She began mixing some of her herbs and flowers in a small pouch, measuring precisely as she went. When she was finished, she tied it off with a white piece of ribbon and offered it to me.

"When you're ready—and you make good and sure you know what you're doing before you start—you burn that little man with this."

I took the pouch from her and examined it.

"It won't bite you, child." She laughed. "That's only a bit of fennel, bloodroot, and hyssop. Nothing at all to hurt you there. Those is meant for purity and protection."

"Protection?" I looked up at her.

"Just in case."

I didn't want to ask what else I might need protection from. "How much do I owe you for the—" I wasn't sure what the little pouch was called.

"The gris-gris," she told me. "And it's no charge, as long as you promise to be safe."

"I promise." I tucked the small pouch into my bag with the figure. "Thanks. I really appreciate this."

"You got a long way to go." She considered me a moment. "But I think you're gonna do okay in the end."

I sighed. "One can only hope."

She smiled warmly. "Hope can only take you so far—just like fate. The rest is gonna be up to you."

38

The drive back to Le Ciel gave me time to think. If Mama Erzulie was right, the effigy I'd found in the cabin was likely the binding charm that tied Alex to Le Ciel. If I destroyed it, there shouldn't be anything keeping him in this time or place. He'd be free, and maybe so would I.

I still didn't understand how I was connected to Alex and Armantine. I didn't know why fate had chosen me, directed me to this moment. But if I had the means to free him—and to end this—I would.

The only question remaining for me was about Silas. Technically, the tiny figure belonged to him—or to the Foundation. I'd seen how Leonard reacted when Mama Erzulie suggested he destroy the other voodoo doll, and I couldn't imagine any of the Foundation's trustees would allow anyone to destroy this one.

I considered telling Silas about it. But I knew how important preserving the past was to him What if he wouldn't let me destroy the charm? Alex might never be free, and neither would I. We'd never have a chance at a real future together.

By the time I returned to the plantation, I'd made up my mind.

But all those thoughts were forgotten when I pulled into the main gate to Le Ciel and saw the flashing lights of an ambulance. I parked Leonard's car haphazardly near Silas's Audi and jumped out as Piers was stepping through the front doors.

"Is everything okay?" By the look on his face, it wasn't. "What's going on?"

"It's Silas," Piers said. "He collapsed a little while ago. They're in there working on him now."

I started toward the offices, but Piers snagged my arm. "You need to stay out here."

Mina emerged from the building a few minutes later. She was talking to someone on her cell phone, and when she saw Piers and me waiting, she headed our way.

"Is Silas okay?" I asked as soon as she hung up the call.

"We're not sure yet," she said, her expression tense. "They're trying to get him to wake up before they move him."

Panic clawed at me. "But he's going to be okay."

Mina gave me a hug, enveloping me in her amber- and- herb scent. "I know you two are close," she said before releasing me. "We just have to wait."

It felt like hours before they finally wheeled Silas out. But he wasn't awake. His eyes were closed, and an oxygen mask covered the bottom half of his face. They were moving too fast, too urgently for him to truly be okay.

I rushed toward the gurney, but the EMTs pushed me back. I wasn't a wife or even a girlfriend. I wasn't anything to him.

"I don't know if he has any family," I told them. "His mom died a few years back. I don't know if he has anyone else . . . "

But they still wouldn't tell me anything, and they definitely wouldn't let me ride along.

Mina took my hand in hers. "He'll be okay, baby. He's stable now, or they wouldn't be moving him. We just need to let them do their jobs."

"I can't just sit here and wait. I need to go. We were supposed to talk—" My voice broke, and I swallowed to keep from crying.

"The Foundation will keep us updated," Mina said softly. "If I hear anything, I'll be call you directly. For now, you need to go home and get some rest."

"Come on, Luce." Piers's arm was around me. "Let me walk you home."

39

Because of the weather, the grounds were quiet and mostly empty as Piers walked me back to my cabin. Neither of us spoke, until we were nearly at my door.

"Have you heard from Chloe?" I asked, glancing over at him. I wasn't sure whether I was asking because I was worried about her or worried she'd said something to Silas.

His jaw tensed. "She's needed some space after what happened with Shaunda."

The lack of details told me everything I needed to know. It wasn't just me she was being distant with. But I wasn't sure how I could help her, not until I figured out my own problems.

When we reached my cabin, I pulled out my key, but I didn't get it in the lock before my gaze caught on shards of blue on the ground. The bottle Mina had gifted me that first night had been shattered into a million pieces.

"Are you going to be okay?" Piers asked.

I nodded. "I'm just worried."

"He'll be okay, Lucy," Piers promised. "He's a young guy in good shape, and he's stable. He's going to come out of this."

I pressed my lips together to keep myself from saying

anything. I didn't trust my voice not to give away everything I was feeling.

Piers waited until I was safely inside, but I finally convinced him to go. He was worried. I could tell he didn't want to leave, but I needed to be alone. I had a piece of evil in my bag, a million questions on my mind, and the fear that somehow whatever had happened to Silas was connected to everything else.

Inside my small cabin, the air still held the faint scent of something warm and woodsy—the ghost of Silas's cologne.

Maybe I should have waited for him, trusted him to help me.

Outside my window, thunder rolled in the distance, but the gray sky hadn't opened up again yet. The day felt as oppressive as the weight I'd been carrying with me my entire life.

I took the charm from the bag, and it pulsed hot and angry against my skin again. I didn't want this to touch Silas. Maybe it was wrong to destroy the little doll, but I knew instinctively it wasn't any kind of past that needed to be preserved.

Grabbing some matches from a drawer, I considered using the sink, but my cabin was too small to risk burning something as potentially dangerous as the charm. Instead, I grabbed the coffee can, emptied the grounds into a bowl, and took it and the matches with me.

The clouds were ominous in the west as I walked away from the quiet row of employee cabins, and I could smell more rain in the air. I didn't have a real plan for where I was going at first, but I headed toward the line of trees to the east almost out of instinct.

The clearing was empty when I arrived. I wasn't sure why I expected Alex to be waiting for me here, but I was almost disappointed he wasn't. My bag felt too heavy for the small bit of wood and thread it contained. Thunder echoed in the distance again. I had to hurry.

The tree. It felt right somehow to do it there, where so many of my dreams had brought me. I'd destroy the charm and, with any luck, leave the past there in the clearing, where it belonged.

The branches rustled in the unsettled air above me as I knelt in the damp grass and arranged my supplies. The empty coffee tin was just large enough to hold the gnarled figure and the bundle of herbs Mama Erzulie had made for protection. I hoped there was enough space for it to burn. I lit a match and held it to the gris-gris, waiting for the fabric to ignite. It began to smolder, but it took two more matches before it finally started to burn.

"What are you doing, Lucy?"

I turned. Alex stood behind me, watching with a guarded expression.

"Where have you been?" I asked as the strange earthiness of the smoke from the gris-gris filtered through the air around me.

He was staring at the coffee can. "What is that?"

"It's the charm we found."

His eyes were wide. "You're destroying it?"

I nodded. "I'm finishing this, Alex. Once and for all."

The fire inside the tin was burning in earnest now, and thick black smoke was pouring out. The air around us thrummed with unsteady energy, and suddenly a gust whipped through the clearing.

"Lucy," Alex warned, taking a step toward me. But then he paused, grimacing as though in pain. "This isn't safe. If the witch discovers—" Again his expression flashed with pain.

"It doesn't matter." The wind was picking up more now, and the energy in the air felt almost electric, like lightning before it strikes. "You'll be free. We both will be."

"Lucy—" He reached for me, but air had whipped itself into a frenzy, and I couldn't hear the rest.

I used my body to shield the small fire inside the can, coughing when the acrid black smoke filled my nose and clawed at my throat. But I couldn't let the fire go out. Not until the charm was destroyed.

Thunder crashed overhead, and the first drops of rain fell, icy and sharp against my overheated skin. But still I shielded the fire. As the tiny figure was consumed, it glowed bright within the night-dark smoke.

"Lucy!" Alex screamed for me, but everything felt impossibly far away. The rain on my back. The smoke burning my nostrils, filling me. And then the world flipped on its head, and I was pulled under.

40

Thisbe's house stands in the shadows of the grove. The day is hot, still, and yet the bottles hanging from the trees clink together, stirred by an impossible wind. I shouldn't have come here. I should have stayed far, far away.

And yet . . .

There is no choice but to go forward. Onward.

I am approaching the steps when the old woman appears in the darkened doorway. *Thisbe.* She knew I would come, and now she watches me with cloudy eyes.

"You back so soon?" Her smile is vicious with delight. "Greedy little thing, ain't you?"

"I've changed my mind." I clasp the locket in a shaking hand. "Please. You must help me. You must undo it."

I've made a mistake. A terrible mistake.

The smile is gone now, but still, the old woman looks strangely pleased. "What's done is done, child. I warned you to be sure before you worked the spell." The bottles rustle, clinking an uneven rhythm, and Thisbe gives me—Armantine—a slick, sickening sneer. But I don't run. I promise the moon and stars and my entire being, and I beg.

"Get off your knees," Thisbe says finally. "Come on inside."

The cabin is cooler than the day outside, but the air is murky and filled with the cloying sweetness of some herb smoldering on the fire.

"Sit." She points to a low three-legged stool by the table.

I do as she commands, my hands still clasped in a half-prayerful hope. She will help me. She will fix the mistake I made, and he will never, ever have to know.

Thisbe taps one craggy arthritic finger thoughtfully on her chin. "You can't just undo a love charm, girl. But there might be something for your problem. It'd be dangerous, but if you're willing to try . . ."

"I am. I'll do whatever I must."

"Magic like this can' t be worked from afar. You got to get me close enough for it do any good at all."

"How close?"

Thisbe's mouth curves up into something that should've been a smile, and suddenly, I know. She—Armantine—doesn't know, but I know. Thisbe will never free him.

"Close enough to touch," the old witch says.

41

"Lucy?" The voice pulled at a memory, but I couldn't quite reach it. "Come on, now."

A sharp pat on my cheek had me opening my eyes to a dark sky. No. Not a dark sky. A broad black umbrella. Piers was crouched above me, and for a moment I was Lila, bloodied and broken, looking up at the men who'd found her. And then I came back to myself.

Groaning, I tried to sit up, but the world tilted wickedly. The sharpness of the smoke was still in my nose, still thick in my throat. It clung to my clothes.

"What the hell are you doing out here?" Piers asked, helping me to my feet.

My clothes were soaked with rain, and my hair was plastered against my cheek. Alex was nowhere to be found. The smoldering can was still lying nearby in the grass, and the hot metal singed my finger when I touched it.

I hissed a curse before trying again, more carefully.

"Were you *burning* something out here?" Piers asked, his tone more incredulous than angry. "Lucy!" His hands were on my arms, trying to pull me away from the can.

"I need to make sure it's gone." I jerked free of his grip. "I need to make sure it's over."

He put up his hands and stepped back, but I could feel him watching me.

Finally, I righted the can and saw the charred remains inside. Nothing but ash was left. "You didn't put this out, did you?" I needed to be sure.

Piers shook his head. "I didn't touch it. It was already like that when I found you."

"Good," I said, more to myself than to him. "That's good."

"Lucy . . ." His voice was softer now, coaxing. "We need to get you inside. The storm's almost here, and you're already soaked to the bone."

I didn't fight him as he helped me up, but I considered taking the can with me. I wasn't sure if there was something more I should do with the remaining ashes—Mama Erzulie hadn't said.

"You're burning up," Piers said, pressing the back of his broad hand against my cheek. "How long have you been out here?"

I had no idea. The sky had been an ominous gray all day. It could have been twenty minutes since I started the fire or it could have been hours ago. "I don't know," I mumbled, the words strangely sluggish on my tongue.

Loose curls trembled before my face, and I frowned—I was shivering.

"Come on," he said, tugging me along. "Let's get you inside."

As he walked me slowly back toward my cabin, I was only barely aware he'd pulled out his phone. "Yeah, Leonard? Can you or Sam come over to Lucy's place? She's going to need some help."

42

I don't remember much of what happened next.

Piers managed to get me back to my cabin, and I was vaguely aware that Leonard and Sam took over at some point and put me into dry clothes. They helped me into bed, and someone kept watch over me. Once, I thought I smelled the familiar woodsy scent of Silas's cologne, but mostly, I existed in a feverish haze of dreams.

I had destroyed the charm, but it didn't matter, because once again, I dreamed of Armantine.

It was after Alex's proposal, after that day in Armantine's studio when he'd knelt before her, when he'd worshiped her with his mouth until the world tilted and broke.

"You're more a fool than I thought, girl." Jules paced as Armantine stood in front of his desk, her hands clasped before her and her head bowed, just as he preferred. "How could you do anything but accept his offer? Don't you *want* to be his wife?"

Her eyes pricked with tears at the thought. "Of course I do," she whispered softly. "More than anything." But the intensity of that wanting, it scared her.

"Then why not accept his offer?" Jules asked.

270 | CELIA CROSBY

She glanced up at him. "You and I both know he can't marry me."

"Not here, no," Jules agreed. "But in France there's no law against it."

"And what if he changes his mind once we arrive?" she asked. "I would be trapped in a strange land with no friends, with no one to help me return. I'd be ruined."

Uncle Jules frowned. "If you don't think you can trust him—"

It wasn't that, not exactly. She grasped the locket. "I believe he loves me now, but what assurance do I have that his heart won't change?"

"You doubt yourself, then," he said, understanding dawning in his voice.

"I doubt the *situation*, Uncle."

"Then you must change the situation." His jaw firmed. "You fear he will be inconstant? There are means to make sure that doesn't happen."

She shook her head. "I won't sign any contract."

"You always have been a practical sort, my girl. But I wasn't talking about a contract."

She frowned. "Then what?"

"An old conjure woman lives out on the River Road. Not too far from the Dutilette place." He pulled a small, thin cigar from his jacket pocket and made a show of lighting it and taking a few slow drags before he went on. "She's helped me in the past. She might have your answers."

Armantine remembered the day Solomon had driven her back to the city. That day, Thisbe had held up hope like a poisoned apple, daring Armantine to take a bite. She wondered if she could.

"I thought you were a man of science," she said carefully.

"I am." He took another deep drag on the sharp-smelling cigar.

"But you don't need science. You need something stronger. You think about it." A knock sounded at the door, and he glanced down at his watch. "But for now, our ten o'clock appointment is here."

Armantine did think. She considered the idea for days, convincing herself of one decision and then hours later changing her mind, but she was running out of time. Finally, the thought of him leaving without her, of knowing she would never see him again, had her walking up the River Road toward Le Ciel on a wickedly hot day in August.

It took Armantine most of the morning to make her way, even with the use of Jules's carriage. So it was well past noon before she finally came to the small grove of trees where the old conjure woman lived. Brilliantly colored bottles hung from bright red cords and danced in the wind to welcome her. But the dark shadows thrown by the trees sent a chill down her spine.

Armantine squared her shoulders. She had made her decision. She would have Alex, and she would be assured he would not leave her as so many protectors left their women. She would keep his love—with Thisbe's help.

Just as she reached the steps leading up to the wide shady porch, a wizened figure appeared in the doorway. "Took you long enough, child," Thisbe said. The old woman gestured for Armantine to approach. "Come on, then. We have work to do."

The inside of the cottage was a surprise. The outside looked humble enough, but within, the walls were washed with a pristine white, and fine furniture was organized to give the effect of comfort and wealth. It was all so much more than a woman in Thisbe's position should have had.

The old woman glanced at Armantine and chuckled, as though she knew the direction of her thoughts. "People are generous when they're thankful." She winked. "Maybe someday, when you're a great lady, you'll be thankful, too." She motioned for Armantine to keep walking, and they made their way to the back of the cottage.

Unlike the front of the house, the back room was furnished for function. Now the shelves were lined with bottles filled with dried flowers and herbs. A low fire burned in the hearth.

Without a word, Thisbe began to gather supplies from her cabinets.

"I'm still not sure why I'm here," Armantine confessed.

"Now that ain't the truth, not at all. You know exactly why you came to see me. You're here for the same reason girls have been coming to me for years." She grinned, a gap-toothed smile that made Armantine cringe. "You got yourself a beau, and you want to make sure you keep him."

Armantine's face heated.

"Nothing to be ashamed of, girl." Thisbe sat across from Armantine at the table. "We women have to do what can be done, but you best be sure before we start, now. My services ain't cheap, and they can't be undone."

Armantine swallowed hard and nodded. "I'm sure."

"Well, then. This is what we'll do—a binding spell to keep your love true." Thisbe placed a thin stick of bloodred wax on the table. "To anchor the spell, I need something from the person you love."

Hesitantly, Armantine removed the locket from her neck and handed it to Thisbe. The old woman raised her brows in surprise. She opened the locket, and when she found the hair inside, she whooped in delight.

"This will work just fine, child. This spell is gonna hold him tight." The way the old woman gazed at the lock of hair, like it was some rare and treasured prize, sent a trickle of unease down Armantine's spine.

Thisbe placed a knife on the table. It reminded Armantine far too much of the knife Alex had been holding when he knelt by Lila's body. A clear vision flashed in her mind—her body instead of Lila's, running its blood into the ground—and she started to stand. To flee. But she was unsteady on her feet and tumbled back into the chair.

"Settle down, child," Thisbe said dismissively. With a movement quicker and surer than Armantine had expected the old woman capable of, she reached out and deftly severed a lock of Armantine's hair. She twined it around the golden strands from the locket. Carefully, she lit a candle in the smoldering fire, melted some of the wax, and let it drip onto the intertwined hair.

As the wax was drying, Thisbe went to a nearby cabinet and unlocked it with an old skeleton key. She brought back a tightly-wound ball of reddish string. Threading the string through a rusted needle, she offered both to Armantine.

"Love magic has to be done by one of the parties involved. You take this thread and pierce the charm while you ask the spirits to bind his love to yours." She offered it to Armantine again. "Go on."

With shaking hands, Armantine accepted the needle and the charm. She looked at them hesitantly before finally closing her eyes and running the needle through the still-warm clump of wax. "Bind his love to mine," she whispered with shaking breath. A cold breeze rustled through the room, and she opened her eyes, unsettled by the uncomfortable sensation crawling across her skin, like the pricking of a thousand tiny pins.

Thisbe nodded and retrieved the charm with the needle still piercing it. With a few deft movements, she looped the thread around and tied it off, then tucked the wax-covered hair back into the locket.

"You hold this charm, you hold him," she told Armantine. "You keep it close to you, girl. You're all wrapped up in this too, now. A love charm ain't never a one-way binding. You understand?" When Armantine nodded, Thisbe handed the locket to her.

She held it in her hands like it had suddenly become extraordinarily delicate. "He'll love me forever now?" she whispered, her voice thick with hope.

The old woman cackled again, a dry wheezing like nails across glass. "This here charm will keep him *steady*. The love is up to you."

"But I thought—" Panic rose in Armantine's throat like bile. Had she made a mistake? She'd wanted to be sure Alex's feelings would remain true. The last thing wanted was to bind him to her if they weren't.

The old woman pursed her lips and shook her head dismissively. "You go on now. I have things to do." She turned back to her jars and bins, effectively dismissing Armantine.

On unsteady legs, Armantine walked back to the city. The air was blistering, but the heat never touched her. She was too cold deep down in her bones even to feel it.

43

My fever broke sometime the next day, and the dreams dissipated along with it. When I finally woke, I had the feeling I wasn't alone.

"Silas?" I said, the memory of what had happened flooding back over me. The evil little effigy. The ambulance's lights. The thick black smoke.

A movement in the corner stopped the words in my throat. *Alex.* I'd taken the risk and burned the charm, and it hadn't worked. Alex was still here. Still haunting me.

Alex stepped forward. His eyes were hooded with concern, and he wore his usual outfit, but something was different about him. His shirt was loose around his neck, and he'd rolled up the sleeves, exposing his strong forearms. He looked uneasy.

"What are you doing here?" I asked him.

"I came to check on you," he said softly. "You collapsed by the pond, but there wasn't anything I could do."

"But I burned the charm," I insisted. "I freed you."

"You *did* free me from the witch's land . . ."

"But you're still *here.*" My stomach sank along with my hopes as I gestured toward him. I had hoped if I got rid of the charm, everything else would be fine. Alex would be free. Silas would wake up.

"Do you have some unfinished business or—" Anger lanced through my tone, spurred by my own impotence. "Why are you still here?"

The question seemed to unsettle him, as though he hadn't ever thought beyond the moment when the doll would be destroyed. "I explained already—I'm not a ghost."

"Then what *are* you?" I demanded.

He shook his head. "I don't know anymore." He frowned. "I'm not even sure I'm quite dead."

"Of *course* you're dead. Even without whatever Thisbe did, you should have died more than a hundred years ago. You shouldn't *be* here."

"But I don't think I did."

"I don't understand." My head was spinning.

"When I—" He paused as though unsure how to continue. "When what happened to me *happened*, I wasn't quite dead. I remember being torn apart from myself, and I watched the old witch do something to my body. But then suddenly, everything went dark until I woke up by the clearing as I am now. I don't know what she did."

"You remember?"

"Not everything, but most of it." He rubbed his hand over his face, and I had the sense he was far away, reliving what had happened to him. "I know that somehow she separated a part of me —my spirit or soul or whatever you might call it—from my body." He cringed, like the memory was still fresh. "I know that she made me into . . . this."

"How do you know you didn't die?"

"Because I *wanted* to. The pain of being apart from myself was so great that I would have been thankful for death. I *prayed* for it. I still pray for it." He looked up at me, his brows bunched in confusion. "I don't know how it happened, but I'm certain the witch stopped my body from dying. She's kept my soul bound to this patch of earth ever since, but my body? It's still out there. Keeping me in this world. Preventing me from ever moving on."

"That's impossible." I explained what Mama Erzulie had told me. "The magic shouldn't have lasted longer than the person who cast the spell. Thisbe can't still be alive, so the magic should have ended as well."

"And yet." His jaw clenched. "For more than a century I've been here, Lucy. I've attempted to discern what happened, to learn how to change it. For more than a century, I've been alone in my quest. Until you, no one could even *see* me."

"But why me?" I demanded. I still didn't understand my part in any of this, and I was tired of it. Tired of the dreams, tired of a past I could not shake.

"Because I've been waiting for you," His voice was soft, laden with the hope of more than a century of waiting.

"But *why*?" I demanded. "Why do I have to be the one? Why do I have to spend my nights dreaming about you and . . . *her*?"

"*Chère —*"

"She loved you."

He flinched at my tone, but regret in his eyes had the fight draining out of me.

"I still don't know the whole story." I looked up at him. "I need to know the rest."

"I don't know the whole story, either," he admitted.

"You're still protecting her, aren't you?" The truth was clear. "After everything she did, you still love her."

"I always will." His voice was steady with resolve. "It is a rare thing to find your other half."

"But you lost her." They'd loved each other, and it hadn't been enough.

His expression crumpled, and a sadness shone in his emerald eyes that stole my breath. "Don't think of it, Lucy. Armantine is gone. Now we must focus on what we *can* do. If I'm no longer bound to this place, then I can find out what the witch did to my body. If I could find it—find myself—perhaps I can be truly free. We could go now and—"

"I can't." I shook my head. I'd already risked everything to try and free him, and I couldn't shake the sense that whatever had happened to Silas, it was my fault somehow.

At the very least, if I hadn't gone chasing after Mama Erzulie, I would have been here for him, *with* him.

"Lucy—"

"I have to go, Alex." I still felt weak from the fever, and I definitely needed a shower, but I needed to see Silas more.

His mouth pressed into a determined line. "I'll come with you."

44

The morning was hazy from the rain that had fallen the previous day, and the temperature was already climbing close to the triple digits when we started toward the city. I'd found out from Leonard which hospital they'd taken Silas to, and he again let me borrow his car so I could go visit. But I couldn't talk Alex out of coming with me. Now that he was no longer trapped on the estate, I couldn't really stop him from going anywhere.

At one point, I glanced over to find Alex watching the New Orleans skyline draw nearer. I was so used to the skyscrapers in Chicago that the neat grove of shining buildings ahead of us had done little to impress me. But for someone who had spent the last hundred and fifty or so years on the same small parcel of farmland? The gleaming windows and soaring heights must have seemed miraculous. Or terrifying.

"This must be like a strange dream for you."

"It is . . . unsettling," he agreed. "So much time has passed, and I've only been aware of glimpses of it, trapped as I was." His gaze darted restlessly from building to building as they grew larger.

"If it's too much . . ." I started.

"No. I will be with you today, Lucy."

I glanced at him again. "Can anyone else see you?"

"No one has before—except the witch you were with." He frowned. "I am not exactly sure how that could be possible. It worries me."

The hospital was buzzing with activity as we made our way to Silas's room. I hesitated at the door, afraid to enter, and when I finally gathered the courage to go in, I was almost sorry I had. Silas was the kind of guy who filled up a room, but lying in that bed he looked frail and almost hollowed out, hooked up as he was to all the monitors and tubes.

I eased into the room, excruciatingly aware of Alex behind me.

"He means something to you." It wasn't a question, but there was a note of some emotion I didn't understand in his voice.

"Yeah," I said, my throat tight. There was no denying that fact now. Maybe I had wanted to push Silas away or deny there was something real between us, but seeing him like that made it impossible to lie to myself.

Tenderly, I cradled his hand, but he didn't respond. His skin was cool to the touch, and his color was off. He looked like a faded version of himself.

I don't know how long I stood there, my thumb tracing gentle circles on the back of Silas's hand, as I watched him take slow, painfully shallow breaths.

A small knock sounded at the door and roused me from my vigil.

"Lucy?" Mama Erzulie peeked into the room. "Is that you?"

I glanced at Alex, who had gone completely still. I knew he didn't trust Mama Erzulie, but I wasn't sure why. After all, she was the one who'd given me the information to help free him from the estate.

She hadn't taken even three steps into the room when she

stopped short with a sharp intake of breath. After a moment, she continued on to his bedside, where she let her palm hover above him for a long silent moment.

"Did the doctors happen to tell you anything?" I asked. A nurse had come by, but I wasn't family, so she hadn't shared anything about his condition.

"What's wrong with him can't be touched by any doctor," Mama Erzulie said darkly. "He ain't completely there, child."

"What are you talking about?"

I glanced at Alex and saw the same question reflected in his expression.

"I'm talking about his spirit," Mama Erzulie said. "That part of Silas that makes him who he is. His *soul*. I can see them. Same as you can see that boy there, I can see the energy that makes us who we are. Yours is still shining out bright, but Silas's? His ain't nothing more than a dim and fading glow. Someone's cursed him. His spirit's been bound up tight."

Panic lashed through me. "Is he dying?" I could barely force the words out.

"Not yet, but if he doesn't reunite with that other part of himself soon . . . "

"It's too much of a coincidence," I murmured.

"What's that?" Mama Erzulie asked.

"He fell ill after I took the binding charm from Thisbe's cottage," I admitted. There wasn't any sense in hiding it, not when she'd been the one to help me burn the damn thing.

Mama Erzulie's brows rose at the information. "Nobody else knows about that charm, do they?"

I shook my head. But then I thought back over the day before, especially about how Chloe had caught me in the cabin. About how strangely she'd been acting. Maybe she hadn't been there on behalf of the Foundation. But maybe she'd been there for herself.

"This is my fault," I said. "I never should have gone there. I never should have touched that thing." Suddenly, I couldn't breathe.

"Lucy, *chère* . . . " Alex's voice was a quiet plea. "Please, calm yourself."

But I couldn't. My chest was as tight as if water was rushing into my lungs. A seeping cold washed through me, like I'd just been plunged into icy depths.

Alex muttered under his breath about being useless, while Mama Erzulie came over and wrapped her arm around me and she whispered soft bits of nonsense in my ear. Little by little, my breathing settled. But the guilt, the knowledge that Silas might die because of me, was unshakable.

"This isn't the end," she promised. "Silas is gonna be just fine once we break the binding."

"How are we supposed to do that?" I pointed to Alex. "I thought I could help him, but I couldn't. He's *still* here. And Silas —" I couldn't say the words. Refused to accept them.

"You have to think, child," Mama Erzulie urged. "To bind someone, a spell worker needs something of the person they're binding. I already explained, to bind a person's soul is strong magic. *Dark* magic. They need something more than personal— something that contains a bit of the person themselves. You have to think about who could've gotten to him and what they might have."

Chloe, something inside me said, but I pushed that thought away. She'd been acting strangely yesterday at Thisbe's cabin, but she was mourning Shaunda. She only knew about Voodoo and magic through Mama Erzulie.

"I've made a mess of things." I never should have come to Louisiana.

"All this started long before you stepped into it," Mama Erzulie said. "There's nothing you could have done to avoid it."

"I could have stayed away. I could have kept myself far from

Le Ciel," I said, listing off all my mistakes. "I should have left that charm alone."

"Maybe you should have, but I don't think you *could* have," she said. "Haven't you been having strange dreams your whole life? What makes you think fate isn't stronger than what you want? You didn't start any of this, child. But maybe you'll be just strong enough to stop it."

"You're right." I deflated at the thought. Alex was watching me with a careful expression. "I've been dreaming about the past for so long, I think it would have come for me one way or the other. But I never intended for anyone else to get hurt."

EVENTUALLY, visiting hours were over, but we were no closer to figuring anything out. On the way back, Alex and I didn't speak much. Neither one of us, it seemed, knew what to say. When the station we were listening to took a break for the local news— another girl found murdered in the next parish over, another murder without any leads—I clicked off the radio.

As we drove through the heavy Louisiana night, all I could think was it was happening again. Just as it had so many years ago. Somehow, I had to stop it.

Alex watched quietly as I dropped off Leonard's car and went through the motions of giving him an update about Silas. We walked the short distance back to my own tiny cabin in silence.

I wasn't hungry, but I forced myself to choke down a granola bar and a Diet Coke as we discussed how we could find the person that had Silas bound up and close to dying.

"Are you sure there aren't any others who might know you removed the charm from Thisbe's cottage?" Alex asked.

"Mama Erzulie's the only person I told about this. She's the only one who knows anything about what's going on here."

"What about the girl who discovered you that day?"

"Chloe?" My stomach sank. I'd thought of Chloe earlier. "I don't want to believe she's capable of it."

He looked like he wanted to argue with me, but decided not to.

I grabbed my tablet and fired it up to search for the pictures I'd taken at Thisbe's cabin. It all revolved around place and whatever curses had been born inside those walls. There had to be some clue, something I was missing.

Alex came up behind me, looking over my shoulder as I flipped through the images. "You've certainly captured the darkness of the old witch's place."

I frowned as I shuffled through the reel of images again. "This isn't right."

"What is it?" Alex asked as I went to get my camera from its bag.

"I'm missing something." I'd taken a photo of Silas at Thisbe's cabin. I knew I had. I'd even printed it for him later that day. I could picture it: he'd been walking back across the field, and I'd captured him with the bright blue of the sky behind him. I'd even printed it out. But the file wasn't here. "One of them is missing—a photo I took of Silas the day of the cleansing."

"Are you sure?"

"Positive," I said, checking once more. But I wasn't wrong; the image was gone. "I thought I had misplaced the print I made or someone threw it away that day, but now all the files are gone as well. Even if the printed image is lost, the original should still be here on my camera or on the storage card. But it's not. Someone deleted it. Why would anyone want to erase my pictures?"

"Maybe they didn't simply destroy the image." He crossed his arms and scrubbed at his chin as he considered the problem. "Maybe they stole it."

"But why?"

His expression was stony. "Long ago, there were those who believed photographs had the power to capture part of the soul. Taking an image of a person was feared by many in these parts, especially those who believed in the spirit world."

"That's just on old superstition," I said, dismissing the idea.

"Perhaps. But some would say the same about spirits or Voodoo or even ghosts."

He had a point. "You think someone took the print I made to work a spell on Silas?"

Alex nodded, his mouth grim. "I can't be sure, but it's the best explanation we have."

"It would explain why the file is missing," I admitted. Without the file, the print would be the only record of the photo I'd taken.

"Who else would have had access to your work?"

"No one, usually." But then I paused, remembering. "Except that day, I left my camera and the computer in the offices while I went to lunch with Chloe."

When he lifted a single brow at Chloe's name, I shook my head.

"Chloe was with me the whole time. And besides, it could have been anyone in the offices: Byron or Mina or even my uncle who took the print and erased the image."

"But it was Chloe who confronted you in the cabin when we found the charm, yes?"

"Yes," I admitted. And she *had* been at the bayou when Shaunda was killed as well. "There has to be another explanation. It could just as well have been Mina."

"Perhaps." But he didn't sound sure. "I could go and search for you."

I considered his offer for less than a second before I refused. "No. If either one of them is behind all this, then that person is probably connected to whatever happened to you as well. She might even be connected to Thisbe somehow, which means it's not any safer for you to go." I took a deep breath that did nothing to calm me. "We stick to the plan and stay together, Alex. Tomorrow, we'll go talk to Chloe. If she doesn't know anything, we'll try Mina. Then Byron. We'll see if anyone in the offices knows anything about the photograph I'm missing, and then we'll pay Mama Erzulie a visit."

45

Thisbe's house stands in the shadows of the grove. The day is hot, still, and yet the bottles hanging from the trees clink together, stirred by an impossible wind. I shouldn't have come here. I should have stayed far, far away.

And yet. . .

There is no choice but to go forward. Onward.

It happens again—Armantine's visit to Thisbe. Her begging the old woman to break the love charm she's spun.

"I'll do whatever I must," she promises, desperate.

And she doesn't notice how Thisbe's mouth curves. She doesn't see that Thisbe will never free him.

"I need to be close enough to touch," the old witch says.

The girl's thoughts race—how will she convince Alex to come to Thisbe's cabin? She will do anything, *anything* to undo her mistake.

But I know with an absolute certainty. This is the beginning of what happened. This is the moment that determined every one that came after. Every day of every year Alex has been trapped all leads back to here.

But the moment tumbles and twists, and I'm falling into

nothing. And then I'm in a room where a steamer trunk stands open. I am Armantine again, and using her eyes, I judge each piece of my clothing as the people in France would. Every frock seems suddenly provincial, and so she leaves most of them hanging like limp bodies in the wardrobe.

She reaches for her canvases and paints, charcoals and paper. These are who she is. These are what she cannot leave behind.

It is dark by the time we finally reach the docks. The night is so thick I can hardly see the ship that will take the girl from the only home she has ever known.

It does not matter. When she straightens her back, stiff against fear, the small vial Thisbe gave her shifts against her skin.

"Tomorrow, *mon coeur*," Alex tells her, squeezing her hand. His eyes shine like emeralds, alight with anticipation. "Tomorrow, you'll be mine."

Tomorrow. Tomorrow he will be safe, and we shall be wed, she thinks. *Tomorrow the past will not matter.*

The ship's cabin is small but comfortable, and happiness wars with nerves. The vial is frigid against her skin. It will be over soon.

He orders a dinner of cold chicken and bread slathered with thick, sweet butter, and she pulls the vial from her corset when he goes to find more wine. Thisbe is waiting for the signal. And then all will be well.

But I know otherwise. And I hate her for not knowing as well.

Armantine takes the wine from him when he returns, and turning her back on him, she pours the scarlet liquid into pewter cups, where it sits dark as death. Then she slips the vial from its hiding place . . .

I scream, words only I can hear. Pointless words to warn her.

Because she's opening the vial. She is pouring one . . . two . . . three drops, as she's been instructed.

I struggle, and I fight, and I scream for her to stop.

But she doesn't.

And suddenly, unexpectedly, I am not in her body any longer. I am standing apart from her in the close quarters of the cabin, watching with horror as Alex accepts the cup.

I try to stop him, but my arms slip through him. I can do nothing but watch as he drinks, as he falls unconscious. I try to wake him, but I'm no more than a ghost in a dream. Armantine signals to Thisbe, and I cannot stop her. I cannot protect either of them as Thisbe enters with two large men. When Armantine realizes her mistake, she launches herself at the men, trying to protect Alex's unconscious form. But she fails.

46

When I woke the next morning, Alex was there, watching me with the same intensity that often took Armantine's breath away. For a moment, I thought maybe I was still dreaming.

"It was her, wasn't it?"

His expression shifted, but I couldn't read the emotion in his eyes. "You had another dream?"

I nodded and attempted to describe for him what I was still piecing together from the disjointed images of my dreams.

"She was so afraid to trust you." The words caught in my throat, but I pushed on. He needed to know. "She didn't think she was enough on her own. It's why she had Thisbe do the love charm. She was so stupid."

"Not stupid, *chère*." His voice was tinged with sadness. "She was blinded by fear. I should have done more to make sure she understood. I should have done more to fight for her."

Pulling myself out of bed, I started pacing I pulled together the pieces of the dream. "I don't know why Armantine couldn't see Thisbe was lying." I stopped and looked at him. "She didn't mean to hurt you—she didn't know what Thisbe was going to do. But she set everything in motion with that love charm, and then she led Thisbe right to you when she attempted to break it."

"But in the end, she was trying to free me from that charm?" he asked, his brows drawn together thoughtfully.

I nodded. "She thought Thisbe would break the love charm. She couldn't see Thisbe's promises for the lies they were. When she went to drop the sleeping potion into your glass, I knew it was going to hurt you. But I couldn't do anything. I struggled against what she wanted to do, and somehow, I can't really explain it, but *somehow* I changed perspectives. I wasn't *in* her anymore. I was near her, watching everything play out like a bad movie. I'm always trapped in her body. Last night was different, though."

"You were separate from her within the dream?" He frowned. "How is that possible?

"I don't know," I told him. "But I was like a ghost to them. They didn't even notice me there. Not that it mattered—I couldn't stop her." I looked up at him. "There was nothing I could actually do."

He moved closer. "It is impossible to change our pasts, Lucy." His voice was softer now. "We can only learn from them."

I knew I couldn't change the past. Whatever had happened to Armantine and Alex had taken place more than a hundred years ago. And I was about to tell him exactly that when the words he'd used registered.

"What do you mean, *our*?" I asked. "This dream was about you and Armantine."

Alex's eyes shifted away, as though he was afraid to look at me, and suddenly everything made sense.

"No." I shook my head in denial. "*No.*" I repeated, as though saying the word could change what was. "They're just dreams. I can't be her. I'm *not* her."

"No, you're not," Alex said, his voice rough with a sadness

that broke my heart. "You're yourself. You live this life, and you *are* this person. Wholly and completely." His eyes lifted to meet mine. "But there was a part of you, once, which lived a different life."

I retreated until the back of my legs hit the bed and I sat with an inelegant plop. *"No.* I don't believe in reincarnation," I told him, as though that solved everything. "It's not possible."

"Why isn't it?" He shoulders hunched as he released a heavy breath. "A few days ago, you would have not believed I was possible. You and I," he said, smiling gently. "Once, long ago, we found each other. Now we have found each other again. Perhaps one day, we will find each other once more. It is as simple as that."

"That's why all this is happening," I realized. "Because I'm *her.* The dreams, this *place—*" Things began to click into place. "Is that why I could never settle down? Any time I started to relax, any time I found happiness, the dreams—the *nightmares—* would come back with a vengeance. They were pushing me here, weren't they?"

"Perhaps," he admitted.

"So, what? This is my fate?" I demanded. "Am I just supposed to keep suffering for something I did in a past I can't change?"

His jaw tightened. "Fate may give us opportunities, Lucy, but I don't believe it controls us. We make our own futures."

I let out a strangled laugh. "What future?" I asked him. "Every time I let someone into my life, the dreams—the past— destroy any hope for a future." *Until Silas.* He hadn't changed or rejected me, even after he knew about the dreams. He'd been a chance at something more. "I'm not Armantine, Alex. I don't love you. I can't."

"I would not expect it of you," he said sadly.

"No?" It felt like a trick—the dreams, how I'd been lulled into feeling what Armantine felt. How her desire sparked mine. *All of it*. The day before, I'd thought I had chosen Silas of my own free will. Now I wasn't sure.

"Love is always a choice, Lucy," he said softly. "It isn't a blind tying. It's an action, a practice. I don't expect you to love me, *chère*. I don't expect anything at all. Not when I have nothing to offer you."

"Then why is this happening?" I asked, my head in my hands. "What am I supposed to do, knowing everything about a past I can't change?"

"I think, perhaps, it's not I who has unfinished business."

I considered that. Was it enough to simply free him? Could I free myself by righting the wrongs of the past?

"Did you know who I was from the very beginning?" I asked. "Did you know what she—what *I*—did to you in the past?"

"I knew who you were the moment I laid eyes on you that morning," he admitted. "But I didn't know what Armantine had done."

"You must have suspected?"

He looked almost faded, like he wasn't quite there. "I pushed you once before—pushed you before you were ready. Before, I asked you to give up far more than was right. It is the reason everything else happened. This time, I forced myself to be patient. To give you the time you needed. This time, things had to be different."

"She understood that she was wrong. She died trying to save you," I told him.

"I know," he said. "Through the haze of whatever was in that wine, I could hear everything. And I could do nothing to help her."

"It didn't work," I said numbly.

Although Armantine had tried to stop the two large men Thisbe had brought that night, they had easily pulled Armantine off and pinned her to the wall.

I had awoken from the dream at that point, but I instinctively knew what came next. It all made sense now. All those nights I had dreamed about drowning, it had always been her. And it had always been me. The guilt made sense too, now that I knew what she had done. What *I* had done.

"Why don't you hate me?" My voice shook, and I couldn't blink back the tears any longer. "You *should* hate me. You asked her for trust, and she betrayed you. You asked her for love, and she trapped you here. But she wasn't trapped. She might have died fighting off Thisbe's men, but I'm here now, in a new life. A new skin."

"I don't hate you because in this life, you bear no blame." His jaw tensed, and I watched as he struggled with what he wanted to say. "I am not sure I can explain to you what it's like to live on for years beyond when one should have died, but when I'm with you, I can remember what I once was."

"You could have told me."

"You needed to discover it on your own." He smiled softly. "It's not the sort of thing that is easily believed."

That much was true. If he had told me that very first day in the clearing that I was his love in another life and he was a ghost trapped in a Voodoo-induced limbo, I would have been on the first bus back to Chicago. But there was one question I still needed the answer to. "What do we do now, Alex?"

"We find who is controlling all of this, and we end this, once and for all."

47

Alex still wasn't on board with me talking to Chloe. In his estimation, it would have been safer for him to go and simply search for the missing photograph. But if she was really the one behind everything—if she was also somehow connected to Thisbe—he would be in just as much danger.

The clouds hung low in the sky, threatening to crush us beneath their weight as I pulled Leonard's car up the drive to the house where Chloe and Mina lived not far from Le Ciel. I hadn't been to their house since the day after Shaunda's murder. That day, I'd thought the house was charming. Today, the bottles hanging from trees reminded me of hanged men waiting to be cut down.

As we walked up to the porch, the door opened and Chloe stepped out, blocking the entrance.

She smiled at me, but it wasn't Chloe's smile that spread across her face. The surface of her face rippled. My stomach twisted. It was Chloe, but it wasn't. Something else moved behind her eyes. But I didn't know if it had always been there.

"I knew you would come," she said in a voice as flat and life-less as her eyes.

"Lucy, we need to leave. *Now.*" Alex's voice was urgent in my ear.

I shook him off. I wasn't leaving until we got the answers we needed.

Chloe watched me—or the thing inside her did. "Is he here?" she rasped, addressing the empty spaces around me. "Did you bring him with you, or is he tucked away safe somewhere?" The voice wasn't hers, and wondered if maybe Thisbe could be behind this. Or if there was some other evil we didn't know about.

But how could Thisbe be involved? Was she also some kind of ghost? How she somehow possessed my friend? Maybe my dreams had somehow unleashed her. Or maybe she'd somehow always been around . . . waiting? There was another option: Maybe Chloe had always had part of Thisbe inside her, the way Armantine had always lived within me? Whatever the case, I swore that I would do what I could to make it right.

I *had* to make it right. If I wanted a chance at a real future, I needed to put the past to rest. Once and for all. I drew strength from that thought and squared my shoulders to cover the terror building inside me.

"I know what you did to Silas."

"Do you?" Her mouth pulled into a curve that couldn't be called a smile. "Then why are you here?"

"Because I want you to undo the spell he's under."

Chloe cocked her head at an odd angle. Then she laughed. "And I want what's mine. The charm. The Frenchman."

Alex vibrated with tension beside me, but I ignored him. She didn't seem to know he was there, and I didn't want her to figure it out.

"What charm?" I already knew, but I needed to hear it for myself. Everything was too precarious to take any chances.

"The one you took from my home," she snapped, her anger making Chloe's body tremble.

My home. I'd been right. Thisbe *was* behind this somehow, within Chloe somehow.

"You want your man whole again, you'll give it back to me," she shrieked.

She wasn't acting like she knew the charm was already gone.

That thought was a tiny pinpoint of hope. Maybe, just maybe, Thisbe wasn't all *that* powerful. Maybe she didn't know who I was, or what I knew.

"I'll give you the charm," I promised. I didn't know how I would do it, but I needed to buy us time. "But I want you to end the curse on Silas in exchange."

"Maybe I should kill him instead," Chloe hissed. "Maybe I should kill all of them—Leonard and Sam and Erzulie—one by one, until you break."

"If you touch anyone else, I'll destroy it," I growled. "I'll burn your precious charm in a fire so bright and hot that you'll never get it back."

Chloe's nostrils flared, but it was the fear scuttling through her eyes that indicated that I was right. Thisbe needed the charm, and she didn't know it was gone. She wasn't all powerful; she could be defeated.

"Lucy!" Alex hissed into my ear. "You don't bargain with the devil."

I ignored him. "I want the piece of Silas that you used to bind him. I want whatever you cursed him with."

She smiled viciously. "A trade?"

I nodded. "You get your charm. I get Silas. Or your charm is gone. For good."

The Chloe-thing hissed.

"Lucy!" Alex was frantic. Warmth pulled at my shoulders, and I knew he was trying to move me. His wisps of energy were charged with the burn of his desperation and fear. I couldn't turn to him, couldn't let Chloe know he was so close, if she didn't already know. Silently, I willed him to trust me.

"Very well, child," Chloe said. "We'll make your little trade."

"Today," I demanded. "I have to go get the charm, but I want this finished today." From what Mama Erzulie had said, we couldn't afford to wait.

"Come to my home at sunset," she said with a serpent's smile. "You'll get your picture."

"Sunset," I repeated, knowing she spoke of Thisbe's cottage.

"*Lucy!*" Alex's voice was frantic. I had finally exhausted his patience. But I kept myself composed. I didn't want Thisbe to sense any weakness.

Turning from him, I left, walking slowly and deliberately to my car. The second I sat down I started shaking. I took a few deep breaths that helped a little.

Alex's jaw was tight. "You took too many risks out there."

I winced at his tone. "I knew what I was doing."

"You couldn't possibly know what you were dealing with. The danger you were in." His jaw clenched.

"It's okay," I told him. "*I'm* okay."

"That girl could have hurt you. And I could have done nothing to stop her."

"She didn't, though." I needed him to understand. "It's not Chloe, Alex."

"I know. Your friend may be in there somewhere, but she is no longer in control." His voice darkened. "Perhaps she never has been."

I started the car and spared only one glance in my rearview mirror as I drove away. Chloe no longer stood on the wide porch, and the house looked like any other home again. Anyone passing by would never guess that behind its cheerful blue shutters lurked darkness thicker than a nightmare.

"Lucy, we do not have that charm," Alex said, his tone betraying his worry.

"I know that, and you know that, but she doesn't, Alex." I glanced over at him. "If she knew we'd already destroyed it, she wouldn't have asked for it. She definitely wouldn't have bothered with a deal."

He thought about it. "Even if you're correct, even if she's not merely setting another trap for you, she won't give you the picture freely, Lucy. She was lying."

"I know that, too." I was already feeling steadier as we moved farther from Chloe's house. "We'll just have to be smarter. Lie better. And be a whole lot luckier."

When we passed the turn for Le Ciel, Alex looked over at me in confusion. "Where are we headed?"

"The next step of our plan, Alex. We need a charm, and I only know one person who can get us one."

48

During the drive into the city, Alex made clear his unhappiness about visiting the Voodoo queen on her own turf. But after what had happened at Chloe's, we didn't have time to waste.

When we walked into the shop, Mama Erzulie was rearranging the glass jars on the shelves.

"I been expecting you," she said before we were even completely through the door.

"Did you tell her we were coming?" Alex whispered.

"No." I was confused as he as by Mama Erzulie 's greeting.

"Well, come on back." She set the last jar in place before wiping her hands on her skirts.

We followed her through the narrow hallway and seated ourselves on the deep couch while she finished brewing more of her fragrant tea.

"We need your help," I told her.

"I figured that much." She handed me a brightly colored mug. This time I took a sip and found that the flowery-smelling liquid was sweet. "Well, go on, then. What do you need?" She motioned for me to speak.

So, I did. I started at the beginning this time and explained everything, about the dreams I'd been having since I was a child and the dreams that had started when I arrived at Le Ciel. And about my most recent dream—the one where I'd stepped away from Armantine's body.

When I finished, she slapped her leg in delight. "I *knew* you were gonna be one to watch." She seemed entirely too pleased with the whole situation, and I couldn't begin to guess what there was for her to be happy about.

"But I don't understand what any of it means," I said. "All I know is that because of me, Silas is hurt."

She leaned forward in her chair and rested her hand on my knee. "It takes a powerful soul to separate their spirit from their body. You must be one of those, child."

"Because I was Armantine?"

"She was probably just one stop on your journey, just like this body you're in now is another stop," she explained. "There are old souls, and there are young souls, child. Every time we take a body, we grow and change. Every time we come back to this place, we have inside us all we ever were before. Remember?" She took a long sip from her mug and considered me. "Most people don't ever figure out what they've got inside them."

"But I've been dreaming about it."

Mama Erzulie nodded. "Dreams are powerful parts of our lives, child. Even the newest souls use dreams to free their spirits momentarily from their human condition. They get to dance free of their worries, of all the pressures and expectations holding them down in this world. Because when we dream, we can move beyond—we can see the bigger picture stretching out before us.

"Most people wake," she continued. "And they don't remember a thing. Other people, they forget their dreams and then, in sudden flashes—" She snapped her fingers. "They realize they've been somewhere before. Done something already." She glanced at me. "Some people call that déjà vu."

She settled back into the plum-colored chair. But then she grew serious. "For some, dreams are more than just a playground. For *some*, dreams are an actual opening to the past. What happened to you last night, I ain't heard of in a long, long time. To pull free of your past self and walk alone?" She paused as though she was weighing her next words carefully. "It's a great gift you've been given, but it's also a dangerous power to have."

"But I couldn't *do* anything," I explained. How was being a powerful soul supposed to help anything if I was powerless as a ghost in those dreams?

"Lucy, just knowing the past gives you power. Our history —our past—it all shapes us. Think of this: without your dreams, you wouldn't be in a position to help Silas. You wouldn't understand all that led us to this moment right here. You'd be like those doctors in that there hospital, wondering why none of their tests work, instead of asking the questions that can give real answers. In fact, you might already have those answers."

"I don't see how." If I had the answers, I would have already used them to help Silas. To help Alex. I would have ended the misery of the nightmares years ago, before they ruined everything.

"You ain't listening to what I'm saying," she admonished. "What you did last night? You ain't chained to your past no more. Think about it. Think how you could use it."

"She could separate herself from Armantine in the dreams," Alex said. "She could see beyond what Armantine herself knew."

"Sure enough," Mama Erzulie confirmed, pleased someone was finally catching on.

"It might work," Alex said to himself. "If you could follow my attackers instead of following Armantine's fate, you may be able to tell what Thisbe did to me. You might be able to discover her weakness."

"You really think it's as easy as that?" I asked. The pieces were growing closer, but I still wasn't sure they fit. It seemed almost too simple to just dream up a solution.

"There ain't nothing easy about it, child," Mama Erzulie warned. "It might even be deadly. But it's *possible*."

I ignored her talk of danger. Difficulty I could deal with, and I could definitely work with possible. But then a thought struck me that made my hope crumble to ash. "But you said this is all dependent on me dreaming. What if I never have that dream again? Or what if I don't have that dream for another three weeks? We don't have that kind of time." I slumped back into the couch as "possible" seemed farther and farther away. "It's not like I can control what I dream about."

Mama Erzulie smiled at me gently. "Can't you?"

"No, I—" And then I remembered all those days after the Saint John's Eve festival, when I'd been so alone. I remembered how much my dreams had taken on a life of their own at night. Because I'd looked forward to them—because I'd *wanted* to see more of Alex and Armantine.

"You seeing the light yet?" Mama asked wryly.

"Maybe." I chewed on my bottom lip and worked through the logic. "It's about concentration, isn't it?" That's what she had meant by it being difficult.

She nodded. "You aren't trained, but you've already done more than you should be able to on your own." She patted my knee affectionately.

"You said it could be dangerous," Alex said. "When she separates herself during the dream, what could harm her?"

Mama Erzulie glanced at him. "'Bout as much as anything can hurt you, boy."

"That does not signify at all," he argued. "She's not in the same condition I am."

Mama Erzulie stared at Alex thoughtfully for a minute before conceding his point. "Nothing can hurt a spirit in a dream, boy. What you have to worry about is the body waiting behind. But we'll make sure nothing happens to her." She tilted her head, considering him. "The question is, what do you know about your own self?"

Alex's jaw tensed.

"You the missing piece in a lot of this," Mama Erzulie told him. "You shouldn't be here unless there was something your spirit is anchored to—some physical part of who you once were. You want Lucy safe? You better tell her whatever you know about what happened to you. Any little piece of this might be the one we're missing."

He remained rigid for a few seconds longer. "I don't know much," he said, his voice rough. "It was only when I woke up by the pond that I realized I was trapped there."

"That was when, hundred fifty years ago or so?" She shook her head. "No, there's something else going on. The kind of magic that's pinned you here is as dark as it comes. It would take more than a piece of hair or bit of nail to keep a spirit on this plane for so long. It takes the kind of energy that only resides in living, breathing flesh."

"But no body can last that long," I told her

"Not naturally," Mama Erzulie said, eyeing Alex.

"What could the old witch have done to my body to effect that result?" Alex asked.

Mama Erzulie frowned. "Something that breaks the very laws of nature. It isn't the kind of magic I deal in, but I've heard of black magic's that more than capable. If someone is willing to cross into the darkness and make the right sacrifice, they can perpetrate all sorts of evil."

"They sacrificed him?" I asked, confused again.

"No, child. But they likely used the power from a sacrifice to keep him here." She glanced at Alex. "Innocent blood could be used to fuel all sorts of evil."

"The girl," Alex whispered.

"What girl?" Mama Erzulie asked. "Not the one who was just killed—that's too recent."

"No. Before this all happened, we found a girl who'd been murdered on Roman's land. One of the enslaved women who worked for my sister."

"Lila." I shuddered at the thought of the girl's blank eyes and the thick blood clotted at her neck.

Alex nodded. "Her death wasn't natural. When we found her body—" He swallowed hard. "There were markings over most of her torso. Runes and symbols had been carved into her skin. And her body had practically been drained of blood."

"That might be part of this, sure enough," Mama Erzulie said. "If the blood had been collected, if it had been charmed, the power from it could have been used for any number of spells or rituals." She glanced at us both. "It doesn't calm me none to know girls have been dying again around these parts in the same kind of way."

"Shaunda," I realized.

Mama Erzulie nodded. "And the way I hear it? Her body was all marked up too. Hardly a drop of blood was left in her veins. Sounds like too many similarities, you ask me."

"It can't be the same person who killed Lila," I protested. "It has to be a copycat or someone else. No one could live that long."

"Maybe. But then again, no spirit should be anchored to this world for so long, either." Her eyes slid to Alex. "We're missing some pieces, all right, but they're all connected somehow." She looked at me with an unwavering gaze. "Might be the answers are waiting in your dreams."

"There's not time." I told her about Chloe and about the

trade I'd set up with the monster that lived inside her skin. "We have to be back by sunset. By tonight, it might already be too late."

"You don't need to wait for the night to dream, child." Mama Erzulie patted my leg gently. "You only have to sleep."

49

I snuggled down into the pillows on Mama Erzulie's couch as she filled the air with an incense that made me drowsy with its thick headiness.

She'd given me some chamomile and lavender tea, to help make me drowsy, and I could already feel its warm pull. Closing my eyes, focused on my most recent dream. I imagined Armantine's excitement as she carefully folded her best gowns for the long journey. I remembered the delight in Alex's eyes as he led her up the gangplank of the ship. I imagined their laughter and joy ringing through the small cabin as they ate their dinner. For a while, I thought it wouldn't work. And then suddenly, I was there.

Alex was across the room from me, watching me with those dancing green eyes of his, and Armantine was about to put the potion into his wine.

I focused on that. On stopping her. With every atom of my being, I attempted to pull her back, to stay her hand. And then, all at once, we were apart.

She was handing him the deadly cup.

I couldn't stop her as she signaled to Thisbe or as she let the witch and the two large men into the room. When Armantine realized the plan had changed, she panicked, just as she had before. She tried pushing the men out of the room. When that didn't work, she threw herself across Alex's unconscious body, shielding him. The men were stronger, and pulled her off easily.

This time, I didn't wake.

This time, I watched as Thisbe laughed at Armantine as the girl struggled to get away from the two men. Then she ripped the locket from Armantine's neck. Opening it, she removed the charm, broke open the wax, and removed the intertwined locks of hair. Only then did she direct her attention to Alex.

"You're not going anywhere until I get what I need from you," she said, her cloudy eyes bright with anticipation.

"Don't touch him," Armantine begged. "I'll give you whatever you want."

"What do you have that I want?" Thisbe mocked. "You ain't got nothing at all, girl. You never did, except this here boy."

Armantine struggled again to break free of the arms holding her, but Thisbe waited, unimpressed, before she grasped Armantine's chin tightly in her craggy old fingers. "I don't think I'll be needing you anymore." With a movement so sharp I couldn't have predicted it, the old woman drove a knife into Armantine's stomach.

Armantine lurched with a sickening groan, grasping at the handle of the blade, but she couldn't seem to make her hands work as blood seeped from the wound. Her mouth was moving, but only a terrible, pained keening came from her lips. Fear —*regret*—clouded her eyes, and I knew in that moment, Armantine understood she'd failed in every possible way.

"Take this one out and dump her." Thisbe's voice rang out from behind me. "She ain't worth nothing to me now."

The pull toward Armantine was so strong—I wanted to be with her, to follow her slow descent when they tossed her into the depths of the harbor. The effort to resist, to stay separate from her was draining, but I used every ounce of energy I had left to follow Alex's body through the dark night instead.

When they arrived at the cottage, the two men dropped Alex's limp form onto the low bed in the back room, and then Thisbe ordered them to wait outside.

She bent over him and poked. "You can't imagine how happy it made me when that there girl came to me for a love charm." She spoke to him as though he was still conscious as she moved around the room, making her preparations. "A charm like that on a rich man like yourself? I thought to myself, *yessir*, that's gonna be worth something. But then I heard you were taking her away. And I couldn't let that happen. I'll be taking my payment now, instead. Turns out, you're just what I need." She tapped him twice on his chest. "You're gonna give me more time. You're gonna give me *everything*."

She opened the locked cabinet and brought out a small gnarled figure—the charm we'd destroyed. Using the still-bloody knife, Thisbe sliced into Alex's hand until his blood flowed from the open wound. When it began to pool, she smeared it on the doll before wrapping the tiny figure carefully with the remaining red string. Then she allowed Alex's blood to continue saturating the fibers as she chanted in strange syllables.

As she chanted, the energy in the space began to build. The air felt like a living thing, swirling and prowling around the room, until suddenly Alex's body lurched upward from the table and the power in the space seemed to shatter. Thisbe only smiled, laughing softly to herself. She held up the charm and examined her handiwork before burying the effigy beneath the stone of the hearth.

Then she turned back to Alex, and grasping Armantine's locket tightly in her hand, she smiled darkly. "Whoever you were, you ain't gonna be that no more. And no one's never gonna know you're gone. They're gonna think you ran off with that girl and forget all about you."

She returned to her cabinet and pulled out a larger skein of red thread. "The spirits have been whispering to me for a long while now, telling me an opportunity was coming. I didn't know the meaning, but I ain't stupid enough to ignore the signs. I got myself ready. I made the sacrifices they require, and I waited." She patted the skein of thread, still talking to Alex's nearly lifeless body. "The spirits did me a great honor when they gave me sweet little Lila. Her blood sang to me while I took it." She tapped the crimson thread again.

"So now, I'm gonna do *you* a great honor as well, *mon-sir*. I'm gonna take *real* good care of this here body of yours. And you . . . " She crouched near his feet and began to wrap the thread around him. "You're gonna help me live forever."

Chanting in her strange language, Thisbe worked methodically, until Alex's entire body was encased in a red web of string. When she reached his head, she tied off the thread and chanted a final invocation.

She cut him again, this time deeply on the other hand. Carefully she collected more of his blood as it dripped from his hand. It pooled in her palm, seeping through her fingers and dripping to the floor. When she could hold no more, she dipped a wizened finger into it and traced her brows.

She repeated the process until her face was coated. As she painted her grotesque mask, she chanted, and as she chanted a strange metallic buzzing grew until a solid wall of frenzied vibrations filled the air with its song of death. Then she filled Armantine's locket with more of his blood and fastened it around her neck. The liquid trailed a dark path down into her loose dress.

The air in the cabin grew hot and thick, pulsing with the same sinister energy as Thisbe began to change. Her shoulders straightened. Her arthritic fingers uncurled. Her cloudy eyes cleared. Her hair lengthened and darkened into the mane of a much younger woman. The blood sank into the deep creases lining her face, smoothing the ashy skin before disappearing.

"No." I repeated that single word in a pointless attempt to deny what I was seeing, *who* I was seeing the old woman transform into before my eyes. It was a face I recognized easily. And when the transformation was complete, her age had melted away and revealed the youth beneath.

When I finally woke up sometime later, I was so weak and disoriented I could barely stay upright.

"Do you know what happened?" Alex asked, once I'd finally regained some of my strength.

I nodded. "And I know where Thisbe put your body."

50

"We can find another way, Lucy." Even as we made our way to Thisbe's cottage, Alex was still trying to talk me out of the plan we'd come up with after I woke.

"We've only got one shot at this, Alex. It's now or never if we're going to save Silas."

It wasn't lost on me, the similarities between Armantine's choices and my own. She hadn't trusted Alex, and because of her fear, he'd ended up caught in some kind of endless curse, pinned to the world and unable to move on. I'd been too afraid to trust Silas with the whole truth of what was happening to me, and because of it, I'd taken the effigy from the cabin. Now Silas was caught between life and death, because the person responsible wanted that evil little charm back. Armantine couldn't do anything to save Alex, but I was going to do my damnedest to make sure Silas didn't suffer the same fate.

As we walked through the forest, I gathered small sticks I planned to use as kindling to build a fire. I would only have a matter of minutes, maybe seconds, before it would be clear to Thisbe that the doll I had tucked into my backpack wasn't the real charm. We needed to be ready to destroy the picture as soon as we had it. Mama Erzulie had explained that fire cleansed all.

We arrived early, and I started the small fire near the edge of the grove. As the sun dipped below the trees, she appeared at the far edge of the clearing. Until that moment, I hadn't known who would come. I wasn't sure whether to be relieved it wasn't Chloe or terrified because Thisbe had finally decided to stop hiding.

She didn't rush across the field. Instead, she walked toward me slowly, like she was leading some invisible procession, forcing us to wait like supplicants in the uneasy silence of the clearing. Apparently, she still had a thing for drama. I couldn't say I appreciated the suspense. Finally, she stood across the fire from me.

"Mina," I greeted her coldly. I could see Thisbe's features in her face so easily now, but the shock of realizing Mina was less than human and more than monstrous hadn't quite worn off. "I see you left Chloe at home today."

She smirked. "I wouldn't leave a task this important in the hands of someone else."

"You brought the picture?" I ignored the pinpricks of fear setting the fine hairs at the nape of my neck on end.

She pulled out a small rolled piece of paper tied with a familiar red thread.

"I want to see it," I demanded. "Show me."

When she hesitated, I thought she would refuse, but then she began to work the thread off. She pocketed it before unrolling the paper itself. She held it close to her chest, but showed me the image of Silas's figure, a dark silhouette against the sky. "Did you bring my charm?"

I nodded and pulled out the old bag—luckily, I hadn't burned it with the charm.

"Take it out," she directed. "I want to see, too."

My hands shook as I pulled out the tiny figure. It was the moment of truth. In the next few seconds, I would know if our plan would work. Mama Erzulie had assured me the charm was close enough that Mina—Thisbe—shouldn't be able to tell it wasn't the original until she had it in her hands.

She nodded when she saw it, and I struggled to keep my features from broadcasting the victory we'd just achieved.

"I want the picture." I was pleased at how calm and steady my voice was. We were close to freeing Silas, and that knowledge gave me the strength to keep going.

She sneered. "I'm sure you do, girl, but you're not getting anything until I get what's mine."

"The picture first, or this goes into the fire." I held the charm up, ready to throw it.

"You wouldn't." Her anger and fury transformed the atmosphere. The air went cold as a strange wind started to whip around me.

I kept my focus on the only thing that mattered. "How much are you willing to bet?" I asked, trying to keep my voice level. "Are you willing to throw away your chance to get this back? Are you willing to let Alex go?" I took a step toward the fire, and anger hardened her expression. "What would that mean for you, Thisbe?" I asked, poking at her like a tiger in a cage. Her lip curled, and a low inhuman growl sounded from deep in her chest, but I didn't allow myself even to flinch. "Are you running out of his power now that I'm in control of him?" I sneered with all my hatred and contempt for the woman, the *thing* the woman had become long ago.

She hesitated, and I could tell she was trying to figure out a way around me, so I lifted the charm higher, prepared to throw it. Her eyes flashed, not with resignation but with a hate so sharp and furious it was almost tangible in the air around us. I hadn't really understood the evil we were dealing with until this moment, but my bluff had worked. That minor victory gave me the strength to continue.

"At the same time." I knew I'd pushed far enough. "You put that picture in the fire, and I'll toss you this charm," I said with a casualness I didn't feel. "A life for a life, Thisbe. Ready?"

Her lip curled in a feral growl. There was something no longer completely human about her. She was permitting me see behind the façade she wore as Mina.

"On three," I said. Her face hardened, but I recognized the desperation in her eyes and I knew I had her where I wanted her. "One . . . Two . . . Three!" I waited the fraction of a second before she released the picture, and then I tossed the charm. Straight into the fire.

Mina howled in anger and dove for it, shoving her hands into the flames to try and retrieve the charm. I watched until I was sure the paper was curling in the flames, and then I ran.

It's done, I thought as I raced across the field to the line of trees, the cold wind whipping around me like an angry breath. I needed to make it to the pond. Mama Erzulie had built up protection charms in the clearing there for me. It was far enough away, she'd said, that Thisbe wouldn't sense them from the grove. If I could just get to that clearing, I'd be safe.

The pond was so close.

The light from the clearing filtered through the edge of the trees. I ran as fast as I could, refusing to let myself trip over branches or limbs in my way. I was almost there.

So close, I thought as a shot rang out and pain ripped through my arm. *So close,* as I fell into the sunlight, and the world went black.

51

I woke up in a hospital bed, tangled in plastic tubes and with Leonard and Sam nearby. A dull pain ached in my shoulder.

"Lucy?" Leonard's voice sounded so far away. "I think she's waking up."

"Luce?" A second voice. Familiar, with its low timbre and softly rounded Southern drawl. "Come on, sweetheart. Open your eyes for us."

"Silas?" I blinked my eyes open and tried to focus on their faces. Slowly, the world came into focus. Silas sat next to my bed, his warm eyes glinting with gold. Something about the sight of him here felt like my world clicked into place, like bringing the perfect shot into alignment through the viewfinder of my camera.

"Hey," I said, smiling up at him. There were dark circles under his eyes, but otherwise, he was as gorgeous as he'd always been. He didn't look as though he'd recently been wasting away, unconscious in a hospital bed. "You're okay."

"I'm fine," he said, taking my hand. His hand was warm and

sure, like an anchor around mine. "You're the one who had us scared there."

"I'm okay," I said, my words slurring a little from whatever drugs they'd given me.

"You were shot, Lucy." Silas's jaw was tight.

"Shot?" That would explain the dull, persistent ache in my shoulder.

Silas looked like he wanted to murder someone, which was kind of adorable. So, clearly, they had me on some excellent meds.

"Do they know what happened?" I asked, wondering how much Mina—Thisbe—had revealed.

"Piers found you bleeding in the overgrown area near the pond."

I tried to sit up, but the effort was too much. Without my asking, Silas assisted me by lifting the head of the bed and offering me a glass of water

I sipped some through a straw. "Do you know who did it?"

"Not yet, but whoever it was, they were probably the same people who've been causing problems all along. They set Thisbe's place on fire, too. Luckily, the fire department already had paramedics on the scene, so they got to you before . . . " His voice went tight.

"I'm okay," I said again, laying my hand on top of his to comfort him. "I'm still here."

"The doctors said the bullet went straight through, but you had us all worried, Luce." Leonard's voice cracked with emotion.

Silas's voice was hard when he spoke again. "We're going to find out who did this to you."

But I already knew who'd done it. I just didn't know how to explain to them what had happened, not yet at least.

"Was anyone else hurt?" I asked, poking for more information. "What about Mina? Or Chloe?"

"Mina's been on vacation all week," my uncle said. "Chloe too. They weren't anywhere close."

She'd covered all her bases, it seemed. It didn't matter. Eventually, we'd find her.

My eyes met Silas's. "I'm okay." I grimaced as pain rocketed through my shoulder. "I'm just so *tired.* And it hurts."

"I'll get the nurse," Sam said. "They can give you something for that pain."

Silas lifted our entwined hands and kissed the back of mine. "You need to rest."

I started to shake my head, but the world spun. I didn't have time to rest. I needed to figure out where Thisbe was keeping Alex. I needed to end this, once and for all.

The nurse came in a few minutes later and gave me more pain medication. I relaxed as warmth crept over me, dulling the pain and making the world seem round and soft.

"Need to tell you things," I said to Silas, but my words were garbled and thick from the morphine. "Need to tell you everything. About what happened. About Alex."

Silas frowned at my mention of the name, but movement in the corner of the room drew my attention. Alex was there, with his golden hair and emerald eyes. A ghost. A dream. A past I had to put to rest.

"You're here," I said, wondering how Alex had found his way to the hospital.

"And I'll stay as long as you want me," Silas said, thinking my words had been for him. "You can tell me everything when you're well." He tucked the blankets up around me. "For now, sleep. We'll be here with you."

The words were comforting, but my gaze slid beyond the group of people around my bed to Alex. "I'll be here as well, Lucy."

I closed my eyes, and drifted into a long and dreamless sleep.

SILAS WOULDN'T LET me go back to my small cabin after I finally surfaced from the haze of drugs and was discharged from the hospital a few days later. He wouldn't take no for an answer, and I was too tired and sore to fight him as he loaded me into his sleek Audi and drove me to his place.

He had a house on Dauphine Street, a couple of blocks from the noise and crowd of Jackson Square. It was a two-story building with coral stucco and sage-green shutters that matched the wrought iron of the balcony. It was also enormous, with a small courtyard in the center that held a gurgling fountain and beds filled with colorful and fragrant flowers.

He'd set up the guest room for me and left me alone, so I had time to settle in. The room had dark wood floors, polished to a shine, and was decorated in soft blues and yellows. It had its own bath, with an enormous antique clawfoot tub and windows that opened to a balcony overlooking the courtyard. Another door led to an adjoining parlor, which I was surprised to find set up like an artist's studio. A powerful Mac with an enormous screen sat waiting on a broad desk that held my camera equipment, and my canvases were leaning against a far wall. I walked over and ran my fingers over the canvas propped on an easel, the one where Alex's green eyes watched my every move.

My ghost had been conspicuously absent on the short drive to Silas's place, but I felt his presence now behind me. I knew he blamed himself for my injury. He hadn't left for one second at the hospital, but simply stood a silent vigil alongside Silas.

"I need to tell him," I said, speaking as much to myself as I was to Alex. "About us. About what's happening."

"If he doesn't believe you?"

I considered Alex's question. There was a better than good chance Silas *wouldn't* believe me, or worse, would think I'd lost my mind. But it didn't matter. Everything I'd been through, everything I'd learned to this point had to have been for something.

"I have to trust him enough to try."

I found Silas in his office on the first floor. His desk was cluttered with papers and ledgers, with double monitors displaying a series of documents and spreadsheets. I stood at the doorway for a second and watched as his face creased in concentration as he sorted through the papers in front of him. Occasionally he ran his hand through his dark curls as he worked, making them stand on end.

Knocking softly to draw his attention, I stepped into the room. It was lined with dark wooden shelves filled with books and other small items. He looked up as I entered, his expression guarded at first. But when he saw me, his heart was in his eyes, and mine beat unsteadily in my own chest in return.

Had I ever been looked at like that—*seen* like Silas seemed to see me?

Only with Alex.

But that had been Armantine. Not me. Whatever I'd been in another life, I couldn't go back there. Whatever Armantine might have felt for Alex, whatever I *still* might feel for Alex, was nothing but a dream. And I couldn't live in a dream.

Silas stood, as though to come to me. "Are you okay? Is there anything you need?"

"I'm fine," I said. "The room's beautiful. Perfect. That studio—"

"I hope I wasn't overstepping?" He looked adorably worried as he approached me.

I tilted my chin up to look at him. "Thank you," I said, lifting a little to press a soft kiss against his mouth.

His hands cupped my face gently. "I like you here, in my house," he admitted. He kissed me again, a brush of lips and breath.

But I pulled back. I couldn't let myself get swept away, though. Not until the truth was out, stark and glaring in the light of day. "There are things I need to tell you," I said, stepping back. "Things you need to know."

52

"He's here?" Silas asked, shifting his gaze to take in the room.

We were tucked into the worn Chesterfield sofa that anchored the fireplace in his front parlor, where we'd been for the last hour or so. The tea he'd made for me had long since gone cold, but I hadn't managed to drink any. It had been enough to have something to hold on to as I spoke. Something to anchor me and remind me what was real.

I nodded toward the place next to me on the sofa where Alex was perched. "He's here."

Silas set his empty bottle on the coffee table. He was processing everything I'd just explained about what had happened, but I wasn't sure which way things would go.

"I want to believe you." He glanced toward my end of the sofa.

"It's a lot to ask of you," I admitted. "I wouldn't believe it myself if I hadn't been living it."

He let out a long frustrated breath. "Okay, fine. If you say this is what's happening, then I believe you."

"You do?"

Silas nodded, and my relief about bowled me over.

"But Lucy, I can't compete with a ghost."

Before I could respond, a knocking echoed from the front of the house. Silas frowned, as though he didn't want to answer it, but when the sound came again—louder and more insistent—he pulled himself out of the couch. "Don't go anywhere. We're not done."

When he returned, he had Piers with him.

I got to my feet at the sight of him. He looked terrible. His usually neat clothes were a rumpled mess, his cheeks held days' worth of stubble, and dark circles lay beneath his eyes.

"You look like you're feeling better," he said, his voice rough with exhaustion. He stared at me for a long minute, and then his gaze focused on the space next to me—on Alex. "Still hanging around, huh?"

"You can see him?" Silas asked.

"Faintly," he admitted.

"That day at Thisbe's cabin," I realized. "You knew he was there in the woods."

"I thought there might be something there," Piers said. He looked between me and Silas. "I just got done talking with Mama Erzulie. I was looking for Chloe—she's not answering my calls or texts. But Mama Erzulie explained everything. Chloe's not on vacation, is she?"

"I don't think so." I glanced at Silas. "But I don't think she's gone willingly," I added, remembering the way her face seemed to struggle against Thisbe's control. "I think she's more a victim than anything."

"I was afraid of that," Piers said darkly.

"We need to find her," I said. "Before Mina can do anything else."

"Where should we start? " Silas asked. He moved closer, slipped his hand into mine.

I looked up at him, measuring the air for some sense of his

thoughts, but there was no pity, no frustration or fear. Only determination and trust shone in his soft brown eyes.

"I have no idea." The world was broad, the game was long, and Thisbe had made an art of biding her time.

"I think," Piers ventured, "the first thing we need to do is work on finding Alex's body."

"But Chloe could be in real danger," I argued.

"I know. But his body is probably the best way to weaken Thisbe. Maybe even to draw her out, so we can find Chloe." He addressed Alex directly. "Do you have any idea where you might be?"

Alex shook his head. "But I think Lucy may." He looked over meaningfully at me.

"Thisbe's men put his body in a tomb in one of the cemeteries in the city." I explained how I'd made the choice to follow Alex instead of Thisbe when I'd dreamed at Mama Erzulie 's shop. I still didn't know if I'd chosen correctly, though.

Piers was obviously disappointed by my information. "There are hundreds of tombs in the city's cemeteries."

"I know. But they moved so fast, and I don't know New Orleans all that well. And it looked different then—older, you know?"

"Right." He ran his hand over his smooth head as he sighed. "Do you think if you walked in your dreams again, you could find out?"

I started to answer, but Silas and Alex both interrupted.

"No," Alex snapped. "I will not have her risking herself for me again."

"Absolutely not," Silas said at the same time. "She just got released from the hospital. She needs to rest."

Piers glanced between the two of them, before finally speaking to Silas. "I can appreciate you're nervous, man. I'd do the same, but we need to—"

"Just give me a second to think." I closed my eyes and brought my memories of the dream to the surface of my mind. It wasn't as clear as being there and walking in it, but I could picture the place Thisbe's men had carried Alex's body to. "It looked like a temple—one of the old Roman or Greek ones. And there was something on top, a tall spire or an obelisk of some sort." The rest was too indistinct for me to get anything more. I opened my eyes. "Does that help at all?"

Piers considered for a moment. "Maybe." He glanced at Alex. "What year was it when this happened to you?"

"1851," Alex told him.

Piers nodded. "That limits it some too." He looked up at me. "Would you know the place if you saw it again?"

I thought about the dream. The night had been bright because of a large full moon hanging low in the sky. It had taken the men who worked for Thisbe a while to open the tomb before they could place Alex's bound body inside. The memory of the dream was foggy, but I'd remember the place if I saw it again. Its strange carvings set it apart from the other tombs that night.

I nodded. "I would know it anywhere. It was covered in markings like that doll." And like Lila, and probably like the ones on Shaunda as well.

"We can try tonight if you're feeling up to it," Piers said.

"I am. But we should plan on Thisbe trying to stop us," I said. "She'll be desperate, so we should expect anything and everything."

"Maybe Mama Erzulie could work some protection charms," Silas suggested.

Piers nodded. "That's a good plan. We'll get Alex back where he belongs, and then we'll rescue *my* girl."

"You *will* keep Lucy safe." Alex's voice was quiet but firm. It wasn't really a question.

"You know it," Piers said simply as Silas blinked in confusion. But it wasn't a statement I had any interest in translating for the living.

53

It took us the rest of the afternoon to organize our plan. Mama Erzulie had made us each protection charms, to help shield us against whatever Thisbe might throw our way. She also gave Silas a bracelet woven of multicolored strings with a series of small charms. It didn't give him second sight or anything, but when he tied it around his wrist, he could sense Alex's presence. I'd caught him looking sideways in Alex's direction more than once since he put it on, but he hadn't said anything more.

We piled into Silas's other car—a large Land Rover SUV that held us all comfortably—and headed out of the Quarter, toward the cemeteries.

"I think our best bet is to try one of the Saint Louis Cemeteries," Piers told us. "They probably have the most tombs from the mid-nineteenth century."

"There's more than one Saint Louis Cemetery?" I asked.

"Three," Silas confirmed. His fingers were laced through mine, and I had the sense that every time he'd touched me since learning Alex was around was a way to mark his territory. He glanced at me. "You have a lucky number?"

I glanced back to Alex, who was sitting stone-faced. His eyes were fixed on Silas's hand interlocked with mine on the armrest between us. I wasn't sure how to feel about it—about *any* of it. He was a ghost, or something more than a ghost. Maybe we'd been together in a past life, but there wasn't a future for us.

Still . . . I felt guilty.

"Might as well start at the beginning of the list." I disentangled myself from Silas and tried to ignore the confusion—the hurt—in his eyes.

There was no winning, it seemed. No matter what I did, I'd hurt one of them. But I'd already hurt Alex enough.

Saint Louis number one was a bust. After hours of looking at tomb after tomb in the eerie quiet, I didn't think I'd ever feel warm again. Saint Louis number two looked much the same as the first cemetery. It was surrounded by the same high, impenetrable walls and populated by the same precise rows of tombs that rose out of the ground to surround visitors with the dead.

The cemeteries would be creepy enough during the day, but when night fell, the silent tombs cast menacing shadows and the presence of death was overwhelming. And at night, people more dangerous than the silent dead roamed between the rows.

I didn't ask Piers where he'd gotten the key that opened the gates, and I pretended I didn't see the snub black pistol he'd handed to Silas or the one he checked over for himself. I didn't say anything when Silas tucked it into the back of his waistband and covered the gun with his shirt before we entered the second Saint Louis Cemetery.

They took up their usual places, Piers leading the way and Silas in the back. I knew they were doing it on purpose, to protect me from all sides. Alex moved silently, close to my right, his eyes shadowed. He hadn't said much since Piers arrived at Silas's place earlier.

We'd barely made it down the first row when I looked over at Alex. A trickle of blood dripped from his hand.

"Your arm." My voice was barely above a whisper, but it drew the other two's attention.

Alex rolled up his sleeve, revealing the source of the blood—a long, ragged gash on his forearm. "It's never happened this close together before."

"What's going on?" Piers asked.

We'd already explained how we believed Thisbe had been using the blood in Alex's body to keep herself alive and young.

Silas frowned as Piers leaned over to examine Alex's wound. Dark liquid seeped from the cut in Alex's arm and trailed down his forearm.

"She's probably with him right now," Piers said.

"If she moves his body—" I couldn't say rest out loud. Because if Thisbe moved him, I had no idea how we'd *ever* find him. And without his body, there was no end to any of this.

Piers frowned. "If she's there now, she could be gathering more strength. We'll need to be extra careful."

"Lucy shouldn't be here," Silas said, his expression like flint. "It's too dangerous."

"He's right," Alex agreed.

"No." I faced Silas, determined. "I'm staying. All of this started with me, and I'm going to be the one to finish it."

Silas began to argue, but Piers stopped him. "We don't have time to argue right now."

Alex glanced at me, and I could tell he was still thinking of ways to convince me to go back and wait in the safety of the car.

"Come on." I stepped toward the shadows. The guys were forced to follow.

We were working down the second row, searching for the tomb with the strange carvings, when a strange scraping echoed in the still night. Piers and Silas exchanged a look.

"I'll go," Alex said. "Keep her safe."

Piers nodded before Alex faded into the darkness. A moment later, he reappeared and gave Piers a quick nod.

"Stay here, Lucy," Piers commanded. "Silas, you ready?"

"You're not going anywhere without me." I didn't want them to rush into anything, and I definitely didn't want to be left alone in this city of death.

"It's not safe, Lucy." Silas came closer. "Please. Go back to the car and wait for us there."

"How many are there?" Piers asked Alex.

"Just the woman. Mina, I think you call her now."

"It's just Thisbe," Piers told Silas, already cutting me out. "This won't take long. I promise."

I opened my mouth to argue, but Silas took me gently by the arms. "I need you to be safe, Luce. Please. Go back to the car and wait. *Please.*" There was a desperation in his eyes I hadn't seen before. "When I heard you were shot, I thought I'd lost you before we even had a chance. I can't go through that again."

"She hurt you, too," I countered. "Do you think it's any easier for me?" I'd watched him lying in that hospital bed, and I'd known it was my fault. When Thisbe used her dark magic against him, I was the one who'd put everything in motion.

Alex watched, silent and stone-faced, a few paces away. I was hurting him. But how could I not? The truth was that even if he had been my past, he couldn't be my future. Maybe I'd been Armantine once before, but now? I was only Lucy. Armantine's memories would always be with me, but I couldn't live in a dream. Silas, though, he offered something more than dreams. He offered something real.

"Nothing is going to happen to me, Lucy." Silas pushed a wayward curl back from my face.

He couldn't promise that. Not with what I knew Thisbe was capable of. "I'm not going back to the car, Sy."

My use of the nickname had his expression softening. "Fine. But stay here." He looked toward the place Alex was standing, but his eyes didn't completely focus on the spot. "Will you stay with her?"

Alex's jaw was tight, but he nodded. "I'll keep watch."

Piers nodded to Silas, to let him know Alex had agreed.

I caught Silas's hand. "You better come back to me."

He smiled softly. "I'm not going anywhere."

Silas and Piers left us there, following the row of tombs before disappearing around a corner. We were alone then, Alex and I, surrounded by the uneasy quiet of the dead. Separated by all that was still left unsaid.

The tombs in this part of the cemetery were more than a hundred years old. Time and weather had worn down the inscriptions and darkened the white marble, but they still made an impressive statement about the importance of the lives they commemorated.

I ran my fingers along one of the inscriptions. *My Beloved Angel*, it read. I whispered the words out loud, my voice soft as a breath.

"You've found someone," Alex murmured. "Silas. He seems like a good man."

I turned to face him. He was nearly swallowed by the shadows. "I . . . " What was there to say? There was no denying how I felt about Silas, no denying I wanted a future with him without the past pulling me back. "I'm sorry, Alex. I didn't plan this—I didn't plan on him."

He smiled sadly. "You don't owe me your future, *chère*. I'm grateful enough I've had your past."

"I thought you might be lurking in these here shadows," said a voice oozing out of the darkness behind me.

I turned to find Chloe standing there, her eyes glowing in the dark night. Thisbe clearly hadn't released her. In fact, it seemed like whatever hold Thisbe had on her had grown. I couldn't tell if the Chloe I knew was still in there somewhere. Her face didn't ripple and pull, as it had before. Now, it seemed that Thisbe had taken her completely.

"You best come with me, child." She tilted her head at an odd angle, like she was trying to crack her neck. "We don't want to miss the party, now do we? Gonna be a good time, too." She smiled, all teeth and no joy.

I grasped the small charm that Mama Erzulie had given me.

"You keep holdin' your little bit of juju all you want," the Chloe-thing hissed, sounding more like Thisbe than she ever had before. She grinned a wicked grin and pulled out a gun. "But I ain't never heard of no charm that could stop a bullet, so you best start walking. Tell that boy to come with me too. If he tries anything, I'd be more than happy to end you."

54

I thought about making a run for it, about shouting to alert Piers and Silas, but I'd had enough experience with being shot to last a lifetime, so I did what she demanded. On leaden feet, I followed the path the guys had used a few minutes before. Alex walked silently by my side.

I moved as slowly as I could without sparking her anger, trying frantically to think of a way out, a way to protect the guys. But I couldn't think of any plan that wouldn't put someone at risk of getting shot. Probably me.

A few rows over, we turned a corner, and I saw it—the brilliantly white tomb from my dreams. Unlike the surrounding tombs, it looked freshly installed. Only the date confirmed it had been there for more than a century. The strange carvings were still in sharp relief, and the letters of the name Bookman showed no wear from the wind and weather.

Unlike the other tombs lining the row, the slab that sealed it was missing, leaving the doorway to the crypt dark and empty.

As we approached, Piers stepped out, holding Mina by the arm and pushing her out of the tomb with the muzzle of his gun. He started to say something to Silas, who was standing with his back to us, when he saw me.

Silas turned, following the line of Piers's vision, and his face blanched. "Lucy!"

"I'm fine," I assured them.

Silas took one step toward me, and Chloe wrapped her arm around my neck and pressed the gun to my temple in response. She laughed, but it was a dry husk of her real laugh. And when she spoke, it was Thisbe's voice I heard.

"I wouldn't be so sure of that," she said in eerie unison with Mina.

Silas froze. He had the gun in his hand, but as his gaze swiveled between Mina and Chloe, the color drained from his face. Without warning, he collapsed to the ground, like a marionette whose strings had been cut. He lay motionless there, and I couldn't tell from that distance if he was still breathing.

"No!" I struggled to get away, but Chloe had me pinned tight.

"Let her go, Thisbe," Piers said as he pulled Mina's arms back roughly and lifted his gun to her temple, a mirror of Chloe's position over me. "It's over."

They laughed again—Chloe and Mina both. Together. In perfect synchronicity, their mouths moved in unison and their voices rang through the air, melding into a discordant harmony as they spoke as one. "It's nowhere close to over, boy. It's barely even begun." Then they let out a cackling laugh that had my skin crawling with fear.

"Let her go, Chloe," Piers begged. "Come on, baby, you don't want to do this."

"Don't I?" the Chloe-thing asked, her head cocked unnaturally to the side. She pursed her lips, like she was thinking, and then tightened her hold around my neck until I could barely breathe. "I think I *do*," they said in unison. "I think I'd like nothing better than to break this girl's delicate neck for meddling where she's never belonged."

"Let her go, Thisbe," Piers said, jerking Mina against him more tightly and pressing the muzzle of the pistol more firmly against her temple. "There's no way out of here that doesn't go through me and this gun. Let Chloe go or I'll end you right now."

Chloe and Mina laughed again, a wild and barely sane cackling that made the hairs on my neck stand on end. "Did you really think you could outmatch me? Did you think I'd go without a fight?" Their voices echoed off the walls of the tombs that stood as silent witnesses around us. "All I've done for more than a hundred years is fight. I know more than you can imagine. I know things you can't even dream. And I ain't even close to done here. *Children,*" she spit. "No better than sniveling babes playing at games they should have stayed far clear from."

"Chloe, baby. I know you're in there," Piers said, his voice more urgent now. "I know you don't want this. You have to fight her, baby. Fight her for me."

"Chloe. *Baby,*" the two mimicked in a sickening singsong voice. "How sweet. You think true love is gonna come on in here and save you? Save *her*? Ha!" Mina's eyes brightened with an otherworldly light, revealing the monster lurking behind them. A terrifying smirk crept across her face. "Love, true or not, never saved no one or no thing. You want true love, boy?" Mina only smiled as Chloe moved the gun moved away from my head and aimed at Silas, who was still unconscious on the ground. "You make your choice, then."

Horror passed across Piers's face.

"Lucy!" Alex was near me now. "Lucy, you have to get away from her."

"Can't," I whispered, barely able to get the breath to say even that much. Chloe had me in a strangling grip that was so much stronger than it should have been.

"You don't think I can kill them both?" the Chloe-thing asked, focusing for the first time on Alex. "I can snap this one's sweet neck as easy as a twig underfoot and put a bullet into the other one's brain before you can even blink."

Mina's body went suddenly limp in Piers's arms, and Chloe alone spoke. "Who are you gonna save, baby?" she asked in a voice almost her own. *Almost*, but there was a metal edge to it, a buzzing hum that vibrated through its tone. "You can save *me*. Just let my momma go. Please, baby. Just let her go."

Piers's his eyes flashed with indecision. "Chloe? That you, baby?"

"*No,*" I rasped.

"Piers, no," Alex said. "It's a trick."

Piers blinked, like he was finally realizing what the rest of us had immediately seen.

"Make your choice, boy," the Chloe-thing repeated, this time sounding less like Chloe than ever. "You let me go, or I'm gonna move this little finger here, just a little bit, mind you. But it would be more than enough for you to lose them both."

Piers pressed the gun into Mina's temple again. "You think I won't kill you, old woman?"

"Piers, wait," Alex shouted. "You can't kill her."

A wave of relief washed across Piers's face.

"You kill her now, and she could have control over Chloe for good," Alex finished. "You don't want that. You'll get another chance. Another time. Save Chloe."

Piers nodded with a jerk of his head and lowered the gun from Mina's temple. "Get out of her body, old woman. Now. Or I swear to the heavens and all the spirits in this world and the next that I'll kill you both." He raised the gun and aimed it directly at Chloe.

"You wouldn't!" the Chloe-thing spit. "You *love* her!"

Piers nodded. "Enough to free her from you if I have to, Thisbe." He dropped Mina's limp body to the ground and stepped forward slowly, keeping the gun trained on Chloe. "Get out of my girl and get back into your own self. And then you get the hell out of here, before I change my mind."

Silence stretched between us as we waited to see who would make the first move. Chloe breathed in heavy, hissing breaths by my cheek, her arm still tight around my neck. Piers's gaze darted between Mina's limp body and Chloe, as though waiting for the devil himself to jump out of one of them.

It was harder and harder to breathe, and my vision went black around the edges . . .

Suddenly, the arm around my neck released me, and Chloe collapsed to the ground. Air rushed into my lungs, and I fell onto the pathway beside her, gasping for breath on my hands and knees. Warmth tingled across my skin. Alex was there. Nearby, Silas moaned, and began to pull himself up from the ground.

"Lucy?" His eyes found me, and panic was etched into his features.

"I'm okay." But my body was already starting to shiver and shake.

The moment Chloe collapsed, Piers ran to her, forgetting completely about Mina's body—Thisbe's body—on the ground in front of the tomb. He cradled Chloe in his arms and rocked her. "Chloe, baby, come on. You have to wake up, girl. Please, baby." Over and over, he crooned to her.

Silas was crouched next to me now, helping me to my feet, even though he'd collapsed first. He pulled me into his arms, wrapped me tight, and simply held me steady for a long, long moment. Then he released me a little, bringing his hands up to frame my face. His brown eyes glinted golden in the shadows as he checked me over.

"You're okay?" he asked. "She didn't hurt you?"

My neck felt bruised, but considering how much worse things could have been, I shook it off. "I'm okay," I assured him. "I'm okay," I said again, assuring myself.

His gaze shifted, and his expression hardened. "Piers—she's getting away."

I turned along with Piers to see that the ground in front of the tomb was already empty. Thisbe was gone. But Piers was wrapped around Chloe, who still hadn't come to. He looked down at her, then off to the darkness behind the monuments. An impossible choice.

"We can't let her get away," Silas said, already moving, already going for the snub little pistol he'd dropped when he'd been taken down by whatever charm Mina had cast.

"Don't go," I said, grasping his wrist to stop him.

"We need to finish this," he insisted.

But I couldn't watch him walk away from me for a second time tonight, not when I knew what Thisbe—Mina—was capable of. I couldn't let him go off alone. And I knew that there was another way to bring Thisbe's power to an end, a way that didn't involve any guns.

"Stay with me, Silas. She can't get far or do anything more as long as we have Alex." Thisbe needed Alex's body. And she'd just left it—and her chance at immortality—behind.

Silas hesitated, glancing over at Piers and Chloe. More of her color was returning every second, and already her breathing seemed more even. But she still hadn't opened her eyes. "Is she. . .?"

Pies shook his head. "She's breathing. She'll be okay."

The tightness in my chest unwound. But I wasn't sure Piers was right. Maybe Chloe wasn't dead, but what she'd just been through? I wasn't sure how you could be anything close to okay after that.

Piers brushed Chloe's braids back as he supported her head. "I've never seen anything like that." His eyes were locked on Chloe. "For a single soul to inhabit two bodies—" He shook his head as though trying to deny what we'd all just seen. "It should be impossible. Unless there was something to link them." He lifted a piece of Chloe's braided hair.

A thin red string woven into the braid, held tight by the silver bead at the end.

"Thisbe must have planned this from the beginning," I said, horror coloring my voice. "That thread is charmed with sacrificial blood. She used it when she bound Alex years ago and when she cursed Silas. She used it on her own daughter—if Chloe even is her daughter." But with how similar Chloe and Mina looked? Chloe likely was Mina's daughter—Thisbe's daughter—and I wondered how much more powerful that had made the link between them. "Thisbe must have been planning on using her for years. Maybe even since before she was born."

"Her braids will have to be cut off," Piers said miserably. "Your beautiful hair, baby," he crooned. "We're gonna make you better, though. I promise." He looked up at the two of us.

With every passing second, Chloe's color returned a little more. As her breathing evened out, the tightness strung throughout Piers's body finally began to ease.

"We need to finish what we came here for," Piers said after he was sure Chloe was stable. "Do you need my help with Alex?"

Alex. How had I forgotten he'd been here a few minutes before? But looking up to the open tomb, I knew where he must be. "No," I argued. "I need to do this on my own."

Silas took a knife from his back pocket, a small switchblade with handle inlaid with mother of pearl. "It was my mom's," he said with a wobbly look. "I'm sending her with you, to protect you and guide you in there."

I had to press my lips together to hold back the tears pricking at my eyes. But I left Silas there with Piers and Chloe. I didn't look back as I ducked under the lintel and entered the tomb.

55

The tomb wasn't an overly large structure compared to the monuments around it, but it was covered in delicate carvings that had gone dark with age. It was flanked by thick columns, which made it seem more opulent than the flat marble of its neighbors. As in my dream, it was topped with an obelisk. The doorway was a dark mouth leading into the coolness of its depths.

I was surprised by the size of the interior—it seemed bigger than it should have been. The walls were covered in more of the strange markings, but those weren't darkened like the ones on the outside. Instead, they glowed with an eerie light, bathing the space in a soft amber. On a shelf built into the back wall, a long form lay wrapped in what looked like a rusted cocoon. Alex was standing next to it, his eyes fixed on the red string it was wrapped in.

"When she originally tied you up, I could still see your skin in places," I told him. "She's added more thread over the years." I ran my hand over it—over him—tentatively. The blood-soaked string had become a shell over the years. But it was warm beneath my hand, and it moved rhythmically with the shallow breaths of the body withing. The body that was still somehow alive.

When I looked up at Alex, my chest felt impossibly tight as I thought about what he'd been through. What Armantine—what I'd—done to him. "Oh, Alex."

"It will be okay, love." He reached for me, but must have realized it was pointless because his hand dropped to his side again instead of trying to touch me. "It is almost finished. But I need you to cut away the thread."

I nodded and firmed my grip on the knife Silas had given me. Slowly, I worked it under the edge of the shell near his feet and then slid the blade up, slicing away more than a century of binding as I went. When I was done, the hardened string fell open like a chrysalis, revealing Alex's body.

I would never have guessed he'd been there for more than a hundred and fifty years. He looked so peaceful, his chest rising and falling slowly. The only sign anything was wrong were the thin lines of hundreds of scars covering his body.

"Are you ready?" I asked, turning to him.

His eyes were tight, and his throat bobbed as he swallowed hard, but he didn't answer me.

"What's wrong?" I asked. "We found you. Everything is going to be okay now."

He shook his head. "Lucy—"

I knew before he said the words. "No," I argued. "I was fine. When Silas went back to his body, he was fine. You'll be fine, too. You'll have another chance at the life you should have had all along." A thread of hysteria wound through my voice.

"Lucy," he said again, his voice sounding as miserable as I felt. "When I go back to myself, the unbinding will be complete. My body will return to the state it should be in."

"You mean—"

"I should have died more than a century ago, Lucy. I am not supposed to be here."

I looked up into his face, and the reality of the situation sliced through me sharp as a knife. "No—" I took a step back.

I hadn't heard Silas enter, hadn't sensed him approach, but now I felt him at my back, his strong hands on my arms. His strength supporting me. I glanced up at him, and he must have seen the pain in my eyes, because he wrapped me in his arms.

"There's no way to save you?" I felt as numb as I sounded.

"Please, Lucy, I would like you to do something for me. One last request." His voice was strained, and he gazed longingly at the prone body on the altar.

"Anything," I whispered. And I meant it.

His mouth curved into a pained smile. "I need you to walk away. Let go of the past we shared. Choose a new future. Claim it and live only for yourself."

I took a deep, shuddering breath and nodded. "I will," I promised. "But I won't forget."

"I can't hold myself away much longer." His voice was soft, but pain threaded through it. "I want you to remember me like this, not—" His voice caught, and he closed his eyes. "Go, love. Don't turn back."

I granted his final wish and left him behind without looking back. Silas walked next to me, his steady presence a support and his arms anchoring me to this world. As we emerged from the darkness of the tomb, I knew it was over. There was no going back.

Grief, relief, and some unnamable emotion consumed me as I collapsed in a heap of tears on the cool, uneven ground.

EPILOGUE

S ilas took me back to his house in the quarter after everything was settled at the cemetery. As we rode through town, there was no discussion about what would happen next, but the silent sureness that Silas always carried about him filled the car, a comfort after all we'd been through. He didn't say much that night. I'm not sure what he was thinking as he guided me into the quiet of his beautiful house or tucked me into bed as chastely as a big brother might.

He kissed my forehead before he left the bedroom, and somehow that was the final straw. My body convulsed into sobs as I cried for all I'd lost, past and present and future too, but at some point, the tears gave way to exhaustion, and I slept. It was a dreamless, uneven sleep, one without Alex or Armantine. One free of nightmares as well, but when I woke, I felt hollowed out. Empty and missing something I hadn't known I needed.

I sleepwalked through the next few days. Eventually Piers brought Chloe, but she was too self-conscious about what had happened to stay very long that first time. Most of her hair was gone now, but it didn't affect her beauty. She had the kind of face that could pull off a closely cropped look as easily as she'd worn her braids.

She apologized for her role in everything, but I assured her there was really nothing to forgive. She had lost a mother, lost even the memories of who she'd thought her mother had been. I wasn't not sure anyone could really understand a loss like that. Not even me.

Silas gave me space, gave me time. I sensed him, a spirt haunting his own house as he stayed out of my way. And I knew he was waiting for me to come to him, to decide.

I can't compete with a ghost. Those had been his words when I'd told him about Alex, and he'd been there that night to catch me when I'd collapsed with the grief of losing Alex again. He understood—too much. And he didn't understand enough.

A few days later, I woke from another dreamless sleep, feeling more rested and well than I had in maybe my whole life. The sun was already shining brightly over the courtyard, and as the murmuring hum of the Quarter drifted through the window, I thought about the promise I'd made to Alex in that cold tomb.

After my dad had died, I'd pulled inward. I'd avoided my friends, ignored Leonard and Sam's invitations, too, even before they'd moved for the job at Le Ciel. I'd let hurt and grief tear me out of the world. And I'd been wrong.

I'd given up so much to my nightmares over the years— friendships, relationships, any chance of a real future. I couldn't keep giving up my life to dreams, even if those dreams were more like memories. At some point, I had to go on. Mama Erzulie had been right when she'd read my cards. It was time to choose.

I climbed out of the rumpled bed and trudged into the bathroom. I took a long shower, letting the steaming water cascade over me until it started to run cold. After, I considered going down to the kitchen, but I was restless, not hungry. Instead, I opened the other door—the one that had been closed tightly since we returned from the cemetery—and I stepped inside the studio Silas had created for me.

My canvases were all still here, lined up against the far wall and waiting. On the easel, Alex's emerald eyes still haunted me on the unfinished piece. Looking at them now, though, I frowned. I'd gotten them wrong. The emotion I'd captured on the canvas was all sadness and pain, but that wasn't who he'd been. It wasn't how I needed to remember him.

Closing my eyes, I thought of the dream about that day in the clearing, the one where Alex seemed relaxed and utterly happy. The day Alex had pressed Armantine against a tree and made her shatter in his arms. Then I pulled out my paints and supplies, and I started working.

The light had shifted and twilight was already softening the room when I finally came back to myself. The canvas had been transformed, and I'd finally gotten it right. It was finished. I studied it, pleased with what I'd done, and the tightness in my chest loosened. My whole body seemed to unwind in relief. And the emptiness I'd carried with me for so long felt smaller now, less painful and obvious.

"It's incredible," Silas said from the doorway.

I don't know how long he'd been standing there watching me, but his soft brown eyes were wary. The expression on his handsome face was pensive. Everything about his posture seemed to be asking a question, one he probably would have never spoken aloud.

"I finally understood what I was doing wrong." With the painting, with my life. I'd been holding on to fear, closing myself off to stop from hurting. In my past life, and in this one, I'd made the same mistakes—decisions born of fear. But no longer. "It's a new direction for me."

I turned back to the canvas with critical eyes. It was more colorful than any of my past work, relying more on straight painting than the mixed media I'd been working with before. I'd still made a collage, blending images to form something new: the columns of Le Ciel, the shadows of a tomb, and in the center, a tarot card—two lovers intertwined beneath angel wings. It felt like the Quarter and the past and everything that had touched me these past few weeks was there.

I bit my lower lip. "Do you think your gallery friends will like it?"

He didn't answer the question I asked. Instead, he stepped toward the canvas, his brows drawn together. "This is Alex?"

I nodded. I'd captured him in paint, golden hair and emerald eyes. Joy and a love stronger than fate.

"But this isn't you?" That unasked question still hung between us.

"Maybe once it was," I told him, gazing wistfully at Armantine's painted figure. They were finally together, acrylics and oil and iridescent ink twining them together. *The Lovers*.

I faced Silas, tentatively interlaced my fingers with his. "But I haven't been her for a long time. All that is over now. I'm never going to be her again."

He didn't speak, just kept watching me with careful eyes, and I knew in that instant he was every bit as afraid as I was.

"Armantine might have been my past, Silas, but she's not going to be my future."

His jaw tensed. "No?"

I shook my head. "But I was kind of hoping maybe you would be."

"You're sure?" His tone was hopeful, his voice no more than a whisper.

"There's no competition, Silas." I gave him a small hopeful smile. "Whatever this is between us," I said, squeezing his hands gently as I moved closer, "I want to give it a chance."

"But you were so devastated." His voice was still wary. "I saw what leaving that tomb did to you, so I know what he meant to you."

"Of course," I said with a small shrug. "Loss is hard. We both know that. And we both know how to move on from loss, even terrible loss. It doesn't have to determine the rest of our lives."

Silas hesitated only a heartbeat longer before he dipped his head to mine. "Be sure, Lucy," he whispered, his breath sweet against my mouth. "Because I don't think I have it in me to survive losing you again."

I wrapped my arms around his neck, pulled him into me and was relieved when his arms tightened. "You only lose me if you let go."

His mouth was on mine then, our lips moving together until I wasn't sure where one of us ended and the other began. Breath and fire, he tasted like hope.

Silas pulled back long enough to catch his breath. "I have no plans to let go." He took my mouth again, steered me back, back toward the wide table that held my supplies, and lifted me onto it. Standing between my open thighs, he stripped off my shirt, my shorts. Then kneeling before me, he slowly, methodically drove away every memory that had haunted me. When our bodies finally came together, heat and need ignited, burning away the past. Forging a new future.

Thisbe was still out there somewhere, Chloe was still reeling, but in that room—in Silas's arms—suddenly my world righted itself. The memories would always be with me, but they would never again haunt me. I would carry who I'd been without letting it overtake me, and together we'd build something new. Something brighter than before.

ACKNOWLEDGMENTS

This book wouldn't have been possible without the help and support of the team behind me:

Danielle Stinson read early versions of and offered keen insights.

Nia Quinn provided brilliant edits and proofreading—any errors on these pages are mine alone.

Angela Haddon designed the gorgeous cover that fit the mood of this book perfectly.

Jaye Robin Brown, Sara Raasch, Lexi Ryan, and others gave me invaluable insights about the independent publishing journey.

Jason, Max, and Harry all lived with me and loved me while I was wrestling with this project.

To my readers who might have read the first version of this story years ago, thank you for returning! To my new readers, welcome! I hope you'll take a moment to follow me on social media, join my newsletter, or take a look at the work I've published as Lisa Maxwell. I couldn't do any of this without you!

ABOUT THE AUTHOR

Celia Crosby is the pseudonym for *New York Times* Best-selling Young Adult author, Lisa Maxwell. She still loves writing fantasy for teens, but her first love has always been Romance. These days when Celia isn't writing books with kissing in them, you can probably find her hanging out with her husband and two boys or taking them on some kind of adventure.

ALSO BY CELIA CROSBY

If you enjoyed *Sweet Unrest* be sure to check out my books written as
Lisa Maxwell

The Last Magician

The Devil's Thief

The Serpent's Curse

The Shattered City

Unhooked

www.ingramcontent.com/pod-product-compliance
Lightning Source LLC
Chambersburg PA
CBHW031316280626
47169CB00019B/1637